NICOLA DOHERTY

The Out of Office Girl

headline
review

First published in 2012 by HEADLINE REVIEW
An imprint of HEADLINE PUBLISHING GROUP

1

Cataloguing in Publication Data is available from the British Library

ISBN 978 0 7553 8684 0

Typeset in Giovanni-Book by Palimpsest Book Production Limited,
Falkirk, Stirlingshire

Printed and bound in Great Britain by
Clays Ltd, St Ives plc

Headline's policy is to use papers that are natural, renewable and recyclable
products and made from wood grown in sustainable forests. The logging and
manufacturing processes are expected to conform to the environmental
regulations of the country of origin.

HEADLINE PUBLISHING GROUP
An Hachette UK Company
338 Euston Road
London NW1 3BH

www.headline.co.uk
www.hachette.co.uk

The Out of Office Girl

To my parents
and to all the Alices out there

ONE

I'm lying on my bed, watching Luther undress. I've seen this so many times but it never fails to mesmerise me. First the T-shirt slips off, white against his tanned skin, leaving his dark brown hair even more messed up than before. The expression in his brown eyes is hard to read – he looks passionate, intense, vulnerable. His hands drop towards his jeans. Slowly, he starts to undo his belt . . .

My phone is ringing. I answer it reluctantly, my eyes still on the screen.

'Hi Alice!' It's Erica. 'I know it's last minute but we're meeting some people in the Dove. Want to come? Or are you out somewhere? I hear voices.'

'No, no.' I find the remote and press pause. 'I'd love to but I'm working.' I instantly regret saying this, because I know what Erica's going to say.

'Oh, come on. You're always taking work home. You should be more assertive. Work–life balance.'

Oh God. I love my sister but I can't deal with her tonight.

'I will. Listen, I'm sorry about tonight, but next time definitely.'

'You should. You don't want to sit sulking at home, you know,' are her parting words.

That's where she's wrong. Sit sulking at home is exactly

1

what I want to do right now, that and veg out in front of Luther Carson films (which counts as work) and eat Pringles and drink white wine and generally avoid thinking about the fact that after two months together, Simon doesn't care about me enough to break up with me officially.

Although I know I shouldn't have, I've saved all my text messages from Simon. It's like a mini history of our eight-week relationship. There's the first one he ever sent – 'Hi Alice, great to meet you last night. Drink next week? Simon x'. It reads like a really precious memory of a golden age when he still liked me. They continue nicely for a while – 'Thanks for a great night. See you v soon S xx'. But over the past few weeks, the 'x's started to disappear and the texts became more casual and infrequent, saying things like 'Running late sorry' or 'Not sure. Will let you know next week.'

'It's constructive dismissal,' Erica said when I first told her what was happening. 'He hasn't actually fired you, but he's changed the terms of your employment so that your previous job – the relationship – no longer exists.'

It's good to have an employment lawyer as a sister, I suppose, but sometimes Erica can be a bit *too* businesslike. The very last text from Simon says: 'Sorry can't do Weds. Will call to rearrange.'

That was over a week ago. At first I tried not to worry about it, reminding myself that he's very busy at work (he's just been promoted). But deep down I knew he was losing interest. Yesterday I swallowed my pride and sent him a quick, friendly text just to give it one last chance. That was over – I check my phone – twenty-eight hours ago, and he hasn't replied. I still can't quite believe it. How can you dump someone after you've been together for two months, not even via phone or text or email but via silence?

2

My flatmate Martin must be back now, because I can hear the football in the room next door. Martin's favourite activities are watching European Cup football at top volume – he actually records them and watches his favourites over and over during the summer – and cooking weird meals, like pasta bake with salami and avocado, that take hours and take over the entire kitchen. He drives me crazy, actually, but I really like my other flatmate Ciara. She's very easy-going: she always has a bottle of wine in the fridge and she didn't say anything when I woke everyone up with the smoke alarm by making toast at 3 a.m. She'd just broken up with her boyfriend when I first moved in, so she was a bit depressed, but she seems much better now.

Someone must have scored a goal; I hear roaring and cheering. My room was originally the dining room, and the wall dividing it from the living room is actually a pair of doors with rectangular glass panes. It means you can hear everything next door, and vice versa. When I moved in, I bought some thick white textured paper from Paperchase and took some cardboard boxes home from work, and filled up all the squares with white textured card. It took me an entire weekend. It's not *Elle Decoration*, but it doesn't look too bad. Simon hated it – he thought it was tacky and studenty. Is that why he went off me? Does he think I'm too studenty to be his girlfriend? Come to think of it, he never actually referred to me as his girlfriend, though I introduced him as my boyfriend last time we met some of my friends . . .

OK, that's it. I'm going to stop torturing myself by thinking of all the things I might or might not have done wrong with Simon. I settle back on to my duvet and pour myself another glass of wine. It was a bit of a last-minute request from my boss but I'm very happy to watch *Fever* again. I think it's up there with *Footloose* and *Dirty Dancing*, though some would say it's a shameless nineties rip-off of both. We're publishing Luther's autobiography, and Olivia wants me to pick a still from *Fever* to use in the picture section of the book. Which isn't exactly a hardship. I make a note of the time on the LCD, writing 'L topless' beside it and a star.

Soon the all-too-brief bedroom scene is over. There's a scene with Jimmy and Donna's family, where they make it clear that they hate him. The headmaster from *Ferris Bueller's Day Off* plays the father. Now Jimmy is trying to persuade Donna to leave her uptight Harvard fiancé and run off to New York with him. They start arguing about it, and then he stops and just asks her to dance with him instead. They don't say anything while they dance, but when the dance is over she tells him she'll go with him.

I love this scene. It sounds crazy, but when I watch it, I don't feel that Luther is acting – I feel that he is living it, and means it. He really wants to persuade her to trust him and stay with him, not by arguing with her but by showing her what they mean to each other. It's so romantic. What a pity that life isn't a teen dance movie, and that real men don't do things like this. Instead, they dump you via the silent treatment.

Maybe I'll have a therapeutic DVD marathon this weekend. I own about thirty DVDs, mostly black-and-white romantic films, or dance or teen movies. I've got all the classics: *The Breakfast Club*, *Footloose*, *Dirty Dancing* (obviously), *Girls Just Want to Have Fun* . . . then I have a few randoms: *Coyote Ugly*, *Heathers*, *Point Break* (Patrick Swayze *and* Keanu Reeves in wetsuits), *The Last Legionnaire* (not my kind of film, but Luther is brilliant in it) and my favourite, *Working Girl*. I also have *All About Eve*, *To Have and Have Not* (I love, love, love Lauren Bacall), *Spellbound* and *Brief Encounter* (though, in my current state, that one might push me over the edge). Then there's an Audrey Hepburn box set Erica gave me – my favourite is *Roman Holiday*. My friends all take the piss out of me for how much I adore these films. But when real life and relationships are the way they are, who can blame me?

I can hear my ringtone again over the music. I press pause and scrabble around on my duvet and my bedside table, and finally locate my phone under the bed. I still always have that slight hope that it's going to be Simon with some explanation – death in the family, doubts about our relationship, even a dead pet would do – but of course it isn't. Missed call: Olivia. Oh God. Why is my boss calling me at 9 p.m. on a Wednesday night?

It's not that I'm scared of Olivia exactly. But she's unpredictable. Most of the time she's great, but occasionally she can go berserk over something completely unexpected. I call her back right away but there's no answer so I just leave a message. I hope there isn't some catastrophe at work and that I haven't done anything wrong – again.

On my screen, Jimmy is paused with his arms around Donna, looking down at her as if he never wants to let her go. Donna is played by Jennifer Kramer, who was a big star at the time but has never really been heard of since. *Oh, Luther,* I think. *How I wish I were on that dance floor with you right now, far away from my life.* But that's not going to happen, so I finish watching the film, write up my notes for Olivia, and go to sleep.

TWO

As I rattle in to work on the Tube the next day, I can't stop chewing over the whole Simon thing, trying to figure out where it all went wrong. He seemed so keen in the beginning, taking my number the night we met and texting me the very next day. I couldn't believe it when he kept calling me – secretly I thought he was out of my league. He's got a fairly hectic lifestyle: he's a marketing manager for a big drinks company that sponsors lots of events, and he does some freelance journalism on the side. He also was, is, gorgeous – very tall, taller than me for once, with dark curly hair and dark blue eyes. And he's smart, and good company, and most of the time we had a lot to talk about – he reads a lot of interesting books and we used to discuss his free-lance writing and all the high-profile events he organises. So what changed? What did I do?

It's true that he's been a bit distracted lately, and our last date was a disaster. We went to an exhibition he had to go to for work, where he knew a lot of people. Rather than cling to his side, I tried to circulate as much as possible, but I didn't know enough people and somehow I kept on being circulated back in his direction. Afterwards we walked around Chelsea for ages trying to find somewhere to eat: everywhere was closed or too expensive and we ended up in Pizza Express, which was bad because Simon hates chains. I should never have suggested going for dinner in the first place. He had a cold and seemed a bit off, and I was going on too much about a problem at work. He didn't want to come home with me because he had an early meeting the next day. In fact . . . he didn't come home with me after our previous date, either. And the time before, he did come home with me, but—

Aargh. I'm not going to think about it any more: it's too depressing. I reach for the copy of *Metro* wedged behind the man opposite me, smiling apologetically at him, and flip straight to the Guilty Pleasures section. There's Luther, papped on his way to the airport in Rome where he's been shooting a remake of *Roman Holiday*. I happen to know he's on his way to Sicily, to finish writing his book. He's older now than in *Fever* – thirty-three – but I think he looks even better these days, with his brooding dark eyes and spiky brown hair. He's effortlessly elegant in grey jeans and black cowboy boots, which would make any other man look ridiculously camp. The publicity department will probably clip it, but I put it in my bag just in case.

The thing that gets me about Simon is that this always seems to happen to me. I go out with someone, he's super keen at first, and after about two months I get dumped. I wish I knew what I was doing wrong, but the one person who could probably tell me is Simon, and I'm not going to ask him. Imagine if, after a relationship ended, you had to fill in an evaluation form. I would score Simon quite highly on everything except the way he's ended it. Even if he went off me for some complicated reason that has nothing to do with me, and even if we were only together two months, I deserve more than this silent treatment. I'm beginning to think I should send *him* a text saying there's

7

no point getting back in touch – he's dumped. Though I suppose it might be a bit too late for that.

It's early when I get into the office, and there's nobody there but Poppy. She's sitting at her desk, holding a hand mirror and placing something carefully on to her eye, mouth half open. If it was anyone else, I would assume they were inserting a contact lens or something, but I know that Poppy is putting on her fake eyelashes. She must have something special on today; she doesn't normally wear those in the office.

'Morning, darling,' she says out of the corner of her mouth, waving to me with one crooked finger.

Before I met her, I would never have believed that people like Poppy could exist, let alone be let loose in offices. Her clothes are mainly vintage or customised or both: often they're almost costumes. Today's outfit, a white crochet mini-dress that looks very cute with her brown Afro and long legs, is pretty understated by her usual standards. She has what practically amounts to a dressing-up box under her desk, and she insists that we clock off every Friday at four for tea and cake. I didn't know what to make of Poppy at first – I was a bit shy of her, in fact, as she has such a big personality. But despite her frothy exterior she is totally down-to-earth, and by now she is a real friend. Unlike Claudine, who is my bête noir – appropriate because she's French, as she frequently reminds us.

'You look nice,' I say, hanging up my jacket. 'Is that dress new?'

'Thanks!' She sounds pleased. 'It's from a charity shop in St John's Wood. Full of lovely rich ladies' cast-offs. We should go there some time.' Poppy is always finding gorgeous things in charity shops – a useful skill when you're on a salary like ours. She puts down her mirror and turns round to face me.

'How are you? Any word from Mr Dempsey?'

'Nope,' I say. 'I think that means it's over.' I'm glad no one else is around and that I can just tell her privately now. Somehow the humiliation is as bad, or worse, as the missing-Simon part.

'Oh, that's rubbish,' Poppy says sympathetically. 'I can't believe he hasn't even called you, what a bast— what a pity. I'm so sorry.' It's nice of her to say that because I don't think she ever really liked Simon, for some reason.

'Is there any chance he might be unwell or something?' she asks. 'Trapped under something heavy? Amnesia?'

'I wish. That's what I thought at first, but it's never that, is it?'

'No. They're never dead, they're just not calling.'

Poppy can always make me laugh, even when I don't feel like it. While I wait for my computer to wake up, I slip out of my ballet flats and put on the slightly less flat shoes I wear for work. Poppy nearly died laughing the first time she saw me do this. In contrast to hers, my desk is pretty boring, just endless piles of proofs and papers. My only decoration is a giant poster of Luther that she and the other girls gave me when we got the book. They meant it as a joke, but I like having it up there to inspire me.

'Are you free for lunch today?' I ask. I'm suddenly craving a carb- and grease-fest.

'I'd love to, but I've got an agent lunch,' Poppy says. 'Could do tomorrow, though?'

Poppy was promoted to editor last month, so she's doing more grown-up lunches these days. I have to admit, I was jealous at first. We joined around the same time – in fact, she joined a month after me. But she deserves it: she's incredibly bright, and she works very hard. With her bargain-hunter's eye, she's just snapped up a brilliant first novel and everyone is excited about it. Anyway, I hope that if I keep my head down and work hard, I'll be promoted some time in the next year. I've been here long enough; four years is make-or-break time. I want to make editor before I'm twenty-seven; so I still have about six months.

My emails have loaded now. I can feel the stress rising in my chest as I see them queue up relentlessly. Olivia tends to copy me in on her emails, and then people copy me in to their replies, so it all adds up. My title is assistant editor, which means that I edit a lot of Olivia's books, and then I'm also her assistant, which means a lot of juggling. It's all good experience, though. I hope so, anyway.

'Cup of ambition?' says Poppy, waving her coffee mug.

'Yes, please.' Come to think of it, where is Olivia? She's normally in by now. And what was she calling about last night? I have had my fair share of disasters over the years, but I thought I'd done quite well lately. None of her emails look too serious – there's an agent complaining about a cover, and an author who's upset about his Amazon ranking, but nothing catastrophic.

It must be something to do with Luther's book. That is a code orange situation: it's running very late and everyone is getting panicked about it. We've just had the first draft in, and it's terrible. It skips over all the interesting parts – such as his relationship with his father; the drugs and rehab; his whirlwind marriage and divorce; the time he disappeared for a year . . . I think Olivia's been slightly taken aback by how much I know about Luther Carson. It's not that I have a crush on him exactly. Well, OK, of course I do – who doesn't? – but I also think he's a very intriguing character. In fact, I was the one who suggested him as a subject for an autobiography.

I decide to try Olivia again. There's still no answer: that's strange. Just after I hang up, my phone rings. I wonder if this is her now, but the display says Daphne Totnall – our managing director's PA.

'What does she want?' I ask aloud.

'Who?' Poppy asks, coming back from the kitchen.

'Hello,' says Daphne. 'Can you come up and see Alasdair please?'

'Of course.' I hang up. What the hell is happening this morning?

Poppy hands me my coffee. 'What's up?' she asks curiously.

'The MD wants to see me,' I say. I'm already walking towards the lift. More people have arrived by now, including the horrible Claudine, who is channelling Audrey Hepburn today in skinny black trousers and pearls. They all hear Poppy call after me, 'Good luck! Don't jump!'

As I ride the lift up to Alasdair's office, I wipe my clammy palms on my skirt and examine myself in the mirrored wall. What possessed me to wear a black skirt with a white shirt? I look like a waitress. Otherwise, I look the same as ever: straight, long blond hair, embarrassingly pink cheeks, anxious expression. Daphne barely looks up from her spreadsheets as she tells me to go straight inside.

I've never actually been in here before. The office is enormous, with floor-to-ceiling windows and a panoramic view over the Thames. There is Alasdair's spaniel, asleep in a basket beside the window. And there is Alasdair himself getting up from his desk.

'Alice. Thanks very much for coming up,' he says smoothly, shaking my hand and motioning me to sit down, just as if I was a powerful old buddy of his. He is about my dad's age, with badgery grey hair, twinkly dark eyes and a deep tan from his frequent sailing and shooting holidays.

'I'm afraid I have some bad news,' he says.

What bad news? Am I being fired? But if I am, there should be someone here from HR, surely. And shouldn't I have had a few warnings first? I'll have to call Erica . . .

'Olivia has to have emergency surgery,' Alasdair continues, 'for a double hernia. She's in hospital and they'll operate as early as they can tomorrow. She'll be out of action for at least two weeks, maybe more.'

I put my hand over my mouth. 'Oh God,' I say. 'That's awful.' Poor Olivia. That sounds gruesome. Though I have to say I'm also relieved that I'm not going to be fired. How did this happen? She was completely fine yesterday.

'We've just spoken on the phone, about her various projects,' he continues.

'Of course.' I know Olivia's schedule by heart, so I can help him with this. It's going to mean a lot of extra work. I imagine I'll keep working on the books I have already, and take on most of the others – maybe we can farm some out . . .

I suddenly find that Alasdair is talking and I haven't been listening.

'. . . Luther Carson. I believe the manuscript isn't up to scratch?'

'Oh! Well—' Now I realise I have my arms folded, and my legs crossed and folded round the chair legs, like a pretzel. Slowly, so it doesn't seem too obvious, I rearrange myself into a more confident-looking posture. 'No, it's not. It's just not personal enough. It leaves out all the most interesting parts. Brian's very good, so I'm sure he's done his best,' I add quickly. Brian is the ghostwriter. 'It just looks as though he hasn't had any proper input from Luther yet.'

'Well, we'll have to fix that,' Alasdair says. 'I'm not expecting *The Moon's a Balloon*. But it's got to be readable. It's got to have drama; it's got to have a bit of misery – not too much, but we have to have his lows as well as his highs. He knows that. It's in the contract. We put in a specific clause stipulating that there would be significant content relating to his childhood, the drugs and the divorce, and the time he disappeared for a year.'

I nod. The mention of this clause gives me a strange, uneasy feeling – I can't quite put my finger on it though.

'So, as you know, we need a finished manuscript in about . . .?' He looks at me expectantly. *Get it right.*

'Four weeks.'

'Four weeks at the latest, in time to have copies in early September. We need this book to turn over a million pounds this Christmas, or we won't make budget.'

I do know all this, but it sounds extra scary when Alasdair says it.

'So, as you know, we've provided Luther with somewhere to stay in Sicily – a very nice place, near Taormina, at our expense, to sort the book out. The ghostwriter is there with him. Before Olivia got ill, she and I talked about her going over there to help him, to apply some pressure, edit the book as it comes out. I think you should go.'

What? Me go to Sicily? Has he lost his mind?

'Well, of course, if you think that's the best thing,' I hear myself saying. 'And work with Brian?'

'No, work with Luther. Sit him down and exercise your influence and generally sit on him until he finishes this book.'

I boggle at the picture he's just created – for a number of reasons. Is he serious? How on earth am I going to exert my influence on Luther Carson? I don't have any influence.

'Alice, we have given this some thought, and I do think it's the best option. Normally we would prefer to send someone more senior, but you're the most familiar with

13

the project. Olivia tells me you know everything there is to know about him. And I hear great things about your editing. She was very impressed with your work on the pet rescue memoir.'

The pet rescue memoir: what a nightmare. Three horses, twenty cats, twelve dogs and assorted birds and reptiles, and one author who loved animals as much as she hated humans. A batty pet lady, though, is not the same as an A-list film star. I'm about to try to phrase this in a more tactful way, but Alasdair is still speaking.

'I suggest you spend a day or so wrapping up here and as soon as you can, book yourself an open return to Sicily. Daphne will help you with the details, flights and so on. Have a word with Ellen and the team downstairs to reallocate all your other work, but this takes priority.'

This is all happening way too fast. An hour ago I was Olivia's assistant and now she's in hospital and I'm on my way to – to work with *Luther Carson*. To handle a book more important than any I've ever worked on before, with an author who, gorgeous as he is, is probably pretty bloody difficult. I can't do it. I'm not senior enough, and I don't have enough experience. I'll have to tell him I need time to think about it, or something.

Alasdair looks up and says, 'Is there anything else?'

I open my mouth to say yes, but something stops me.

I've just realised something blindingly obvious. This might be scary, but it's a huge opportunity. He's giving me the keys to the kingdom. What am I doing, second-guessing and dragging my heels like this? I should be flattered that they're even asking me. I need to stop wimping-out, right now, and step up.

'No,' I say as firmly as I can. 'That's all very clear. I'll handle it.'

Alasdair smiles and stands up to shake my hand.

'Excellent,' he says. 'Keep in touch and let me know if you need anything.'

I'm halfway to the door when he calls me back.

'Alice,' he says, 'your current title is assistant editor, isn't it?'

'Yes,' I say, turning round. Is he going to rethink because I'm too junior? *Don't change your mind*, I think frantically. *I want to go! I can do it!*

'Well, we'll have to see about changing that when you come back with the book in your bag,' he says. 'Editor, or senior editor, even.'

I force myself not to let out a shriek of joy. 'That sounds – good,' I say in a measured tone. 'Thanks.'

I head out the door in a total daze. I forget to say goodbye to Daphne, and I walk straight into a big pot plant on the way to the lift. My cheeks are flushed and I feel sick and elated at the same time. *My big break.* That thought keeps repeating itself in my mind, but at the same time there's another one, that's even more insistent: *I'm going to meet Luther Carson.*

THREE

'Did he really say: I want you to sit on him until he writes his book?' asks Ruth, almost crying with laughter.

'Yes, he did,' I say happily. We're sitting at a tiny table outside The Cow on Westbourne Park Road, near where Ruth lives. It's not especially handy for me, but much as I love her, Ruth is one of those friends whom you travel to see, not the other way around. Beautiful people are swarming all around us, but Ruth cleverly arrived early and bagged us a table outside. This was meant to be a commiseration-about-Simon drink but it's turned into a celebration. It's a lovely July evening, the summer is finally here. Life is good. Actually, life is great.

'Well, I can't get over it,' says Ruth, which I'm not sure is flattering. 'Not that you don't deserve it,' she adds quickly. 'It's just so surreal. My best friend from school is going on holiday with Luther Carson. What next? Is Mike going to start playing basketball with Leonardo DiCaprio?'

Mike is Ruth's current boyfriend, an Irish banker she met through work. Before Mike there was Jonny, and before Jonny – was it James or Chris? I can't remember. Ruth is one of those people who just skips effortlessly from one man to the next. There is never a gap of longer than a few weeks, and sometimes there's an overlap. I don't know how

16

she does it. Of course, she's very pretty, with big brown eyes and a sort of tomboy look, and she also works in financial PR which seems to be a better source of men than publishing. In contrast, before Simon, I was single for about nine months – total tumbleweed except for a couple of awkward dates. But who cares about Simon when I have Luther Carson?

'I'm not going on holiday with him,' I remind her. 'I'm going to work and I'm terrified. I've never handled an author as big as him before. Stop laughing!'

Eventually Ruth calms down. 'It'll be fine,' she says, wiping her eyes. 'You'll get over there, worm all his dark secrets out of him, and he'll cry on your shoulder and fall madly in love with you.'

'You think?' I'm laughing, because it's so ridiculous, but secretly I quite like that idea – strictly as a fantasy, of course.

'Totally! He'll find your down-to-earth English charm *so* refreshing after all the Hollywood bullshit. He'll say, "Alice, I'm tired of these Botoxed bimbos. All they want is to be photographed on my arm. I need you."'

'Hah.' I wish I had Ruth's confidence. 'That's a nice idea. But it's not going to happen.'

'Why not?'

I look at her to see if she's serious. 'Because – he's a major star. He works with the most beautiful women in the world on a daily basis. He was married to Dominique Rice. I'm not even going to be on his radar.'

'You never know,' says Ruth.

'I do know. But even if he did have some sort of interest in me, which he won't, there's no way we could ever have a – a romance.'

'Why can't you?'

'Because the book is too important. If I don't do a good

job with it, it will be a disaster for the company. It's a major part of our budget.'

'So why don't you have a fling with him *and* do a great job on the book?' Ruth asks. 'Simples.'

'I don't think so.' I start counting reasons on my fingers. 'First: I have to be able to tell him what to do and I can't if I'm – you know. Second: it would be totally unprofessional. And third, I would be fired and my career would be over.'

'But you won't need a career once you're married to Luther Carson. Joking! I'm joking, Alice! You shouldn't take things so seriously.' She pats my arm. 'It's about time Olivia gave you a fun job like this. You've edited enough nightmare books for her. I'm glad she's finally recognising what you can do.'

I'm about to say that I haven't actually had a chance to talk to Olivia about it all yet, but Ruth is taking a call.

'Hi honey! Yes, fine . . . I'm here in The Cow with Alice. Really? Why don't you come along?' She looks at me with an 'Is that OK?' expression. I mime back, 'Of course.' She continues to chat – it's obviously Mike – and I check my own phone. Two texts. One is from a friend asking if there is any news on Simon. Oh God, I wish I hadn't told so many people about my problems with him. And one from my flatmate, Ciara: 'Great news! R u celebrating? Where r u?' I text back: 'At The Cow Westbourne Pk Rd. Come!'

Ruth is off the phone now. 'That was Mike,' she says, blissfully and unnecessarily. 'He'll be here any minute.'

'That's great,' I say, swallowing my disappointment. Mike's nice. It's just that I haven't seen Ruth on her own in ages . . . and this was meant to be our commiseration-turned-celebration drink . . . oh well.

'Anyway.' She tops up my glass. 'Listen, Alice. You'll be completely fine. You can handle this guy. Just don't rule anything out. A fling with him could be just the thing to help you get your confidence back after Simon.'

I'm about to ask if she's still joking when Mike arrives. He's come in a black cab, which tells me that a) he's dying to see Ruth and b) he's pretty rich. I approve of a) and I'm not that bothered about b). I've never been into rich City types. I prefer creative people, which Ruth would say is part of my problem.

Mike gives Ruth a quick but enthusiastic kiss, and nods pleasantly at me. They make a nice couple. She's petite and dark, and he's short, too, but built for rugby, with sandy hair and freckles. As soon as he's got back from the bar with his pint, Ruth fills him in discreetly.

'GUESS WHAT? Alice is going on holiday with LUTHER CARSON!!!'

'Who?' says Mike. I make frantic 'shushing' sounds to Ruth – even in this achingly cool spot, one or two people have looked around curiously.

'The actor? He was in *The Last Legionnaire*, you know, and *Stars on the Water*, about the man whose wife dies—'

'Oh, your man. He was in that other film, wasn't he, about the two cowboys?' Mike surprises us by saying. 'That was a good film.'

'*Brokeback Mountain*. Um, that was Jake Gyllenhaal,' I say tactfully.

'I didn't know you liked that film.' Ruth gazes at Mike in wonder, as if he's just saved a child from drowning or discovered a cure for cancer.

'There's more to me than multiplexes,' Mike says. 'So how come you're going on holiday with him?'

I explain. Mike nods thoughtfully, then says, 'Is he not a bit young to be writing his autobiography?'

'Well, he is,' I say. 'But he has quite a story to tell. He was a star at twenty-four, when he did *Fever*—'

19

'Then he was incredibly successful, and then he went off the rails and disappeared for a year,' Ruth adds. 'Nobody knows where he went.'

'And then he had a big comeback with *The Last Legionnaire*. And his upbringing was crazy. He and his family were homeless for a while.'

'And, and, he was married to Dominique Rice – you've got to get him to do lots on that,' says Ruth to me. 'Honestly, how can you not know all this?' she asks, turning to Mike.

'OK, fair enough,' says Mike, holding up his hands. 'You two are well informed. It's your job, Alice, but how do you know so much about this guy?' he asks Ruth.

'Well, duh,' she says. 'It's general knowledge.'

'Is it,' says Mike, raising one eyebrow. 'So what's he got that I haven't, for example?'

Ruth and I exchange looks.

'Aside from being a multimillion-dollar-earning, good-looking film star,' Mike concedes. 'What's the big fascination?'

'I suppose . . . it's the bad boy thing,' I say shyly.

'Completely,' says Ruth. 'He's always out on the tiles and getting into trouble . . .'

'Not so much now, that was a few years ago,' I say.

'But you just know it's because of some kind of pain in his past . . . his crazy childhood . . . the divorce . . . and he's so talented . . .' Ruth looks dreamy; Mike looks sceptical.

'I'd say you'll have your hands full with him, all right,' he says.

'I'd love to have my hands full with—'

'Well, yes,' I chip in hastily, before Ruth gets herself into more trouble. 'He probably is difficult, but I'll just have to do my best.'

'Ah, listen, I didn't mean to worry you,' says Mike. 'I'm

20

sure he's a delightful character. Just head out for a few scoops with him and you'll be sucking diesel.'

'What?' I say. This doesn't sound good.

'He means, just go out for a few drinks with him and you'll be fine. Is that right?' Ruth asks Mike. 'He's been teaching me Irish slang,' she adds to me.

'Ten out of ten,' Mike says to Ruth, and raises his glass to me in a toast. I smile, clinking my glass against his. Mike is nice. I hope he lasts.

'Oh look, there's Ciara,' says Ruth. 'Ciara! Over here!'

I shouldn't make comparisons, but in contrast to Ruth, Ciara has come all the way from her job in Bermondsey, where she works for a charity, to join us in Westbourne Park. And she would have seen me at home in Hammersmith anyway. We introduce her to Mike, and as they're both from Dublin they start swapping acquaintances. Before they get into it all, though, Ciara goes to the bar to order champagne, and Mike follows her to fight over who's paying for it. I hope he wins because Ciara doesn't earn much money. When they come back, Ciara hears all about Luther all over again from the three of us. She's very pleased for me, especially when I mention what Alasdair said about a possible promotion.

'So what's happened with Simon?' she asks at one point. I haven't seen her properly for a couple of days so she's not up to speed. I appreciate her concern but I'm getting so sick of telling everyone; it's like a broken engagement or something. I almost need to take out an ad somewhere: *Attention: To whom it concerns: Simon has dumped Alice.* At least I never changed my relationship status on Facebook.

'Oh – he hasn't been in touch. No big deal,' I say.

I don't want to go into more detail with Mike there – there's nothing worse than having your romantic failures rehashed in front of your friend's new boyfriend. But Mike insists on hearing the full story. When he does, he doesn't say, 'Well, why don't you call him?' or offer excuses. He says Simon sounds like a gobshite and that I should forget all about him. I'm beginning to think he's absolutely right. It's a fun evening and everyone is on great form. I love my friends; I love London. I can handle Luther Carson.

Just after eleven they kick us out. There's some talk of going on somewhere – maybe to one of the clubs in Notting Hill – but we all have work tomorrow so we say our good-byes and Ciara and I head to the Harrow Road to get some chips, and then weave our way back down to Westbourne Park station. And on the way there, I get a text message. It's from Simon, and it says, 'Sorry, Alice, been v busy at work and can't see you again I'm afraid. Have a good one.'

FOUR

Have a good one. Have a good one? Have a *good* one?

I cannot believe Simon chose to break up with me with the phrase, 'Have a good one.' Simon wants to be a journalist, for God's sake. Isn't he meant to have a way with words? Couldn't he have come up with something a little more appropriate? What does it even mean? Have a good what? Life? Rejection? 'Can't see you again I'm afraid.' That sounds as if he's been taken to prison or something. He should be, for breach of relationship rules and common decency.

'Maybe he means, kind of . . . go in peace,' Ciara said cautiously when I showed her the text. 'You know? Sort of, you'll go your way, I'll go mine, beautiful memories . . .' She read the message again. 'No, there's no good way to spin this.'

'Have a good one.' I repeated. I wanted to send him a text telling him exactly what I thought of him but Ciara said it was better not to. Two days later, on the plane, I'm still seething. I'd actually have preferred silence to a horrible, heartless, spineless text like that. I had no idea he could be such a pig. As well as being angry at Simon, I'm angry at myself. How could I have got it so wrong? I thought that, after all my other disastrous relationships, this one was going to work out; but it was just another mirage.

At least I've had some distraction with the mad dash to get ready. After agonising over what to pack, I think I've managed it; some light shirts, shorts, sandals and a little black dress, in case we go out for dinner to talk about the book. Plus my swimsuit, as the villa has a pool: I plan to do some lengths every morning, before we start work. Ruth was trying to persuade me to have a Fake Bake, but I'm not brave enough for fake tan. Anyway, it's been too hectic. I've been in the office until eight every night for the last few days sorting everything out.

I didn't manage to call my parents until last night. I was glad to have the good news about my work trip and possible promotion to distract them from hearing about yet another failed romance. My dad kept talking about travel insurance and my mum asked me if Sicily was 'safe', which I told her I wasn't even going to reply to. They both worry a lot – about me, that is. When Erica was twenty-six she was an associate in her law firm, was buying her first flat and was engaged to Raj. In contrast, I sometimes feel I haven't got off the starting-block.

I've also spoken to Olivia. In fact, she called from the hospital, right after she woke up from her procedure, to tell me it wasn't her idea to send me at all.

'I told Alasdair . . . to send Ellen . . . but he insisted,' she rasped, her voice still hoarse from the operation. 'He wants someone young and on . . . Luther's wavelength.'

There was always the chance that she might just have been delirious from the anaesthetic, but she sounded pretty lucid to me. It made me feel even less confident about going, and also somehow guilty. She sounded so feeble: it was as if some dying aunt had told me on her deathbed that she wished she hadn't left me her favourite cameo brooch after all. But this is my big break, and I am determined to make it work.

What gives me hope is that Luther has such an extraordinary story. I know some people think of him as a sort of pretty-boy action star, but I don't think that's right. I've read some really interesting and perceptive things he's said in interviews, and I genuinely think he's very talented. The scene I love so much in *Fever*, where they dance in silence, was apparently his idea. In any case, you don't get the kind of career he has without having a pretty good head on your shoulders.

So why on earth is Luther writing this book at all? It's a very unusual move for someone who's as big a star as him. It's not as if he needs the money. I think there is more to this than meets the eye. Maybe it's to do with his disappearance from the public eye for a year; maybe it's something else, but there is definitely some reason.

I get a little shock every time I remember: I'm actually going to meet him. Not just meet him: if everything goes well, I'm going to get to know him in the most intimate way possible – well, one of the most intimate ways. I'm going to talk to him about things he's possibly never told anyone else, ever. With everything he's been through, it's not surprising he should want to look back, reflect, talk to someone. And that person could be me.

And if that's the case . . . I would die if anyone knew I was thinking this, but maybe, just maybe . . . something could happen. After all, actors fall for their PAs and their make-up artists all the time, because they're the people who are closest to them. Why not their editor? I treat myself to a daydream about the two of us, after a hard day working on the book, having a romantic dinner together, Luther confiding in me all about his life: 'I've never been able to talk about this before . . .' I'd have to go back to London, but we could go long-distance for a while. Then I'd move to LA and we'd live in a little house in Malibu – wherever that is . . . I'm pretty sure there are literary agencies in LA where I could work . . . I have a blissful vision of Simon opening up a magazine and having to read about my new celebrity romance, or seeing a picture of me and Luther and wishing he could have me back . . . but then I snap out of it. I couldn't even keep Simon interested for longer than eight weeks: I'm certainly not going to end up with Luther Carson.

Bing-bong! It's another bilingual announcement. We're landing. I can see Sicily: the coast with its lights, and the sea in darkness, and more darkness in the interior of the island. It's my first time in Italy, and I'm excited. As is everyone else – people clap spontaneously when we land. The Italian girl beside me puts away her book and we start chatting. She's been working in London but she's thrilled to be home; in fact, when we finally step down from the plane, she touches her fingers to the tarmac and kisses them joyfully. I've never seen this at Gatwick.

It's ten o'clock at night and dark, but the air is still balmy. Entering the airport, I'm surprised to see lots of military-looking types swaggering around in light blue uniforms, brandishing sizeable weapons. Our bags take ages to arrive, and I have the usual fear that mine has got lost, though as yet this has never actually happened.

Twenty minutes later, it has happened. There is, officially, no bag for me. An Italian family is also missing a buggy, and I tag along with them to enquire. The father rants and raves, but all we get is a long form to fill in. As the arguing reaches a crescendo around me (the father is gesturing at me, I think to illustrate some point about helpless foreigners let down by Fontanarossa airport) I decide to postpone my meltdown. I will cope. Everything crucial is in my hand-luggage, including Luther's manuscript and a jar of Marmite that Brian, the ghostwriter, has asked for. And at least it means the queue for passport control has shortened, though my passport is checked very thoroughly, the guard's eyes flicking up and down between me and my terrible passport photo.

'*Inglese?*' he asks.

I can guess what he's saying. 'English, yes,' I reply. He shrugs, as if to say, 'Can't be helped,' and gives me back my passport.

'*Grazie,*' I say.

Emerging into arrivals, I feel like a giantess – the tallest person, as well as the palest, by a mile. Everywhere there are short, snappily dressed men and gorgeous women talking their heads off. There's a lot of bling: white jeans; designer T-shirts, and barely a flat shoe to be seen.

I look around for someone with a sign – I've organised a driver. I could have hired a car, but it's expensive and I'm not totally confident about driving in Sicily. I don't see anyone likely, though. Just as I'm wondering whether they've left, a tall man with brown hair, wearing glasses and a faded grey T-shirt that says UCLA, steps forward.

'Olivia?' he says.

'No, I'm Alice Roberts,' I say. 'I work with Olivia. Um . . . are you from Italicar?'

He raises an eyebrow. 'No. I'm Sam Newland.'

Oh, God! It's Luther's monster uber-agent. I've seen some very scary emails from him. I had pictured him in his forties, but he can't be that much older than me. What is he doing here? He's meant to be in LA.

'Oh, sorry. I had no idea you'd be here.'

'Clearly,' says Sam. 'I wasn't expecting you, either.'

'Well, Olivia's unwell, so I've come instead.' How does he not know this? I told him, or at least I told one of the entourage.

Sam is looking at me as if he's ordered prime rib and

has just been served a steak tartare. I obviously look way too young to be handling Luther. Well, he's not exactly an old-age pensioner himself. He's fairly good-looking in an identikit American way: tall, well-built and tanned, with perfect teeth and a square jaw. His only unusual features are his slanted grey eyes, which are slightly bloodshot. He doesn't look like a Hollywood agent, more like a preppy college boy or a young banker let loose to play football on the weekend. Ruth would probably love him, but he is definitely not my type.

Sam is tapping a foot and looks impatient to get going. 'So are you good to go? Where's your bag?' he asks.

I explain, and before I can stop him or ask him what he means, he's gone off to buttonhole an airport official in what sounds like rather fluent Italian. He gets no further than I did, which makes me feel relieved. It's bad enough to lose my luggage and find he's installed himself here, without him instantly sorting out my travel disasters.

'I did organise a car,' I say as we head to the exit.

'Yeah, I cancelled it.' Sam is easily the tallest person in the airport, and I'm struggling to keep up with him as he strides along. 'I wanted us to have a chat and get a couple things straight before you arrived.'

That sounds ominous. We arrive at a dusty little rental Fiat – what, no Porsche? – and Sam opens my door for me before walking around to the driver's seat, though I get the feeling this is done out of habit rather than any particular desire to charm me. As we get into the car, he takes his glasses off and rubs his eyes.

'I haven't been boozing, by the way,' he says. 'My eyes got a little bloodshot in the pool today.'

It's nice to know he's been enjoying himself in the pool, but I wish I knew what he was doing here: not just at the airport but at the villa. And what does he want to talk to me about? I thought I would have the drive to prepare myself for everything, instead of being plunged into it like this. I also realise, looking surreptitiously in the mirror, that I'm a mess; my hair is all over the place from dozing on the flight and I look tired and tiny-eyed.

Before long we're on a motorway. Sam has the air conditioning turned up full blast and I'm glad I still have my wrap. Maybe I can wear it as a kind of sarong tomorrow. Or maybe there will be some curtains at the villa that I can convert into dresses, like in *The Sound of Music*. I keep thinking of important things that were in my luggage – like my medicine bag; swimsuit; my phone charger and, oh no, my huge bottle of Factor 45 suntan lotion. Like Miley Cyrus, I have literally hopped off the plane with a dream and a cardigan, except that in my case it's a dream and a pashmina.

'Is the villa nice?' I ask, trying to make small talk. We're paying for the villa, but Team Luther chose it.

'Sure,' says Sam. 'Luther wanted someplace quiet after Rome and he asked me to pick a spot. He was thinking Sardinia, but that's too much of a party island – we'll be more private here.'

He might not have finished charm school, but he obviously has a lot of influence with Luther. I'd better get him onside.

'Where did you learn to speak such good Italian?'

'I spent some time here at one point,' he says, in a tone that doesn't invite any more questions. I'm trying to think of some more subtle enquiries, when he beats me to it, launching into a series of interrogations.

'So . . . what exactly did you say was wrong with Olivia?'

I explain about the double hernia.

'Right,' he says, sounding as if he thinks she should have pulled herself together, popped a few aspirins and got on the plane. 'Why didn't she let me know you were coming in her place?'

'Didn't Brian mention it?'

'No, he just said that Luther's editor was coming. Which I understood was Olivia.' There's a loaded pause. 'You're the out of office girl, aren't you?' he says abruptly.

'What?'

'I mean, you're the person who's named on her out of office email.'

'Oh. Yes.' Shit. Shit. Now he knows I'm her assistant. 'Yes. I . . . I work very closely with her.' I hope that sounds sufficiently vague.

'Right,' he says again. 'Well, whatever. You're here now.'

And it's lovely to meet you too, I think.

'The thing is, though, there really wasn't any need for you to come,' Sam continues. 'Luther is already working with Brian. And he's delivered a perfectly good book. They're just polishing it.'

'Well –' This really isn't the way I wanted to bring this up. 'It needs a little more work, to be honest. We just need some more personal detail to bring it alive. If I'm here with Luther, it means I can work with him more closely.'

'But we never intended for this to be some kind of kiss-and-tell. Even if Luther did have any skeletons in his closet, which he doesn't, by the way, he's a pretty private guy and he wouldn't be comfortable sharing.'

We're off the motorway now and winding around some hairpin bends; mountains tower on our left and I can see the sea and some steep cliff edges, a little too close for comfort, on the right.

'Well, we don't want this to be a kiss-and-tell either.' Oh dear. Should I have said that? 'But it does need to have more life than it does at the moment – and he needs to give us more on things like his relationship with his father,

30

and rehab . . . it doesn't have to be salacious.' *Although salacious would be great.* 'Luther does have a great story. And I presume he wants to tell it, or he wouldn't have signed up for it.'

I look at Sam, whose eyes are fixed on the road. I'm feeling sick from nerves; or it could be all the bends.

'Listen, Alice,' he says, in a deceptively reasonable tone that rings all my alarm bells, 'Luther did sign up to write a book. But we never intended for it to be some kind of exposé. That was clear from the start. Someone like Luther is not going to benefit from the public knowing every last thing about his life. I don't want their perception of him as a person interfering with his range as an actor.'

Then why on earth did you agree to let him write a book? I think. But even as I do, my heart is sinking. This is exactly the kind of speech I was dreading; I just didn't know I would be getting it less than an hour after landing. I grit my teeth and decide to bring out the big guns.

'But it's in the contract. We put in a clause saying that he would be required to include –' I frantically try to remember the exact phrase – 'significant content about his childhood, the drugs and the divorce. And the year he disappeared.'

To my horror, Sam laughs. 'You're kidding, right? There is no way we would ever agree to something like that.'

'But you did,' I say, uncertainly. Though at the same time, I'm having a nightmarish feeling of doubt.

'Seriously,' he says, glancing at me. 'There's no such clause.'

Oh, God. Is it possible he's right? We did add that clause at a late stage. That is, Olivia asked me to add it to the form we fill in when we create a new contract. And I added it. Didn't I?

Or did I?

My mouth is dry, and I'm swallowing repeatedly and having to catch my breath. Instinctively my fingers reach for the door handle and for a mad moment I contemplate opening the car door, jumping out and running straight back to the airport to get the next plane back, so I can check that bloody contract. But that's not possible, so I try to keep calm. I'll ring Poppy. She'll know what to do. At least, she'll be able to tell me one way or the other if I really have left it out. I just can't think about it now: what with the late night, and no luggage, and Sam, I'm flattened.

For the rest of the drive, there's no more chat. He's clearly not going to bother making any more effort at conversation, so neither am I. Before too long we're rattling downhill, along a rough track with no lights that leads to a bay. A bank of cypresses is shielding something white: the villa. We arrive at high walls and electric gates. Sam leans out and zaps something, and we drive in. As he parks alongside two other cars – one a sleek-looking vintage number – I see a name written up on a pillar: Al Plemmirio.

We walk around the side of the villa, to a terrace over-looking the bay, with a pool that reflects thousands of stars. I can hear the sea, and crickets. There's a table here under a canopy, with several bottles on it – I spot champagne and red wine – and some chairs; it looks like it's been recently abandoned.

'I guess you can meet them tomorrow,' says Sam.

Inside, I'm so tired that all I can take in is the delicious cool, the stone floor, and a vague impression of spacious rooms. Sam shows me to a bedroom at the end of a passage, and he strides away. Finally I've got rid of him. The first thing I do, once I'm on my own, is pull out my phone and call Poppy. There's no answer, but I leave her a message asking her to call me back as soon as possible. Then I text my parents to let them know I've landed safely – though that's debatable.

FIVE

I'm woken by an unfamiliar feeling: warm sunlight on my face.

Squinting, I can see the sun is coming through some shutters, which are painted pale blue. The room is small but with a high ceiling. The walls look old and whitewashed, and there are dark stone tiles on the floor. There's no furniture aside from a massive chest of drawers with an old-fashioned mirror on top. So here I am: in Sicily, in Luther's villa, with no clothes. I think I can hear the sea outside. I check my phone: 9.05 a.m., local time.

There's an en suite bathroom, and I'm thrilled to see it's equipped with towels and some posh toiletries including, thank goodness, a toothbrush. I had a mini deodorant in my bag so at least I have the basics. After my shower, I pull on the clothes I wore on the plane – cream linen trousers and a navy T-shirt – and brush my hair. It could do with a wash, but I don't see a hairdryer and I don't want to have to waltz around on my first morning with dripping-wet hair.

I put on a discreet coat of mascara, and stare at myself in the mirror, wondering if there's anything else I can do to improve my appearance. I can't believe I have to make my first impression on Luther with dirty hair and wearing a crumpled, day-old ensemble. Why, why did I have to check in my bag? Well, it can't be helped. I'm never going to resemble, even vaguely, the women that he sees in LA. He'll probably have seen *Bridget Jones:* everyone knows English girls are scruffy and badly dressed. I'll just have to rely on personality.

I emerge from my room. The place is much bigger than it looked from outside; everywhere there are high ceilings with oak beams, and tiled floors, and a feeling of calm, in contrast to the butterflies in my stomach. I head towards the back of the house, where I can hear voices. I step outside, and what I see takes my breath away.

The terrace overlooks a little bay with steep, forested sides that slope down to a huge blue sea, which meets a huge blue sky. At the far left end of the terrace is a pool, with nothing behind it but green hillside – I can make out pine trees and here and there a palm tree – and the sea. To my right is the long table I saw last night, now completely tidy and half shaded by a vast canvas canopy. Sam is sitting there in the sun. He's working through some papers and tapping on his BlackBerry, while drinking espresso and eating bread rolls with butter. I imagine he misses his protein shake or wheatgrass or whatever he normally has in LA.

'Um – good morning,' I say.

'Hi,' he says briefly, barely glancing up. I sit down, wondering where Luther is.

Hearing a noise in the pool, I turn around and realise that there is someone in it, at the far end – I can just see his head and shoulders above the water. There's a splash, and he disappears underwater, emerging at the end closer to us a few moments later. He hoists himself out. It's definitely him. There's that tattoo on his arm. And there's that bare, brown chest and those broad shoulders – defined but not overdeveloped, tanned and glistening wet. Oh, my God. This is like some sort of fantasy being enacted before my very eyes. With unhurried movements, he wraps a white towel around his waist, tucking it in around his gorgeous washboard stomach. Now he's walking over, dripping wet, with his easy, athletic stride. He holds out a hand – which is completely wet – and I shake it. I'm touching his hand!

'You must be Alice,' he says. 'I'm Luther.'

He knows I know that, and I know he knows I know: it just adds to the surreality of it all. It's hard to describe the experience of meeting someone very famous. It doesn't feel as if they've entered your world; it feels more like you've entered theirs. I feel as though I'm in a film: one of Luther's films.

'Hello,' I say, spellbound.

He's not as tall as I expected – in fact, he's only slightly taller than me. But he is every bit as good-looking – in fact, more so. I've never seen such a handsome face in real life: long, lightly stubbled jaw, high cheekbones, a beautiful mouth; light brown eyes, squinting in the bright sun. It's not just his looks, though; it's a magnetism that he has. I can almost feel myself inhaling it. Standing there, with the burning blue sky behind him, he looks like something out of an ad or a film – which, of course, he is. I'm not even conscious of my wrinkled clothes or my three-day-old hair; I'm just drinking him in.

He throws himself into a chair opposite me, still dripping.

'So, Alice, how are you?' His accent is broader than I'd expected – more New York-sounding. My brain starts reciting bits from his Wikipedia entry: Michael Luther Carson, born in Camden, New Jersey . . . later moved to Queens . . .

'I – great!' is all I can muster. My hand is still wet, and

I'm not sure what to do with it. Do I wipe it? And if so, where?

'I'm excited you're here,' he says. 'I never had an editor before. Lots of directors, but no editors. How's that going to be?'

I smile at him, I hope reassuringly. 'I'm here to help!'

'Good.' He looks at me thoughtfully. His eyes aren't brown, as I thought, but a sort of honey-hazel colour . . . or amber, even? 'I'm kind of having writer's block at the moment and I could use your help.'

'Well – that's what we're here for!' This is encouraging: it already seems as though he's motivated.

'You know, Sam here doesn't think I can finish the book, but we're going to prove him wrong, OK?' He gives me a wicked grin, and my stomach flips.

'Sure, man,' says Sam, smiling but not looking up from his paperwork. 'You prove me wrong.' I can tell he's been listening to our entire exchange, not missing a thing.

Someone's coming out of the house. An elegant lady with beautifully coiffed grey hair, wearing a blue apron over a black dress, has appeared with coffee, which she pours for me and Luther. Of course: the staff.

'Alice, this is Maria Santa,' says Sam. He adds something to the lady in Italian, which I don't understand. She looks at me and then at Sam, asking him something; he smiles and shakes his head and they both laugh – he's being uncharacteristically charming to her, I notice.

I watch, fascinated, as Luther adds milk to his coffee, and starts eating some figs. *I'm watching Luther Carson have his breakfast.* Maria Santa gives me some bread and butter, but I'm not totally sure if I can eat anything right now. Sam's phone starts ringing. He excuses himself and walks away, talking.

'What a wonderful place to work on the book!' I say to

Luther. My heart is racing with adrenaline and I'm pretty relieved to find myself talking so fluently.

'Hey, I'm glad you like it,' Luther says. 'I'm just sorry it's not Ibiza; I know how you Brits love it there.'

'I've never been,' I tell him. Though he could probably tell that just from looking at me.

'I guess the best part about this place is we can lose the photographers, more or less,' Luther continues. He points to the bay with his knife. 'Unless they sneak up in a boat with long-range cameras.'

'We've been pretty discreet,' says Sam, rejoining us at the table.

'It's so beautiful,' I say. I feel as if I'm in a huge blue heaven, suspended between the sky and the sea. I can see lemon trees in the terraced garden beside us, and cactuses, and growing over the white walls is a brilliant hot-pink flower, the one you see everywhere in films set in the Mediterranean – bougainvillea, that's it. I realise for a second I've almost forgotten where I am. It's a shock to come back to earth and realise I'm here in Sicily, discussing the possibility of a paparazzi approach with Luther Carson and his agent.

So the good news is that he seems utterly charming and down-to-earth, just as I knew he would be – much nicer than his agent. He's not necessarily spilling his innermost thoughts yet, but that will come. The bad news is he's so attractive that I'm going to have to keep calm and concentrate, and do my best not to stare at him. I decide to gently introduce the topic of the book.

'So – I don't know what your plans for today are, Luther, but maybe some time this morning, we could sit down together and – talk about the book so far?'

He nods. 'Sure thing. We can have a creative chat.' He smiles at me. Wow. I've seen that smile so often on film, but to be on the receiving end of it – I'm almost knocked sideways. I'm so happy he seems to like me; maybe this is going to be easier than I thought.

'Want me to sit in?' Sam asks.

'No, I got it. Hey, lady.' For a second I'm confused, but then I realise Luther's talking to someone behind me.

Padding across the terrace, wearing a white bikini with a transparent pink shirt floating over it, is one of the most stunning girls I've ever seen outside the pages of a magazine. For an awful second I think it's Sienna Miller, but it's not. Her bikini is effortlessly set off by a few different slender and chunky necklaces – I can never accessorise like that. She's my height and also blonde, but the resemblance ends there. Where I'm a pale size twelve, she's incredibly slim, and tanned a perfect gold, and while this morning my hair is hanging in limp curtains, hers is rippling down her shoulders in buttery, beachy waves and curls.

'Annabel, this is Luther's editor Alice; Alice, this is Annabel,' says Sam.

'Luther's what? Oh. I *think* someone mentioned you,' says Annabel in a voice that is as sweet, fake and ice cold as Diet Coke. She's English! How funny: I thought she looked American. Her Sloaney accent instantly reminds me of school bullies, the King's Road and lots of things I want to forget. Is she Luther's girlfriend? I really, really hope not, for all sorts of reasons.

'Annabel and I just finished shooting *Roman Holiday* together,' Luther tells me.

'Gosh,' I say, like an idiot. 'Who did you play?'

Annabel gives me a big, false smile. 'I played Jane? She's the Princess's main lady-in-waiting. It's a supporting role. I have a lot of time on screen.'

She doesn't look very nice – that is, she does look very nice in a stunning model or actress way, but she is looking at me in a way that makes me feel even more crumpled than I am. So much for English girls being badly groomed: she's perfect. Even her nails are beautiful: not painted but buffed to a shine. She sits down beside Luther, props a lovely foot up on the chair beside me and takes a dainty sip of coffee.

'That sounds great,' I say, to make conversation. 'It must have been so exciting working with Natasha Pullman. I love her. She reminds me of Audrey Hepburn.'

The words are barely out of my mouth when I realise this remark was a big mistake. Annabel is looking at me with complete loathing. Her eyes are a beautiful turquoise colour, like a swimming pool, but there's also something slightly crazy about them.

'Alice's luggage got lost on her flight,' Sam tells Annabel. 'Can you lend her some clothes?'

I look at him, surprised. That's unexpectedly helpful of him.

'I can *try*,' says Annabel. 'If I have anything big enough. But Luther, are we going on Federico's yacht? Or do you have to do boring book stuff now?' She looks at Luther with a sad face, pouting.

'Hey, yeah,' Luther says. 'Let's do that. Alice, my buddy Federico has a beautiful yacht, a Sunseeker – you like boats? He's going to call in at our bay this morning, and we thought we'd take a little cruise, maybe round the headland as far as Lipari . . .'

'Oh!' I say. 'But weren't we—'

'As far as Lipari?' says Sam. 'That's over a hundred miles.'

'A hundred bucks,' Luther says immediately. 'No, a hundred euros. A euro a mile. That baby can go, dude.'

'Whatever,' laughs Sam. 'I'll swim there. Race you.'

With all this banter, we seem to be forgetting something: the book? I'm worried that a word from Annabel has made

Luther forget our plan for today, but I don't see how I can tell him to cancel his friend's yacht. Well, we're getting on, so maybe I should just build on that. Then, when he's in a more receptive mood, I can coax him into some work.

Also: it is incredibly hot. It's not even 10 a.m., and it must be nearly thirty degrees. I don't think we would get much done if we stayed baking here. On a yacht, we'd at least get some air, and I could get to know Luther a bit better.

Annabel has been examining me closely while this conversation has been going on.

'So, Alison, you're an editor,' she says in her most patronising tones. 'Does that mean you just sit around and read all day?'

'It's Alice,' I say. 'No, I have to—'

'I love reading,' says Annabel. 'I was in *The Tudors*. But I get so many scripts to read, I don't have time to read books.'

I'm confused. Does she think *The Tudors* is a book?

'Oh, good morning, Alice,' says a voice behind me.

I never thought I'd be so happy to see Brian Reynolds, the ghostwriter, who is now shuffling towards us, looking as if he hasn't slept in days. With his pink face, bald head and glasses, he is reassuringly familiar. It's nice to have someone around who doesn't look like a model. He responds to Luther's high-five with a weak pat, and sits down heavily.

'I'm glad you're here,' Brian says, and starts tucking methodically into his breakfast – Maria Santa brings him tea. Brian enquires after Olivia, but I don't go into huge detail – not that this lot cares what we're saying. Annabel is talking to Luther in a low voice, very rudely, I think, and Sam is absorbed in his BlackBerry. Brian looks exhausted, and I notice he doesn't seem especially thrilled to see Luther. I wonder, with Luther so charming, what on earth can be going on with the book.

40

'Brian, I've got those papers for you that you wanted,' I say. 'Do you want to come inside, and we can look over them?'

The others look at me, and I feel like a nerd. Annabel smirks; Sam looks watchful. Luther alone looks totally unconcerned. Brian, though, bless him, is already on his feet and coming with me.

'See you all shortly,' I say with a smile, and hurry off.

Inside, Brian and I find a corner of the big reception room, which is full of beautiful abstract art, with a low coffee table made of brown mosaic and thick red and blue rag carpets on the stone-tiled floors. We sit on an immaculate white sofa.

'So, how's it going?' I ask. 'He seems very nice and normal – is he just not being co-operative?'

'Not really,' he says. 'I'm worn out. He talks a good talk, but whenever we actually sit down to do any work, which isn't very often, it's like catching quicksilver. He's very charming, and he chats away, but it's impossible to pin him down on anything personal.'

'But why not?'

'I just don't know.' Brian looks despondent. 'Maybe he's in denial about the fact that he is actually doing the book. Or maybe he thinks I'm not an interesting enough audience. I can't get a handle on him, which doesn't often happen. And his agent's been a nightmare. He keeps sitting in on our interviews, interfering, trying to censor everything we talk about – it's been very intrusive.'

'I can imagine,' I say. 'Look, don't worry. I'll talk to Luther. We seem to be getting on so far, and I'm sure now that I'm here, he'll realise it's a real project and buckle down more. It doesn't look like he has any time this morning, but I'll have a word with him later on.'

41

I remember about Brian's Marmite and go back to my room and present him with it; he goes off to show it to Maria Santa and to make a phone call. I'm about to head back out to the terrace to do some more bonding with Luther when Annabel floats in, presumably on her way back to her room. And I remember: I have nothing to wear on Federico's yacht – or indeed, anywhere else.

I ask her again, very reluctantly, about borrowing some clothes, and to my surprise she's suddenly all smiles. 'Of course! Come with me.'

Where is she going to take me? She'd better not be sharing a room with Luther. But there's no sign of anyone male in her room, which is bigger than mine with the same view of the sea. Instead, it's like a girl bomb has exploded: brushes, tubes, lotions, hair straighteners, giant rollers and huge professional-looking make-up cases are crammed on to every surface and all across the floor. A big full-length mirror is propped awkwardly in one corner – it looks as if it's been taken from some other room in the house. Piles of colourful clothes are also strewn around, falling out of every shelf and hanging in the wardrobe. If she wanted to, she could probably have an entire fashion show here.

Annabel roots around, and produces what looks, at first, like a bikini, but what I then realise is a swimsuit: one of those scary ones that plunge right to the navel with huge cut-outs at the side. It's a neon lime-green colour that would look fantastic on someone very skinny with a tan, and I absolutely know, without even trying it on, that it will look horrendous on me, with my pale skin and chunky thighs.

'Now this is cute! The straps are adjustable, so it *should* fit,' she says, sounding dubious.

'Thanks,' I say helplessly.

'No problem!' She turns away and sits down at her

dressing table, and starts slapping on some expensive-looking lotion.

'Um . . .' I hate to ask her another favour, but for the moment I don't see the alternative. 'I don't suppose you could lend me – a T-shirt or something? Just to have something spare, until I can sort out getting my suitcase back, or buy something . . .'

'Oh.' She gets up reluctantly. 'Oh, dear, oh dear.' She sighs and flicks through some rails. 'I'm not too sure what I have that will fit you . . .'

Is she for real? We're not *that* different in size, surely. I have never met anyone as breathtakingly rude in real life – not since my all-girls school, anyway.

'You *could* try this . . . it's elasticated so it might work.' She hands me a wrinkled linen knee-length brown dress, with cap sleeves and a white frill around the neck. It's pretty hideous, but the look in her eyes tells me there's not going to be anything else on offer.

'Thanks,' I say. And then I remember about my Factor 45; that's the only thing I definitely can't do without. 'I hate to be a pain, but do you have any spare suntan lotion? Don't worry if you don't . . .'

'No,' says Annabel. 'I mean, I have this Sisley stuff but it's extremely expensive.' She just looks at me as if no further explanation is needed. Which it isn't.

'OK,' I say. 'I'll manage. Thanks again,' and I make an exit.

What a cow. I know it must be annoying to have a stranger ask to borrow things, but still. Thankfully, Brian has some waterproof Factor 50 for kids. It's very white and gloopy, and difficult to rub in, but at least I won't get burned. He won't need it, he says, because he's not going on the yacht.

'I don't want to get sunburnt again,' he says. 'My head got burnt the other day and it was terrible. I am going to

43

reread this draft, and see if there is anything remotely salvageable in it. Could we just make it all up, Alice, do you think?'

I leave him setting up his laptop in the shade, under the canopy. Maria Santa has brought him more tea and some little lemon biscuits, and I'm consoled to think that, even if he is having a terrible time, he has a nice place to have it in.

I stand for a minute on the terrace, drinking in the scenery. It's like being on the prow of a ship. I've never seen anything so blue. To the left I can see a town high up on the cliff-top – that must be Taormina. In the terraced garden below, I can see chickens scratching among the olive and lemon trees. Aside from the chickens clucking, the only noise is the hypnotic sound of the sea. I'm picturing how lovely it will be on the yacht when I remember, to my horror, that I still need to ring Poppy and find out about the clause. I hurry back to my bedroom and close the door and the window so nobody can hear me: I can just picture Sam lurking outside in the bushes.

Thankfully, Poppy answers her phone after a few rings.

'Alice!' she says. 'Ciao, bella! How is Italy? What's going on? It is such a miserable rainy day here! You're so lucky to be—'

I've just noticed I only have one bar of battery left, so I cut her short.

'Poppy. I think I'm having a disaster. I need you to check something for me . . .' I explain as quickly as I can. Poppy says, 'Give me five minutes. I'll go and look.'

As I wait for her to get back to me, I fan myself with my passport. It's a little cooler inside, but I'm still melting. I'd love a dip, but can I really brave Annabel's neon horror suit? I think longingly of my faithful black M&S swimsuit, which is now having a holiday of its own somewhere . . . But then I reproach myself. This isn't a holiday. If this clause is missing, I'll have a lot more to worry about than unflattering beach wear.

'OK, I'm back,' says Poppy. 'Look, it's not there.'

'What's not there – the contract?'

'No. The clause. I've read it through twice. I'm sorry.'

I close my eyes and sit down heavily on the bed. I knew it. I remember now. Olivia emailed me at the last minute, asking me to do a whole load of things and at the very end was the clause. And I *forgot*.

'Alice? Are you still there?'

'Just about.'

'Look, it's not necessarily the end of the world. He could end up telling you about these things in the clause anyway.'

'But he doesn't have to. It means we can't hold it over him as a threat. And if the book goes wrong we have no legal redress, and it will be my fault and I'll be fired.' I feel so sick, I can barely talk.

'You won't be fired. People make mistakes. It's not ideal but it happens. I think you should just tell Olivia, or Alasdair, so then at least they know, and they're prepared if there's a hitch.'

I knew she was going to say this. Poppy is so straightforward. I don't know if she's confident because she's straightforward, or straightforward because she's confident, but she's both, and the truth is I'm neither.

'I can't.' I add miserably, 'Olivia already thinks I'm not up to it.'

'What?'

I hadn't planned on telling her about my deathbed conversation with Olivia, but it all comes out.

'Well, that's Olivia for you,' Poppy says bluntly. 'She's not exactly supportive. Look, you won't get Luther's story out of him with legal threats anyway. You'll just have to get him onside another way.'

'I suppose,' I say unhappily. 'Listen, I'd better go. We're about to go on the yacht and I think everyone's waiting for me.'

'There you go! You're already bonding with him. Just be your charming self and get to know him properly, and you'll have him eating out of your hand.'

My despair gets even worse once I climb into Annabel's horror suit. It looks every bit as horrific as I'd imagined; the green colour makes me look like a plague victim and I'm falling out of it, too: the straps give me a hideous side cleavage. Maybe I should just wear the linen dress instead? Unable to decide, I get back into my own clothes, and go back to the terrace to try and calm myself down by admiring the view.

'Did Annabel lend you something to wear?' a voice behind me asks.

It's Sam. Looming behind him is a huge, snow-capped mountain, seemingly right behind the house, though I know it's miles away. This must be Mount Etna: I can't believe I haven't noticed it before. It looks sort of ominous, actually.

'Oh – yes. I mean – she did, but I think I'll still try and get my bag back.'

'Don't bother. It's probably halfway to Beijing by now. You should just borrow more stuff from her; she arrived with about eight suitcases.'

I can tell he doesn't like her either, but I don't care. Why this sudden interest in my clothes? I'm not a child. I can look after my own wardrobe, for God's sake.

'It's fine. I don't need a huge wardrobe to edit Luther's book,' I say shortly.

'Sure,' he says. 'But if you get tired of wearing your pyjamas all day, let me know.' And he walks off.

I no longer think he's being helpful about my clothes:

46

he is *horrible*. Do my trousers really look like pyjamas? I thought they were fairly smart, but then I didn't envisage them having to last for the entire trip. I suddenly wish I was here with Simon, on a romantic holiday instead of on a stressful work trip. But before I go into another slump over Simon, I remind myself: I'm about to go on a yacht with Luther Carson! I'm not going to let a hitch with the contract, or his nasty agent, stop me from getting to know him.

SIX

'. . . So I don't know if you knew this, but it came down to me or – guess who? Rosamund Pike. And the director doesn't like Rosamund Pike. He hates her! He thinks she's awful! He can't stand her! But he was forced to have her because she's a big name. He would have much preferred me though. It's a real shame for him.'

As I listen to Annabel ranting on, it occurs to me that things would be much easier if we were doing *her* life story: she's certainly very ready with information.

This yacht really is something. I've never known what all the fuss about yachts is, but this is wonderful. We're going fast, but you can't tell – it's so smooth, it's almost like flying. The coast looks so beautiful and green from here, and the sea is intensely blue, except where it's foaming white behind us. The only thing that's letting down the perfect scene is me.

I decided not to wear the scratchy linen dress, which felt a bit like a hair shirt. Instead I've thrown yesterday's navy T-shirt on over the lime-green horror suit. Annabel, of course, looks sensational in a turquoise and blue bikini, with her hair in a cute turban. This suit is so indecent I have to stay covered up in my T-shirt, probably looking like an Amish schoolgirl, with my white legs providing a lovely contrast for Annabel's tanned, smooth limbs. To add the finishing touch to my outfit, I'm carrying my handbag with the scratchy dress tucked inside it just in case. Annabel of course has a beautiful striped cotton beach bag.

Our host, Federico, is also extremely elegant in a natty orange polo shirt and shorts. He is about Luther's age or a little older, and handsome in a kind of cartoon-hero way, with crisp curly black hair and bright blue eyes, and friendly enough, but with a strangely blank expression. When he and I were introduced he looked at me in a puzzled way as if he wasn't sure what I was doing there.

'This is Alison,' Annabel told him. 'She wants Luther to write a book.'

'It's Alice, actually. Hello,' I put out my hand. As he shook it, he looked me up and down and I could tell he was wondering where on earth Luther found me. As far as I can make out, he and his wife are friendly with Sam and Luther, but how or why I don't yet know.

Federico and Sam are now doing something manly with ropes towards the front of the boat. Luther and Annabel are lounging on the white sofa area below me, drinking champagne. She's putting her hand on his arm and laughing away at something he's said.

I've crept away to the top deck to get a few moments alone just lying in the sun. I had hoped to talk to Luther some more, but Annabel kept bringing the conversation back to *Roman Holiday* and also some independent film she's been in. I get the impression she wants Luther to do something to help the film out. Sitting there with the two of them, I felt like a lime-green gooseberry. I just keep telling myself this is only a temporary hiccup, and I will get to talk to Luther properly at some stage. I decide to get some sun, horror suit and all, and take off my T-shirt.

I've had my eyes closed for what feels like about five

minutes, when a shadow falls across me. I look up; it's Luther. Every time I see him, it's as if reality bends and I have to get used to him all over again. He's carrying two champagne flutes – chilled from the fridge – and a bottle of Moët. It's like a daydream. My first reaction is embarrassment that he's found me skulking up here – but of course, I'm thrilled, flattered, and amazed that he's tracked me down. I bet Annabel's not pleased.

'Hey,' he says. 'Can I pour you a drink?'

He sits down gracefully beside me, one knee propped up, the other leg stretched in front of him, and leans against the little cabin wall behind us. He looks even better with his clothes on, if possible: frayed white knee-length denim shorts and a faded blue Penguin shirt. Even his bare feet are beautiful. Most men's feet are not their best feature, but Luther's are lovely. I'm suddenly abashed again when I compare his lean, bronzed limbs to my pallid body. Why didn't I get a pedicure, like Ruth suggested? I discreetly put the T-shirt back on, pulling it down over my thighs.

'So what brings you up here?' he asks. 'Were you maxed out on movie talk?'

'Not at all.' I don't want to sound rude. 'I'm just enjoying the view.'

'It's so peaceful after Rome. It was a tough shoot.' He closes his eyes briefly. 'I mean it's a fun romantic comedy, but you're doing it in the shadow of a huge classic. And there were some restrictions on the locations, so we had to shoot at odd hours – it was pretty exhausting.'

'Oh, gosh, of course. Did you – think it went well?' I feel uncertain asking him about his craft.

'I hope so. She's a tough director, though. Sometimes, in the bigger scenes, we'd have to do thirty takes one after the other, without being told why, and then sometimes when it was just me and Natasha, she'd only let us have one.'

I nod, thinking I'll have to get a handle on all this acting talk if I'm to bond with him.

'And it's been kind of non-stop – a couple of other people from the cast were here last weekend, and with Annabel still here, it's almost like I'm still on set.'

'Oh! So there was a group of you?' I'm pleased to know that Annabel didn't get a special invitation.

'Yeah, Annabel's stayed on. She's a good kid. I like British girls.' He glances at me, half smiling. Wow. Is he flirting with me? I must just be imagining it.

'Anyway, we had fun. There were some dance scenes; that was interesting to do. It's a while since I did any of those.'

'Of course! I know! I loved you in *Fever*,' I say sincerely. 'I am such a big fan of dance movies, and I think it's one of the best. You were amazing in it.'

He looks very pleased.

'Yeah?' he says. 'Thanks.'

'There are such great social undercurrents in it. Like, when all the couples are lining up after the formal dance, and the principal won't shake your hand . . . that was so moving, and such a terrible indictment of society in those days.' I shake my head, realising, as I do, that the champagne is going to my head.

'It's interesting you should say that. You know, something a lot like that happened to me in high school,' he says.

'Really?' I'm enthralled. This is more like it: personal reminiscences! I sit up, and tuck my legs under me, tugging the hem of the suit down as I do.

'Yeah. I had this real ass of a principal . . . I was going to be in the school play, which was *Our Town*, and the week before I got busted with a buddy who had some weed on him. We weren't even on school property – we were just outside in his car. But anyway, we got caught – I didn't have anything on me but they claimed he was selling it to me.

There was a huge row and the principal – Mr Spelling, can you believe that was his name – wanted me suspended and out of the play.'

'What happened?'

'The drama teacher said it was impossible because there wasn't an understudy, so he let me be in the play. But, if you'll believe this, he wouldn't let me take the curtain call.'

'No!'

'Sure thing. The rest of the cast came out and took their bow and everything, but I had to stay backstage in the naughty corner.' He swigs some champagne. 'I didn't give a damn but my mom and grandma were in the audience, and I felt bad for them. People were talking about me and what happened, this nosy neighbour lady gave them a hard time . . . it was such bullshit.'

'So what were you doing while they were taking their bows?'

He grins. 'I was backstage getting high!'

I can't help laughing at this; the champagne makes it seem even funnier. I'm thrilled that he's already talking about two of the things in the contents clause: drugs and childhood – sort of. That could be Chapter One, in fact – though we'd have to change the principal's name, of course. We're still laughing when Sam emerges on to our deck.

Somehow, what with the champagne and my state of undress, I feel like we've been caught doing something illicit. But after a quick glance at us, all he says is, 'Hey, Luther. I talked to Paula and they're sending over the *Fur Coat Blues* script.'

'Yeah?' says Luther. 'I don't know, man. It sounds so weird.'

'I think you should read it. I'll let you know when it's here,' says Sam, and disappears. God, he's bossy. Does Luther just let him talk to him like that?

'Sam is a great guy,' says Luther soberly, once he's gone. 'He's saved my ass so many times. And he got me *Roman Holiday* which is a terrific part. If you decide to move to Hollywood and break into movies, Alice, make sure he's your agent.' He raises his glass in Sam's direction, then clinks it with mine.

'I don't think I will,' I say. 'Move to Hollywood, I mean.' The champagne doesn't seem to be helping my repartee.

'It's hard to get in with the real agents,' Luther says. 'A lot of kids coming to Hollywood end up with crappy managers instead. They just set up from their bedrooms. They're not allowed to find work for you, but they all do. Some of them take huge percentages on crummy jobs they didn't even get for you, charge you for headshots – some of them are basically just pimps.'

Wow. I'm not sure what to say to that, so I just nod, thinking how unbelievably handsome he looks, frowning, with his hair ruffling in the wind, and the sea behind him. I decide to try and turn the conversation back to him, do a little gentle probing.

'So . . . who was your agent, when you did *Fever*?'

He shrugs. 'I didn't have one. My mom found me a lawyer who read the contract – though I doubt he knew what the hell he was doing, because all he mostly did was fake insurance claims. And we signed it. That was it. It seems incredible now, when I look back. The truth is I was lucky.'

'It must have been exciting.'

'Yeah, it was great. But I'm at the stage now where I do need a team. You know, I hate that whole Hollywood circus thing. I'm not one of those people who's like, this is my manager, this is my manager's manager, these are my seven agents . . .' He pauses, looking at me and I nod.

'I only have one agent now, and that's Sam. And I have my publicist Sandy, I guess. And my attorney and my accountant. And my assistant. So maybe it's a little circus, but that's it. No nutritionist, no Feng Shui expert, no trainer. At least, I do have a trainer but I haven't seen him for a while. But for this trip, I decided to go solo.'

I nod again. I know enough to realise that this is genuinely unusual for a Hollywood star. He could have a far bigger entourage. I was right after all: he is down-to-earth.

'So is your assistant . . .'

'My assistant is back in LA, looking after my dogs. I've got a Rhodesian ridgeback and a greyhound. They get the blues if they're left alone. You want to see a picture?'

'Of course!' I'm not the biggest doggy fan, but these are not just any dogs. He whips out an iPhone and shows me some pictures, and I think, *I'm looking at Luther Carson's dogs.*

'But it's definitely good to have Sam here with me. You know, the cool thing about Sam is, he has integrity, you know? He's not all, "Sequel, bitch". He lets me say no to stuff.'

I'm sure he does. 'No' is probably Sam's favourite word. I'm a bit at sea, and it's hard to know what to ask next. So I ask the first random question that springs to mind.

'So did you ever have a manager?'

'Oh . . .' Out of nowhere, it's as if the temperature has plummeted. Instead of his usual eye contact, he's looking very interested in the far distance. 'No, I never went there. Hey, it looks like we're stopping. You want a swim? I might take a dip.' He gets to his feet and holds out a hand for me. I take it. It's a pretty dangerous thing to do, because I instantly want to keep holding it, but thankfully, I manage to let go.

My head is whirling as we go downstairs, and not just because of the champagne. I wish I'd taken a Dictaphone or notebook, but on second thoughts, that would seem a bit crass. But this is all such great material. Despite what Brian said, he's already given me two great scenes: the curtain call he couldn't go to, signing the contract with the two-bit lawyer . . . But why did he react like that when I asked him if he had had a manager? Oh, no. Was I showing my ignorance – is it so terrible to have a manager? Surely it can't be that unheard of. I watch as he heads to the rail, and looks out over the water. Maybe he just wanted a swim? No, there was definitely something that he didn't like about that question.

'Alice!' says Federico, coming out from the bar. 'You should swim.' He looks at me dubiously. Maybe he's wondering if I *can* swim.

'I don't think I will,' says Annabel. She's reclining on a sun lounger, wearing enormous sunglasses. 'I'm all slippery with sun factor and I can't be bothered to reapply.' Luther turns away from the water. I can see him giving her a good long look, and I can't blame him – she looks stunning.

'Suit yourself,' says Sam. 'I'm going in.' He's already wearing his swimmers, and seems to have abandoned his glasses somewhere. I notice again how athletic he is: broad shoulders, powerful arms and a flat stomach. I know some women love that type, but it just makes me think of all the hours he must spend in the gym. Simon didn't have a six-pack, but unlike Sam he had interesting conversation, which is far more important, if you ask me. Sam dives off the boat with barely a splash, and Luther and Federico cheer.

'OK, I'm there,' says Luther. He starts stripping off there and then, and I notice Annabel is sitting up to watch him, as am I. This is something you don't see every day. He's utterly divine: not too muscular, just lithe and gorgeous. Absolutely no need for body doubles there. He dives off the boat, and starts ploughing away with a vigorous front crawl.

Annabel casually sits up and stretches. 'Perhaps I will go in after all,' she muses, and takes off her sunglasses. How can she be so obvious?

Federico and I watch as she lowers herself down, her beautiful arms flexing on each side of the ladder, until she releases the last rung with a dainty squeak at the cold, and starts swimming straight towards Luther.

'Are you going to swim, Federico?' I ask.

'No! I have to look after the boat.' He pats the rail proudly. I suddenly realise that my initial impression of him was correct: he *is* a bit empty-headed.

Federico sits down beside me, no doubt for want of anything else to do, and starts chatting away. I'm grateful for the company, but I'm a bit taken aback when he tells me his entire life story. First he explains how difficult it is to get the right kind of yacht these days. Then it's the best places to buy clothes in Italy – Rome or Milan, apparently, not Sicily – then about his apartment and how beautiful it is, and the stresses and strains of running the family business, which sounds as if it's something like 'semen' – but that can't be right.

'I don't think I know what that is,' I say cautiously.

'To make houses, roads,' Federico says impatiently.

'Oh, sorry. Of course,' I say.

Unfortunately, cement doesn't last long as a topic. I observe that Sicily is very beautiful, Federico agrees, and we lapse into silence.

It is very hot and I do want to swim, but the thought of exposing myself in this hideous suit – in fact, the thought of stripping off in front of this gang at all – is daunting. Eventually, though, I decide to brave it. I abandon my T-shirt and head towards the ladder. I would normally dive in, but not in this thing – the straps have an alarming tendency to go walkabout.

The water is beautiful, cool and silky under the hot sun. I feel instantly refreshed. I dip my head under the water, then swim away from the others. Swimming always makes me feel so free. As I look up at the sky, I manage to forget about everything for a few moments and just enjoy floating . . .

Suddenly, something thwacks against my leg, and I jerk upright into a treading-water position. My heart banging, I look around to see if it's a shark, but it's Sam. He must swim like Michael Phelps; he was nowhere near me a minute ago.

'Ow! That hurt,' I splutter, though it didn't really.

'Sorry,' he says ungraciously. 'You know, you shouldn't float so close to a boat. You can get sucked under.'

'Or get kicked to death,' I retort, under my breath.

I notice Sam glancing down, and follow his gaze. *Oh, God.* One strap of the stupid suit has come away, exposing me to his startled eyes. I adjust it instantly, and look up, but he's already swimming towards the yacht, which is probably the best thing he can do, under the circumstances. As he hauls himself up the rope ladder, I notice two heads bobbing together in the distance, one dark and one gold: Luther and Annabel. Bugger.

We've come ashore for lunch. Hiding in the tiny bathroom of the restaurant, and trying to make myself presentable, I feel as if I've reached a new low point. My T-shirt had a huge blob of sun-tan lotion down the front when I got back to the boat. Annabel looked all innocence, but I suspect sabotage. So I've changed into the brown dress, which is now damp from my wet hair. My nose is sunburnt, and there's a huge red burn on one shoulder. In fact – I lean closer – that's not all that's become burnt. I've forgotten to apply suntan lotion on my upper lip, and it's now red to match my nose. That's bad enough, but if it goes brown,

I'll have a tan moustache. And, just to round everything off, Sam has seen me topless.

I look at myself in the mirror, and I can feel the panic rising in my throat. What am I doing here? How am I ever going to get this book done? What happens if Luther just keeps on evading it and leading me on a dance around the hot-spots of Sicily? He's being friendly enough in a distant way, but I'm paranoid that I've antagonised him somehow. I could call Olivia or Alasdair, but I don't know what they could do. I'm on my own now.

Outside, everyone is already gathered around the table on the restaurant terrace. The town is very pretty, with ochre and white houses tumbling down the steep hillside to a bustling harbour. The restaurant overlooks the marina, where sleek yachts are clinking away gently. On the waterfront, crowds of beautiful couples, families and one intrepid roller-blader are gliding back and forth, seeing and being seen. Everyone, even the children, it seems, is wearing sunglasses and beautiful light-coloured clothes. The men here are unbelievably gorgeous, but Luther still stands out – in my opinion anyway.

As I approach our group, I can see how glamorous everyone looks – except me, obviously, in my sackcloth. Luther's got shades on and is facing away from the seafront: a couple of people have obviously spotted him and there's a little ripple of interest and buzz that ebbs and flows around him, but nobody has actually approached him. The others are lounging around looking bronzed and healthy. Annabel is making a big fuss about the fact that she's facing the sun – she wants Sam to swap with her, but he refuses. In retaliation she moves her chair so that she's out of the sun *and* sitting beside Luther, and is scanning the crowds hungrily – I imagine for any signs of paparazzi.

'That's better,' she says, shaking out her blond mane and

re-adjusting her silk headscarf. 'I don't want to get lines. But then I think it would be nice to have a tan in my new headshots. And I do take the sun very well.' She looks at me with false concern. 'You're *very* red, though. And – is that a sunburn on your upper lip? If it goes brown you'll have a moustache.'

'I'm fine,' I mutter, sitting down beside Federico. This brown dress is the worst possible thing to be wearing on a day like today; I am literally roasting in the sun.

The waiter arrives with our food. I've ordered linguine with scallops and cream, and I'm famished, not having had anything at breakfast. My linguine is delicious; silky and creamy, with a touch of lemon, and beautifully meaty scal-lops. I know it's misery eating, but at the moment I feel only food can cheer me up. The prices are sky high, and I've belatedly realised I never agreed an expenses budget for this trip. Are they going to expect me to pay?

'Is that pasta nice, Alice? You're going to end up in a carb coma if you're not careful,' says Annabel.

'In Italy we eat everything,' says Federico ponderously. 'And we smoke. I love to smoke.'

'Oh, yes, absolutely, I eat what I want too. Life's too short,' says Annabel, carefully fishing a crouton out of her salad.

'Nobody smokes in LA,' says Sam. 'It's illegal almost everywhere. Even the bums have given up.'

'Except weed, that doesn't count,' says Luther. 'And I smoke, and Dominique smokes.'

'Does she?' I'd like to hear more, but Annabel is saying, 'I hope it won't be smoky in Tesoro.'

'I don't think we're going to Tesoro, Annabel,' says Sam.

'We could go,' says Luther. 'What the hell.'

'You'll get papped,' says Sam, and, seeing Annabel's face, I realise that's exactly what she's hoping.

'What's Tesoro?' I ask Federico discreetly.

He waves his hand. 'It's a nightclub, near Taormina, very nice, very . . . not everybody can come. I know the owner. Yes, let's go.'

My heart sinks even further. More outings for Luther. Even if he's not raising hell, he's certainly not going to be tucked into bed at 10 p.m., eager for an early start on his book tomorrow morning. This project is slipping completely out of my control.

'How about tonight?' says Annabel.

Luther shrugs. 'Sure, why not?' He turns to me. 'Do you want to go, Alice?'

'I don't think I can,' I say. 'I've basically only got this dress to wear. I'll have to go shopping at some point, but I can't go if it's tonight. Don't let me stop you, though.'

'Yes, I imagine they have a strict dress code,' says Annabel. 'It's such a pity none of my stuff would fit you,' she adds, so nicely and normally that, for a second, I wonder if I've forgotten some sort of trying-on session. Even once I've remembered, I can't believe that she's actually lying. I have a new-found respect for her acting skills.

'No, I forgot,' says Federico. 'It's closed tonight. Open tomorrow.'

'Then let's go somewhere else tonight,' says Luther.

'We can go to Pearl Bar,' says Federico. 'They have a private room, it's quite nice. I'll ask Marisa.'

'Great,' says Luther.

'So I'll reserve a table for five . . . six? You're coming?' Federico asks me.

'It sounds like Alice isn't up for going out,' Sam says. 'But count me in.'

My mouth is still half open. Thanks, Sam, for telling me what I want to do. I'm suspicious: does he want to keep me out of things deliberately?

'Let's get out of here,' says Luther, and everyone starts getting up to go.

'Um, did we pay?' I ask, confused.

'We don't pay for stuff here!' says Luther, standing up. He says this in a generous way, as if I've had a cup of tea at his house and he's telling me not to wash up.

We do, though, because I can see Sam signing something and taking back a card. Great. Now it's official: he's paid, and he's in charge of this trip.

'Hey, it's a pity you can't make it tonight, Alice,' says Luther jovially, punching me gently on the arm. I'm so relieved that he doesn't seem to be cross with me any more.

'But we'll go again,' he adds.

Smiling at him tentatively, I think: that's what I'm afraid of.

SEVEN

As we drive back that evening, my heart is in my boots. It's all the fault of my stupid luggage. If only I hadn't checked it in: why didn't I just carry it on? But even if I did have my clothes, what good would it do me? I'd still be following Luther around, asking him if he could spare a second for the book, which he clearly has no intention of doing. I've been here a whole day, and we're no closer to working on it than we were before I came. I might as well still be in London.

When we get back, everyone goes off on separate errands. Federico has gone home to meet his wife – I knew she existed but he didn't mention her during his monologue to me earlier. Luther has disappeared: from the sounds I can hear from behind his door, I think he's playing a video game. Sam is making more of his endless hiring-and-firing phone calls. Annabel has gone to pamper herself and choose from her million outfits for her night out: soon the sound of Madonna is pounding from behind her door. I love Madonna and irrationally, I'm annoyed that Annabel likes her too. Brian comes out to meet me from the reception room, his glasses shining in the dusk.

'Any progress?' he asks hopefully, in a low voice.

'Not just yet,' I say shortly, going past him. After all my

talk of how I'm going to bond with Luther! He must think I'm a total idiot.

I'm going to have to ring Olivia. I'll come clean, explain the situation and ask her what to do. I get to my room, compose myself and dig out my phone from my bag.

It's dead. And where is my charger? Why, it's in my luggage, of course. I sit down on the bed for a minute and look at myself in the mirror, as anxious and pink-cheeked as ever. What would Olivia do? Well, whenever there's a problem, you talk to the agent. I'm going to tackle Sam. We might disagree about the content of the book, but he has to accept his responsibility to make Luther deliver a proper manuscript.

On my way out, I notice that Brian is sitting in the corner of the reception room. He's talking very quietly on his mobile, and saying, 'We can only hope for the best. I know, I know. Let's just take it one day at a time.' Who on earth is he talking to? Olivia? Are they talking about me and how badly I'm doing? I hurry out before I can hear any more.

Sam is standing on the terrace, talking on his BlackBerry as ever, making a big noise about the size of someone's trailer. Honestly, who cares how big a trailer is? Across the bay, a spectacular sunset is glowing orange and gold over the water. Behind us, Maria Santa is setting the table and lighting candles for dinner. As I walk over to him, I think how idyllic this place could be, in another context, with a completely different set of people who didn't hate me and whom I didn't hate. Sam hangs up, puts his phone into his pocket, and sees me standing there.

'Sam, I need to talk to you.'

He turns back and leans against the balustrade, looking at me. I wish he wasn't so tall.

'Shoot.'

I take a deep breath. 'Look. I know I've only been here

a day, but it's pretty clear to me that Luther is not prepared to focus on this book.'

'So?'

'So I'd expect that as his agent, you would use your influence to make him fulfil his obligation to us.'

'Why?'

'Why?' I'm stunned. 'Because he signed a contract! Because he's already accepted an advance, and he's meant to have delivered a publishable book about six weeks ago.' I try to keep my voice down, in case Luther is anywhere near us.

Sam shrugs. 'We can return the advance.'

'It's a little late for that.' I hesitate, not sure if I should say what I'm about to say, but then continue regardless. 'If we don't get it, we'll certainly investigate legal options.' I'm totally bluffing here, because there are no legal options – not the ones we want anyway.

'Go ahead. We'll bankrupt you.'

'But why did you let him sign this contract in the first place?'

'I didn't. He signed it through his commercial agent without consulting me.'

'Was that Marc?' This was the person we dealt with before Sam, who disappeared one day without a trace. 'What happened to him?'

'He's no longer with us,' Sam says in a bland tone that sounds very ominous. 'Look, Luther isn't one of your home-grown nobodies who are desperate for exposure at any price. He's a star. I know you wouldn't hesitate to exploit him if it meant you could impress your boss with a trashy kiss-and-tell, but it's not going to happen. As far as I'm concerned, Luther's delivered what he promised and now he needs a vacation.' And he walks off, pulling out his phone.

For want of anywhere better, I start walking towards my

room. My heart is thumping. I'm furious. How *dare* he say I'm out to exploit Luther? And simultaneously, I'm terrified. I feel as if I'm falling down a very steep cliff, at the bottom of which is the company in ruins, the missing clause discovered, disgrace, my career over . . . *What if there is no book?*

'You look like you just saw a ghost.'

It's Luther. He's emerged from his room, which is opposite mine, looking heart-stoppingly handsome. He's dressed for going out, in a grey linen jacket over a blue T-shirt and narrow jeans, but his hair is all messed up, as if he's been having a nap. He's carrying a FedEx package.

'Check this out,' he says. 'I just got a little care package from Sandy with some mail and products.'

'Products?'

'Yeah. People send a ton of stuff so they can say I use it. I get to keep whatever Sandy's assistant doesn't cream off. They've sent me the latest iPhone. Also some male grooming products.' He looks at one of the packages. 'Great. Another one for Lucifer Carson.'

'Luther,' I blurt out, 'I'm worried about the book.'

That probably wasn't the best way to put it, but at least now the cat's out of the bag.

'About the book? Why?' He lights a cigarette, even though I'm sure we're not supposed to smoke indoors. God, listen to me. Smoking indoors is not the worst thing he's ever done.

'Well – we haven't done any work on it yet.' Just in time, I remember to start putting things in a more positive way. 'I'd like us to focus on it soon.'

'We will,' he says. He looks at me seriously. 'Alice, we will. But, you know, you've only been here a day! I thought it would be cool to get to know you first,' he adds softly, his eyes resting on my face. 'You know, hang out and spend some time together, before I start telling you my life story!'

He puts his hand on my arm. I look down at it.

'Oh. Right.' Now I'm totally confused. Does he mean it, or is he just fobbing me off?

'You seem like a pretty cool girl,' he continues. 'I think you should just kick back, come out with us on a night out, we can party . . . Oh, no. You can't come tonight, can you?'

'No, I'm afraid not – I'm going to have to sort out my clothes tomorrow, but I can't go in this.' I pluck at the hair shirt.

'You look cute in that,' he says. 'It's kind of – English chic.'

'Annabel lent it to me,' I say quickly. I don't want him to think I'm wearing it voluntarily.

'Exactly, English chic,' says Luther. He throws an arm around my shoulder and starts walking me towards the terrace. 'So listen, don't worry. We will do the book – I promise. Has Sam been giving you the big chief talk? Don't listen to him. He works for me, not the other way around.'

'So we'll do some work tomorrow?'

'Sure,' says Luther. And he looks so serious that I begin to feel, for the first time, a little reassured. I mean – I suppose it does make sense for us to get to know each other before launching into such intense work together.

'Come and eat, guys,' Sam calls from the table. I can tell he's been watching the end of our conversation, and he's decided it's time it was over.

As we all sit down, there's some noticeable tension in the air. Annabel is all over Luther, and she's looking more glamorous than ever in a slinky yellow playsuit that shows off her tan and blond mane. I'm unsure how friendly to be to Luther so I'm staying pretty quiet. I'm not even looking at Sam. He's still watching us both like a hawk – he obviously wants to make sure Luther doesn't mention anything remotely interesting. Brian is a bit distracted. I don't blame him; he was probably hoping for something better than me to appear.

'Are you all right?' I ask him quietly.

'Oh, yes, yes, absolutely. That's a nice colour,' he says, looking over his glasses at Annabel. 'You don't often see girls wearing yellow.'

'I wore this colour to the BAFTAS,' says Annabel. 'And at London Fashion Week. Now, it's funny, it's almost like my signature colour. The press are always going on about it. I'm definitely wearing yellow to the Oscars next year.'

'Are you expecting an invitation?' asks Sam.

'Of course – once *Her Master's Bite* is released.'

'What's this?' I ask Brian in an undertone.

Annabel looks at me patronisingly. 'It's my next big feature, about vampires. I've got the starring role. We're just waiting for a proper distributor and then it's going to be huge. My agent thinks it's one of the best things she's ever seen, and she's very well-connected. She's one of Martin Scorsese's best friends. You've probably heard of her. Terry Heverige? She was an actress herself, she was really huge in the nineties . . .'

I can just picture Annabel playing a bloodsucking fiend, I think to myself, as she rattles on. We've had tomato and mozzarella salad to start, and now Maria Santa is serving us all delicious-looking pasta with some kind of rich tomato and meat sauce.

'Though I could do with some representation in LA as well,' Annabel says. 'Just to deal with all the demands out there.' She looks pointedly at Sam. The table goes quiet. It's a bit of a tumbleweed moment.

'Sorry, Annabel,' he says. 'I already have someone on my books who is a lot like you.' I get the feeling he's said this to her before, probably several million times.

Annabel is only briefly thwarted before turning her attention to me.

'Do they have awards ceremonies for books, Alice?' she enquires innocently. 'Red carpet events? Paparazzi?'

My mouth is too full of pasta to answer. Brian helpfully chips in, explaining about the Nibbies and the Man Booker and other literary awards.

'Sounds very glam,' Annabel says. 'Just think, Luther, once you've written your book you won't have time to go to the Oscars – you'll be jet-setting off to – what is it, the Nibbles?'

'Hey, I could check out the Nibbles,' says Luther. 'Sounds like fun. I could meet some hot intellectual chicks.'

'As long as you don't miss the Oscars,' says Sam.

While the rest of us have been downing wine, I notice he's making one small bottle of beer last all through dinner. He is a total control freak. How can Luther stand him?

'Ah, here's Marisa and Federico,' says Luther.

Federico's coming through the archway, with – of course – a very striking woman beside him. She's not tall, but she has a slender and shapely figure, set off by a simple, fifties-style pink dress with silver sandals. I don't think she's all that beautiful – she has quite a Roman nose – but she's very elegant. Her black hair is swept into a perfect up-do, and she's beautifully made up, with winged eyeliner ringing her green eyes. I feel even more mortified in my brown dress, but Marisa doesn't seem to notice. She greets Sam and Luther affectionately and kisses us all, even me and Annabel. Federico, who is poured into grey sharkskin trousers with a white shirt, greets us more languidly, but Marisa begins chatting to us all at once.

'*Ciao a tutti!* How are you all? I am sorry I couldn't join you today. I had to go and look at an apartment. Did you have a nice time? Did you make friends with Federico's boat? He loves his boat more than me.' She smiles at Federico, briefly putting her hand on his thigh as they sit down. He smiles back, but it doesn't quite reach his eyes.

'It was lovely,' says Annabel. 'I got a nice tan but poor Alice had to stay out of the sun the whole day to stop getting frazzled.' She reaches out her own not-at-all frazzled golden arm and admires it.

'Alice is clever,' says Marisa. 'She stays out of the sun, and she will look young for ever. Me, I'm going to look like a crocodile in twenty years.'

'But a very hot crocodile,' says Luther.

'You won't, Marisa. You'll be like Sophia Loren – a young Sophia Loren,' Sam says, which is uncharacteristically charming for him. He can obviously turn it on when he wants to.

'Yes,' says Annabel. 'Italian women age so beautifully. Personally, I can't wait to get old. Even women in their thirties or forties can be incredibly elegant.'

I don't think this is the most tactful line of conversation, especially as Marisa can't be more than thirty or so, but she continues to rabbit on. Maria Santa appears again, and I'm surprised that she and Marisa seem to know each other – Marisa kisses her very affectionately. I'm also surprised that she's producing another dish – what looks like chicken. I thought we'd had dinner? I don't think I can eat any more, I had so much pasta.

'This is the second course,' Annabel tells me patronisingly. 'Italians eat pasta for their first course, then meat or fish second. Didn't you know that?'

Once I'm home, I decide, if I ever see Annabel in a magazine, I'm going to scribble moustaches on every single one of her stupid faces, if I have to buy the whole shop. Meanwhile, I'm zoning her out. The conversation moves on to a lot of movie gossip about how much things have grossed and who is attached to which project and something being in 'turnaround'. Marisa seems to know people in common with Sam. Annabel, meanwhile, is trying to explain the story of *The Tudors* to Federico. In the end she gives up, and tells him, 'You should look me up on imdb.com.'

I chat mainly to Brian and Marisa. There is something very likeable about her and I'm wondering what she's doing with Federico – he is nice enough, but I still think he's a personality vacuum.

Luther pushes back his chair.

'OK, folks, let's hit the road,' he says. Everyone downs tools and starts getting up from the table.

'Goodbye,' I say.

'You don't come with us?' asks Marisa, but before I can reply, Annabel chips in,

'Oh, Alice doesn't approve of nightclubs. She's going to stay here with Brian and have a nice civilized evening, aren't you? They're going to talk about books.'

I'm about to attempt some sort of a swipe back, when Brian appears in the doorway.

'Look what I found, Alice,' he says, obviously making an effort to be cheerful. 'Scrabble!'

'Great,' I murmur. I don't want to hurt his feelings, but I wish the ground would swallow me up.

'Byeee!' says Annabel. 'Don't go mad, you two!'

They all look so glamorous: Federico, Marisa in her pink dress, Annabel in her playsuit – and, of course, Luther. They make a stunning group. The only one who hasn't made any effort is Sam, who's wearing jeans and a T-shirt – a white one today – and still has his glasses on. He has a cheek, talking to me about pyjamas. As their voices echo through the courtyard and out in the drive, I feel like the kid being left behind with a babysitter while all the grown-ups go out.

'It's a pity we don't have a dictionary,' asks Brian, who's busy clearing a space for the board.

I turn to him, shamefaced. 'I'm sorry, Brian. I don't exactly have him under control yet, do I?'

He shakes his head, but doesn't quite meet my eye as he replies. 'Let's just enjoy a nice quiet evening. You can make a fresh start tomorrow.'

I still feel miserable, and I'm very glad that nobody knows that I'm here playing Scrabble with the ghostwriter while my author is off having a wild time without me. Luther seems really nice and genuine, so why can't I get a handle on him? I know that there's more to him than the partying and the yacht-going, and I think I could get to it, if I could only keep up with him, or if I could get rid of Sam – and Annabel. It's so frustrating. To be so close, but not able to do anything . . . a little voice inside says, *What if Olivia was right? What if you're not up to this?* I do my best to ignore it, but it keeps on long after I've gone to bed.

EIGHT

I wake up feeling marginally better. After all, the first day is bound to be a bit messy. Today I'm going to get going on Project Luther. Last night, after Brian beat me at Scrabble, I washed the brown dress and my T-shirt in the sink. It's so hot that they've dried already. The suntan lotion mark hasn't completely come out of the T-shirt, so I put on the brown dress, wondering if the others think this is some sort of monastic dress that book editors wear. At least it covers up some of my burnt shoulder – though my nose and upper lip are still bright red. I almost laugh when I remember my worries that Luther or Sam would somehow rumble me as not being a 'proper' editor. I could be the post-room boy for all they care.

There's nobody outside, but the table is set with bread and butter, yoghurt, olives and fruit. Maria Santa appears miraculously with coffee and fresh orange juice, which I take gratefully. I heard the others coming in last night around three or four. There were a lot of voices – more than five, definitely, and lots of Italian – and I think I also heard some splashing in the pool. Aside from the chairs being crooked, everything looks relatively normal, except I notice a bra stuffed behind one of the cushions in the seating area. Goodness. I wonder if there will be any new faces at breakfast? Or is it Annabel's? I pick it up and inspect it, trying to guess from the size.

'Gosh, whose is that?' says a voice behind me. I drop the bra immediately, but it's only Brian.

'Good morning,' I say. 'Um, I'm not sure. Where's Luther?'

'He's gone to a vintage car rally.'

'You're kidding! When? He must have left at the crack of dawn!' I look at my watch. 'It's only nine.'

'He left about fifteen minutes ago, I'm afraid.'

I can't believe it. That is, I can believe that Luther's gone gallivanting, but I can't believe I just let it happen – again. He said we were going to work on the book: I should have got up earlier and made sure he didn't forget.

'Didn't you want to go?' I ask. 'Did he ask you?'

'No, and I didn't feel like it,' says Brian. 'To be honest, Alice, I didn't come here to go on a yacht or go to vintage car rallies. I'd sooner stay here and fiddle on that ruddy book. I'm sorry he left without you, though. I think there was a particular race he wanted to see.'

Well, if Luther's gone off for the day, I'm going to take the opportunity to sort out my clothes.

'Can I borrow your mobile, Brian?' I ask. 'Mine's out of battery.'

'Oh,' he looks awkward. 'I'm sorry – I'm waiting for an important call myself. Do you mind? There is a landline though.'

'Fine.'

I'm going to call the airport, and insist on speaking to someone about my bag. If it's turned up, I'll get a taxi there and get it, and if not, I'll just go into Taormina or Catania to buy some basics. I can't afford all this, of course, but I'll put it on my credit card and just pray that I can expense it. I don't relish explaining my lost bag to Olivia – she already thinks I'm pretty scatty – but this is definitely an

73

emergency, if ever there was one. I can't keep sitting at home in my brown dress while Luther chases around town.

Just then, as if in answer to my prayers, Maria Santa materialises behind me. She's holding out a cordless land-line and indicating it's for me. Great! Then fear grips me: this is going to be Olivia, and she won't be pleased at my lack of progress.

'Hello?' I say tentatively.

'Alice, *bella*. It's Marisa!'

'Hi, Marisa! What's up? Has something happened?' I'm suddenly worried: has there been an accident? Has Luther wrapped himself around a tree or something?

'No, nothing!' she says. 'Sam told me about your problem with your bag. I have to go to Catania today. You can come with me. We'll stop at the airport and we'll get your clothes, or we'll get some money from them. If we get money, we'll go and buy you a dress. *Va bene?*'

I'm stunned by her kindness.

'Marisa, are you sure?'

'I'll see you in half an hour,' she says, and hangs up.

Marisa arrives just before ten, driving a little Cinquecento. She's looking very chic in Capri pants and a sleeveless shirt, with a scarf tied around her head.

'Did you have a good night?' I ask as I get into the car, wondering whether to mention the bra.

'Good – yes. Very late!' she laughs, revving skilfully up the steep lane. 'We brought back some friends and went swimming in your pool!' I'm impressed at how fresh-faced she looks. I hope I'm like that when I reach my thirties.

Our visit to the airport is like a hit-and-run. We arrive at top speed, Marisa parks her car in a totally illegal pos-ition, and we're in and out within about twenty minutes. I stand by, speechless, as she makes mincemeat of the baggage official, talking without interruption in a very firm

74

voice, hands on her slender hips. I can't understand anything she's saying, of course, but I can see him crumpling and crumbling by degrees, until, after making a hushed phone call to somebody, he hands over a cheque.

'What did you say to him?' I ask, fascinated, as we leave.

She shrugs. 'He said your luggage was still lost, so I reminded him that they had to pay compensation if it doesn't appear after three days.'

'But it's only been two days! And wouldn't I need to make an insurance claim or something?'

She shrugs again. 'You have the cheque now.'

Clearly there was more to it than that – but I'm incredibly grateful. I look at the cheque, and I can't believe my eyes.

'Marisa, this is far too much. My luggage wasn't worth that.'

'No? Never mind, you can buy some new things!'

'Just something very simple,' I say cautiously.

Catania doesn't immediately knock my socks off. We drive through some fairly dull suburban areas, and I notice a lot of the buildings look quite dark and grimy. But after we park, and start to walk to the centre, it improves. There are some very handsome baroque-looking buildings, and I catch glimpses of ruined Roman or Greek monuments here and there. Apart from the squat palm trees everywhere, it almost looks the way I imagine Rome to be. Everywhere we go, we can see Mount Etna, looming at the end of almost every street. It's strange to see a snow-capped mountain when it's so incredibly hot.

We emerge into a beautiful square lined with imposing buildings, dominated by a huge church – a cathedral, in fact – and with a magnificent stone fountain in the middle. It's ringed with cafés, where people are sitting outside, drinking coffee and watching the world go by. A man walks past us, dressed in a navy blue suit and a pink shirt, carrying a briefcase and with a little poodle on a leash. Everyone, even the men and women who are clearly dressed for work, looks as if they're on holiday. This is more like how I imagined an Italian city to be.

'Wow,' I say involuntarily. 'It's lovely.'

Marisa laughs and squeezes my arm. She steers me into a large pedestrian street off the square, filled with people drifting up and down in no particular hurry, going in and out of some extremely smart-looking boutiques. We find an electrical store where I buy a charger for my phone, then Marisa suggests we do some clothes shopping. I'm worried she's going to take me into one of the expensive shops, but instead we go to a department store with the mysterious name of Coin. I hope that gives an indication of the price.

While Marisa inspects some scarves, I take the escalator upstairs. I'm conscious of her waiting, so I don't want to spend ages choosing things; anyway, this stuff is just to tide me over for this trip. My first priority is underwear: I choose two plain white bras and some multipacks of cotton briefs. I pick out a few more navy T-shirts, which are quite like the one I have already, a white T-shirt, which I reckon will go with my trousers, a pair of linen shorts, and a black dress which is on sale, for going out. I also find a navy cardigan which looks very useful and cosy. Feeling pleased with myself, I head towards the till. I don't think I need to try these on, I can tell they'll fit.

Marisa comes over to me as I'm queueing. 'What did you get?'

I show her, and she literally recoils, as if I've shown her a bag of snakes.

'Alice!' she says. 'No!'

'Why not?' I'm totally bemused. 'What's wrong with them?'

She just shakes her head, looking very serious. She brings me back upstairs, where she marches me around, pulling things off the rails and handing them to me. First she finds a couple of little white shirts and cotton tops in different designs, a black halter-neck top, and a pink tulip-shaped skirt. I wouldn't have picked them myself but I have to admit, they look great. She also picks out a striped black-and-white cotton blazer, a gorgeously patterned blue-and-green silk scarf, a white sundress, a pale blue ballet-wrap cardigan and a white shirt, and makes me try them all on. Then we add some flat gladiator sandals and a pair of high heels with wooden soles. I want to keep the shorts, but Marisa finds me a flared navy skirt instead, as well as some big sunglasses and a wide-brimmed hat. I also find a beautiful pale blue bikini, and a navy silk bra-and-knicker set to go with my cotton basics, and a nightdress. Marisa reminds me to buy a new travel bag and beach bag, which would never have occurred to me. None of my new outfits is expensive, but it's the way she's put it all together; I look so much more sophisticated and stylish.

'They all look lovely, Marisa,' I tell her.

'Then why didn't you pick them yourself?'

'I don't know,' I admit. I know that I have a tendency, when feeling panicked, to pick out very safe outfits – 'boring', Ruth would say. 'Maybe because they seemed too fancy?' I realise how lame that sounds. 'And I didn't want to delay you too much.'

'Don't worry, *brava*,' she says. 'I don't have much else to do today.'

She looks a little sad as she says this.

'Anyway there is something I need to do in town,' she adds mysteriously.

After I've stocked up on suntan lotion and a few more toiletries, we leave the store, and go back down the street to a large café on the corner, opposite the entrance to a botanical garden. Marisa leaves me here, saying she'll come back when she's finished her errand. I go inside with my bags, feeling thrilled at the thought of all my nice new things.

The café is thronged with short old men in white shirts and grey trousers, teenagers in T-shirts and jeans, tiny old women in brown and black dresses and gorgeous women my age or older, beautifully dressed and made up. They're not all at tables; most of them are standing at the bar chatting at top volume. Waiters in blue waistcoats and white shirts are rushing around behind the counter, serving drinks at the speed of light and banging down change and receipts on little metal saucers. On the counter, under a plastic hood, there is an extraordinary array of pastries, cakes and treats I don't even recognise. Listening to the roar of Italian voices, I realise I haven't seen a single tourist all day.

Everyone, even the tiny birdlike old lady beside me dressed in black, looks so stylish that I suddenly decide I have to get out of these linen trousers, which are almost standing up by themselves. Sam was right: they do look like pyjamas. I go into the tiny bathroom, and get changed into the pink skirt and the black halter neck. I don't have a strapless bra, so I decide to go without. I give my hair a quick once-over with a brush, and twist it up behind my head. Emerging back out, I feel like a completely new person. Is it my imagination, or am I suddenly getting a few more looks than previously?

I stand at the bar to order my coffee, as all the locals are doing. I ask for a cappuccino, but the waiter shakes his head at me and points at the clock. He gives me an espresso with milk instead. I have no idea what that's all about, but when in Catania, I suppose.

When Marisa arrives, she almost walks past me, before I reach out and tap her arm.

'Ah, you changed!' she exclaims approvingly, seizing my shoulders. 'Beautiful!'

'Thanks! I might wear this tonight.'

'No. We'll go somewhere else for your evening clothes.'

She's so bossy: I kind of love it. 'Would you like a coffee?' I ask her. 'I'll buy you one. Just don't ask for a cappuccino; he wouldn't give me one.'

She laughs. 'Cappuccino is for breakfast, that's why. It's twelve o'clock!'

How bizarre. For such a seemingly laid-back country, they seem to observe a lot of rules: pasta before meat, no cappuccinos after breakfast . . . Marisa knocks back a coffee with me, and we leave and return to the car. I hadn't realised we were making another car journey, and I feel a sudden pang of conscience. I'm not actually supposed to be spending the day shopping.

'Marisa . . .' She looks at me expectantly. 'Um – is it far, where we're going?'

'Half an hour. Why?'

I'm wondering if maybe I should tell her that I don't need evening clothes, and head back to the villa instead. But then again, I don't know if Luther is even back yet himself. And I do know that he's going out again tonight, so it probably makes sense to get something I can wear if I join him.

'No reason. Just wondering!' I tell her, getting back into the car.

Soon we're heading out of town and on to another motorway. After the strain of yesterday, I feel so much more relaxed, and Marisa is lovely company, chatting away to me about Sicily, asking me about my family and life in London. She reminds me a little of my sister Erica. She also asks me if I have a boyfriend, and she's very sympathetic when I mention the break-up with Simon.

'He didn't deserve you,' she says confidently. 'Somebody better will come.'

I'm not sure I believe her – if Simon didn't deserve me, why don't I still have him? But I appreciate the thought. I'd like to ask her what she does for a living, but I don't because I have the feeling that she doesn't exactly do anything.

After half an hour or so, we arrive at a little town high up on a hill, seemingly in the middle of nowhere. Getting out of the car, I can see ripples and ripples of green and sandy-coloured hills spreading away in the sun, with ancient towns perched on top here and there. The town we're in looks newer; it's not especially picturesque, just one street with a bar, a hairdresser's, and a garage – and a shop without a sign on front.

'In here,' says Marisa, guiding me inside.

It's much bigger inside, and it doesn't look at all like a normal shop; instead, there are racks and racks of clothes, all squashed together and lined up in a very businesslike fashion. A tall woman in a green dress with tortoiseshell glasses comes over, and after a brief exchange between her and Marisa, she leaves us to look around.

It's not quite like the shop scene in *Pretty Woman*, but it's close. Marisa makes me try on tons of dresses, including a beautiful pale pink silk halter-neck dress, and a blue-and-green beaded dress that makes me feel like a peacock. I don't think I would have tried on either of them by myself, but I love them both. I almost don't recognise myself in the mirror. I wish Simon could see me like this. Would he even know it was me?

'You don't think they're a bit too much?'

Marisa waves her hand. 'Being beautiful is never too much.'

They're both reduced – I've belatedly realised this is a

discount store – and I can afford them, especially with my miracle cheque. I also try on a black wrap dress, which looks useful, and is reduced by 75 per cent, but Marisa shakes her head.

'Blondes look good in black, but that style is too old for you,' she says. 'And don't you already have lots of black?'

I'm about to ask how she knows, but then I realise she's teasing me. I don't mind. For the *pièce de résistance*, I unearth a biker jacket of very soft petrol-blue leather, close-fitting, light as a feather and extremely flattering. Marisa suggests I try it on with the dresses, which I never would have thought of doing. It is so beautiful, but I'm afraid it's too expensive.

'You shouldn't buy it if you don't love it,' says Marisa seriously. 'But you do love it, and so you should.'

She's right. I hurry over to give it to the woman behind the counter before someone else snaffles it. I hesitate for ages between the two dresses, and find myself wondering which one Luther will prefer. Then, putting that thought out of my head, I decide to go crazy and get both. Marisa tells me it's a good investment. She herself tries on a pair of jeans, then decides against them because of some minute imperfection.

It's already after two o'clock, and I tell Marisa I'd like to buy her lunch. We go to the little bar down the road. There's a handful of locals inside, who all glance up curiously when we go in, losing interest when they see our shopping bags. Marisa says a general '*Buona sera*' and everyone replies. A teenage girl breaks off from texting to show us to a table, and brings us two bowls of gnocchi with fresh tomato sauce, some bread and red wine. I suddenly realise I am starving. Marisa attacks the pasta with equal gusto, sprinkling parmesan over it. I'm so grateful for her help today when she could have been on the yacht with Federico, or even at the car rally with Luther.

'How do you and Federico know Luther, Marisa?' I ask.

'I met Sam at Cannes a few years ago, and then one of his clients was in a movie I produced. We kept in touch . . . and when he came to Sicily with Luther, he called me. And now Federico and I are very happy to know them both.'

'I didn't know you worked in movies.'

'Yes, I was a producer for five years, in Rome. We did many co-productions with UK and French companies, Japanese and Korean companies . . . many beautiful films, with incredible directors.'

'And what happened?' I ask. 'Why did you decide to leave?'

'We went bankrupt.'

'Oh.'

'And then I married Federico. His work is here. He can't leave Sicily, so I left Rome and moved back here.'

'Aren't there any films in Sicily?' I ask.

'Not really. The Italian film industry is quite small compared to France or Spain, and most of it is in Rome. There is very little work here in general. It's beautiful, as you see, but not very rich. Almost everybody I grew up with has left our town, and moved to Palermo or Messina, or the mainland.'

I'm shocked. Has she given up her entire career for Federico? But I can't ask that, so I just say, 'So you're from Sicily?'

'Of course. You've met my mother!'

'Have I? When?'

Marisa looks mischievous. 'You didn't see her at breakfast this morning?'

'Maria Santa? Is she your mother?' I'm amazed, but now that I think of it, it seems so obvious – there is a real resemblance. 'How come she works in the house?'

'Mama is retired, but she and my father used to run a

hotel, in Cefalù, on the northern coast. Since my father died, she likes to be out of the house from time to time. I was telling Sam this, and he asked if she would like to come and work in the villa. So she did.'

'I had no idea.'

'We even have the same name, you know – Marisa, it's short for Maria Santa. A few years ago, I think looking after Luther would have been too much trouble for her, but from what Sam says, it seems he's better. Not too much party.'

I'm thinking about Sam. It was quite nice of him to give Maria Santa the job, I suppose, but is there anything he doesn't micromanage? I realise, with a terrible lurch of guilt, that I haven't thought about the book for hours. I've thought about Luther, certainly, but not the book.

'So *bella*, how is everything going with Luther? Is he doing his work?' Marisa asks me, as if reading my mind.

'Well, not just yet.'

'Ask Sam to help you,' says Marisa. 'Sam can get things done.'

'Right,' I say non-committally.

Marisa smiles. 'Don't you like him? He is a great guy. Not at all a typical Hollywood agent.'

'Really?' I'm dubious, on both counts. 'To be honest, I think he's very rude and . . . unhelpful.'

'No! Alice, you have no idea how lucky you are. Sam is so reasonable, so trustworthy. He's just being protective of Luther. Once you have him on your side you can do anything.'

I definitely don't recognise this glowing version of Sam. And more importantly, I don't have him on my side.

'Luther's not a bad person,' she continues. 'Really, he is very easy, compared to how he could be. But he's powerful, and he's not used to working on anything that's not movies. So you need to go gently with him, but be firm. He likes

83

you, that's important. Once you have his trust, you can push him, and he'll follow your lead. Believe me,' she says, seeing me droop. 'I've worked with many actors. They all want a director.'

I just wish that all the people who gave me advice about handling Luther had to handle him themselves. But it is a good point, and I can imagine Marisa being quite formidable in a work setting.

'Do you miss producing?' I ask her curiously. I normally wouldn't ask such a question, but I'm on my second glass of wine.

'Maybe,' she says. 'Yes, probably. But this is the choice we make.'

I wonder, exactly, what choice she has made. She doesn't seem madly in love with Federico – in fact, there seems to be something very amiss between them. And I wonder: does she have some kind of interest in Sam? Hardly, or she wouldn't have praised him so openly. Would she?

'Anyway,' she says. 'Never mind about all this. Tonight we'll go to Tesoro, we'll have a good time, we'll all make friends and tomorrow your artistic collaboration with Luther will begin!'

She raises her glass, and we toast to me and Luther.

NINE

Marisa suggests that, instead of going back to the villa, I should get changed in her place, which is on the edge of Taormina. We drive back there, listening to the radio and chatting away. The drive is beautiful, all along the coast, and we climb ever higher until ahead I see a small and very picturesque town clinging to a cliff way above the sea – the same town I saw from our villa.

We park near Marisa's apartment, which is a modern building on the edge of the town. Federico's not home. It's not very big, but it feels spacious, and they (or presumably Marisa) have done it up with real style – there are flowers everywhere, a big paisley-patterned silk scarf is thrown over one of the white sofas, and there's a beautiful rag-worked rug on the stone floor that looks as if it cost hundreds of pounds.

'My aunt made it,' Marisa says, when I compliment her on it. 'Would you like a Campari?'

I don't actually know what this is, but it sounds extremely sophisticated, so I say yes. Marisa tells me to go to the terrace, and she'll bring it out. Before I do, I remember to plug in my phone – I'm so happy I was able to get a charger. I have a ton of messages. There's a text from Erica wishing me luck, and *three* texts from my mum – one asking how

I am, and one telling me about some friend of a friend of hers who lives in Rome, who I should get in touch with if I need help, and one asking why I haven't replied yet. Honestly, it's as if I was in Outer Mongolia. I text her and Erica the same message: 'All well. Place beautiful, Luther v nice, book going well.' It's mostly true. There's also a missed call from Olivia. Oops. I'll wait till I've had a quick sip of Campari, and then I'll call her back.

I step outside, on to the terrace, and my jaw drops. I can see the entire town spread out before me in a jumble of red-tiled roofs, stone arches and beautiful old houses, coloured golden, ice-cream pink and peach. There are two golden beaches far below, curving like scimitars and meeting at a point in the middle, where there's a tiny green island. The sea is navy blue, dotted here and there with white yachts ploughing across the bay, their white trails criss-crossing. The town is perched on a cliff-top that's lush with pines, cactuses and the ever-present palm trees, falling steeply down to the coast. With all the exotic greenery, it almost looks tropical. Below me I can see a Greek amphitheatre spread out on the edge of town. If I look further to my right, there's Mount Etna again with its snowy top. I wish I had my camera.

'Beautiful, isn't it?' says Marisa, coming outside with our drinks.

'I can't believe you actually live here,' I tell her, taking my Campari. I take a sip, and almost gag; it tastes like cough medicine. Marisa sees my face and laughs.

'Campari's not for everyone,' she says. 'Would you like some lemonade?'

'No, it's OK. It's an acquired taste, but it's growing on me.' It still tastes medicinal, but I'm finding it refreshing – it makes a change from white wine. And it feels exactly the thing to be sipping on this balcony, looking down at this beautiful view. We spend an hour or so lounging on the terrace, drinking and chatting, until Marisa suggests we start to get ready.

She has an actual dressing room, with a dressing table and built-in wardrobes on two sides. It's not just for her clothes, though; one whole side is full of Federico's suits and shirts. I can't decide between the pink and the blue dress – the blue dress is stunning, but I feel it's too much of a dramatic leap from how I used to look. With all the beading, it feels a bit like fancy dress.

'It's a very fancy nightclub,' Marisa points out.

But I feel the pink dress is more me. It really is very pretty – it clings seductively, and the colour flatters my pale skin. It's such a pity about my sunburn. I've never worn anything with such a low back before, and I'm taken aback to see how sexy it looks. I can't wear a bra with this either, but I think I can get away with it – that's one upside of not having much cleavage to speak of.

'You're lucky,' says Marisa, shaking her head. 'Without a bra, I look like a monster.'

Anything less like a monster than Marisa would be hard to imagine – she looks a million dollars in an emerald-green strapless dress, with a thin diamond bracelet around one slender brown wrist. I watch, fascinated, as she does up her hair in heated rollers and wraps a silk scarf over them while they cool.

'Would you like me to do yours?'

I shake my head. 'Oh, no, I wouldn't suit curly hair.'

'It won't make you curly. It's just for volume. Come on.'

She's like a girl with a doll, as she sits me down and puts some big Velcro rollers in my hair, and blasts me with a cold hairdryer. I'm dubious, but I'm going to trust her.

'And now, your make-up! Can I do it?'

I'm not sure if she's joking or not.

'I've already done it,' I tell her. I've covered up my red nose and lip with concealer, and put on mascara, brown eyeshadow and lip gloss. Can she really not see it?

She shakes her head. 'Invisible make-up is fine, but not for the night,' and she gets to work.

I'm worried she'll make me look like a drag queen, but she doesn't. She uses some of my own stuff, but she applies it with her own brushes – she has a set of about ten of them – and she spends ages brushing, blending and shading. By the end, I look like me, but better: my eyes are bigger, my lips look fuller, and my skin looks absolutely flawless – even my cheeks look flushed and pretty rather than just pink. She also uses my foundation, mixed with body lotion, to cover up the burn on my shoulder. Finally she takes out my rollers and shakes out the groomed waves. I hardly recognise myself: I look so different. I'm exclaiming over the result when my phone starts ringing.

It's Olivia. Oh, shit. I take it out into the hallway.

'Alice!' the line is crackling. 'Finally! I've been calling and calling you!'

'Oh – I'm so sorry, Olivia. I lost my charger –'

I can hear her sighing all the way from London.

'Alice, you've got to learn to be more careful. So how is it going? Have you made any progress? We're all waiting to hear, you know.'

'Um –' My expression in the hall mirror is guilty. I'm infinitely relieved that she can't see me, dressed up to the nines with a Campari in my hand. 'Well, I've mainly been getting to know him.'

'Getting to know him?' Olivia sounds incredulous. 'And how much progress have you made on the book?'

I shut my eyes briefly and take a deep breath.

'Olivia, I'm doing my best. But he's tricky. He's just finished shooting a film. He's got a few friends with him, and he wants to relax. At the moment I'm just trying to build a rapport with him, and then I hope we—'

'A rapport! Alice, you don't have time to build a rapport. The point of you being there is to put pressure on him. You need to sit him down right now and make him do some work.'

While this speech has been going on, I've taken the phone into the living room. I'm kneeling on the edge of a chair, staring out of the window where the sun is glowing over the golden town.

'I will, Olivia. I promise. I've only been here two days.' I know I sound like an idiot. What I want to do is to ask her how to do it – *how* to make him buckle down – but I can't.

She continues, 'If I weren't banned from flying after my surgery, I'd be over there right now sorting it.' There's a bad-tempered pause.

'How are you feeling?' I ask.

'I'm all right. But I'm still not very mobile. And I'm very worried about this book.'

I take another deep breath.

'It'll be fine, Olivia, honestly. He's very nice, and he does seem keen to do the book. I think I just need another day or two, sort of building his trust.' As I look at myself in the mirror, I can see myself blushing, because, if I'm honest, I don't know if I'm dressed to build his trust or do something else.

'Well, get on with it,' says Olivia. 'And use his agent. He's there, isn't he? Get him to lean on Luther for you. Remind him about the contents clause.'

'I will,' I say, feeling sick. Oh, God, the clause.

'I can't do everything for you, Alice,' she says. 'You've got to learn to take control of things and to make decisions.'

'I know,' I say humbly.

89

'I've got to go.' She's hung up.

'Everything OK?' Marisa's appeared behind me.

'Oh, fine. Just my boss asking about Luther.'

Marisa obviously sees the glum look in my eyes. 'Don't worry,' she says. 'There's a Sicilian proverb, "How we trouble . . ."' She's obviously trying to think of the right translation. '"How we trouble ourselves, and then we die." In a year's time, what will this matter?'

Well, I want to say, it will matter if we haven't got the book and we've lost millions of pounds and I've been fired for incompetence. But there's no point going into all that right now.

'Can I have another Campari?' I ask.

TEN

As we walk down the apartment steps in our high heels, both spritzed with Marisa's *Acqua di Gioia*, I've pushed Olivia's call to the back of my mind, and I'm feeling excited about tonight. Finally, I can be seen in something other than the hair shirt. It suddenly hits me: I'm going out for an evening with Luther! I may not have seen him all day but it was time well spent. I'm finally going to be able to keep up with him, and get to know him on an equal footing, in a relaxed, informal setting. And tomorrow, we'll do great work on the book. I almost forget about my shopping bags, but Marisa says one of her cousins is going over later to see Maria Santa, and can drop them off.

If the view from the balcony was spectacular, the town itself is like a film set. We walk down through narrow, winding medieval streets, catching glimpses of the sea at the end of little alleys where red and hot-pink flowers spill from black wrought-iron balconies perched up high on the walls. Stone arches and palm trees everywhere give the place an almost Arabic look. As we walk along, I realise how slow our pace is compared to how I normally walk in London. People here seem to stroll, or glide instead. It must be partly because it's so hot – I can feel my silk dress sticking to my skin already. Also, walking around seems to be just as much of a social activity as sitting in bars or cafés: the whole town is one giant catwalk. Marisa seems to know everybody, and stops more than once to exchange 'ciao's and kisses. Each person she greets is more glamorous than the last and they all look at me curiously as Marisa introduces me.

As we pass a church, a gorgeous woman with streaky dark blond hair, wearing a long black dress, comes out holding a baby and followed by a dark-haired man in a grey suit. Their chat seems amiable enough but I pick up on some kind of tension – I think Marisa is getting a little annoyed over something, though she doesn't show it.

'Who was that?' I ask Marisa, after they've gone.

'I was in school with her. She's always asking me when we're starting our family, can you believe it? People are so rude.' She looks infuriated, and I don't blame her.

'That happens to my sister Erica as well,' I tell her. Funny that even in this place, which looks like paradise to me, people are bothered by the very same things as back home.

The restaurant where we're meeting the others is in an old stone building in one of the main squares. It's like the square in Catania, but even prettier. Walking along with Marisa I get that same feeling of being in a film. I picture myself coming back here with Luther, late at night, his jacket over my shoulders . . . OK, I need to get a grip.

Inside it's very slick and modern, with white walls and quirky artwork everywhere, and waiters whisking around in black jeans and white T-shirts. The tables outside look very inviting, but apparently we have a private room indoors. As Marisa and I go inside, I can feel heads turning. Everybody is staring at her, of course, but I realise a few people are also looking at me. I can hear bits of Eurotrash conversation in English as we walk through the restaurant:

'I know her. Isn't she that French actress? You know, the one that—'

'French, my ass. Is that what she told you? She's Lebanese.'

'Did you know Luther Carson is here? I'm going to try and meet him! I heard he's going to Tesoro later.'

Our party is in a private dining room, and everyone is already sitting down. Annabel's even more bronzed this evening. She looks beautiful and extremely smug in a sleeveless, high-necked black dress with a feather trim around the collar, and her hair done up in a fabulous beehive. Her face falls when she sees me.

'Alice, you look so much better,' she says, puzzled. 'It's astonishing.'

Luther gets to his feet. 'That's a very hot dress,' he says, kissing me on the cheek. He's never done that before, and it gives me a jolt, almost like a mild electric shock. He holds out the seat beside him, and I slide into it. I feel a bit self-conscious as I slip the biker jacket off my shoulders – the dress really is very revealing. Luther's about to take it for me, but a waiter beats him to it, pouncing on it immediately. He gives me a big gilded key which I presume is for the jacket. Sam has also done a double-take, and is staring at me.

'So did you have a nice day shopping, Alice?' Annabel asks me. 'Brian's been working hard at home. Still there, in fact.'

I'm about to reply, when Sam says, 'As a matter of fact, I went and did some shopping myself today.' He's wearing a very smart-looking jacket and blue shirt. 'I'm going to Venice for the festival in September, and I want to go undercover as a European.'

He does look surprisingly elegant, considering I've never seen him in anything but a T-shirt before, and he's not wearing his glasses.

'Nice try, Elder Newland,' says Luther, lazily hooking an arm around the back of my chair. I sit uber-upright, hardly daring to lean back. 'You might be a closet Euro-fan but you'll always look like a Yank. I mean, look how tall you are, man. It's not just the clothes, it's the way you wear them.'

'I agree,' says Federico ponderously. 'Style is very important to Italians.' Marisa pats his arm approvingly, though I notice she's not looking at him but at Sam.

'Whenever I go visit my grandparents in Salt Lake, if I so much as wear a shirt that's not plaid, people say I look very LA,' says Sam. 'I can't win.'

'I think I have an international look,' says Annabel. 'Though maybe I should get my teeth whitened again so I can play Americans.'

'Yeah,' says Luther, barely listening. Annabel's jaw drops; I don't dare to look at her. I'm acutely conscious of Luther's arm on the back of my chair. I've seen him sit like this before, though; it doesn't mean anything, he just likes to sprawl.

'Alice, can I swap with you?' Annabel asks me.

'Um – why?'

'I want to be able to see myself in the mirror,' she replies. This is pretty bonkers even by her standards, and I'm lost for words. Luther rescues me.

'Let's stay where we are,' he says. 'I want to order. What's everyone having?'

'Veal Marsala,' says Federico.

'Swordfish for me,' says Marisa.

'I can't decide,' I say. I've read the menu about five times, and I can't take it in. 'It all looks delicious.'

'Would you like me to order for you?' Luther says. 'It can be a surprise.'

'Sure, why not!' I say. Luther suggests white truffle risotto, followed by poached chicken with asparagus. I notice Sam watching me with a very sceptical expression, but I don't care. When the waiter comes, I order exactly what Luther suggested.

The waiter has now reached Luther, who's still studying

the menu. Everybody's waiting, but he's still reading. Then he says, 'Can I get a medium steak, with fries?' I do a slight double-take: that wasn't on the menu. But the waiter nods and hurries off.

The meal passes in a blur. Luther is on great form, pouring me endless glasses of wine, and making us all laugh by deciding that he's going to learn to do an English accent. As the wine flows, a feeling of euphoria steals over me. I can see us all reflected in the mirror; we do look like such a glamorous group. I look at the blonde girl in the pink dress, chatting to Luther. Is that really me? I wonder if people looking at us think that we're in couples. In which case, with me sitting beside Luther, that would make me . . . I know this is all a bit of fun and a fantasy, but every time I look at Luther, I feel pretty overwhelmed at the way he looks back at me.

Annabel, meanwhile, is acting like a spoiled toddler, issuing an endless string of demands: 'This mineral water tastes weird. Can we get another bottle? I'm too hot. Can we get them to turn the air con up? Sam, I asked for this salad without oil – what's the Italian for 'without oil'?'

'There is no Italian for 'salad without oil',' he tells her.

A young English girl approaches our table. 'Luther? I love your films! Can I take your picture?'

Luther says, 'Sure – just as long as you snap my date too.'

He puts his arm around me, and pulls me close, so that my face is touching his.

'Thanks!' The girl leaves, beaming. My heart is beating fast; I can still feel the brush of Luther's cheek against mine.

'Do you want me to have a word with the owner?' says Sam.

'Don't sweat it, big guy,' says Luther lazily, grinning at me. 'We should've asked her for a copy, right?' he says to me, and it's funny because it's exactly what I'm thinking.

Annabel is looking more thunderous by the second, her black dress seemingly matching her black mood. She's glaring at Luther who seems totally oblivious. I take another slug of wine. It's hot in the restaurant, and I'm glad my dress is so skimpy, purely so that I don't melt.

The girl comes back, and addresses Annabel. 'Sorry,' she says, 'I forgot to say, I think I know you too.' Annabel smirks modestly.

'Aren't you from that late-night shopping channel?'

Annabel doesn't even bother to reply; she just blasts the girl with a withering look. I manage not to laugh, but as I look up I catch Marisa's eye and we exchange smiles.

'That is so tacky,' says Annabel, once the girl's gone. 'And they haven't even offered us champagne on the house. I'm never coming here again.'

'I might get a coffee,' says Sam.

'No. Let's go,' says Luther.

As we get up to leave, I realise that I've had a lot to drink – the room isn't spinning, exactly, but I can sense a very gentle tilt, like being on the yacht. I think I could have done with a coffee but it's obvious Luther is impatient to get going, so we all file out. I almost forget about my jacket, until one of the waiters rushes up after me after with it. I try and put it on but he insists on helping me with it, which is a good thing because I'm actually having trouble with the arms.

'You certainly did make an effort. I hope you won't feel overdressed in the club,' Annabel says to me with a little laugh, as we head towards the waiting car. 'I notice the foreign girls always dress up loads, while the Italians are more casual.' I don't think this is true, from what Marisa said earlier, and she's not looking especially casual herself, but I don't bother to reply – in fact, I'm not sure I can: I definitely need a minute just to breathe. I had hoped the fresh air outside would revive me, but I'm still swaying slightly. Sam notices me half stumble but doesn't say anything.

The car, a huge jeep, is already revving up as we arrive, and we all pile in. Luther's heading to the front seat but at the last minute, he says to Sam, 'Hey, man, you're the tallest – you ride in front.' Before Sam can protest, he scoots around the back and gets in beside me.

I can smell his aftershave and, during the entire drive, I'm acutely conscious of his body pressed beside me. 'Gotta love these bends,' he says to me, smiling wickedly. Having him so close to me is completely dizzying.

The club is seemingly in the middle of nowhere, and looks like a private house at the end of a long drive, where we park. As we walk closer, the noise of crickets is gradually drowned by the deafening sound of music. There's a long queue of beautiful people, smoking and chatting as they wait, but we are rushed straight in through a back entrance. A man wearing a headset shows us to a smaller, cordoned-off area upstairs, where there are a few other tables with little groups of even more beautiful people. Everyone has seen us coming in, but they immediately pretend not to have noticed, though all of the women are staring at Luther.

We've barely sat down when several bottles of champagne arrive in silver buckets, distributed by very efficient-looking young men with headsets. I suddenly realise I need a glass of water, and I ask one of the young men, who says, 'Pronto, signorina!' Pronto! I could get used to this.

Luther comes over and sits beside me, and the next minute, Annabel is right behind him, practically stepping on me in her haste to sit on his other side.

'Luther, guess what,' Annabel says. 'Tessa called and she thinks she can definitely get Martin, I mean Marty, to screen Her Master's Bite. Isn't that great?'

'Yeah, excellent,' Luther says vaguely. He pours me a glass of champagne, then drains a full one himself. Federico and Marisa come over and they all start chatting. Annabel looks insanely furious. She glares at me, and for a second I wonder if she might hit me or something. Instead she purses her lips and starts looking around the room.

'Now *there's* an attractive man,' she says loudly. I follow her gaze towards a man in a cream-coloured suit. I suppose he is handsome enough, but he has a very low forehead which gives him a slightly prehistoric look. He sees her looking and lifts his glass to her in the most cheesy way imaginable.

'I'm going over to say hello,' she says and, shooting an evil glance at Luther, who doesn't even notice, she stalks off towards her prey.

'Good riddance,' I think, and then realise I've said it out loud. Luckily no one seems to have heard. A girl has come over on the pretext of talking to Federico, but really to stare at Luther. Luther turns back to me.

'Hey, lady,' he says. 'What do you think of Tesoro?'

'It's fantastic!' I say, looking around properly for the first time. It seems to be made to look like a cave, but with lots of Perspex tables and chairs, red velvet carpets, and big gilt mirrors everywhere. From our upper room, we can look down on the dance floor below, which is already filling up. My glass of water hasn't arrived, but I see I have some champagne, so I knock that back instead. It will hydrate me, sort of, I suppose.

'Good old Moët,' says Luther. 'I hate that Cristal crap.'

He's sitting very close to me, and has his arm around the back of my chair again. Because of the music, anything he says practically has to be said right into my ear. Sam is sitting opposite us, chatting to Marisa, but I can see he keeps glancing over in our direction.

Despite my hazy state, I decide we should probably be having a conversation, so I say to Luther over the music, 'Is it true your favourite drink is a frozen margarita?'

'No,' he says. 'I hate tequila. But I do talk dirty in Spanish.' He gives me another one of his wicked, wolfish grins. I don't get it, but I smile back anyway.

Three of the girls have started to dance to Shakira. Their dancing seems slightly weird and stilted to me, but they're all gorgeous, and they all appear to be performing for Luther, especially one very stunning one in a white tube top.

As I watch them dance, I think: they're so lucky. They're free just to enjoy themselves on a night out without having to be on their best behaviour or worry about work. Isn't that what being young is all about? I drink more champagne, savouring the sharp, bittersweet taste, and the bubbles. Suddenly the strains of the last few days – weeks, years – seem irrelevant. I'm here with Luther. It's going to be fine. Luther starts talking nonsense to me about Shakira, making me laugh. I know I should pay attention because Shakira is on Olivia's list of people she'd like to write autobiographies, but I can't quite follow his story, which is something about meeting her backstage: I'm just gazing at him. He is so outrageously handsome.

After a minute the tube-top girl comes over to talk to Luther, totally ignoring me. He chats to her for a few minutes, but it soon becomes obvious that he wants her to leave.

'Listen,' I hear him shout over the music, 'I'm here with some friends. I'll talk to you later.'

'What?' the girl says, pretending not to hear him.

'I'm here with my girlfriend,' Luther says this time, indicating me. 'I'll talk to you later. It was nice meeting you.' And with that, he turns away from her, ostentatiously putting his arm around my shoulder. The girl looks furious and storms off. I'm in shock. *Luther Carson just called me his girlfriend*. It was part of a ruse, but still!

'There you go,' he says. 'Now she'll tell the nearest journalist what an asshole I am.' He tops up my glass. 'Thanks for being my alibi. I'm just going to head to the bathroom,' he adds, getting to his feet slightly unsteadily, 'and then I'll be back, baby.'

He strokes my shoulder briefly with one finger as he goes. It sends a shiver down my entire spine. Oh, wow. If he can do that with one fingertip . . .

I notice Sam, who is still opposite, looking at me and obviously taking in the entire exchange. Well, to hell with him. It's Luther's business who he wants to talk to. I see that on his way to the bathroom, Luther has met another girl, and they're having a brief conversation. Oh, no. Is he chatting her up? But I can't see, because the next minute, a boy in a crazy-looking catsuit has materialised and is asking to take a photo of Luther. The girl turns on him, and during the ensuing argument, Luther slips away inside the bathroom.

I suppose this could be my cue to sober up, but I don't want to. I know I'm drunk, but I feel as if my drunk self is full of wisdom that my sober self could learn a lot from. It's telling me life is for living. I worry about everything, all the time, and when has it ever done me any good? Ruth is always telling me to relax and not take things so seriously. I'm on a night out with a film star in a nightclub in Sicily. When has this ever happened to me, and when will it ever happen again? Why ruin it? As I'm thinking these thoughts, I'm gradually slumping down lower and lower in my seat, until I suddenly realise I'm almost falling off the edge. I make myself sit up again before anyone notices.

Sam and Marisa come over and sit beside me, and the

next minute, Annabel appears, flushed with success about her Cro-Magnon catch.

'He's a millionaire! He's really great,' she adds hastily. 'His name's Nikos. He's from South Africa. Or maybe Greece. He's really, really into film and he says he's interested in finding out more about *Her Master's Bite!*'

'Finding out more about her master – what?' I say. I know I'm not in full possession of my faculties, but that doesn't sound good.

'As in, to finance it, duh!' Annabel says.

'*Bella*, did he just tell you he's a millionaire?' asks Marisa gently.

'No, it just slipped out,' says Annabel. 'It is true though.' A look of doubt crosses her face, and she turns to Sam. 'Sam, how can we find out if he's a real millionaire?'

'I think there's an iPhone app,' Sam says.

A very handsome older guy with curly hair approaches us.

'Hello, I'm Giancarlo, I'm the manager of this club,' he says. 'I'm very sorry not to introduce myself sooner – Mr Carson, it's an honour,' and he shakes Sam's hand.

I'm expecting Sam to bite the guy's head off, but instead he just smiles and says, 'That's very kind.'

The music has changed, from ambient stuff when we first came in to more fun, danceable songs. The dance floor, even in our little area, has filled up. My foot has started tapping, and I'm dangerously close to chair-dancing myself – I can see Marisa and Sam are laughing at me, but I don't care. Suddenly, my favourite song of the summer comes on.

'I love this song!' I yell to Marisa and Sam.

'So does my eight-year-old cousin,' Sam says, but he's smiling – for once. Annabel rolls her eyes.

'Let's dance!' says Marisa. I jump up instantly. Sam and Federico are looking amused, but I don't care. I love this song – I know it's always going to remind me of this summer

– and we're dancing, and I'm singing along, and thinking how true the words are, about things being crazy and people being famous. That's my life right now. Now Luther's joined us. He's found a cowboy hat from somewhere and he starts doing line-dancing moves, and people are watching and laughing. He's camping it up madly, and I can't stop laughing either.

'You're a great dancer,' he shouts in my ear.

'Really? No!' I say breathlessly.

'Yeah, you are,' he says, and he pulls me into a twirl. And we're dancing together.

Even though I watch a lot of dance movies, I'm a pretty awkward dancer myself. But this is effortless. All I have to do is follow Luther wherever he leads, pulls or twirls me. I can vaguely register the others staring at us, but it's like a dream; it's just me and him, his arms around me, my dress flaring out, his eyes catching mine. He is an amazing dancer – of course he is, I know he is, I've seen him on screen. But I had no idea what it would be like to dance with him. He makes me an amazing dancer too. He's Jimmy in *Fever*, and I'm Donna, the uptight uptown girl whom he falls in love with and rescues . . . I realise now that I'm completely hammered, but that's fine. That's a good thing.

When the song ends, he doesn't let go of me.

'That was fun,' he says, as the music changes to 'La Isla Bonita.'

I reluctantly start to move away, but he pulls me back. He holds me close against his body, moves me away, then pulls me in closer and sets a slower, sexier pace. I can feel the heat of his body, so close to mine, his hands on the silk of my dress. This is a little dodgy, but it's fine. Friendly. Although, at this stage, we're pretty much dirty dancing.

'You're a very beautiful girl,' he says. 'Do you know that?'

I can't believe my ears. 'Oh, no . . .' I say. 'No, I'm not.'

'Sure you are. You just don't know it. You're kind of an English rose type, you know? Sort of fresh faced and innocent . . . but not *too* innocent . . .' His mouth is beside my ear as he's saying this, and his lips are almost – but not quite – brushing my skin.

I feel my eyes closing, then I open them suddenly and realise that absolutely everybody around us is staring at us. When the song ends, I decide through my haze that I need to get away from Luther right now, and pull myself together.

'I'll be back in a second,' I tell him.

He says in my ear, 'Don't be long.'

I've never found a bathroom so fast in all my life. Thankfully there's no queue and I'm in and out in minutes. I check my reflection in the mirror. *You're a very beautiful girl.* Did he mean that? My reflection seems to be moving from side to side ever so slightly, because I'm swaying a little, but I can see my make-up is intact; my eyes are wide and my cheeks are flushed but not red. Even my hair looks good. I had intended to use this bathroom break as a time of reflection, but that doesn't happen. I just don't want to take the risk that Luther will leave or start talking to another girl. There are thoughts circulating in my mind that this isn't wise, but those thoughts aren't in charge right now.

I'm walking back out when I literally run into Sam – I almost crash into him, in fact. He disentangles himself, giving me that look again. I'm sick of having to be polite to him. He hates me and I hate him; what's the point of pretending?

'Well, what?' I ask him. 'Are you about to lecture me or something?'

'Would it do any good if I did?' His eyebrows are raised, and he looks contemptuous. I try to match his stare, but I can't so I just walk off. I can see that a little group of girls has formed behind Luther, but he has his back to them and is still talking to Marisa.

'Hey, where have you been?' Luther asks me.

'Nowhere, I just—'

'Let's dance,' he says.

He pulls me in close and slides his arm around my shoulder. They're playing a slow song in Italian. I've never been held the way he holds me: so firmly, and so confidently. As we move together slowly, I breathe in the scent of his skin, his hair. His right hand is on my neck now, and I can feel him gently moving it over the nape of my neck, under my hair. I inch my free hand up so it's just touching the back of his neck. I can feel his body pressing against me. I can't look at him. If I look at him, he'll see how much I want to kiss him.

Kiss him . . . I imagine his lips closing on mine, how soft they would be. Even though we're hardly moving, my pulse is throbbing and my knees are shaking. Suddenly I feel very strange – as if all the blood is rushing to my head and then draining away again, leaving me weak. I take a breath and the feeling goes away, then comes back. I suddenly have to hang on to him tighter, to steady myself.

He says something I don't catch. 'What?' I ask, and I look up. Oh, no. I'm looking in his eyes. His face is so close to mine. He's bending down, and he really is about to kiss me —

Blackness.

ELEVEN

I'm lying on a couch, in some kind of office. There are some concerned faces hovering above me. Giancarlo is there – the manager – and Sam, and Marisa. I can hear music playing faintly outside.

'What?' I ask, bemused. 'What happened?' *And where's Luther?*

'You fainted,' says Sam. 'While you were, ah, dancing with Luther.'

I close my eyes. I *do* not believe this. It's clear from his tone that by 'dancing' Sam means, 'making a complete show of yourself'.

'Take some water,' says Marisa, handing me a glass. I sip it.

Sam starts barking questions at me: 'Have you taken anything? Are you prone to fainting? Are you hypoglycaemic?' He pauses. I bet he wants to ask if I'm pregnant.

'I just have low blood pressure. I've fainted before in the Tube,' I say. 'But never at a nightclub.' The full mortification is just beginning to creep over me. Oh, my good God. I fainted like a schoolgirl in assembly.

'You were lucky Luther caught you before you hit the floor,' says Sam.

'Where is Luther?' I ask quietly.

'I don't know,' says Marisa. 'Oh, look, here he is.' I look up; Luther's coming in through the door, drink in hand.

'Hey, lady! You gave me quite a fright.'

'Sorry. I'm fine,' I say, sitting up, with an effort.

'Let's get a car and take you home,' says Marisa. 'Giancarlo –' she addresses him in Italian and he nods and leaves the room.

Now they've all left, leaving me alone with Luther. I feel utterly extinguished with shame. I can barely meet his eye.

'Well,' he says, 'I've never made a girl faint before. I hope it wasn't my breath.'

'I have fainted once or twice before, but never in a nightclub. Maybe I've had a bit too much to drink,' I admit. 'Or a lot too much.' My head is already starting to throb, and I'm really thirsty. 'I am so sorry.'

'Why? It's flattering.' He pushes my hair back from my face. I shiver at his touch, but I'm amazed. How can he still like me?

Just at that moment, Sam returns. He takes in the scene, but says nothing except, 'The car's ready. Are you guys good to go?'

'Sure thing,' says Luther. 'Come on, baby.' He holds out a hand to me, but I pretend not to notice and stand up alone. As we walk out, I am cursing myself. *What* an idiot. I know why I fainted: it was the drink, sure, but I was also, literally, knocked for six by Luther. And now he knows that. What was I thinking? Do I have some kind of career death wish? He is my *author* – my very difficult, important author who I need to get to buckle down asap. I need to earn his respect, not snog him in a nightclub.

As we join the others, I can see there's a bit of a scene going on. Annabel is having a hissy fit, just for a change.

'I'm just not,' she's saying. 'You lot can suit yourselves.'

'Fine,' says Sam.

'Sam, we can't,' says Marisa.

'What's going on?' I ask.

'She doesn't want to go home. She wants to stay here with her new friend,' says Marisa.

'So why don't we let her?'

'I don't think we should,' says Marisa.

Oh, for God's sake. 'She is a grown-up, pretty much,' I say tetchily. I'm suddenly almost swaying on my feet. 'Look, if you guys want to stay, do. I can get the car alone.'

'I'll go with you,' says Luther.

'Whatever. Just go!' says Annabel. 'Take Cinderella with you before she turns into a pumpkin.' She turns her back on us and marches over to her new beau, who's now taken over the VIP table we were at before.

A pumpkin: that's quite witty, I think foggily, as we make our way out. My sobriety seems to be coming and going in waves, I realise, as I nearly crash into a big red velvet chair. I brace myself as we pass the mirror, but in fact I still look good. Wow! I wish Marisa could get me ready every night. Everybody seems to be staring at us. They probably think I collapsed from drugs, which is fine by me – it's better than the truth, which is that I passed out from the unfamiliar proximity of a devastatingly attractive man.

We're nearly at the back entrance when one of the headset-wearers rushes up and says something in Italian to Sam, glancing at Luther.

'There are photographers outside,' says Sam. 'Let's go out the front.'

'That's great,' says Luther. 'I was starting to think they'd forgotten me. Come on, baby, this will be fun,' and, slinging his arm around my shoulders, he marches towards the door.

As soon as we go outside, the flashing starts. I think there are only about half a dozen men, but I can't be sure. It seems like more. The barrage of lights isn't as overwhelming as I'd expected; it's the shouting that gets me, mostly Italians speaking English but a few English accents as well:

'Luther! Over here!'

'Luther, who's your friend?'

'What's her name?'

'Sweetheart, give us your name?'

I'm being papped! I'm just glad I'm dressed for it. I start smiling out of habit, before I remember that we don't like them, and frown mysteriously instead. Then I remember what I've read in magazines about putting your arm on your hip and angling your waist. I give it a go, but I'm far too drunk and Sam is dragging me into our car. I get in reluctantly, clamping my legs together in case they take some awful up-skirt shot. Once I'm in, I turn to look at Luther, but Sam's wedged himself in beside me instead.

'That was unnecessary,' he says to Luther, who's on his other side.

'It was fun for Alice,' says Luther, sounding petulant.

Everyone is quiet except Federico, who's become inexplicably chatty and launches into a long, boring monologue about Giancarlo's success with the nightclub, and how he himself would like to do something similar. Marisa, who's sitting in the front with him, replies in monosyllables.

After we've dropped them, it's only another fifteen minutes to our house. My eyes are beginning to close. The evening is running through my head again: the dressing-up, the dinner, the club, the paparazzi and oh, God, the dancing . . . the dancing was wonderful. Even if it was unwise, it was wonderful.

We're here. The car drops us off, and the three of us walk towards the house. It feels strange to be here without Annabel. Strange, and very nice. It's as if the house has been possessed by a malevolent spirit, and now it's been exorcised.

The bay is as calm as ever; the air is so lovely and fresh I can feel it instantly making me feel better.

'Who's for a nightcap?' says Luther. 'It's only, like, two a.m. The night is young!'

I know I should probably go to bed, but it's so nice out here. I am definitely, definitely not going to get up to anything untoward with Luther. But it might be wise just to have one drink with the two of them, so there's no awkwardness between us.

'I'm fine,' says Sam.

'Can I have a Sprite?' I ask Luther.

Luther shakes his head. 'I'm disappointed in you both,' he says, and he goes off inside the house. A minute later he pops his head back out: 'Have you noticed that I am getting you guys drinks? That's very good of me, don't you think?' And he disappears again.

I collapse on one of the sunloungers and look up at the stars, which are perhaps rotating a little bit.

'Goodnight,' says Sam.

I look at him in alarm. 'Are you going to bed?'

'Yeah,' he says. 'I don't want to cramp your style.'

'I don't know what you mean.'

'You know exactly what I mean. Your speech yesterday about legal options and all the rest of it made you sound very committed to your work. Looking at the floor show you gave us tonight, I'm not so sure. Are you here to work or to score yourself a celebrity boyfriend?'

'We were just dancing. What's wrong with that?' I can feel myself flushing. I know what was wrong with it. And what was right with it.

Sam looks disdainful.

'If that's what you want to tell yourself, go right ahead. But I would have expected a little more professionalism.' And he's gone.

I glare at him, wishing I could think of a scathing reply. Bastard! Self-righteous pig. How dare he be so preachy? What business is it of his anyway?

I'm feeling rattled, all the same, and I should probably go to bed. I haul myself reluctantly off the sunlounger, and head towards the house, where I almost collide with Luther. He's got an open bottle of champagne under one arm, and two glasses in his hand, one of which is full.

'Hey, not so fast,' he says. 'Where are you off to?' He puts the champagne down on the table, and hands me the full glass. 'Here's your Sprite.'

'Luther, I know that's champagne. And I'm going to bed.'

'Oh, no you don't. We're going for a swim.'

'A swim?'

'Yeah, a swim.' Looking at him, I realise this isn't the romantic Jimmy from the dance floor any more: he means business. This time he's not going to stop at a few twirls, and fainting won't be an option . . . I still think he's gorgeous, but I also feel as if I've got a tiger by the tail. He takes a step closer, and takes my hand. And I see something clinging to the inside of his nostril; a minute white lump.

I mean, I'm not an idiot. I know what he's been doing every time he spends a quarter of an hour in the bathroom. It's not that that brings me to my senses. I am very drunk, true, but there's a tiny, tiny part of me that retains the power to think. And it's telling me I have two choices right now. I could kiss him, sleep with him, maybe even have an affair with him. But if I do, I can kiss goodbye to his book, and to my career.

'I can't,' I say. 'I'm really sorry.' Before he can say anything, I crash past him, and stumble into my room. I hope that Sam hears my door closing.

TWELVE

I must be dying.

My tongue is stuck to the roof of my mouth, and my head is full of pounding hammers, like a factory. I'm parched – even my hands and feet feel dry, as if my body has been completely leached of moisture. I've got to drink something. I lever my head up off the pillow and the pounding increases, as does my nausea. I think I'm going to be sick. I spot a half-empty glass of water beside my bed – it's like an oasis in the desert. With a huge effort, I lean out of the bed, successfully grab it and drink it down. It's warm, but at least it's liquid.

I'm still in my pink dress. My pillow is covered in mascara. I go cold and hot as I remember the horror. Oh, God. I was dirty dancing with Luther. I almost kissed him, and then I literally swooned in his arms. The humiliation makes me curl up in my bed. I was papped with him, and then . . . Phew. We came home, and I went to bed. *Thank God.*

Through my nausea, I realise that I've had a very lucky escape. Sam, though – he thinks I've slept with Luther, I bet he does. And everyone will have seen me making puppy-dog eyes at him . . . slow-dancing with him . . . fainting . . . Suddenly there's an unbearably loud cheeping noise. I lean over and feel around on the floor for my phone. It's a text from Ruth. 'How is it all going over there?? Is LC hot? Don't do anything I wd!' And there's another from my dad, sent yesterday evening: 'Glad all going well. How is book coming? Did you bring traveller's cheques or are you using ATMs? If latter be careful re fraud.'

I groan, and drag myself out of bed. I have to have something cold to drink. I manage to get to the kitchen by shuffling along very slowly in a semi-erect fashion. Everyone seems to be still asleep. I have no idea what time it is. I find some water and gulp it down. As I stagger back to my room, I see the swimming pool outside, and remember my resolve to do lengths every morning, before spending a civilised day working on Luther's book.

There are footsteps behind me. I turn around; it's Annabel. I suppose I should be relieved that her Cro-Magnon brought her home instead of cutting her up into little bits and dumping her somewhere, but it's a close thing. I'm pleased to see that, like me, she looks a bit the worse for wear.

'Have a nice time last night?' She steps right up to me, so we're almost nose to nose. 'Whose bedroom did you end up in?' she asks aggressively.

'I can't deal with you right now,' I tell her, and I stumble off to bed. Gosh, that was feisty of me. Maybe I'm still drunk? I get back to bed and lie down carefully. Then I realise I'm definitely going to be sick. I hurry next door to my bathroom, just in time.

I feel marginally better afterwards. I contemplate having a shower, but that would mean standing up. I decide the only thing that's going to make me feel better is to go in the pool. My shopping bags are lined up neatly just inside my door, but it takes me ages to locate my new bikini and put it on – I almost don't have the strength to pull off the tags. I inch my way outside, head down, moving like the Kia-Ora crow in the ad and squinting at the sun. As I lower myself into the water, which is blessedly cool, I can feel myself magically regenerating. Soon I can even swim a few strokes. That's a bit much, though, so I just lie there on my back, floating motionlessly, letting the water heal me.

Suddenly I hear shouting. Someone jumps in and starts splashing towards me. Before I can even turn my head, I'm being hauled across the pool by a pair of incredibly strong arms.

'What the—' I splutter. It's Sam. He lifts me out of the pool and dumps me on the side.

'What are you doing?' I finally manage to say.

'I thought you were drowning!' he yells, in a voice that cracks my head open again. 'You scared the shit out of me!'

I put my hands over my eyes. 'I was just floating,' I complain. I squint at him. He's crouched beside me, wearing a T-shirt and jeans. He must have jumped in fully clothed. I hate to admit it, but the wet T-shirt look suits him.

'How was I to know that? And you did faint last night, in case you've blacked that memory out.'

I laugh weakly. 'Did you think it was like the beginning of *Sunset Boulevard*, with the dead body in the pool?' Then I start to cough. 'Oh God, I feel awful. You made me swallow some water.'

'You need it,' he says tartly, 'after all the booze you drank last night.'

'I wasn't the only one, you know,' I tell him. 'What time is it?'

'You're lucky my watch is waterproof,' he says, looking at his wrist. 'It's noon.'

As late as that? Oops. 'Where is everybody?'

'Brian's down on the beach. I think Annabel just rolled in from her, um, date. And I've been reading a script, and saving your life. And Luther—'

'I haven't seen him since last night,' I say quickly.

113

'I know. He's gone out with Marisa and Federico.'

Oh. From the way he says that, I think he knows nothing happened with me and Luther. But how? Did Luther tell him?

Sam gets to his feet. 'I'm going to get changed. Try not to drown.' And he's gone, leaving me sitting on the edge of the pool, my relaxing swim well and truly over.

I've just thought of someone else who might also be annoyed at me. Luther. He's probably going to be furious with me for leading him on all night, and then for backing away at the last minute. What if his film star ego is in shock, and he takes it out on me? Why, oh why did I go to that nightclub with him in the first place? Why did I have to dance with him like that? I was meant to be getting to know him on a deeper level, instead of – well, instead of what happened.

I pick up my phone and look at the date. This is my third full day, and I've managed to get myself into the worst possible situation I could have imagined – second only to sleeping with him. I groan out loud. To prevent the panic rising again, I start to think about damage limitation. If Luther is annoyed at me, there's not much I can do, except cast myself on his mercy. I'm going to have to make an appeal to his better nature. I'll tell him we need him – I need him. I'll tell him how much we want to hear his story . . .

Then I remember – he's already given me some of the story! The curtain call with the high school play, and the local lawyer who signed the contract for *Fever*. It's only a page or two, but it will at least be something for Brian to work on.

As Sam had told me, Brian is down on the little shingle beach that belongs to the house, trying to skim stones into the sea. I suddenly feel desperately sorry for him. I bet he

114

wishes he was at home. Since I arrived, things have probably been even worse for him.

He turns around to face me, and I get a real shock. Even though he was at home last night, while we were carousing, he looks absolutely awful – his normally ruddy face is pale, and he has huge bags under his eyes.

'Brian! What on earth is wrong? Are you ill?' I take a step towards him.

He shakes his head. 'Just a few – just some things on my mind. I'm fine. How was your evening?'

I hang my head. 'It was all right. But it's not getting us any closer to the book. When Luther gets back, I'm going to – talk to him. I swear. Meanwhile, I've got some little bits for you to write up, if you don't already have them.' I tell him the high school curtain-call incident and the lawyer story.

He nods. 'Thanks. It's not much, but I can weave it in – for what it's worth.'

While Brian's working, I pace up and down the terrace, psyching myself up for Luther's return. I'm not going to think about last night. I am going to get him to do some work. I *am*.

Annabel's installed herself on the terrace, where she's sunbathing and listening to her iPod. Sam is beside her, still reading his script. Now she's applying her expensive suntan lotion – bloody cow. Sam glances up from his script, and looks at her. I wonder if he's going to ogle her, but instead he keeps reading.

Seeing Sam read his script obviously stirs Annabel's competitive instincts. She zips into the house, and before long she's reappeared with her own script. She ostentatiously marks – I count them – three lines, and starts muttering them under her breath.

At about 3 p.m., there's a crunch on the gravel outside.

Luther's back – alone, thankfully. He comes in, wearing his shades and looking a bit crumpled and unshaven and very much as if he's been out on the town the night before. It's a particularly devastating look for him, but I'm going to try not to think about that.

'Hey, lady,' he says, and walks right past me.

Oh, shit. I hurry and catch him up.

'Luther – can I talk to you? I really, really need your help.'

'What's up?' He pulls down his shades, and I'm relieved to see he doesn't look particularly annoyed after all, just exhausted. OK. This is a good sign.

'I just—' I'm about to mention last night but I decide not to. 'I need two hours of your time this afternoon. To work on the book.'

He gives me a long, cool look. Amazing how his hangover makes him look like a sexy, hot mess, whereas I just look a mess. I plough on.

'We're all such fans of yours. Everybody I work with is so thrilled that we're going to be telling your story. I promise there doesn't have to be anything in it that you don't want,' I add, throwing caution to the wind. 'But we are nearly out of time. And, to be honest, my job's on the line. I really, really need you.'

'OK.'

'OK?' Wow. Is it going to be that simple?

'There's a back terrace. Let's go out there.'

'I'll get Brian.'

He turns around. 'No, let's leave it just the two of us for now.'

116

THIRTEEN

I run in and grab Brian's Dictaphone, and hurry out to
follow Luther into a small, square back terrace that overlooks
the other side of the bay. I didn't even know it was here;
this place really is rambling. One wall is taken up with a
long sofa-shaped padded seat, and there's a sunlounger on
the other one. Luther flings himself on to the sunlounger,
puts an ankle on his knee and hooks his hands behind his
head.

'So what do you want to know?' he asks. I can't read his
expression.

'Well – maybe we can start with some of your early life.
What about the time when you were temporarily
homeless?'

'Really? You want to hear about that?'

'Yes! I'd love to!' As he begins to talk, I turn on the tape.

'That was a crazy time. It lasted about a year. My dad
moved out when I was thirteen, and my mom couldn't
afford the mortgage any more. At first we stayed with some
friends of hers, but that didn't work out.'

I just nod.

'Around that time my mom got a new boyfriend. Amos.
What a hick. Definitely not your regular Camden dude. He
was the brother of Mom's friend – the one we were staying

with. He was a hippy, I guess, or a pothead, anyway. He kept talking about this place he knew in Mexico where people could come and stay for free. Me and my sister just hoped he'd take himself off there soon, and never come back.' He looks at me through his lashes.

'One day, I came back from school. My mom and my sister were sitting at the kitchen table and Amos was there too. I remember it so clearly. She told us to pack our bags. We were going to Mexico.' He shakes his head. 'So, we packed up all our stuff and the next day we got in his van and started driving.'

'A long way.'

'Sure. It took about three weeks, and we had to sleep in his crummy van the whole time. Mom didn't have a car at the time, by the way – she sold it. By the time we got to the border, we were so tired we were almost hallucinating. We didn't even have passports, so we had to sneak out past the border police. Luckily, they don't pay as much attention to people coming *out* of the US.

'Then we got there. Somewhere near . . . Tijuana. It was a weird, weird scene.' He leans back and looks up at the sky. 'I don't know how to describe it. It was basically a cult. They dressed in white, and called themselves the Children of God, and—'

'The what?'

'The Children of God?' He looks at me blankly. I'm not sure why I've interrupted him – it's just that it was so totally unexpected, I wanted to make sure I didn't mishear. It also sounds familiar for some reason.

'Sorry. Go on.'

'They made all us kids sleep together, away from the parents. They said there were no such things as children, or parents, we were all children of God together.' He shakes his head. 'Me and my sister used to sneak away as often as

118

we could. We'd sing songs in the streets to try and get money.'

'Why?'

'I was saving up to run away.' He looks down. 'That was a bad scene. No kidding. The older kids were talking about some kind of initiation rite. I didn't know what it was, I just knew I didn't want to be there when it happened.'

I can't quite believe what I'm hearing. Is it true? How is it possible that all this happened and that I've never read or heard a word about it? Yet it does sound vaguely familiar. I'm simultaneously reeling from these disclosures, feeling sorry for Luther, wondering about the legal issues and thinking that this is certainly pretty revelatory material.

He tells me that his mother had a falling-out with Amos, came to her senses and managed to leave with both Luther and his sister. He's very funny on the subject of their journey home, talking about all the crazy experiences they had while hitch-hiking back to Queens to his mother's family. It would sound implausible, except that there's something about the way he describes it that gives it a ring of authenticity.

After a while, he's starting to look tired, so I suggest taking a break.

'OK,' Luther says. 'I'll think I'll go take a nap.'

Gosh. That wasn't so hard. I go and find Brian, who's sitting inside in the cool reception room tapping on his laptop. Nobody else seems to be around.

'I did it! I got an interview from him!' I hand him the tape, which is nearly full. 'You should listen to it.'

'Well done, Alice. By the way – there's something I should mention.'

'Oh, what?' I hope he's going to tell me what's been on his mind.

'Well, I was writing up that school play story, and I spoke

to a woman who was in Luther's class – she's been very useful for background. She says it's not true.'

'What's not true?'

'The whole story about him not taking the bow. She's scanned and emailed a photograph of him, centre stage, taking a curtain call. She doesn't know why he's said he wasn't there.'

'Why would he make it up?' I say in disbelief.

Brian shrugs. 'It's very common. Often people tell you what they think happened, or what they wanted to happen – it's hard to tell the difference sometimes. Perhaps the principal did tell him he couldn't at first, and that's what he remembers. I shouldn't worry too much, anyway. I'll ask him about it.'

'No, I'll ask him,' I say, indignant. 'I don't want him to think he can just lie to me. Oh, shit,' I add abruptly, as a new and unwelcome idea finally hits me.

'What?'

'I think he's just been telling me another pack of lies.'

'What about?'

'About – his mother taking him and his sister off to join a cult. I knew it sounded familiar. He said they were called Children of God.'

'And?' Brian says. 'Sounds odd, but it might be true.'

'No. It happened to River Phoenix. Oh, my God. That is the sickest thing I've ever heard. He's stolen River Phoenix's childhood!' I grab Brian's laptop, and google 'River Phoenix cult'. Sure enough: River and his family were taken off to join the Children of God in Venezuela – not Mexico; that was Luther's invention. 'I don't believe a word of it.'

'Well, it does seem odd that this is the first we've heard of it,' Brian says.

'I'm such an idiot. And him!' I glance up furtively, but there's no one around. 'With all of us dancing attendance

120

on him, trying to pin him down . . . you and I could be at home right now!'

Brian stares down at his laptop. He really does look awful.

'Brian, what on earth is the matter?' I ask. 'I don't want to pry, but I can tell something's up – what is it?'

'It's my wife,' he says. 'I just – she's been having tests. And this morning, we got some bad news.'

'What?'

'It's cancer,' he says. 'Ovarian cancer.' His face crumples, and tears start to run down his plump cheeks.

My hand is over my mouth. I can't believe it. Poor, poor Brian.

'I'm so sorry,' I say. I put my arm around him; I almost feel on the verge of tears too. He doesn't cry any more, but gives big, jerking sighs. As soon as I think he's ready to listen, I say, 'But Brian. What are you *doing*? Why are you even still here?'

'I've signed a contract,' he says numbly.

My mind is racing. I want to tell him that he has to go home immediately, but I can't do that without checking with Olivia first.

'Hang on, Brian,' I say. 'I'm going to speak to Olivia. I think you should go home, but I just need to tell her first. Is that all right?'

He nods. He looks as if he's barely heard me. I quickly walk back to my room, and dial Olivia's landline. No reply. Then her mobile. It rings out. I leave a message: 'Olivia, it's Alice. Something's happened with Brian, and I think he ought to go home. Please ring me as soon as you get this. Thanks.'

I go back into the room, where Brian is sitting and staring at his hands.

'I've left her a message,' I say. 'Let's see if there's a flight this evening.' I gently take his laptop from him and start looking online. There's a flight at seven-thirty, but we'll have to leave in the next half-hour to catch it. The next available one isn't until the day after tomorrow.

'But what about the book?' Brian says.

Good question. What about the book? What on earth am I going to do without a ghost writer? I'm an editor, not a writer – well, I'm not really an editor, but we'll leave that to one side. I'm not even supposed to be doing inter- views and, judging from the way the last one went, I can see why.

'Well . . . we can probably manage something,' I say uncertainly. 'I mean . . . I could do more interviews, and you could work at home . . .'

Brian's looking at me expectantly. The expression of hope in his eyes breaks my heart.

'Is there anyone there with your wife right now?'

'Our daughter Jennifer is finishing her gap year trip. She's in Chile. We haven't told her yet. She only has two more weeks left and it seems such a shame.'

'So – she's at home alone?'

He nods. 'I asked her to get her sister to come and stay, but she didn't want to.'

And I realise that even if it's inconvenient for us, I have to try and get him on the seven-thirty flight tonight. I don't know what Olivia will say, but I can't keep him here. And anyway, didn't Olivia say that I had to learn to make decisions?

I stand up. 'Brian, why don't you go and pack your things right now. I'm going to call for a taxi, and then we'll go to the airport and put you on that next plane. In fact, don't pack yet. Call your wife first, then pack.'

'Thanks,' he says, and begins to dial. He looks up. There are tears in his eyes. 'Do you know, it's the stupidest thing.

I've forgotten the dialling code for England. I dial it all the time –'

'It's zero zero four four, and then your number, without a zero,' I say. 'Here, I'll do it.' He was calm when we first started talking, but now that he's told me, he seems to be unravelling before my eyes. I think he must still be in shock.

After I've dialled for him, I set about looking for a taxi number. Why have I never organised a car service here? It's crazy. What if there was an emergency? What am I saying – this *is* an emergency. I hurry off towards the kitchen, thinking I'll ask Maria Santa, but she's not there.

Suddenly I spot a folder on the sideboard, which looks like a guide to the house. Inside – hurray! – there's a sheet of paper with numbers of local taxi drivers. Unfortunately, the first person who answers doesn't speak English any more than I can speak Italian. I say, 'Airport?' but no joy. Eventually he twigs. *'Un'ora,'* he says.

'Oh, no, I need it now.' I indicate my watch, which, of course, is pointless as he can't see me. Just then, Sam wanders into the room and pours himself a coffee from a pot on the stove. Great. I pointedly turn my back to him, and repeat, 'Now?' The man repeats *'Un'ora'*, so I hang up, and dial the next number.

'Going somewhere?' Sam asks.

'No. It's Brian.' I may as well tell him. 'His wife is unwell and he has to leave for the airport immediately.'

I begin the same conversation with the next person, who does speak English but can't come soon enough either. Sam doesn't leave the room; he just sips his coffee and watches me with interest – bastard. I'm dialling a third number when he says, 'This isn't Fifth Avenue, you know. You can't just click your fingers and get a cab.'

'I'm aware of that,' I say through gritted teeth.

'Look, I'll take him.'

I'm stunned. 'Are you sure?'

'Get him ready in five minutes, or I'm changing my mind.'

'Oh – OK. Thanks.'

Why is Sam offering to help us? I have no idea, but it doesn't matter; the main thing is to get Brian home. After I've told Brian we're leaving, I walk down the corridor towards Luther's room. I am so furious with him right now. When I think of what Brian's been going through – I can't believe that one person could be so selfish and obstructive. Why is he pretending he wants to do this book when he so clearly doesn't?

I'm actually standing outside his door with my fist raised, ready to tear strips off him. But then what? I scream at him, he goes into a strop, he leaves, and there's no book. Or, I scream at him, he miraculously reforms, we do a fantastic book? Not likely. Anyway, I don't have time. I have to get to the airport. I step away from Luther's door and go back to help Brian get his things together.

FOURTEEN

Five minutes later, we're piling Brian and his wheely suitcase into Sam's Fiat. Brian sits in the back and, after a momentary hesitation, I sit in the front with Sam.

'I should have said goodbye to Luther,' he says, as we set off. He still seems dazed.

'Don't worry, I'll tell him,' I reassure him. 'We should be in time for your flight. Can someone pick you up?'

'Yes,' he says. 'Sheila—' His voice breaks and he goes quiet. Ridiculously, I can feel my own eyes welling up.

'We'll get you there,' says Sam, looking at him in the rear-view mirror.

He's driving much faster than he did on the way from the airport with me. I never noticed it before, but he does have a nice profile, with his slightly snub nose and firm mouth. And very good forearms. I love watching men's arms when they're driving; I can see the muscles flexing as he moves the wheel . . . He looks over at me and I look away quickly, before he can see me checking him out.

Oh my God. Am I checking him out? *Sam?* I must be out of my mind. He might be doing an uncharacteristically good deed for Brian but he's still an arrogant bastard. Not to mention the fact that he probably wants Brian gone anyway, so he's really just doing himself a favour.

I clear my throat and sit up straighter in my seat, looking out at the sea and the mountains flying by, lit up by the evening sun. I check my phone. No word from Olivia. I'm glad, because the longer she leaves it before replying, the more of an excuse I have for sending Brian home. But I have to admit, she's not going to like it – in fact, she's going to flip. This whole situation could not be more of a mess. I thought I'd had some nightmare projects before, but this one takes the biscuit.

Thankfully, there's no queue at the sales desk, and we get Brian on to his flight straightaway. I'm braced to put it on my credit card, but Brian says he can do that himself. Just as well – after my shopping spree yesterday, I must be near the knuckle, and I still haven't figured out how to cash my Italian cheque.

'Thanks, Alice,' says Brian, once he's checked in. 'I think I'll leave you this, just in case.' He hands me his laptop. 'It's just one I use for travel. You can give it back to me in London.'

'Thank you,' I say, taking it. 'Oh, wait. What about the tapes and the Dictaphone?'

'I left them in the living room. There's a computer there as well – it's slow but it works – and a printer, if you need them.'

'Great. I'll walk you to the departure gates. Um . . .' I half turn to Sam. I want to talk to Brian alone but I'm not sure how to put it.

'I'll see you back at the car,' he says shortly. 'Take care, man,' he adds, shaking Brian's hand, and strides off.

'Listen, I think we can make it work,' I tell Brian as we walk. 'I'll just have to do the interviews, and I'll send tapes to you at home and you can write them up. It will be fine.' I'm not sure I believe this, but Brian looks so miserable, I want to cheer him up.

'I'm very sorry, Alice. I've never let a client down like this before.'

'Don't be silly. This isn't your fault.' I swallow. We've arrived at the queue for the gate now. 'Brian – oh God. I should have asked you this earlier. Do you have any, I mean – advice?' It's so lame, but I just want to hear if he has anything I can learn from, before I'm on my own.

He thinks for a minute. 'There's so much but . . . one thing is never to jump in to fill a silence during an interview. If you can sit it out, eventually he will say something, and it will probably be something pretty important.'

'Thanks.' I give him a hug, and watch him go off through the departure gates, his small, stumpy figure soon lost in the crowd. I cross my fingers inwardly for him. Then I make my way back out to the car, where Sam is waiting, drumming his fingers on the dashboard and looking impatient – essentially, his usual charming self. I deliberately decide not to thank him again, or apologise for being late.

'What's wrong with his wife?' Sam asks, as we queue for the exit. I explain briefly.

He doesn't express sympathy or say anything else until we're on the motorway. Then he says, abruptly, 'It's going to be pretty hard for you without him.'

'Well, it's not ideal,' I say, instantly on the defensive. 'But I'll manage. We can still do the book—'

'You didn't have to let him go, though. Right? You could have made him stay regardless.' He glances over at me.

What is he getting at?

'I suppose I could have, but it wouldn't have been right.'

Sam just nods. As we drive on in silence, he seems preoccupied. I wonder what that was all about. Was he testing me on something? Maybe he wants to see how determined I am to see the job through. Or he thinks I've finally lost the plot now that I've let Brian go home. And he's probably right. It was stupid of me. I am not looking forward to explaining this to Olivia.

Before long, Sam's phone rings. I assume he'll leave it but he actually has a handsfree thing installed in his car. Most of the conversation is incomprehensible though I do catch something about vacation days and an assistant, and something called 'play or pay'. Suddenly the call is over – I think the person on the other end hung up. Sam swears under his breath.

'I'm going to have to pull over,' he says.

We seem to be taking some kind of back road now; we're off the main motorway and in what looks like a more rural area. He drives until we get to a sloping lay-by, where he stops the car and gets out to make his call. After the call ends, he spends a while punching out an email, and then he makes another phone call. I turn on the radio and listen to Italian pop music, while he paces around outside. It's almost soothing to see him being horrible to someone else besides me.

It's a full fifteen minutes before Sam gets back into the car, looking extremely tense. He turns on the engine, which instantly stalls. He revs it again, but we're on an incline, and as soon as he releases the clutch the car promptly cuts out again. It must be because he's so agitated. Finally, he gets the car going, and we inch up the lay-by.

'Shit!' he exclaims.

Our way is now blocked by an enormous herd of sheep, tailed by a man on one of those three-wheeled cars I've seen puttering about. There must be at least a hundred of them, all baa-ing madly and roving all over the road.

To my immense surprise, Sam starts laughing. He turns off the engine, leans his arms and head on the steering wheel, and turns to look at me. 'I thought the traffic in LA was bad,' he says.

Now I'm laughing as well – in fact, I can barely draw enough breath to point out that more sheep are coming.

'Shit! Literally. And we'll be behind them all the way home.'

After five or ten minutes the sheep begin to disperse, and Sam turns the car around, saying we'll have to go back the other way.

'I hope you didn't have early dinner plans,' he remarks. 'I should ring that asshole back, but whatever. I'll just tell him there was a sheep situation.'

'What time is it in Hollywood?' I ask, suddenly curious.

'It's about nine a.m. – a good time for calls. Though my assistant can't always listen in, which is inconvenient.'

'She listens in to your calls?'

'Sure. Doesn't yours?'

'Um . . .'

'Any given phone call in LA has at least two people listening in and taking notes. Or more, if it's a conference call.'

It sounds ridiculous and also mildly terrifying to me.

'It's just the way it works,' he says, seeing my expression. 'When I started out as an assistant, I would spend the entire morning rolling my boss's calls. He would call me at the office from the gym, or his home or his car, and I had to get him one person after the other while I stayed on the other end, taking notes and putting things in his diary. They all knew someone else was listening. Everyone does, though it doesn't stop them from saying the craziest shit. At first I couldn't believe what I was hearing. But then I started to find it pretty useful.'

This has to be one of the longest speeches he's ever given. I'm absorbed in the vision of a lowly Sam, switchboarding away for his boss. I'm just reflecting on how strange it is that we're actually having a conversation, when he says something even more unexpected.

129

'Hey. I'm sorry for what I said to you last night.'

'What – about Luther?'

'Yeah. I should have called him on it, instead of taking it out on you. And . . . I got the wrong idea. I heard both your doors closing,' he adds. 'Slamming, actually.'

'Oh.' I can feel my cheeks going hot.

'I guess I jumped to conclusions.'

'A bit like in the swimming pool?' I say, wanting to make a joke of it.

'No way. You definitely looked a goner there.'

We both laugh. How did this happen? How am I laughing with Sam, as if we're pals? I can't figure him out. Thinking about Luther I realise I'm glad I've had a chance to calm down. If I had seen him right after all his fibs and after Brian told me about his wife, I would have wanted to rip his head off. Now I feel calmer.

Just as I think that, my phone rings. It's Olivia.

I don't want to talk to her with Sam right beside me, but if I don't answer now, I know that she'll go even crazier. I take a deep, deep breath, wishing that Sam didn't have to hear what is probably going to be a very humiliating conversation.

'Alice? I just got your message. What's all this about Brian?'

'It's his wife,' I explain. 'She has cancer. She was just diagnosed.'

'Oh, no. The poor fellow. I must send flowers. Can you organise it for me?' There's a loaded pause. 'But – what were you saying about him going home?'

'He's just left.'

'Just left? Just like that?'

'No, I – actually, I just put him on a plane.'

There's a silence so long that I say, 'Olivia? Are you still there?'

'You should not have done that,' she says, 'without consulting me.'

She's right, of course. That's what makes it so awful.

'I'm sorry, Olivia. I just – there was a flight this evening, and he was in such a state. I couldn't – I mean, it seemed—'

'Did you hear me the first time, Alice? I said that you should not have done that without consulting me.'

'I realise that.'

There's another silence, during which I don't like to imagine Olivia's expression.

'How do you propose that we do the book without a ghostwriter?'

I shrink down in my seat and lower my voice, hoping that this will somehow magically stop Sam from over-hearing. 'I think we'll manage. Luther wasn't talking to Brian anyway. I think I can do the interviews with him, and send tapes to Brian at home.' *That's if I can get him to tell me the truth*, I add silently.

Another deadly pause, and then Olivia says very slowly, 'Well, Alice. It was a crisis before you went, and now – now, it's a fucking disaster.'

I've never heard Olivia swear before. I'm not surprised when she just hangs up. I dig my nails into my palms and repeat to myself: Do not cry. Do not cry. Do not cry. If I start having a meltdown in front of Sam, then I might as well give up and go home right now.

I don't dare look at Sam. Did he overhear Olivia's end of the conversation, hear her asking me to order flowers, for example? I have a horrible feeling that he did. Even hearing her squawking through my phone would have been enough. Great. Now he knows I don't have back-up. If he finds out I'm not even a proper editor, I'm screwed, especially after what happened in the nightclub. He'll walk all

131

over me or, at the very least, he'll complain to Olivia. I brace myself for what's about to come.

'Have you ever had *caponata*?' he asks.

Before I can reply, he starts talking about some dish that Maria Santa is going to make for us tonight – not that I'm going to be able to eat it. As he rambles on at length about Sicilian food and how different it is from other Italian cuisine, I realise he's deliberately changing the subject. This is very weird. Is he actually trying to save my face? My hangover is making a come-back, and I'm suddenly longing for five minutes alone so that I can pull myself together.

Finally, we're back, and parking at the end of the drive. I fumble with the door handle, but for some reason it won't open.

'Is there some kind of child lock?' I ask Sam, but to my surprise he's already leaned across me and opened it. For just a split second, his arm and upper body are almost brushing against mine; his head is close to my chest; and I feel a strong crackle of something – I don't even want to know what it is. I practically jump out of the car in my haste to get away.

Luther is outside the house, leaning against the wall and smoking a cigarette.

'Hey, where were you guys?' he says, coming towards us. 'I woke up and I felt like Rip Van Winkle. Annabel's out with her new dude and I've been staring at the walls all afternoon.' He sounds genuinely annoyed, and I realise he's not used to being left alone. I decide to let Sam deal with it and I slip inside.

He's not on his own at all. Marisa and Federico are on the terrace about to start dinner. They look pleased to see us. I sit down beside Marisa, as far away from Luther as possible. Sam sits down opposite her, across from Federico.

'You've been to the airport?' Marisa says.

132

I explain briefly about Brian. Marisa exclaims and asks questions; even Federico looks politely concerned – I think so, anyway.

Luther just says, with a shiver, 'I hate talking about cancer.' He immediately starts talking to Sam about the new release date for *The Deep End*, which is the film he's got coming out before *Roman Holiday*. I can't believe he's being so selfish. I'm getting more and more disappointed in him.

'I almost forgot!' says Marisa, seizing my hand. 'What about you? I worried about you! You're feeling better?'

For a second I'm confused – do they know about my conversation with Olivia? Then I realise they mean my fainting fit, which already seems a million years ago.

'Oh, yes,' I say. 'Just a little embarrassed.'

Federico nods. 'Don't worry. We all know. Too much party – boom!' He mimes collapsing. 'A little too much champagne and, how do you say, snow?'

The cheek of him! 'No snow, just champagne. I have low blood pressure.'

'Hypo-something,' says Luther. He's looking more cheerful now. 'I'll play doctors with you any time. I think I'd make a good doctor. Sam, can you get me a doctor part?'

Dinner seems to take for ever. I keep on thinking about Olivia. She was right. I know she was right. I should never have sent Brian home without talking to her; it was idiotic. When she said I had to make decisions, she didn't mean unilateral and stupid ones. Thank God she doesn't know about my performance in the nightclub. Strangely, though, I feel more self-conscious around Sam now than I do around Luther. At one point I glance up, and catch him looking right at me, before he looks away.

I think I'm just over-tired. All the events of last night and today have hit me, and I'm practically falling asleep at the table.

'Alice,' Marisa says, beside me. 'Did you hear me?'

'Sorry, Marisa, what?'

'I said: do you want to come and have dinner with me tomorrow night?'

'Just us?' I ask, tiredness making me tactless.

'Yes, just us girls! Federico is away on business again.' Hearing his name, Federico looks up and says something in Italian, indignant and snappy-sounding. Sam says something to him, equally sharply, also in Italian, and Marisa joins in, conciliating.

'Jesus. I need subtitles,' says Luther.

I stand up. 'I'm going to bed. Goodnight, everybody.' Marisa looks embarrassed, and I smile at her. 'See you tomorrow,' I tell her. As I leave the table, Luther cracks another joke and the conversation starts again.

FIFTEEN

I'm in the water, ploughing up and down, swimming lengths just like I promised myself I would every morning. After thirty, I haul myself out and wrap up in a towel. In contrast to the brilliant mornings of the last few days, today's a little overcast, but it's still very warm. I dry my hair, looking out over the sea. I'm feeling calm. I know exactly what I'm going to do.

'Ready for your therapy session with Luther?'

Of course: Annabel. It would be too tempting to imagine that she would just shack up with her caveman and leave us all alone. However, I've come to a very pleasant decision about Annabel; I'm going to ignore her completely. I don't say a word, but float past her towards the villa. To my surprise, she comes after me.

'It's become pretty boring here, you know,' she says. 'Ever since you came. I'm going to stay with Nikos for a while.'

'Who?' I say, just to annoy her.

'Nikos! My new guy. He's got the most beautiful place on the other side of Catania. I'm really into Australian guys. They're so much more macho than Americans, or English men. Or Italians—'

'I thought you said he was South African?'

Annabel looks confused. 'Well, he's definitely *lived* there . . .'

'Never mind. I get it. He's macho. Have a good time,' I mutter.

What a bird-brain. I go into my room, quickly pull on the pink skirt and a black top, and twist my hair up into a bun. I want to look neat, but other than that, it doesn't really matter what I look like. I go and knock on Luther's door. I realise that by bearding him in his den, I'll be catching him off guard and possibly at a disadvantage, which is fine by me. Anyway it's 10.30 a.m., a perfectly reasonable time for him to be awake. Sam's already been up for hours, and has gone out with Marisa somewhere.

After a long pause, Luther calls, 'Who is it?'

'It's Alice.'

'Come in.'

I walk inside. The blinds are half down and the room is pretty messy; I see several beer and wine bottles, and piles of laundry. Actually, it's like my flatmate Martin's room though admittedly not as smelly. Luther's in bed, shirtless, reading one of a pile of handwritten letters. I'm guessing this is his fan mail.

'What's up?' Luther says. 'Not that this isn't a nice surprise.' He's looking very handsome and rumpled, but right at this moment, I don't care. I find a free chair and sit down.

'I need to talk to you.'

'OK,' he says, staring at me. He lights a cigarette, and offers me one. I shake my head and take a deep breath. I'm going to be very cool and reasonable.

'Listen, Luther. I know that the Children of God thing didn't happen exactly the way you told me. Didn't happen at all, in fact.' He starts to protest, but I go on. 'And neither did that story about the curtain call at the school play.'

'Woah. Who says I lied to you about the fucking Children of God?'

136

I can feel myself getting cross: I *hate* people swearing at me.

'I know you did, because that actually happened to River Phoenix,' I say as gently and calmly as possible. 'And we spoke to someone from your high school who emailed us a photo of you taking that curtain call.'

'How do you know it was the same play?'

'You said it was *Our Town*, and that's what it looks like. Look, I don't mind about the specifics. You're free to take the odd bit of poetic licence if you want. But you need to decide, now, whether you want to do this book, or not.'

'What's in it for me?' he says, sulkily.

I can't believe what I'm hearing. 'What's in it for you?' I repeat.

'Yeah. Why should I do it?'

Something snaps. All my good intentions go out of the window, and I lose it completely.

'Luther,' I say, 'who do you think you are? We're paying you a million pounds to write this book. I know that's just spare change to you, but actually, to some people that's a lot of money, not least me and my colleagues, who are hoping to get paid this year. We've put you up in this place, which is costing God knows how much, and sent you the best ghostwriter in the business, who's been kept dangling here, while his wife was waiting for the results of a biopsy, and you've refused to lift a finger. It's up to you. All you have to do is lie by the pool and dictate ninety thousand words. If you don't want to do that, just say so, and we can all go home. But if you do, you're going to have to stop being such a selfish pig and *actually do some work*.'

He doesn't say anything, just stares at me with his mouth slightly open, cigarette dangling. I stare back at him. I can't believe I said all that.

'So, let me know,' I say finally, lamely. And I walk out of

the room and quietly shut the door behind me. My heart is hammering.

I've just made the biggest mistake of my career.

What the hell am I going to do now?

I need to get out of here and think. Oh, how I wish I had a car and could drive somewhere, anywhere. I decide to take my phone down to the beach and call someone. Who, though? I don't want to call Erica; she could give me legal advice, which might end up being helpful, but she has a tendency sometimes, if you mention a problem, to tell you to think of orphans in war-torn countries. I know she's right but I don't want to hear it right now. I know! I'll call Poppy. It'll be expensive, but I don't care.

'Hello, editorial,' she says after a few rings. Hearing her voice, I can just picture her sitting cross-legged at her desk, wearing one of her crazy outfits – it all seems so far away.

'Poppy! It's Alice.'

'Alice! How's it going?'

'Is Olivia there? Can she hear you?'

'No, she's not back in the office yet,' says Poppy. 'How are you? How is the gorgeous Luther?'

'Oh, well, you know. He's charming, selfish, spoiled and, I think, a compulsive liar, and I just told him to either do the book or go to hell. And I've sent the ghostwriter home.'

'What? You've sent the ghost *home*?'

'Shhh! Someone might hear you.'

'Oh, absolutely. No, in that case it does make sense. Of course. Very sensible. Gosh, the line's very bad. Just hang up for now and I'll ring you from another line and see if that helps.' I hang up and wait, praying she'll get through. After a couple of minutes my phone rings, and Poppy hisses, 'Alice? Hi. Claudine was out there with her ears flapping so I've gone into Ellen's office. What's happening? What do you mean, you told Luther to go to hell?'

I try and explain. 'He's being a nightmare. He won't do a thing, and he sort of –' I decide not to go into the night-club story. 'He's just not buckling down. He pretended to tell me some stuff but it turned out to be a total lie. So then I tried to have a calm chat with him this morning, but I slightly lost it and told him he was a—'

'A what?'

'A selfish pig,' I say in a small voice.

'Oh, boy, oh boy.' There's a silence. 'Maybe it will be like in *Anne of Green Gables*, when she beats the little boy and it reforms him.'

I close my eyes. Sometimes I think we all read too many books and watch too many films.

'That's a nice idea,' I sigh down the phone. 'You are so lucky with fiction, Poppy. Never, never leave it. These auto-biographes are insane.'

'I won't. God, Alice, what are you going to do?'

'I actually don't know. I just walked off afterwards and I haven't seen him since. I'm too scared to think about it. I'll have to wait and see what he does.'

'Bloody hell,' says Poppy. 'And to think all I've been doing is going to my dressmaking class and watching *Mad Men*.'

It's so nice to talk to her that I almost feel myself welling up again.

'Tell me something to distract me,' I say. 'What's up with you?'

Poppy pours out soothing news and trivia: she's read a great book and is taking it to the editorial meeting; she has a new bicycle; she's making a hat. Her biggest news, though, is that her oddball ex-boyfriend, an artist called Crippo, is creating an installation inspired by their relationship.

'He's calling it – brace yourself – *Bitch Done Me Wrong*.'

'*What*? That's horrible! Are you upset?'

'Yes, but he says it's meant to be ironic,' says Poppy.

'Whatever. I just hope he doesn't end up winning a prize for it or something. Hey, would you like to hear the latest work gossip?'

'Of course.'

'It's a Claudine special. A great submission came in, and Ellen wanted me to read it, but Claudine kindly "offered" to read it instead because, she said, it was too literary for me. Honestly. Slap her, she's French.'

It's all so brilliantly petty; I wish I was back there.

'You know she's angling for promotion,' Poppy says. 'She wants to be the next one they make editor.'

'Well, of course she does. We all do.'

'And . . . by the way, I don't know if you want to know this, but – it's probably not a big deal, but –'

'Spit it out!'

'She seems to be having some kind of thing with Simon. They met at a book launch. I don't think it's romantic, but I'm not sure. Maybe it's just a networking thing . . .'

Ouch. That does sting, but actually, not as much as I thought it would. 'Poppy – that's fine. I don't care. She's welcome to him.'

'Good.' Poppy sounds relieved. 'Anyway, what else has been happening? Who else is there? Is it just a totally crazy set-up and is he on drugs the whole time, with groupies? Spill.'

'Not really. He's being very lazy, but actually pretty tame, I suppose. But just – maddening.' I tell her about stupid Annabel, and losing my luggage, and Marisa and Federico, and the yacht, and Sam.

'Oh ho,' says Poppy. 'A hot young agent?'

'Only if you like the clean-cut, angry type. He doesn't want Luther to do the book, so he's a fly in my sunscreen.' I realise I don't quite know how to explain Sam to her. She'll get the wrong idea if I tell her about how he drove

140

Brian to the airport, and saved my face with Olivia. 'He's very arrogant and controlling. He throws his weight around all the time. This morning I was in the pool and he decided I was drowning, and nearly gave me a heart attack dragging me out.'

'He saved your life? That's romantic! But what about Luther? I thought he was the man of your dreams.'

'Not any more. He's – I don't know, he's not how I expected he'd be.' I hadn't really realised this was the case until I said it to her. 'Anyway, I might be going home after today, if he decides to take me up on my ultimatum.'

There's a silence on the other end of the line, then Poppy says, 'Yes, that was a bit of a gamble.'

'A bad gamble?' I ask her tentatively.

'Well . . . I don't know. Perhaps. But look, Alice, no matter what happens, nobody is going to die.'

I think of Brian's wife, and shiver. 'No, of course not.'

'And if all else fails, I'm sure Claudine will give you some freelance work, if you ask nicely.'

'Shut up!' I shriek, and we both laugh. I haven't laughed like this in days. I forgot how good it feels. We chat for a while more, my phone starts to burn my ear.

'I'd better go,' I say reluctantly. 'I don't want to get you into trouble with the phone bill.'

'Alice, would you listen to yourself?'

I can guess what she's about to say: *You've potentially just lost us a multimillion-pound book and you're worried about the cost of a phone call?* But because she is a nice person, and my friend, she says, 'You're out there slaving twenty-four hours a day, even if you are in a beautiful villa full of hot men. The least they can do is spot you a phone call from HQ.'

'You're right. Poppy, it was so great to talk to you. Would you like anything from Italy? I forgot to ask you.'

'Maybe some olive oil,' says Poppy musingly. 'I'm doing a lot of cooking at the moment. Listen, chin up. I'll cross my fingers that Luther makes you the happiest girl on earth and says, "Yes, Alice, I will do your book."'

'Thanks,' I say. 'We'll see.'

After we've hung up, I sit on the beach for a minute and listen to the waves. So: Simon and Claudine. It's so clichéd of him to pick her up at a book launch. *I* met him at a book launch, for God's sake. Weirdly, I'm not as devastated as I would have been even a few days ago. In fact, I've hardly thought of Simon at all since my night out with Luther. Correction: my disastrous, drunken night out with Luther. I think of the first day I was here, of how dazzled I was by him. I didn't even question the fact that we went sailing instead of working on the book. It turns out I didn't even need to worry about people finding out about the contents clause; I've managed to mess everything up all by myself.

Something else is occurring to me. I'm not sure I was right to blow up at Luther about Brian. I was so self-righteous that I didn't stop to think about it from his point of view. He didn't even know about Brian until last night. And I could have tried harder to make him get down to work. It's not his fault that I wasn't able to be firm with him. Now I'm toast. It's even more overcast now, and I'm starting to get chilly. I walk slowly back up to the house.

SIXTEEN

I find Marisa and Sam on the terrace, deep in conversation; they almost don't notice me until I'm right on top of them.

'*Ciao, carissima*,' says Marisa. I can never get over hearing her say things like that – it makes me feel like I'm in a film.

'Hi there,' I say. I get the feeling that I've just interrupted something. 'Um, where's Luther?'

'We thought he was with you,' says Sam.

'His car is gone,' says Marisa. 'He's not with Annabel either – she's gone out with Nikos.'

'I'll try his cell,' says Sam.

It's a little disconcerting – but he can't have run away, can he? I'm sure he's just gone to clear his head, or something. I hope so, anyway.

'Do you mind if we have lunch instead of dinner, Alice?' says Marisa. 'I don't want to get back too late tonight. Federico said he might be able to come home early.'

'Of course,' I say. If Luther's gone off somewhere, I may as well have lunch early – and I also don't particularly want to face him alone if he does come back. 'Do you want to eat here?'

'No, thanks. Let's go into town.'

We don't go back to the same place as before, but to a restaurant in the same square, where we sit outside under

143

a canopy and eat *pasta alla Norma* and drink red wine. It's so pretty, but I'm not in the best state to appreciate it. The waiter is extremely charming and attentive, showing us to several tables in turn so that we can choose our favourite. I wonder if it's always like this for Marisa, wherever she goes. I can't help noticing, though, that she looks depressed, and she's not as chatty as usual.

'Is there anything wrong?' I ask her.

She shakes her head. Her mobile rings, and she answers it. I can't hear anything but her replies: '*Si . . . si . . . si . . . va bene. Va bene. Va bene.*' I know that *va bene* means all right, but it doesn't sound like whatever's happened is remotely all right. Then there's a burst of angry speech, and she hangs up, looking furious.

'Everything OK?' I say, tentatively.

'Federico. He's not coming home tonight after all.' She shrugs.

I look down at my plate. I know that in these situations, almost nothing you say is going to be helpful.

'How did you and Federico first meet?'

'Ah! Probably – in church, or in a neighbour's house.' She looks off into the distance. 'We both grew up in a small town inland, not too far from Cefalù. He was two years older than me. I never knew him very well, but I always thought he was the most handsome boy in the town. I had a crush on him! Then, after school, I went away to university and he stayed here to work on his father's business.'

'Oh yes, the cement.'

'Yes. They have a big factory near Messina. Anyway, after university I went to Rome to work. I got a job in a TV station, then later in a film production company. But I went home for three weeks every summer and two weeks at Christmas, and I used to see Federico every time. Roman men are very arrogant – I mean even more than Sicilians.

144

They think every woman in the world is in love with them. Federico was different, more sincere.'

I'm trying to compute this with the Federico I know. I suppose empty-headedness can be sincere.

She continues, 'After my father died, two and a half years ago, it was a terrible time. I lost my job, and I came here to be with my mother. Fede was one of the only people my age I knew who was still living here. He came to the house a lot, and he did lots of things for us . . . it was good to have him around. We became a couple. Then . . .' She looks at me with a 'can you guess?' expression.

'Oh,' I say.

'We both wanted it. We couldn't imagine – doing anything else. And I was ready to settle down. I was tired of Rome, and I wanted to be here for my mother. And I was thirty. I thought that was so old!' She laughs, but to my horror I can see her eyes welling up.

'What happened?'

'I lost the baby. But by then we were engaged. And I honestly thought we would make each other happy.' She adds quietly, 'It's different now.'

'And since then . . .?'

'Nothing since then. I don't know why. I thought we should have tests, but Fede hated the idea. And I'm not sure now if we should.' She looks down at her hands, beautifully manicured, her diamond bracelet glowing on her wrist.

'I'm sorry,' I say.

She looks up, her eyes bright with tears. 'Alice! I should be sorry. You have enough to worry about without me and my drama. It's fine.' She smiles at me. 'He's a good husband, Fede, really. And he's given my mother a lot of financial support. My father didn't leave a lot of money. And my salary in Rome wasn't enough to support her.'

145

Poor Marisa. I remember, when I first met her, thinking she wasn't beautiful – now I think she's stunning. I wonder whether, if she didn't have her mother to consider, she would have left Federico by now. Poor Marisa, and poor Brian . . . I'm really not the only person with problems.

We pay the bill, and drive back to the villa. It's three o'clock now, and I'm hoping there will be some news of Luther. But, as we park, I can see his car is still missing. Sam is on the terrace, tapping away on his eternal BlackBerry.

'Any word from Luther?' I ask.

'Nope,' says Sam. 'But I wouldn't call the *carabinieri* just yet.'

'I should go and let you both get back to work,' Marisa says, glancing from me to Sam.

'No, stay,' he tells her. 'I'm done for today.'

I say I'll leave them to it, but Marisa insists that I join them. Maria Santa brings us some iced lemonade, and we all collapse on the sunloungers and spend the next hour reading and chatting idly. It turns out to be a surprisingly nice interlude. Sam and Marisa tell me some funny stories about the movie they worked on in Rome, and about directors and producers they've both come across. I'm taken aback to learn that in one of my favourite rom-coms, the leading actress was saying most of her lines to a stand-in because her co-star would go off and rest whenever he wasn't actually on screen. And I'm disturbed to learn about the famous action star who has to weigh every single bit of food he eats. But there's nothing too X-rated.

'Sam, always so discreet,' Marisa teases him. 'You never tell us the good gossip.'

'I honestly don't have the best gossip,' Sam says. 'Crew are the best people for that. They see everything, and nobody notices them.'

'I don't believe you. You have plenty of stories,' Marisa

146

says, swatting him lightly with her magazine. He just smiles, and shakes his head.

I look at the pair of them and think: is there something going on here? They certainly get on like a house on fire. And Marisa is gorgeous – any man would be interested.

Marisa stands up and stretches. 'I'm going to talk to Mama for a while. Excuse me.' And she goes inside the house, leaving Sam and me alone together.

I instantly start feeling self-conscious again. He's lying on the sunlounger right beside mine, just a foot away. When I find myself staring at his tanned arms, I realise this is just way too weird, lying around together in silence. We need some small talk.

'Did you always want to be a film agent?' I ask him, brightly. To my surprise, he laughs.

'No. I wanted to be a professional basketball player.'

'Oh.' I wasn't expecting that. Though he is very tall. 'What happened?'

'I got a basketball scholarship to UCLA, but in my senior year I busted my knee. I haven't played a competitive game since.'

'So how did you get into agenting?'

'Well, I was considering law school but I thought I'd rather earn a salary, even a tiny one, than get into a lot of debt with school fees. I wanted to stay in LA, so I decided to try and get a job with an agency. One of my friends is an actor, and I interviewed for a position with his agent.'

'As his assistant?'

'No, in the mail room. I worked my way up. A whole eight floors,' he says mock-seriously.

'And do you like it?'

He laughs again. 'You know, nobody's ever actually asked me that. Sure, I like it. It's exciting. When the deals go well, it's the biggest adrenaline rush. And I like building a relationship with clients, looking out for them. But it's a pretty crazy job. It doesn't stop. This is the longest vacation I've taken in two years.'

'This is a *holiday*? But you're working!'

'No, officially I'm on vacation. But I have to be available all the time. I can only do this because my assistant is so solid.'

Wow. That sounds a very depressing way to live. I thought Erica worked long hours, but at least she gets to go on holiday.

'How about you?' Sam says.

'How about me what?'

He waves a hand. 'How did you get into publishing? Is it what you've always wanted to do? Do you like it? Take your pick.'

'Oh. Yes, I've always wanted to work in publishing. Ever since I realised that books didn't just make themselves. I love books, and I love being part of something that entertains so many people. And I love working with the authors . . .'. My voice tails off. I was briefly distracted for a minute while talking to Sam about his job, but now I'm worried about Luther again. He should have been back hours ago.

Seemingly reading my mind, Sam says, 'If you're worrying about Luther, don't. He occasionally just heads for the hills. He did it in Rome too; once he learned to drive stick, there was no stopping him. He'll be back.'

'I know,' I say quickly. I'm not going to tell him that the last time I spoke to Luther I told him to go to hell.

Marisa reappears shortly afterwards and stays for dinner. Luther still hasn't come home by the time I go to bed. It takes me ages to get to sleep: I can't stop worrying about where he is and what he's doing. At one point I get up for a glass of water. As I walk back through the reception from the kitchen, I can hear Sam's voice coming in from the terrace. Marisa is still here; I hadn't realised. They're still at the table, their heads very close together. He reaches out and touches her arm. 'Just tell me,' I hear him say in a low voice. 'Whatever you want, I'll do it.'

Good grief, what's this about? Hastily I tiptoe back to bed before they see me. Later, in the spare moments when I'm not agonising about Luther, and replaying our conversation in my head, I wonder what on earth was going on out there.

SEVENTEEN

I'm woken by noises outside: thank God, I can hear Luther's voice. I'm so relieved. Although, what did I think was going to happen? That he was going to throw himself off a bridge because I was mean to him?

After I get dressed, I sit on the edge of the bed for a minute and think. I'm too afraid to go out and face him. In fact, I feel nauseous. What on earth am I going to say? What will he say?

Perhaps he's already called Olivia to complain about the way I spoke to him. I haven't been in touch with her since our last disastrous conversation. Oh, God. If he or Sam calls her, and tells her that I gave Luther an ultimatum . . . But why am I worried about my boss being cross, when the consequences could be much more dire? Olivia might not even be my boss much longer; she might get fired for trusting me with this big job, which I messed up. My head starts to throb steadily from stress and terror.

I stand up and look out of my window at the beautiful view outside. It's a gorgeous day and the heat has started pulsing up again, surging up from the ground in huge waves. The sky and sea are the same incredible blue. The windowsill is too hot to touch. It's such a beautiful place, but after this trip, I never want to come to Italy ever again.

There's a knock on my door. It's probably Sam, or bloody Annabel wanting to borrow something. Or could it be Luther, with flowers and an apology? Yeah, right.

Before I can say anything the door has opened slowly and a head comes around it. It *is* Luther. He looks like he's been out all night, which he probably has.

'Can I come in?' he says.

He comes inside the room in a very circular way, moving around the edges. He goes to my dressing table and picks up the silk scarf Marisa chose for me.

'Luther – I'm so sorry about yesterday,' I tell him. 'It was incredibly rude of me. And stupid. I didn't mean it.'

He doesn't seem to hear me. Instead, he slips the scarf around his neck. 'Suits me?'

'Um . . .' I smile and shake my head, though the strange thing is it actually does look quite cool on him – like everything he wears.

He puts the scarf back on the bureau. 'Let's take a walk,' he says.

We walk down towards the beach. I don't say anything, because I'm not sure what's happening and I want him to talk first. When we get to the beach, he picks up a stone and skims it, just like Brian did the other day, but more expertly.

'I guess I'm the one who should be sorry,' he says. 'You must think I'm some asshole.'

The relief is so strong, it's an actual physical sensation.

'I don't think you are an asshole at all.'

'Hah,' says Luther. He throws another stone. 'The thing is, I do want to do this book. I do. There's lots of stuff . . .' he trails off, and looks back to sea. I wait for him to go on.

'There's lots of stuff I want to tell someone.'

'You can tell me,' I say. He nods. I count to ten slowly inside my head, just as Brian suggested, waiting.

Eventually Luther says, 'It's funny that you said, "Who do you think you are?", because I guess I'm at a point in my life right now where I almost don't know who I am. Do you know what I mean?' He continues, 'I mean, I play all these roles but I don't know who I am when I'm off-camera, really.'

I don't say anything at all; I just nod, hardly daring to breathe. I've never heard him talk like this before.

'So, when I was talking to you earlier, I guess I was stalling,' he says. 'I want to do it, but when it comes to actually talking about that stuff – it's pretty scary actually.' He adds quietly, 'It's just weird to think of it all being out there.'

I don't know what to say. I'm feeling overwhelmed with remorse, and sympathy. He's right. Despite me bitching about how easy he has it – I'm not the one who is about to reveal my life story.

'I know,' I say. 'But we can take it slowly. And we don't have to put things in if you don't want to.'

He nods. 'Good. I'm up for it, I really am. If you are.'

'Of course I am.' I'm so happy.

'So what do we do now?'

'Well, you and I can talk. And then we'll send the tapes to Brian, and he'll write them up. When he's finished, you can read it and we'll make changes together. And then it'll be done.'

'OK.' He gets up. 'You know what?' he says decisively. 'I'm excited. No bullshit. I want to do this.'

I'm so relieved; I can't believe he's come around. It's taken a while but I think I'm finally getting closer to the real Luther.

I let him go on ahead while I send Olivia an update message. I don't want to call her now, because I don't want to interrupt the momentum with Luther. My text says: 'Have

152

had breakthrough with Luther. He and I doing interviews. Expect good progress.' I press send cautiously, hoping that will go down OK.

I approach the terrace, where Sam and Luther are talking.

'Do you know who they went with?' Luther is asking.

'Not yet. I'm finding out. I know it was out to Seph Banks –'

'That guy! He wouldn't know a good movie if it bit him in the ass. Screw it. Tell them I passed. Tell them I'm going to be working on my book instead.'

Sam looks aghast. 'You're working on your book,' he repeats.

'Absolutely.'

'Look. Luther. This is a bad idea. No good can come of it whatsoever.'

'I don't care! I want to do it. And I've told you that about a million times. So stop cock-blocking me, and trying to invent all these projects to distract me with, because it won't work.' He turns to me. 'Are you ready?'

'Yes!' I say. 'I'll just get my tapes and things.' I beam at Sam, and dash into the house.

Sam follows me, looking totally enraged. 'I hope you're happy now,' he snarls, once we're inside. 'You've got Luther started on the worst mistake of his career.'

I can see why he's annoyed, but I don't care.

'Sam,' I say, 'it's not your decision. Luther wants to write a proper book. So if you have a problem with that, you'll have to take it up with him.'

He doesn't say anything, and I know it's because he can't. If Luther has decided he really wants to do this, there's nothing Sam can do to stop him.

'You're going to show me transcripts of every single one of his interviews as they come out,' he snaps. 'Everything he tells you goes through me. No exceptions.'

As I watch him stalk off in a rage, I realise that I was almost beginning to like him. Not in a romantic sense, obviously, just as a person. But it can't be helped. He's had his way; it's my turn now. I gather up my stuff, and before I head to see Luther, I type out a very quick text to Poppy. 'You might be right re Anne of GG. Fingers crossed – will keep you posted!' And I hope and pray it doesn't turn out to be premature.

EIGHTEEN

We're on the back terrace. Luther is on a sunlounger, and I'm sitting opposite him on a chair. The Dictaphone is on. I can feel there's something different about him. It's his demeanour – he looks more serious than I've ever seen him before. It suits him.

'So . . . maybe we could start with what you were telling me earlier, about when you had to move out of home. Was any of it – the way you described it?' I ask. I was going to say 'true', but I don't want to emphasise the sad fact that he was lying earlier.

'Well, sort of. It's true that my dad left home when I was thirteen. And then we went to stay with a friend of Mom's, maybe for a month or two. And she did have a brother, Amos, who Mom started seeing. And that's when her friend asked us to leave. That was all true. And we moved in with Amos for a while. But he didn't ask us to come to Mexico, or anywhere else for that matter. One day he just disappeared. Mom was pretty upset.'

'Oh,' I say. Poor Luther, I think. Two father figures disappearing within the space of a few months.

'We had to leave his place, so that was when we started sleeping in Mom's car. It was hell. At first we didn't tell anyone. We used to just park it different places. My mom was working in Walmart at the time and we parked in their lot. She used to sneak me and my sister in there at six a.m. so that we could wash and get dressed for school. The people on the night shift knew, but she worked days so she figured she could get away with it. But then they found out, and we had to move on.'

A shiver goes down my spine as I contemplate Luther's mother and the two kids, washing and dressing in the employee bathrooms.

'What about your grandparents?' I ask. 'Didn't you have any relatives in town?'

'Not in Camden, because my mom is from Queens originally. And she fell out with her folks when she married my dad – they hated him. So, we were on our own.'

'And did you go to school the whole time?'

'At first. But my mom couldn't stand people knowing about us, where we lived. She was scared everyone in town would find out, though, to be honest, I think they already knew. She worked with a woman who used to go to Florida for harvests. She said she could get Mom a job, so my sister and I dropped out of school and we drove all the way there in Mom's ancient Ford Maverick. You could practically see the road through the bottom of that car.'

'What was Florida like?'

'It was OK,' he says. 'It was good not to be cold any more. It got pretty cold in that car. Though I got sick of eating oranges – we had about ten a day each. In the evenings, we went out, me and my sister, and got more money. Like I told you we did in the cult.' He laughs.

'Um – how?'

'We used to perform to the tourists. We'd sing songs, make up sketches. I had this whole speech from *Back to the Future* memorised.' He shakes his head. 'My mom had a new boyfriend by that time and she was a little distracted.

But when she found out, she came down on us like a ton of bricks. And soon after that, she made it up with her folks and we moved to Queens to live with them. But that was when I first discovered how much I liked to act, I guess. It was a way of getting attention, but also it helped us escape whatever was happening at home.'

My editor brain is registering that this is brilliant material. But at the same I'm feeling incredibly sorry for Luther, and his family. I can't imagine an existence on the edge like that.

As the morning wears on, Luther smokes his way through an entire pack of cigarettes. He tells me more about his early years, before his dad – whom he seems to have worshipped – left. He got into endless trouble: skipping school, shoplifting, trying to steal cars. He tells me about his mother, who seems to have alternated between being very affectionate and being wrapped up in her own chaotic life, and his grandmother, who was much more stable. I hadn't realised she talked him into doing dance classes, which helped him get the part in *Fever*.

'What was it like?' I ask him. 'I mean, we have all the facts and everything, but how did it feel?'

'It was a dream come true,' he says simply. 'It just felt like – all of those trailers and cables and lights and make-up people and caterers, and the director and the assistant director, and all of the crew and the extras, and even the rest of the cast – they were all there because of me. Because I was the star. It was all up to me to make the movie a success.'

'That sounds scary.'

'No,' Luther says, leaning forward. 'It should have been terrifying, but I was so clueless, I loved it. I was addicted to the whole thing: the costumes and the script and the choreography – everything. I had no idea what I was doing – they had to keep reminding me not to look in the camera.

But I had good direction and somehow I pulled it off. I basically wasn't acting, I was just playing myself. And then when the movie went crazy, I just went crazy with it. But the comedown, once the movie had been out for a few months, was horrible.'

'Why?'

'Because it was over. I would never have that particular experience again. I'd already signed for *Stars on the Water*, but there was no guarantee that it would be as big a hit as *Fever*. And I was beginning to realise how out of my depth I was. What if it all ended and I had to go back home with my tail between my legs? It was terrifying. In a way, the fear that I should have felt while I was shooting *Fever* only really hit me after it was over.' He thinks for a minute. 'I guess I also . . .'

I wait.

'The whole time I was going to acting classes or auditions, I sort of hoped that, some day, if I made it as a movie star or a TV actor or was even in a commercial, my dad would see me, and would maybe . . . I don't know what I expected. But that he would think I was an OK kid, I guess, or at least get in touch and let us know if he was alive or dead. But that never happened. *Fever* opened and I did a ton of interviews, and I was on magazine covers, but nothing.'

'Do you know where he is now?'

'Honestly, not a clue. He could be dead, for all I know,' says Luther. 'Or he could be, I don't know, living on welfare or in a trailer park somewhere. I have a feeling he's not, though, because if he was alive, I don't think he would be shy of getting in touch.'

'To see you?'

'No, to ask for money.'

'Oh.' I can't imagine how horrible it must be to have to think that of your own father.

158

'I know that, considering he walked out on us, I should think of him as an asshole,' he continues, 'but actually I remember him as being pretty cool. He was always laughing and joking and he had so many buddies – the room used to light up whenever he came in. He used to play baseball with me for hours. He gave me my first beer when I was twelve. But my big sister doesn't remember him like that.'

'No?'

'No. She says it all depended on what kind of mood he was in when he got home. That she and my mom would pray that he was in a good mood, because otherwise it would be hell. But, if he was in too good a mood, it would mean that he was boozing.' He shakes his head. 'She first told me all that after the premiere of *Stars on the Water*. We were at the after-party. I was telling her I wished he could be there, and she just blew up at me, and it all came out. I guess she was right. I did hate him for leaving my mom and for leaving us, but at the same time, I kind of felt – I remembered him as being a pretty cool guy, and I didn't just want to forget about that. But I guess he was an asshole. I don't know. I don't remember, really.'

He looks so downcast, lying back on the sunlounger. In fact, he looks incredibly handsome right now, and, seeing this side of him . . . I quickly get a grip, and ask him about his current relationship with his family.

'Mom and I get on great now,' he says. 'She's been married for about ten years, to a good guy. Life is just easier for her now, you know? I bought them a house as a wedding gift. I think he felt a bit weird about taking it, but I don't care.'

'And your sister?'

'That's a whole other story. We were pretty tight when we were kids, but now, not so much. I think she feels I took up a lot of Mom's time with my dramas, while she was doing her own thing. But she's done well. She's married, has three kids, lives in a nice neighbourhood. She never lets me buy her stuff, but I give the kids presents, so that's cool.'

This is good to know: we need to know who's likely to complain and who isn't.

'And your grandmother?'

He's silent for a minute. 'She died, actually. The whole time I was shooting *Fever*, she was dying of cancer. I still feel guilty that I didn't spend more time with her. I went to see her as often as I could but it wasn't often enough. In fact, of all the shitty things I've ever done – I think that's the one I regret the most.'

Poor, poor Luther. So that explains why he reacted the way he did when I mentioned Brian's wife. I feel so bad for doubting him earlier.

We talk for another hour or so, until I realise that I can't see my notes any more because it's getting dark. I've been so absorbed I've completely forgotten the time.

'Luther! Can you believe we've been talking for over six hours?'

'Yeah? Did you get what you wanted?'

'Absolutely. You've been fantastic. Well done and thanks so much.' I'm about to stand up, but he stays looking at the ground, his head bowed. In the dusk, I can see that he looks a bit overwhelmed and very sad. Oh, God . . . I just feel the impulse to put my arms around him and tell him I'm sorry he's had such a rough time.

'Are you OK?'

'Yeah, I'm fine,' Luther says, looking up. 'It was pretty good to talk through that stuff. We could go on for longer, you know.' He glances at his watch, and I feel torn. I'm exhausted myself, but if he does want to talk, I want to be there for him.

'Actually, no, let's take a break,' he says finally. I nod.

160

Luther heads off to find Sam, while I stand up and stretch slowly. I realise my neck, shoulders and arms are aching, even though all I've been doing is listening and making notes, and occasionally changing the Dictaphone. But it's brilliant. Today he's given me at least 30,000 words, and it's the most interesting stuff we've had on the book so far.

I find Federico and Marisa talking to Sam and Luther. They're all planning to go out for dinner and drinks in Taormina. They look very smart, whereas I'm a scruffy mess from working all day.

'Are you coming, Alice?' asks Federico. Marisa and Luther look at me too. I notice that Sam pointedly looks away. He probably doesn't want to be around me right now.

'I can't, I'm afraid.' I explain that I have to type up the transcripts of today's interview with Luther, and email them to Brian. I've realised this will be more efficient than sending tapes.

'Are you sure?' Marisa asks me. 'My cousin Giulia speaks very good English. She could help you with the typing.'

'No, thanks all the same, but I have to do this myself,' I say. I'm the only one who knows what needs to be flagged up for Brian, and what can be left out. Not to mention that this is highly confidential material and I don't want anyone else handling it, no matter how many forms they sign. I want Olivia and Brian to be the first people to see this.

I'm relieved when they've all gone out, and left me to think.

I'm still dazed from everything Luther's told me. I've learned more about him in the past six hours than I have in the whole time I've known him. His childhood sounds terrifying. To lose your home and have to live out of a car; to have your father walk out of your life one day and never reappear – no wonder he's mixed-up. Anyone would be. I'm still trying to square the person I know with the things

161

he's told me. I hadn't realised he was so self-aware or perceptive about his own motivations – like when he was describing his feelings of anti-climax after *Fever* ended, or his disappointment that his dad never got in touch. That was heartbreaking.

It just goes to show: you can be as rich and as famous as Luther, but none of it matters if you don't have the important things: love, stability, a home, parents who love you or at least care where you are and what you're doing. Perhaps that's why he wanted to become famous – to try and get that love that he didn't get at home.

I put in my earphones and settle down for an evening's work. The sound of Luther's voice fills my ears, as I begin to type his words.

NINETEEN

I'm on a film set or a stage, and I'm meant to be playing Luther's love interest but, instead, for some reason I'm sitting at a little desk, typing away furiously. All around me, people are rehearsing and putting up lights and arranging cameras. They're all waiting for me and getting impatient, but I can't help it – I have to finish writing the book before I can kiss Luther. The only solution is to type faster, so I do, typing more and more furiously so that I can escape. The typing is getting louder and louder, until I realise it's not typing, it's knocking. I'm awake, and somebody is knocking loudly at my door. I close my eyes, hoping it will stop, but instead it goes on and on.

'Who is it?' I call, or croak.

The door opens. It's Luther. I twitch the sheet over my exposed leg and try to sit up and look respectable. I hope my face isn't all puffy.

'Hey. You mind if we get going soon? I've been up for a while, thinking . . .'

I squint at him. 'Great. Just give me a minute?'

'Don't be long,' he says, and disappears.

I collapse back on my pillow. I can barely open my eyes, I'm so tired. The typing last night took me so much longer than I'd thought. I was up until 2.30 a.m. transcribing the interviews, editing out things we don't need, and writing notes to Brian. I pick up my phone from the ground and check it.

It's 6.40 a.m.

OK. It's a little early, but that's fine. The important thing is that Luther is motivated. This is great! I am a little groggy, but I'll just get in the shower and I'll feel fine.

Ten minutes later, my hair still wet and scraped back in a ponytail, I'm on the back terrace with Luther, in the same positions we were in yesterday. I'm clutching a cup of coffee and a bread roll that I grabbed from the kitchen en route. Luther hasn't shaved, but he looks very bright-eyed and bushy-tailed, and very handsome in a blue hooded sweat-shirt and jeans. He must have the stamina of an ox.

'How was last night?' I ask.

'Fine. They all wanted to go on somewhere after dinner but I wasn't into it. I was preoccupied. I was just thinking about stuff, remembering all these things that I wanted to talk about.'

'That's fantastic. I'm delighted you're – finally getting into this,' I say. And I mean it. It is absolutely brilliant.

Luther and I spend the morning talking about his early film career and the two films he did after *Fever*. He gives me some great anecdotes about some of the actors and directors he's worked with, all printable, I think. It's so entertaining listening to him, I almost forget my exhaustion.

After we've been talking for over three hours, and gone through three tapes, I decide we both need a break. I wait for a suitable moment, when he's just come to the end of a story, and then I say, 'Hey, Luther. It's already ten. How about taking a break for half an hour or so?'

'I'd rather not,' he says. 'I wanted to talk to you about Don.'

164

I'm completely lost. He's assuming I know exactly what he means, and I don't want to be rude, but I have no choice: I have to ask who Don is.

'Dom! Dominique,' he says.

'Oh, of course. Sorry! I misheard you.'

He means his ex-wife, Dominique Rice. From everything I've read, she sounds completely insane. Apparently she had his name tattooed on the sole of her foot after their divorce so that she could walk on him every day. I know this is true because I've seen pictures of her on a sunlounger, with 'Luther' in horrible faux-Gothic script on the bottom of her foot.

'That will be great to talk about,' I say. 'What about a quick break first, though? That way, you can be really fresh, and talk about it properly.'

Luther looks at me for a second, and then he looks out to sea. 'I don't know. I feel like I need to talk about it now, or not at all.'

OK, fair enough. He's about to talk about his ex-wife, after all. I should probably be sensitive about this subject.

'Of course.'

He starts by telling me how much Dominique has changed since she got married, had her two kids and went all holistic, and how hard it is to break up with someone well-known.

'The thing is, when regular people break up, they don't have to see their exes ten feet high on a billboard, you know? I mean, it's hard enough breaking up with someone, without having to see them on screen, and in magazines, and read interviews about how your break-up was mutual when you know it was anything but. Don't quote me on that, by the way.'

'I won't quote you about reading her interviews and

disagreeing about the break-up being mutual,' I say. 'But I like the bit about the billboards.'

'I read an interview after she had her baby,' Luther continues. 'I couldn't believe it was her. All that stuff about the divine mother and life force and seeing rainbows everywhere. I remember her saying that she definitely didn't want kids because they sucked the life force *out* of you, and that was why she hated her parents and vice versa. Kids were not on our agenda. But I guess he talked her into it. And now she's happy. And that's great.'

'He' is Dominique's current husband, and I've already gathered that Luther can't stand him. 'Douchebag' is one of the more polite words he's used.

'I mean, you know what – he acts all arthouse and sensitive and he does his painting and carpentry and all that stuff. And that's cool. But what nobody seems to remember is that he started out on a soap opera and he's basically had about as much formal training as I have, i.e., none. And even though he's meant to be so bankable, half of his movies don't open. The fact is, he has this undeserved reputation which doesn't translate, either to his bottom line or to the quality of the movies he picks.'

'Um . . .' I'm beginning to realise that, like most authors, Luther sometimes has a tendency to go off on tangents. He clearly has a bee in his bonnet about Dominique's husband: I'll have to remember this and steer clear of the subject. 'You were telling me about Dominique,' I say, gently.

'Right. Dominique and the mother life force?' He laughs. Then his smile fades. 'I guess the thing about those conversations we had,' he continues, 'was that they always happened when we were out of it. But then, we were almost always out of it. That's kind of how it worked with us.'

'Right,' I say, trying to look knowledgeable.

'I don't know if you do drugs, Alice.'

'Well, I've—'

'The thing about them is . . . when you do a lot of drugs, and you get together with someone else who does a lot of drugs, it's a kind of like having a third person in your relationship. Do you know what I mean? I mean . . . after a while it's hard to tell if you're doing drugs because you're together, or you're together because you do drugs, or both.'

I make a note of this, thinking again how perceptive he can be.

'The first time I met her was during a read-through. I'd seen pictures of her, but I just thought she was even more beautiful in the flesh, and she had this edge about her. The tattoos – I had never seen an actress with inks before. Now they all have them, but even six years ago it was pretty unusual. But most of all, it was the way she just looked right through me, like she didn't give a damn who I was.'

'And you liked that,' I say. Clever Dominique, I think. The oldest trick in the book.

'Yeah! I'd had two years of women throwing themselves at me. I could have anyone I wanted, and I did. I can remember – I'm not kidding – being at a party where girls were literally lined up in front of me. The line to talk to me was like a line to get into a nightclub. So Dom's attitude was pretty attractive.

'The movie wasn't huge, as you know. But we had fun shooting it. Lots of action scenes. We used to get off on those.' He looks at me lazily, and I sit up straighter, hoping I don't look embarrassed. 'And Dom got me into her hobbies. I already did coke and E and sometimes meth, but she was in a whole other league.'

'Meaning?' I take an involuntary glance at the Dictaphone to make sure it's still working. I don't want to miss a second of this. I suddenly have one of those flashes of surreality that have hit me since Luther started telling his story: *I'm*

sitting here with Luther Carson, hearing things that he's poten-
tially never told anybody else, ever.

'Heroin. She did heroin. The first time I saw her, I could not believe it. I wanted to call the cops, or something. She was "chasing the dragon" – you know, where you cook it up and sort of smoke it. Like a fucking Chinese gangster. But she said it was cool, and I trusted her, so we did it. It was – if you've never done it, I can't describe it to you. But trust me, it was unbelievable.

'The only trouble is, it can kill you. A girl she knew died from an overdose, and Dom stopped, and I stopped too. But we were always doing something. We couldn't even watch a movie together at home without doing a line of coke first. And we always had it before sex as well.' He pauses. 'I guess we overdid it. One time, my mom rented a vacation house in Florida and invited us to visit her. I told Dominique we couldn't bring anything with us, because I knew my mom would have hated it, so Dom said she wouldn't go.'

'So what did you do?'

'I cancelled. I said she was sick. I just couldn't stand to be away from her. But then I realised things were just getting more and more out of hand. One night, I stayed awake all night, sweating and having DTs. My heart was beating so fast I honestly thought I was going to die. I got up and started looking around for a pen and paper to make my will, I was so out of it. You'd think I would have had the sense to call 911 instead, but no, I had to dispose of all my assets first. And then, as you know, one night, someone else did call 911 for me, and I got rushed to hospital. I'd been drinking pretty heavily and then I took some, I don't know, rat poison or something. I don't know what the hell I took. But that's not what got me into rehab.'

'What did?'

'I did something pretty shitty. I had earned a lot of money from my first two films, but somehow I never seemed to have any. By the time I paid my agent, paid my tax, bought a new car, well, a couple cars, took care of my buddies, rented a place, went out every night . . . it just disappeared. Dominique was even worse. One night, I just happened to be between pay cheques and I had lost one of my ATM cards as well. But we needed cash right away. So I stole a hundred dollars from Bruce Willis.'

'You *what*?'

'Yeah. We were at a benefit dinner for AIDS. I was sitting at his table, and I saw him put some money in a donation envelope on the table. When he got up, I just took it and left. Nobody noticed a thing. It was pretty lame, I know, but at the time I thought it was hilarious. And so did she. To be honest, it's not like we were short of cash. I just needed to pay my dealer that night and thought it was easier to take it from the table than go driving around looking for an ATM machine. But later I couldn't stop thinking about it. I thought, you've almost killed yourself twice, and now you've stolen money from AIDS victims. And I just called up a rehab centre and in I went. Dominique was not happy.'

'Why not?' I ask.

'She felt like I was abandoning her, I guess. Like I said, she needed me to be using so that she felt OK about her own drug use. And I think she thought that she was more likely to OD or get in trouble without me around to keep an eye on her. But in the end, she got out of it fine. She's done very well for herself.' He sounds slightly resentful.

'So, is that why you two broke up?' I say. 'Because you stopped doing drugs to the same extent?'

'I guess it was, you know? We were both addicts and we made each other keep using. You know, they talk about co-dependency and all the rest of it. But the truth was that the drugs were what kept us together. Without them, I don't think we would have had a whole lot to talk about. Funny. I knew that I knew that, but it's only really occurring to me now you've asked me that. Don't put all that in.'

I find it hard to believe that talking was really ever what Luther wanted from her, but who am I to judge? But it's interesting to know that he can see deficiencies in their relationship. He's obviously realised that he needs someone with a more stable lifestyle.

'What about that tattoo on her foot?' I ask. 'Is it true that she, um, got it . . .'

'So she could walk on me every day? That's bullshit. She got it long before we separated. She said it was because I was the ground beneath her feet. It's probably faded by now. I told her at the time that's a terrible place for a tattoo because it wears away so fast, but she insisted.'

I make a note, 'Dominique foot – check', and sigh inwardly. This sounds like the sort of thing that will become an unending bone of contention during the libel read, with lawyers asking for proof, Luther swearing blind that that's what happened, Dominique's attorney, if we send him the manuscript, objecting . . . It suddenly strikes me how surreal this situation is. I'm probably going to spend a lot of time in the next week or so, along with several other people, trying to establish the facts around Dominique's foot tattoo. How has this become a normal part of anyone's working day? If I ever thought, for a second, that some stranger was writing memos about my feet, I would think that there was something seriously wrong with the world.

I decide to take Luther back over a few important parts of their relationship: I want to know what his first words to Dominique were, for example. He can't remember, which is unfortunate though not unusual.

'I think I might have asked to borrow her highlighter pen.'

Together we come up with a better opening line. I also want to know when their first date was, but I'm soon corrected: it sounds like there was no first date, just a more-or-less instant falling into bed.

'That will work too,' I say. 'I mean, that's fine, if that's how it happened.'

Luther doesn't say anything. I glance over at him, to see that he's frowning in concentration.

'Hey,' he says. 'You know, that story about me stealing money from Bruce. Or when I invited both those girls to the same premiere. Or learning to hotwire cars. And all the boozing and the drugs and everything . . . sending my assistant to meet my dealer . . .'

'Yes?' I say nervously. *You mean, the best parts of the book? Please don't start saying you want to take them out. Please, please don't do this to me. Not now . . . not after everything we've been through . . .*

'Do you really want to put those in the book? I mean – don't they make me sound like an asshole? Not that I care what people think,' he adds, somewhat unconvincingly. 'It's just, I don't like to talk to interviewers about that stuff, because they twist it. I don't know why people would want to read about it.'

He sounds genuinely puzzled. Does he not understand?

'But, Luther,' I say. 'Those are exactly the kinds of things that make a person interesting, and lovable. If you'd never put a foot wrong your entire life, and been a complete straight arrow, your story would be pretty dull. Despite all the great things you've done,' I add quickly.

He looks sceptical.

'Really?'

'Of course! It's like in any story. Nobody identifies with

a character who's perfect – it's boring. Whereas, someone who messes up – that's much more engaging. It's more interesting, and it's more real, because nobody is perfect.'

He's looking as if this is all completely new information.

'I know that's the case with characters,' he says. 'But I never thought it would be like that for autobiographies. I guess it makes sense.'

'I promise,' I say. 'And, look, Brian is brilliant at making his subjects come across as sympathetic. If there's anything he's good at, it's getting the reader on your side. And that's what we want. It's in our interests to make you look good.'

Luther is obviously mulling this over. 'Right,' he says. 'Well, it's probably going to be good for Dominique also. This is definitely a side to her that isn't so perfect. And, according to you, that'll make her more sympathetic, right?'

Oh, dear.

'Well . . . no,' I say. 'That's different. It would be one thing if she were telling the story herself, but this is your side of the story only. If you sound as if you're being critical or unfair about her, it won't make you look good. So we'll have to bend over backwards to be gentlemanly.'

'That sounds like quite a contortionist act,' says Sam, appearing in the doorway.

'Hey, man,' says Luther.

I'm pretty pleased to see him. For the past hour, I've been dying to go to the bathroom, but I haven't dared leave Luther while he's sharing such intense stuff.

I stand up, saying, 'I'll let you guys chat – I'll be back in a second!' And I scoot away before either of them can say anything.

Once I'm in the bathroom, I take a minute just to slump there and zone out. I can't believe how intense today has been, on top of very little sleep last night and a twelve-hour working day yesterday. But it doesn't matter. None of it matters, as long as we get the book. And Luther is still being brilliant. Wonderful. I'm just beginning to feel dizzy and I think I need fifteen minutes' alone time.

After a minute, I realise I'd better go back out. Sam is still on the terrace. He's dressed a bit more formally than usual, wearing a jacket over his T-shirt and carrying what looks like an overnight bag.

'Are you going somewhere?' I ask, knowing I sound inane.

'Yeah. I have to go to London for a couple days and do some fire-fighting. Not literally fire-fighting,' he adds, seeing my expression. 'I mean – forget it. I'm flying to Rome now to catch my connecting flight.' He looks at Luther. 'I'll come back as soon as I can, though. And I'll be contactable. So call me if anything comes up. Anything *whatever*,' he adds pointedly to Luther. He looks extremely pissed off.

'Don't sweat it,' says Luther. 'We're busy. We're working. We're in the zone. In fact,' he says to me, 'maybe that's the best thing. A closed set. What do you think, Alice? We can have a total lockdown, make sure nobody comes here, so we can work twenty-four seven . . .'

I'm trying to control my expression, but I'm actually feeling pretty worried. It sounds brilliant in theory, and it's what I would have dreamed of a week ago, but . . . if Sam leaves us, that means I'm alone – for at least two days – in the house with Luther, with only Maria Santa as chaperone. Obviously it will be great to spend so much time with Luther and do the interviews freely without Sam interfering. But how am I going to get my work done in the evenings? Luther needs company, especially after such intense days, and I can't keep him company *and* transcribe our interviews. I won't have time. I suppose I'll have to rely on Marisa and Federico.

'Sure,' I say, trying to sound cheerful. 'We'll be fine. Have a lovely trip.'

Sam just gives me a look. 'I'll need those transcripts,' he says curtly. 'Don't forget.' As I watch him go, his bag slung over his shoulder, I get the strangest sensation: it's as if I'm marooned on an island, watching a boat sail off into the distance.

'What was I saying?' says Luther.

TWENTY

By the time evening comes, I'm a shadow of my former self.

It's not that Luther's being difficult: quite the reverse. The floodgates have opened. He's been talking and talking: it's as if he's taken some kind of truth drug. After hearing his stories, I no longer believe anything that's written in the papers; the reality almost always seems to be more bizarre. He's dropped one outrageous fact after another about different A-listers and smaller fry. After he mentioned something about a co-star of his who asked his assistant to break up with his girlfriend on his behalf, I had to explain to him that we can't publish everything he says.

'How come?' he said. 'It's true.'

'Because we could get sued,' I said. 'I'm not a libel lawyer but I do know that if we say defamatory things about people, we have to be able to prove them, potentially in a court of law, and even if we can prove them, we don't want to end up in court. It's just not worth it.'

'No?' Luther didn't look too upset, but I continued.

'We can mention some of these things, provided we disguise people's identities. But it gets tricky, because we could end up creating a fake identity that might then get mistaken for another, real person.'

'Uh-huh,' Luther said. I could see that I'd lost him. I can't help noticing that his attention does tend to wander when we're not talking about him.

In any case, Luther has plenty of anecdotes that are lively without being completely scandalous. There are some great stories about him picking up girls with Leonardo DiCaprio and gatecrashing a party at Tom Cruise's house. The great thing about him is that unlike lots of more – well, mature stars, who have big, pharmaceutically induced holes in their memories, he can remember everything – or most of it. What with this, and his candour about himself, and the stuff about his childhood and early years, the book is going to be fantastic.

So it's been great; but it's been heavy going. My shoulders are aching; in fact, every muscle in my body is aching. I never knew listening could be so much hard work. And it's not just listening; it's concentrating on what he's saying, trying to ask the right questions, keeping him on the subject, getting the facts and chronology, all at once. And I still don't know when I'm going to have the time to type it all up. I've tried calling Marisa to see if she's coming over, but there's no answer.

At 7 p.m., Maria Santa rings the bell for dinner. It's early; I think she probably saw how I was wilting during our quick sandwich lunch, which didn't interrupt the flow of the interviews even remotely. How I wish I could collapse on a sofa and eat my dinner in front of the TV.

Suddenly I realise how weird this is. Here I am, in an Italian villa with Luther Carson, whom I've had a crush on for years, who's been voted MTV's Most Desirable Male, and been officially described as one of the Thirty Sexiest Men on the planet. He's pouring out his heart to me and telling me things that probably no one else knows. We've been left all alone all day, and now we're about to have dinner together. It *sounds* like heaven – and a week ago, it would have seemed an impossible dream – but, when faced with it in real life, it's not at all how I would have imagined it.

'Chow time,' Luther remarks. 'Why don't you take the tape with you? I might think of more stuff over dinner.'

I pick it up, and go to put in a new tape. And I realise something inconvenient, that could also be good news.

'Luther – this tape is full. And it's my last one. We've used up every single one. Which is wonderful!' I add, seeing his face fall. 'It's fantastic that you've been working so hard. But I'll need to download all the files to the computer before we do another interview. It could take a while.'

'I guess we can just talk,' he says, sounding disappointed.

It's a beautiful evening. The sun is sinking across the bay, and the terrace has never looked more inviting. Maria Santa has set the table beautifully, with little yellow and white flower arrangements, and what looks like a new set of plates that I've never seen before. She gives me a special smile as we sit down, and pours us each a glass of prosecco. Help. Does she think this is some sort of romantic occasion? If she has a violin quartet waiting in the wings I'm not sure what I'll do.

'She seems to think we're celebrating,' Luther remarks.

'We're celebrating all your work on the book,' I say, and clink my glass against his. 'Seriously, Luther, you've been an absolute star.'

I'm ravenous. We start to eat our first course, which is my favourite: grilled, marinated vegetables, with slivers of ham and cheese. And I realise something very odd. I've spent the last two days nose-to-nose with Luther, hearing the story of his life, and now that we're not working on the book, I can't think of a single thing to say to him. I'm racking my brains to think of a question to ask him but,

177

on the other hand, I'm worried that he must be tired of talking. So I try to think of something amusing to say, but my mind is totally blank. And then I start to worry that he must be finding me boring.

'Have you ever been to London?' I ask him, thinking that perhaps I can entertain him with tales of the metropolis.

He thinks. 'Yeah, a couple times. I did some PR there, for my last movie. I stayed at The Dorchester. I didn't see the place that much. When I'm in London,' he adds, 'I always book in under Joe DiMaggio. I don't know why.'

'Oh, how funny!'

Silence descends.

As I rack my brains for another topic of conversation, something else occurs to me – an absolutely radical new idea.

Why can't Luther ask *me* a question?

I'm trying to remember, but in the whole time I've known him, I don't think Luther's ever asked me a single thing about myself. I'm learning everything there is to know about him, and he knows absolutely nothing about me. Of course, I am meant to be interviewing him. But surely most people would have asked one or two questions, just out of politeness, if not out of genuine interest. Luther certainly doesn't know my last name. If pressed, he would probably be able to say that I lived in London. But otherwise, for all he knows, I might have landed from the moon three weeks ago.

He glances up, obviously aware of me staring, and I realise that I'm being weird. I might be overdosing on him a bit, but I can't let it show.

'Sorry. The Dorchester sounds lovely. I've been there for tea. Did you have a suite, or . . .?'

And he's away. All I have to do is listen and ask questions, and make a mental note of anything we can use in the book. As we chat – or rather, as he talks and I listen – I realise this is reminding me of someone. Who?

Simon. I'm remembering our last awful date in Pizza Express, when I was racking my brains trying to think of something to say – that is, of a question to ask him. I can't believe I thought I was talking too much that evening about my problems at work. I'd say the ratio of my voice to his was something like 20:80.

As Luther continues to talk, I wonder: are all my conversations with men going to involve me being an audience to a monologue? Maybe I should just put my fingers in my ears and start talking about myself – tell Luther all about growing up in Hertfordshire, my horrible school, how I want to be promoted, my disastrous love life, Simon and how I always end up getting dumped. But he would probably be asleep within minutes.

I can see that he might find me boring. But – another seemingly radical idea occurs to me – *Isn't Luther a little boring himself?* He's had an amazing life and everything, of course. But when we're not doing interviews, is he interesting to talk to? I still think he's a good actor, but would people make such a big fuss of him if he didn't look the way he does? I have to say the answer's no, on both counts.

Finally, after what seems like hours, dinner is over, and Luther stands up and stretches.

'Time for a game of Grand Theft Auto,' he says. He looks at me consideringly. 'Hey. You want to play?'

Oh, God. I can't say no, because that would be rude. But I can't say yes, because I've been in his company for over twelve hours now without a break, and if I don't have just ten minutes by myself, I'm going to go insane. In fact, if my state of mind were a painting, it would be *The Scream* by Edvard Munch. That's how I feel inside, though I'm smiling outside.

'I'd love to,' I say. 'Maybe in a while? I just need to do some work first. I hope you don't mind.'

As soon as he's gone, I try Marisa's mobile again. She answers it with a flood of lively-sounding Italian, whether angry or happy, I can't tell.

'Marisa! It's Alice. How are you? Listen, I need to ask you a big favour . . .'

Two minutes later, I've hung up the phone with a feeling of total bliss. She's not free this evening, but she and Federico will come by tomorrow evening at seven, and take Luther out for dinner and drinks. Tomorrow evening, I'm off the hook. And the day after, Sam should be back. The relief is indescribable. Marisa really is my fairy godmother.

I look at my watch. It's 8 p.m. now, and I should start transcribing. I reckon it's going to take me until at least 3 a.m. this time around. If only there were some computer program that converted audio tapes into words. I bet, in fact, that one either already exists, or will be invented as soon as I stop this typing.

As I resume my station at the computer, I realise I am shattered: bone tired. I think I'll make myself some coffee; otherwise I can picture myself falling asleep over the keyboard and waking up in the middle of the night with with asdfghj imprinted on my cheek. Maybe I should borrow some of Luther's pharmaceuticals to stay awake. But that would mean knocking on his door, and I just can't face him at the moment.

Wow. I never, ever thought I would feel that way.

As a treat, I take a quick look at Facebook. Ruth has declared herself 'In a relationship' with Mike. Lucky Mike. Erica has posted pictures of her new kitten – it's adorable. Out of habit, I find myself looking at Simon's page. He's posted pictures of himself at a party with his arm around some dark-haired girl – *not* Claudine. I'm just about to click on her profile to see who she is when I change my mind. Why am I looking? I'm not even interested. I go back to Simon's page and click 'delete friend'. Great! I feel much happier.

I've recently figured out how to log into my work email from here. Along with all the work stuff there's a message from Ciara, asking how I am and when I'm coming home. It all makes me feel homesick; it will be so nice to get back to London and see everyone. I'm about to reply to her when I see that I have an email from Sam – no subject. Feeling my heart skip slightly, I open it up. What is he going to say?

'Alice: you still haven't emailed me those transcripts. I need them a.s.a.p.'

Huh. That's a very short, rude email. Doesn't he want to know how we are, or what the weather's like or anything? But then I realise I'm being ridiculous. This is what I wanted, after all. I'm winning, and Sam has to ask for my help. I attach the most recent transcripts and press send, trying to ignore my irrational disappointment that he doesn't have anything else to say to me.

TWENTY-ONE

'I miss autographs. The thing is that when someone gets your autograph, that's cool, that's like you're giving them something special. But when they just take a snap of you on their phone, and they don't even speak to you – it's like they're at the zoo and you're the monkey. You know?'

Luther is lying on the lounger, his eyes closed, his hand thrown over his head to shield himself from the sun. He looks like he's on a therapist's couch. I'm opposite him on the chair. We've now spent most of the last few days in this position, and I know this back terrace as intimately as I know my bedroom at home. The red tiles on the ground; that crack in the wall where the gecko sometimes comes out; the windows that look into the sitting room, and Mount Etna in the distance . . . I'm probably going to see it in my dreams for years to come.

Yesterday was so much easier. After his initial manic burst, Luther seems to be slowing down a little. We didn't start until 9 a.m., so I got at least five hours' sleep, and we talked until around 6 p.m., with a quick break for lunch. Then, Federico and Marisa came around in the evening, as promised, to hang out with Luther, letting me off the hook. I was able to spend all evening typing up the interviews, structuring them in rough narrative order, and writing notes for Brian. I finished up, again, around 2 a.m.

Brian seems to be holding up, thank goodness. His wife's cancer is only at stage two, which is good news, and he sounded so much better than he did the day he left. He also said he was happy to have the book to focus on. He gave me a list of questions to ask Luther.

'These interviews are terrific, though,' he told me. 'There is going to be no problem with this. The book's going to be a winner.'

I was so happy to hear this, I actually jumped up and down on the spot. I'm beginning to hope that this book isn't just going to happen: it's going to be really good. The only thing that worries me is that I still haven't heard anything from Olivia, even though I've been copying her in on all my emails to Brian.

Luther is on a detour right now, so I want to nudge him back on to what he was originally talking about, which was the *Roman Holiday* shoot.

'By the way, what was it like working with Natasha Pullman? I never asked you.'

'It was magical, fantastic, such a generous talent, blah blah. Actually, she's a little witch. Can we say that she's a little witch?'

I laugh. 'Is she? Well . . . we could say that you didn't bond, or that you've had other co-stars you've clicked with better. I mean, you can express opinions about people as long as they're just presented as your opinion, not fact . . .'

'Uh-huh,' he says, losing interest. 'No, let's just not give her any air time. That's what she's going to do to me. Wait till you read her publicity. She hates this romance they've manufactured about us, and she's not going to say one word about me in any of her interviews. She's one of the least supportive co-stars I've ever worked with. I could barely even talk to her; everything had to go through the director and her ten managers and PAs.'

'Oh dear.' I'm getting slightly tired of Luther's gripes.

'She's just obsessed with making it very clear who the star of this movie is. I mean, fine, she's number one on the call sheet, and – she is a bigger star.'

I'm very surprised to hear him say something like this. I wouldn't have said that this was the case, at all. I'm about to ask him what he means, but then I decide that whatever it is, it's probably not something I want to get into right now. Luther's anxieties about whether he's a big star might be good in a print interview, but not in our book, which needs to end with him 'in a good place'. So I just say, 'That's crazy. I think you're much bigger than she is. Hey – you know, we've been talking for an hour and a half. What about taking a quick break?'

'Yeah? Has it been that long?'

'Yes . . .'

'That's OK,' he says cheerfully. 'Don't forget, I'm used to fourteen-hour days.'

But I'm not, I want to say. 'I need to change the tape,' I say artfully.

He gets to his feet. 'Fine. Let's take ten. But no longer! I'm going to take a leak and maybe a dip in the pool. But not at the same time, don't worry.' And he's gone.

I've closed my eyes and am taking a few deep breaths when the peace of the morning is shattered by some ear-splittingly loud music – I think it's Aerosmith. Luther some-times does this when we take a break. It's annoying but I suppose he needs to let off steam. Anyway, it's a small price to pay for what he's giving us: his story. Finally. I drift off for a second into a daydream: *Sunday Times* bestsellerdom for Luther, promotion for me, a launch party at which Poppy and I can spot celebrities . . .

I've acquired a nice biscuit-coloured tan, just from sitting out here with Luther, and I'm admiring it through my sunglasses when Sam appears in the doorway. He's obviously come straight from the airport. He's looking very tired and unshaven, with dark circles under his eyes – he must have got up at the crack of dawn to be here. I'm surprised at how pleased I am to see him. I sit up a little straighter in my chair, feeling glad that I had time to wash my hair this morning, for once.

'Welcome back! How was your trip?'

'Short,' he says, tight-lipped. Oh, God, what now? 'As soon as I read those transcripts, I decided to come back early.'

'Oh. How come?'

'How come? Well, let's see. There's the kiss-and-tell. The tales of Luther's bad behaviour, all those stories about other actors. The drugs. The boozing. Do you want me to go on?'

'But—'

'I don't expect you to know this,' says Sam, 'but there's a certain understanding among people like Luther that you don't repeat gossip about your friends. What you get up to on your down time is your own business.'

How patronising can he get? 'I don't expect you to know this' indeed.

'But the stories aren't about Luther's friends,' I object.

'No? That trip to Mexico with Colin Farrell? The unnamed but completely identifiable actress who supplied him with coke on set? The idiot actor who broke up with his girlfriend via his assistant?'

'But – that's just –' I want to say that it's just good clean fun, though I realise that's not the phrase I want. 'But we've deliberately kept it light. I mean, relatively speaking. Most of the book is Luther's story – his childhood and teenage years and everything. As for the Hollywood stuff – it's not that scandalous compared to the stuff on Gawker or

185

whatever. It's colourful, but it's all pretty good-natured. It's not as if anyone's privacy is being compromised.'

'What about Dominique Rice?'

I don't know what to say to that.

'I mean,' Sam continues, 'there is no way she's going to OK what he's said about her. Your lawyers will be telling you that soon enough.'

'Yes, of course, and we can make the changes they recommend. But beyond that, it's Luther's book, and he can say what he likes.'

'And if Luther never works again because of this book? What kind of success story will that be for you?'

'But that won't happen,' I say, uncertainly.

'Really? Can you think of another actor like Luther, who's done a book like this and survived it?'

That idea makes me feel very bad. But I can't let that stop me.

'Look, it's Luther's career. I can't imagine that this book will end it, but if he wants to do it, doesn't he have the right to?'

Neither of us has noticed Luther approaching. He slings an arm around us both.

'Hey,' he says. 'I don't want Mom and Dad to fight.'

I can't help laughing. Sam looks completely unimpressed.

'You said you had some news for me,' Luther says to Sam.

'Yes,' says Sam, recovering himself. 'Very exciting news. Seth's been given a heads-up about a pilot—'

'Uh-oh. No. Not Seth. Not pilots.'

'It's a great part,' Sam says.

'No how. No TV. I don't do TV. I am big screen.'

'Luther, everybody does TV. Glenn Close does TV. George Clooney. Laurence Fishburne. Chloë Sevigny. Gabriel Byrne. Rob Lowe—'

'No! Don't say Rob Lowe! I never made a tape!'

'And the money is good. Do you know how much they're offering, per episode?'

He tells Luther, and I gasp.

'I'm not in this business for the money,' says Luther.

From the look on Sam's face, I can tell he wants to strangle Luther. I sympathise because I know exactly how maddening Luther can be. Sam starts talking about how acclaimed the writers and the producers are.

'Luther, Dustin Hoffman is doing TV now,' he says. 'Don't you think there's something in it?'

'I'll leave you guys to it,' I say, discreetly backing away.

I'm hoping that I can just have a sandwich by myself before I write up some of this morning's interview. I've felt rude leaving Luther to eat lunch alone, but now that Sam's back, I'm off the hook. I am worried about what Sam said about Luther. I don't want Luther's career to be in ruins. And I'm annoyed that Sam is taking it out on me when none of this is my fault.

There's nobody in the kitchen, but half the cupboard doors are open. It's like that scene in *The Sixth Sense*. I know why this is; Luther has been in here earlier making a snack, and he wouldn't think of closing a cupboard door after himself. I close them all, and then I cut myself some bread and cheese and tomatoes, and take a plate out to the front terrace.

Just as I start eating, my parents call. I haven't spoken to them since I arrived, and it's so nice to catch up. They've just been to see Erica and Raj and met their new kitten, and they've bought an electric mower, even though our lawn isn't really big enough to warrant one. My dad is already addicted to riding around on it. 'I suppose it's cheaper than a new car,' says Mum. 'By the way, have you got enough Factor 50? I've been looking at the forecast in Sicily. It was thirty-five degrees yesterday!'

Just then Luther comes out and sees me on the phone.

I cover it quickly. 'I'm sorry – it's my parents. Can I just take five more minutes?'

Luther looks annoyed. 'Well, I'm ready now.' He turns around and leaves.

'Mum, I have to go,' I tell her.

'Is everything all right?' She sounds alarmed.

'It's fine. I'll call you later.'

I follow Luther to the back terrace, where we resume our positions. He's looking a bit depressed, hunched up on his bench and smoking a cigarette.

'TV, huh?' he says.

'Oh, Luther. I'm sure it's a good part. What's the series?'

'It's about estate agents in LA during the 1980s,' he says, sounding moody. 'It's pitched as *Desperate Housewives* meets *Mad Men*. My character – or the guy Sam and Seth want me to do – is a sleazy huckster type who does loads of deals and bangs loads of hot women.'

'But that sounds perfect for you! I mean, sorry – you would be great in that. Why don't you want to do it?'

'I just think . . . so the part might be a good part. But would Clooney do it? No. You know?'

I think I get it: he thinks TV is somehow a sign of failure.

'I don't know what George Clooney would do,' I tell Luther. 'But I really like *Mad Men*. And *Desperate Housewives*. I think American TV drama is outstanding.'

Luther looks at me sceptically.

'Seriously. Something like *The Wire* – I haven't watched it all, but I've seen it – it's a work of art. In fact, I read in a newspaper that if Dickens or Shakespeare were alive today, they would be writing for American TV.'

He doesn't even seem to hear me, just shakes his head and sighs. 'Really,' he says indifferently. 'Let's get back to work.'

We work until six o'clock. Luther goes off to have a workout, and I start my evening's typing. I'm only going to

188

do an hour or two tonight. Federico and Marisa are coming over for dinner, and I think I'll actually be able to join them. We've now pretty much covered Luther's entire story – except the time he went missing for a year. Brian has been working around the clock too, and we should have an early draft in the next few days. And once that's done, we're home and dry. Luther will no doubt want to make changes, but at least we will have words on a page that we can publish – which is more than we had a week ago.

Poor Luther. It probably shouldn't come as such a shock to me that a film star should be self-involved. It's strange that he doesn't seem to feel the intensity of being cooped up with me nose to nose like this, but it obviously doesn't affect him in the same way.

It's probably not a bad thing if he knows nothing about me. The more anonymous I am, the more freely he can talk to me. It's a strange, one-sided relationship, but I imagine most of his relationships are strange and one-sided. What on earth must it be like to be him? The more I think of it, the more horrifying it seems. It would be one thing if you had some sort of normality to retreat to, like a happy marriage or a stable background, or a group of friends who had a foothold in the real world, but Luther doesn't have that. He doesn't have parents who want to tell him about their new electric mower.

As I sit down in front of the computer, I think of how compassionate I felt about Luther when I first learned of his troubled background. But the thing is: even though he's had a difficult upbringing, that doesn't make him any less of a pain in the neck when he chooses to be – like begrudging me five minutes on the phone with my family. It explains it, but it doesn't do away with the effect. I remember trying to decide whether he was a lost puppy or a selfish charmer. I suppose the truth is he's both.

TWENTY-TWO

I've only been typing for twenty minutes when I hear my phone. It's Olivia. I sit bolt upright. Please let her be pleased . . .

'Hi, Olivia. Have you . . . what do you think of the material?'

'I haven't had a chance to look at it all yet, Alice,' she says. 'But I've been looking at the contract . . .'

Here we go. Oh God. I put my hand to my mouth . . .

'And I've remembered, we need to book Luther's publicity days urgently. I can't get hold of his wretched publicist and I thought Sam might be able to help. Can you ask him?'

'Well – he probably could, but—'

'Brilliant. I'll leave that with you, then. Bye.'

My hand is shaking as I put down the phone. Thank God she hasn't noticed the clause yet. Perhaps she won't ever notice it, provided the manuscript is good enough. And provided Sam doesn't kick up a fuss about the content . . .

The door to Sam's room is open, and he's writing on a yellow foolscap. I've never been in here before – obviously. He looks around and sees me, then he turns back to his writing. The room is bare and tidy, with just a few manly things scattered around: a pair of sunglasses, car keys, an e-reader, neat piles of paper scripts on his bed. I wait until he finishes, watching him, or rather, watching the back of his neck. He's wearing his glasses, which I think suit him, and there's a small hole in his T-shirt, which is the grey UCLA one he wears all the time, and his hair's grown a fraction longer . . . He turns around abruptly, and I look away just in time. 'What's up?'

I hope he didn't see me staring. 'Sam – I'd like us to be able to co-operate on this book. Or at least, not be complete enemies.'

'That sounds idyllic. What do you need?'

'The publicity days.'

'I'm glad you reminded me. That's one thing we can lose the memo for.'

I sit down on the other chair. 'Look, this book. Luther wants to do it, you know. He's enjoying it. I think he's finding the process . . . cathartic.'

'He enjoys a lot of stuff that's bad for him,' Sam says drily.

'But is it such a bad thing?'

'In a word, yes. His publicist has no idea what to make of it. I should give her these transcripts but she'd have a heart attack. As would his attorney, probably. But, do you know what I really worry about?'

'No . . .' I'm not sure I want to know either.

'I worry that people will think Luther's doing this book because he needs the money. It's the kind of thing that a has-been would do, quite frankly.'

'What about Michael J. Fox? And Patrick Swayze?' I say triumphantly, before remembering that poor Patrick Swayze died before his book came out. 'They're not has-beens,' I add, more uncertainly.

'It's funny you should mention them. Do you know what the head of our agency said when Marc produced this book deal for Luther? He said, "Is he dying? Is he paraplegic? Does he have Parkinson's? No? Then why is he doing a fucking book?"'

'But that's just—'

'The point is those guys had specific issues they were writing about. Whereas Luther's specific issue seems to be his loose cannon past, which I've spent the last year and a half trying to play down.'

Ouch.

'I'm also wondering how Dominique Rice is going to react when she comes across her ex-husband's description of her smoking heroin like, quote, a fucking Chinese gangster, unquote. Among other things.'

'Well, we don't need to use those exact words . . .'

'Dominique is a powerful woman. She and her husband have a very good relationship with one of the biggest studios. If she reacts badly to this book, it's possible that Luther will never work on one of that studio's films again. They might even decide to extend that favour to all my other clients – not that that's relevant to you, but I'm just letting you know; it might not just be Luther's career you're harming.'

'Doesn't it help that it's only being published in Europe?'

He sighs. 'Maybe. I'm praying it will be like one of those whiskey commercials you do in Japan and that nobody has to know about.'

'And – the other stuff. I mean, the famous friends stuff. Maybe they'll take it as a compliment? Like having a cameo in *Entourage*, or something? He could contact them all, put it as a favour . . .' I've heard about *Entourage* from Luther; he's a bit sore that they've never asked him to do a cameo.

'*Entourage* is fictional,' Sam says.

'I know,' I say, annoyed. This is his problem, after all, and I'm only trying to help.

Sam looks out of the window, takes off his glasses and rubs his eyes.

'I suppose they might OK it. It's more the general impression it creates.'

'You mean – the book making it seem like the end of Luther's career?'

'I never said that,' he says quickly. 'I said that that's how some people *could* see it. He's got a long career ahead of him.'

'Of course he does. And maybe this book could mark the beginning of a new phase.'

'Meaning?'

'The point of these books is that they have a happy ending. Not the end of your career – but, you know, the end of a certain kind of life. We're spinning it as Luther looking back on his bad-boy past – emphasis on the past – and putting it all behind him. Doesn't that help you?'

'Huh,' says Sam. He doesn't sound convinced.

'And it could work quite nicely, couldn't it? If he does the TV part. That's another new phase for him. It's a very different part to any he's played before. I think he would be great doing a more complex, comic role.'

'I'm glad you approve,' he says sarcastically.

'I do. I think the show sounds great. I've told Luther that. And I'll tell him again.'

Sam doesn't say anything for a while. He doodles on his pad, and without looking up he says, 'I can't talk Luther out of this. So I'm going to have to trust you. Can I trust you?'

'Trust me to do what?'

'Not to screw Luther over. Not to make him look bad. Not to produce a tacky book that will damage his career, or mine: all that kind of stuff.'

'Sam, honestly. You can trust me.' I give him my most sincere, trustworthy expression – which for some reason makes him laugh. He throws down his pen, shaking his head.

'OK, fine. I will help you and Luther with this car-wreck of a project. I'll read the book through and point out the biggest trouble spots. And I'll get the manuscript to Dominique to try and smooth things over, and I'll give you the three publicity days. And you will show me everything you're doing, and keep talking the TV show up to Luther. Are we good?'

'We're good,' I say. I really am picking up so many American phrases.

As I'm going out the door, he says, 'I forgot to ask you. How's Brian and his wife?'

'They're doing all right. It seems like the prognosis is hopeful. Thanks for asking.'

'Sure.' He turns back to his work.

I go straight back to my room, delighted that I can give Olivia some good news.

'Olivia? The publicity days are sorted. Sam will call you to arrange them.'

'Fine,' Olivia says. This is one of those things about her; sometimes, even when you do a good job on something tricky, she sounds as if she doesn't care either way. 'And I'll start reading the material tonight. I'll check it against the –' I hear rustling – 'contract too, to see how we're doing on length and on . . . the content . . .'

Oh no. Please, no.

'The content clause . . .'

I'm holding my breath. Should I hang up? Pretend I got cut off?

'Where is it? I'm looking at the contract, and I don't see that clause.'

It's happened. The thing I've been dreading for so long has finally happened. I could lie and say I have no idea why it's missing, but what's the point? With the sensation of jumping off a cliff, I say it quickly before I can change my mind.

'The clause isn't in the contract.'

'What do you mean, it's not in the contract? Why not?'

Deep breath. 'I forgot to put it in . . .'

Apparently there is a French expression: a bad quarter of an hour, meaning an unpleasant experience. This is what happens to me now. I just concentrate on holding the phone, staying upright, and counting the tiles on the floor, while Olivia's words flow over me like a tidal wave. I try not to listen too closely but I hear things like 'stupid', 'unbelievable', 'incompetent' and 'lack of trust'.

'You knew this clause was missing?' she says at one point. 'You've known all along, and you didn't tell us?'

I nod, before I remember she can't see me. 'Um – yes.'

'This is just – we could be within our rights to dismiss you. Do you realise that?'

I say yes.

'This is serious, Alice. I don't think you realise just how serious it is.'

I apologise once more, but it just seems to set her off again. Her final words, which she hisses at me before she hangs up, are: 'This manuscript had better be *outstanding*.'

The ringtone sounds really loudly in my ear. I put down my phone carefully; the battery is nearly gone, so I plug it into its charger. For want of anything better to do I decide to get changed for dinner. I put on a green dress Marisa gave me: it's very pretty, pistachio-green with a low neck. I think I'm still in shock; I just can't bear to think of everything Olivia said to me and what's going to happen next. *Very serious indeed. Dismissal.* I start putting on some eye make-up. *You've known all along and you didn't tell us.* At least she said she *could* fire me. So that means she probably won't. Hopefully. If I don't do anything else wrong. I pile my hair up in a sort of French roll, which luckily works first time. I can hear the others arriving outside. Good. I need a drink.

TWENTY-THREE

I walk out on to the terrace, and I'm almost surprised to see everything looks normal: sun, swimming pool, sea, just as I left it. Except for Brian, the gang's all here: even Annabel has graced us with her presence, and she's brought Nikos with her. She seems to have gone for the Eurotrash look, with a white dress with tacky ripped cut-outs all down the side. Nikos is looking sleazy in the tightest of tight white T-shirts, showing off his steroid arms – I can never understand how straight men think they don't look ridiculous in those. I sit down opposite them, reluctantly, since there is an empty seat. After I've just been blasted by Olivia, Annabel should be easy enough to deal with.

'You look exhausted, Alice,' Annabel tells me in satisfied tones. 'Sort of . . . washed out. Or maybe it's just that colour.'

Nope. Can't deal. I get up again, and move around the table to get as far away as possible from them, ending up opposite Marisa.

'*Carissima!*' Marisa kisses me. 'Good to see you. I hear you are making great progress and Luther's working hard.' She drops her voice. 'What did I tell you? He just needed a firm hand.'

'Yes, I suppose so,' I say. I pour her a glass of wine, and then myself. I am not going to think about Olivia, or Luther, or the trouble I'm in. I'm just going to drink this glass of wine.

Sam approaches the table next. He seems to hesitate over where to sit – there's an empty seat beside Luther and opposite Federico – before sitting down beside me.

'I just spoke to Dominique's manager,' he tells me. 'Apparently Dominique is in Capri right now, taking a few days' vacation, so we can FedEx her a copy there and she might even have time to read it this week.'

For a second I almost forgot who Dominique is. 'Oh, goody,' I say. 'Would you like a glass of wine?'

'Um . . . sure,' he says, exchanging a slightly puzzled glance with Marisa.

Marisa is looking as lovely as ever in a white sleeveless shirt and pink Capri pants which would make me look like an elephant. As I see her laugh at something Sam says, I feel so jealous of them both. They haven't made hideous mistakes at work. Then I wonder, not for the first time, if there might be something between them.

Well, she could do a lot worse. This is a good distraction from everything: I'm going to give this Marisa-and-Sam thing some proper consideration. I have to admit that, compared to all the other men here – Federico, Nikos, even Luther – Sam is in a different category. He may not be drop-dead gorgeous like Luther, but he is definitely attractive, if you like that tanned, athletic, outdoorsy type. He's intelligent and successful. And he's not being difficult about Luther's book for the sake of it. He is trying to do the right thing for him, even when that means arguing with him. And even though we've spent hardly any time together compared to the time I've spent with Luther, he knows a lot more about me than Luther does. He even remembered to ask about Brian; Luther basically still hasn't noticed that Brian's gone.

Wait a second. Has my crush on Luther been replaced by an attraction for Sam?

No, of course not. That would be crazy. It's true that, objectively, I can see he is attractive. He is definitely very attractive. But that's not the same as being attracted to him. Anyway, he and I have nothing in common, and he lives on the other side of the world. Not to mention that he is probably dating Megan Fox or similar.

Sam looks up, and I realise I've been staring.

'Sorry,' I say. 'What were you saying?'

'We were talking about a famous actress who we won't name,' Sam says.

Marisa tells me in a stage whisper who it is.

'Oh, I know her.'

'She was a client of mine,' Sam says to me. 'For about five minutes, before she got huge and dropped me. Did I tell you the emergency blowout story?' he asks Marisa.

He glances around the table to make sure no one else is listening. I'm thrilled: more distraction. I'm so glad everyone has come to dinner tonight. Imagine if I had to sit alone with Luther! I take another slug of wine.

'So she's shooting in New York. And she has her personal hairstylist with her, as per contract. It's his fortieth birthday, and to celebrate, he goes out for dinner with his boyfriend and some others from the cast and crew. They're all having a great time in a really nice restaurant in Tribeca, and she calls him in the middle of it, and makes him abandon dinner right in the middle of the entrée and come back uptown *at once*, because she needs – drum roll – an emergency blowout.'

'She needed a *what*?'

'A blowout. She was just acting up. Probably furious to be left out, even though he invited her to dinner.'

I've heard some eye-opening things in the past few days, but this is definitely the worst.

'But . . .' I'm shocked. 'How was that part of his job description? And he was gay!'

'Well . . .' Sam's looking at me strangely. 'He's her hair-stylist. Lots of them are gay. And it is part of his job, just maybe not during his fortieth birthday party when she has three assistant stylists on call for emergencies like that.'

Aha. I think I see my mistake. I start to laugh.

'What? What did you – oh.' Sam starts laughing too. 'You don't use that phrase, for styling your hair?'

'No. That's a blow-dry,' I say, in between fits of laughter. 'Sorry . . . I'm a bit zonked from all the interviews.'

'I'll have to remember that. So what's a blowout?' says Sam. 'I know you get blowout matches, in basketball . . .'

'Oh, God,' I say, wiping my eyes. 'A blowout, for me, is when you eat a lot. And I just thought it must mean . . . God, I don't know what I thought. Sorry.'

I think I must be slightly hysterical after the conversation with Olivia, because I can't stop laughing. I keep calming down, but then I took at Sam and I start to laugh again. And every time Sam sees me, he starts to laugh too. Soon we're laughing so hard, the rest of the table is staring at us. Even Marisa is looking mystified.

Annabel glances at us, clocks our mirth, and goes on with her own story.

'So then in March,' she says, 'I'm covered in mud, sort of writhing around, very Xenia Warrior Princess. And in April, I'm kind of covered in flowers, but not quite.' She wriggles and smirks at Luther, who's raised his eyebrows appreciatively. 'It's very arty.'

'What's this?' I ask, hoping I won't start laughing again. Though it sounds as though I probably will.

Annabel turns on me impatiently. 'The Pirelli calendar!' she says.

'Pirelli? Really?' Marisa asks, eyebrows raised. Federico looks excited.

'No, no, babe, I told you,' Nikos butts in hastily. 'It's not Pirelli – it's a company that sells to Pirelli. Distributes through them, I mean. Sort of a spin-off,' he adds to Sam, in a man-to-man way. 'She keeps getting it wrong.' He has such a strange accent. It's impossible to figure out where he's from – and I don't think Annabel knows either.

'Right,' says Sam, sounding deeply sceptical.

'The idea is,' Annabel says, 'that this is going to be the money-spinner, and then out of that, we get to finance the distribution of *Her Master's Bite*.'

'Ah, *Her Master's Bite*,' I say. Our old friend.

'How exactly are you going to finance the distribution of a feature film?' Sam asks Nikos. 'And where?'

'I've got some contacts . . . some buddies. It's a very big area, yeah, and one I'm planning on expanding into,' says Nikos. Marisa and Sam start asking him questions at once, but Luther interrupts by saying to Annabel, 'Well, Pirelli girls are hot, and you're hot, so I think it's perfect.'

I smile to think how just a few days ago that would have made me jealous. Now I don't even care. I look at Sam, and we both almost start to laugh again.

'How was London?' I ask him. 'You must be exhausted.'

'It was good, I really like London. My meetings were all in Soho, and I took a walk afterward, down to the river. The view along there is cool.'

'You would have been close to my office, then.'

'Oh, yeah, I know. I looked it up,' he adds, seeing my expression of surprise. 'Where do you live?' he continues.

It's such a novelty to talk to someone about myself that I launch into an in-depth description of Hammersmith and its amenities, and then I tell him about my flatmate Ciara and how she needed someone to move in after her break-up. Sam is telling me about a friend of his who had a similar situation, when Nikos butts in, asking about a big Hollywood star who has a house in Sicily.

'Apparently he's there with his boyfriend right now,' Nikos says. 'Is that true?'

Sam says, 'No, that's just a ridiculous rumour.' Luther says, 'Yeah, that's horse shit.'

But I have a feeling they're both lying. I'm surprised: the person Nikos mentioned is a total heart-throb, and always seems to have some woman on his arm.

The conversation moves on. 'Is that true?' I ask Sam in a low voice. He shrugs, which I understand means yes.

'But he has a girlfriend.'

'She's on a retainer,' says Sam. 'And she's signed a contract, with a confidentiality clause. She's an actress, so it's good exposure for her. Everybody wins.'

'But why does he have to hide it? There must be lots of other gay actors.'

'Of course there are. Just like there are lots of cokeheads and meth addicts and idiots and prostitutes and affairs. Sadly it's seen in the same light, as something to hide. Rumours leak out, the publicists bury it, and it's business as usual.'

'But what about—' I'm trying to think.

'Are you trying to think of a gay leading man?' Sam asks. 'I'll give you a hundred dollars if you can.'

'Rupert Everett!' I say finally.

'And what big roles have you seen him in?'

'*My Best Friend's Wedding*?'

'Where he played a . . .'

'. . . gay best friend. Yes, but surely he's done other films . . .'

'Not all the ones he could have, if he'd been straight. And that was a comedy. You think they would have cast

Jake Gyllenhaal and Heath Ledger in *Brokeback* if they'd actually been gay?'

'So – who are all the gay actors?'

'I'd rather not mention names,' says Sam. 'But there are plenty. Hollywood is an equal opportunities employer, as long as you stay in the closet.'

He pours himself, and me, another glass of wine. I can see he's had a lot to drink. Perhaps his trip didn't go so well. I know the feeling.

'I won't quote you on that,' I say.

'What are you two saying about Hollywood employment opportunities?' asks Annabel.

'We're talking about how Hollywood doesn't like gay leading men,' says Sam.

'No way. Goddamn faggots run the creative industries,' says Nikos.

'Which is more than we can say for you,' says Sam. In the candlelight I can see all trace of laughter has disappeared from his face; he looks furious.

'Hey, easy,' says Marisa, patting Sam's arm across the table.

'What the hell is that supposed to mean?' snaps Nikos.

'It means that I don't know what your real line of business is, but I don't believe for a second that you know anything about movie distribution – you bigoted jerk.'

'How dare you? You fucking Yanks are all the same. You'd want to put your own house in order, before telling everyone else what to do—'

'STOP!' I yell. Everyone looks at me, astonished. Annabel in particular looks as if she can't believe I've dared interrupt her boyfriend. 'I'm sorry, it's just – Luther and I have been working hard today, and we want to relax. We don't want arguments. Please.'

'Sorry – Alice,' Sam says, not looking at Nikos.

'Yeah, whatever,' says Nikos, looking more like a caveman than ever.

'More pasta, anyone?' asks Marisa.

'Who *was* that asshole?' Sam's grumbling. Dinner is over, and we're sitting around on the terrace with Luther. Everyone else has gone home.

'Let's not have the Joneses over for cocktails again,' says Luther.

'For sure. Jesus, where did Annabel find him? And by the way, where did you find Annabel?'

'I don't know. She was on set, and then she came here.'

'Did you ever have a thing with her, Luther?' I ask. It's cheeky of me, but I've always been curious about this.

'No. Well, yes. But it was on location. Which doesn't count.'

'And not since then?' says Sam. I'm glad I'm not the only one being nosy.

'No, I kind of got tired of it. She has the crazy eye. And she kept busting my chops with her vampire movie.'

'What's the crazy eye?' I think I know exactly what he means, but I'd like the official definition.

'It's the look that some actresses have, that means they have to be a success no matter what, and they'll walk over your hands to get there. It can be a little scary. Actors have it too but not as much.'

Poor Annabel. I can think of a few people at work who have the crazy eye, and I've probably had it myself at times. It's not super gallant of Luther to bitch about his ex-conquests, and I feel suddenly guilty about joining in.

'She's so beautiful,' I say. 'When I first saw her, I thought she was Sienna Miller.'

'Actually Sienna Miller is very sweet,' Sam says. 'So there's no danger of mistaking her for Annabel, if you ever meet her. I guess she and Nikos are suited.'

'By the way, why did you go all Sam Seaborn on parts for gay actors?' Luther asks. 'You could say the exact same thing about parts for black actors or whatever. Your kid brother is gay, right?'

'Yeah. But that's irrelevant. I just find the whole thing kind of depressing sometimes, is all.'

Luther turns to me. 'Did you know that Sam here paid his brother's college fees?'

'Wow.'

'That's not true,' says Sam. 'I helped him out in his first year, but he also won a scholarship.' He looks proud. 'He's a very bright guy. How'd you know about that, anyway?' he asks Luther.

'He told me that time we went to the Griddle Café,' Luther says. 'He's hot stuff. If I was gay, I'd be on to him like a shot.'

'You stay away from my brother,' says Sam. 'And my sister. She's still in college.' He pulls out his phone and shows me a picture of the three of them. It looks as though it's taken at Christmas – there's a tree and decorations in the background. They look like a nice family. They all have the same grey, slightly slanting eyes.

'Do you have any siblings?' Sam asks me.

'I have an older sister, Erica,' I say. 'She's married and lives in London.' I'm not sure what else to tell them. I certainly didn't pay Erica's college fees, and she's not gay.

'So we're both spoiled youngest kids,' says Luther. 'And Sam is a responsible eldest.'

'Yes, I am, and don't you forget it.'

'No,' Luther says. 'Don't start on me about the book again. Or the TV. I want to do my book. And I don't want to do the TV.'

'OK, OK, I heard you,' Sam says, pouring him another drink. He glances up and says, 'Alice? You want another?'

I'm about to say yes, but then Luther says, 'Come on! You're on vacation.'

And I remember with a creeping feeling of shame that I'm not here on vacation at all. I'm working, and I'm in big trouble with work. What would Olivia say if she could see me getting sloshed with Luther and Sam, just a few hours after our awful conversation? I look at my watch: a quarter to midnight. I need to go to bed, get up at a reasonable hour, and try and make some sort of amends for everything tomorrow.

'No thanks. I'd better go to bed,' I say, standing up. Luther waves and knocks back another drink. Sam says, 'OK. Goodnight.' As I walk across the terrace, I can feel him watching me go.

TWENTY-FOUR

I can't sleep.

I'm tired enough, and it's the first time in a while that I've been in bed before 2 a.m., but I can't stop thinking about Olivia and my disaster with the clause. And it's so hot. I drank too much at dinner, and had a coffee afterwards. Now I'm wide awake, staring at the ceiling. Looking at my phone, I see it's twenty past one.

Maybe I should go outside and get some air, or even go for a swim. Without turning on the light, I put on my bikini, put my nightdress back over it, and pad outside.

There's a full moon, shining as brightly as an electric light. It's just as hot outside as it is inside, but the water looks inviting. I've just dipped my toe in, when I hear a noise behind me and almost jump out of my skin. Someone is lounging in a seat beside the pool. It's Sam. He's dressed only in a pair of jeans, holding a lit cigarette, and listening to music. In the dark, I can just see the light of his eyes and the glow of his cigarette.

He removes his earphones.

'Can't you sleep either?' he says.

'No. It's so hot.'

'I know, right?' he says. 'Plus, I slept on the plane.'

I take a seat beside him. My nightdress is very flimsy, and I'm glad I'm wearing my bikini underneath it.

'I didn't know you smoked.'

'Only on special occasions. Like when I close a deal. It's like cigars for real men.'

'Did you close the deal in London?'

'No.' He passes me his tumbler of whiskey. 'So I'm drowning my sorrows. Cheers,' he adds, tapping a finger against the glass.

'What about you?'

'We can share.'

I sip it. I hate whiskey, but this isn't too bad. The burning warmth somehow seems to make the hot night feel cooler. I take another sip.

'Cigarette?'

I nod. Sam lights an extra cigarette, and passes it to me. As he leans over I notice his washboard stomach – even though he's sitting down and wearing jeans, I don't see an ounce of fat. Amazing. It's my first cigarette in years, and as I inhale and lean my head back, I can feel a mild buzz.

That's better. I'm so sick of thinking, and fretting, about my job. If I get fired, I get fired. At least, unlike Luther, whatever I do, it won't end up in the papers. I toy with the idea of telling Sam what's happened – I can hear myself say out loud, 'I'm in serious trouble with work.' But I can't tell him, much as I'd like to. Instead, I decide to ask him something else that's been on my mind.

'Can you think of anything worse than being famous?'

He laughs. 'Well, there are a few things . . .'

'No, I'm exaggerating, of course there are. Like being an orphan in a war-torn country. But even an ortorn in a warphan – sorry. An orphan in a war-torn country has something that a famous person doesn't have.'

His eyes are resting on me, serious and attentive.

'What?'

'Their identity. I mean, I won't say privacy, because if you're very poor, you might not have a lot of privacy. But – for me, I can go out in the street, and I can meet people on equal terms; I'm a human being and so are they. But if you're famous – that relationship is impossible.'

'I know what you mean.'

'I just don't think we're meant to relate to each other like that. I mean, Luther's pretty normal.' I pause as I wonder whether I really believe that. 'But that story, about the actress and her blow-dry . . . Nobody should behave like that. It's ridiculous. But it's also wrong.'

He doesn't say anything for a while. Then he says, 'Of course they shouldn't. But the thing is . . . from her perspective, she's given up a lot to do what she does today. The exact same things you're describing: privacy and identity. And the pay-off, for her, is that she gets everything she wants. The people around her give it to her because they know that's the deal. And they're on her payroll, they make money from her. She's not a private person any more; she's an industry.'

'But I don't think that's why she acts up like that. I think it must be terrifying to have everyone say yes to you all the time. It would be like going insane. If I behaved like that, I think it would be because I wanted someone to tell me no.'

'Yes, but that's because you're smart, and a good person. I said no to her, and she fired me.'

'Oh.' At the sound of the word *fired*, I wince in sympathy. I'm about to ask him more about that, but he's continuing, 'Anyway . . . there are plenty of big stars, and powerful people, who don't act like that. Some of them are really nice. And sometimes the ones who are up and coming are the craziest. There's no hard and fast rule.'

Thinking of Annabel, I realise this is true.

'I think it's grotesque, all the same. A person isn't an industry.'

'You're right,' Sam says. 'I agree. But here you are, and here I am.'

I don't know what to say to that.

'Sorry. That came out wrong. For what it's worth, I think Luther is getting something out of this book . . .'

'Thanks,' I say, in a small voice. Does he really think I'm exploiting Luther? Treating him like an industry? I suppose I am.

'Jesus – Alice,' Sam says. 'I'm sorry. I didn't mean to imply anything about you. I think I'm talking more about myself. I mean . . . I compromise myself, a lot. The way I talked at dinner, or the way I'm talking to you right now – I could never talk to anyone that way in LA. You wouldn't believe the way some of the agents I know talk. Homophobic, racist, anti-Semitic, anti-Republican, anti-Democrat, anti-actors . . . you name it. But the flip side is that the rest of the time, we're kissing ass. And we benefit from it just as much. You know, it's not just being famous that makes people treat you differently.'

'How do you mean?'

'Well . . . take me. If I were a struggling actor, or an assistant, nobody in the industry would talk to me. That's fine because they're industry people, but what I don't like is the way it affects my personal life.'

'You mean, the way you work all the time?'

'No. Well, yes, that too, definitely. What I mean is – OK, I'll tell you a story. Not long after I started signing my own clients, I met a girl at a party thrown by some friends of mine. We went home together . . . and the next day, she emailed me her résumé and a head shot.' He takes a drag of his cigarette. 'The irony was, I really liked her, and I definitely would have helped her if she'd just asked me. I just found it so sad that that was what she thought she had to do. Most of the guys I work with, that stuff doesn't bother them at all. They see it as a perk. Me, not so much.'

There's a pause, while he takes the tumbler back from me.

'Maybe you could just not date actresses,' I suggest.

'I don't, but the thing is, it's just an example of how people think there. Even my ex was like that, and she's not an actress.'

His ex. OK, so that sounds as if he's definitely single. Not that I'm interested, of course, but – anyway, he's single.

'I feel like it's turning me into someone I don't want to be. Jesus, Alice, how do you do this?' he asks suddenly.

'Do what?'

'Get people's life stories from them. Next I'll be giving you my social security number and telling you all about my first kiss. No wonder you've got Luther eating out of your hand.'

'Oh.' I'm distracted by the mention of his first kiss. 'Sorry, I hadn't realised I was doing it. Just habit, I suppose. What I think is . . .'

'What?'

He's looking at me, and it's an expression I haven't seen in a long time, maybe ever. It's the look of someone – OK, a man – who's really enjoying this conversation, and is waiting to hear what I'm going to say next. And I don't think it's just because we're talking about him.

'I was just going to say: of course what you do affects people's perception of you. Because it reflects who you are, and the fact that you're intelligent, and you've worked hard, and you've made good decisions. I don't see what's so wrong about that. But if your job is all they care about, then yes, that would be bad. Does that make sense?'

'Sure.'

'But . . . I don't think you're genuinely unhappy about it. Or about the fact that you have to work a hundred hours a week.'

'No?' He looks even more fascinated, and amused at the same time.

'No. I hear people – friends who work in the City, or in lots of different industries – complain about that kind of thing all the time, but they don't change it. Because although they complain, that's how they like it.'

He doesn't say anything for a minute, and I wonder if I've completely overstepped the mark. I can't see his face in the dark. But then he turns to me and I see he's grinning broadly.

'Wow. I have to hand it to you, Alice. That is the best gauntlet throw I think I've ever been given in my entire life. I've poured out my misunderstood agent angst to you, and you've summed it up in five words: Put up, or shut up. No, I like it,' he says, as I start to protest, laughing, that that wasn't what I meant. 'I really like it. And I want you to know, I'm going to give it some serious thought.'

He really does have a nice smile. It lights up his whole face.

He gets to his feet. 'Shall we shelve the soul-searching? Do you feel like a dip instead?'

'Why not.'

Sam takes off his jeans – he's wearing his swimmers underneath, like me. I slip off my nightdress, and we wade in. The water is wonderful. The craziness of the last few days seems very far away, and we're just two people on holiday, having a swim on a hot night. I watch as he swims the length of the pool underwater. I hope he's not too drunk to be swimming like that. He seems sober enough, but I think he has had a lot to drink. Still, I would happily administer the kiss of life.

211

Oh, shit.

During this entire trip, I've noticed, good news has immediately been followed by bad news. The good news is that I don't think Sam is going to interfere with the book any more. The bad news is that my crush on Luther has been replaced by an attraction to Sam – a real one.

He surfaces beside me.

'Have you ever seen the movie *Le Grand Bleu*?' he says. '*The Big Blue*? It's pretty lame, but it has a great soundtrack by Eric Serra. It always reminds me of swimming at night. I was just listening to it before you came outside. You want to hear some?'

'I – OK,' I say. I should go, but I don't want to be rude when he's sharing his music. I'll just stay a minute longer.

He hoists himself out of the pool in an easy movement, and goes to get his iPod, drying his hands on his jeans first. How could I ever have thought he looked bland or identikit? He is so beautiful; I can't take my eyes off him. He comes back into the water and hands me the iPod, but I shake my head.

'Wet hands.'

He looks at me for a second, then he carefully fits the earphones into my ears, pushing my hair back gently. As soon as he touches me, I can feel my heart start to pound. I'm inches from his bare chest; in fact, I could lean forward and touch it right now. I've never been this close to him before – no, I have, when he saved me from drowning, when I wasn't drowning.

He reaches past me, and starts the music. It's beautiful. It sounds so mysterious – like being deep under the sea. He's still standing very close to me, looking down at me. I'm trying not to look at him, so I'm looking past him instead at the stars or down at our waists, close to each other in the pool. But I'm getting a feeling from him. It's

212

that feeling that tells you someone is about to kiss you. I cautiously look up and meet his eyes, just for a minute, but it's enough; I'm completely overwhelmed, and I start to shiver.

'Hey,' he says, turning the music down. 'You're not getting cold, are you?' He puts a hand to the side of my face, and takes the earphones out.

'No. Well, maybe just a little. I think I'd better go to bed.'

But it's too late for that; he's still holding my face, my palm has strayed on to his chest, and now he's leaned down and kissed me, so gently but so firmly that I almost expire: it is the perfect kiss.

I kiss him back. He is a wonderful kisser, his mouth just as soft as I would have imagined, tender but very confident, and soon we're kissing harder. His hands are in my hair and then on my shoulders and my waist, and I'm running my hands down his arms and his back and his chest. His body is rock hard: I can feel how strong he is. I am drowning in the feel of his lips on mine, his hands on my skin. Simultaneously, there is a part of my brain that's saying, *Is this a good idea?* But it's pretty muffled.

After a minute, we stop for breath. He's leaning his chin near the top of my head. I hear him inhale, and I know he's about to say something. Please don't let it be *We should stop.* Instead he says one word, hoarsely, into my ear, and it's 'Wow.'

'I know.' I bury my head in his shoulder, inhaling the scent of his skin.

'This is definitely the highlight of my evening.'

'Mine too,' I say, close to his ear, and then I start kissing the ear.

He starts kissing my neck, down towards my collarbone, and then my shoulder. Now he's kissing my bikini strap – not just the skin beneath it, but the actual strap. My arms

213

are around his neck while I hook one leg around his. Then he sinks underwater, and kneels in front of me, holding my thighs and kissing my stomach, then moving lower . . . Suddenly I feel a bit self-conscious, and I pull him up.

'Hey. I was enjoying myself.'

I lean forward and kiss his chest. I put my arms around him, letting them travel down towards his shorts, and press him closer until I can hear him gasp. Gently, he eases my bikini strap off my shoulder, and starts kissing downwards to the side of my breast. He spends a while there, kissing the curve of it, until I think I'm about to die, melt or explode, depending on what he does next.

'Alice,' he says in my ear. It sounds as if it's taking him all his strength to say it.

'Yes?'

'If you want me to stop, please tell me now.'

'No,' I say, close to his ear. 'I don't want to stop.'

He puts his arm around me, and holds me even tighter.

'Let's go inside,' he says. And – I can't quite believe he's doing this, but he is – he scoops me up and *carries* me up the wading steps, out of the pool, only depositing me to pick up his jeans and my nightdress. Our progress inside is impeded by the fact that we're stopping to kiss each other every few seconds. We tiptoe into his room, closing the door as quietly as possible because, let's face it, the worst possible thing would be for someone – i.e., Luther – to hear us right now.

Once we're inside, he knocks a pile of scripts and papers off his bed and pushes me down on it, climbing on top of me and kissing me again, while I run my fingers through his hair and down his back. We're both still wet from the pool, but it's so hot it doesn't matter. Not that I'd care if it was twenty degrees below zero. I have never been so turned on in my life. It's as if I don't have to think and

214

rules don't apply. I feel completely relaxed and uninhibited, soaking in all the different sensations: his hand on my thigh, his hair and skin under my fingers, his lips on my neck, on my shoulder, on my breasts . . .

I haven't slept with very many people, and when I have it's often been awkward and forgettable. This is a completely different experience in every way. It's not just that he's so incredibly unselfish, or that he doesn't rush me, or that he's so gorgeous and he keeps telling me I am as well. It's not just that he's confident enough to ask me what I want, but doesn't have to ask all the time. It's that, seeing him lose himself so completely in me, I feel that he wants me just as much as I want him; it's totally equal. I don't think I've ever had that before.

TWENTY-FIVE

There's light coming in through the window. I'm lying with my back to Sam, and both his arms are wrapped around me. My hair still feels damp, but the sheets are mainly dry. Which means last night was real, and not a drunken dream. *I am in bed with Sam.* Luther's agent, Sam. *What the hell have I done?* I'm already regretting it: he's *definitely* going to regret it. I begin to edge out of the bed, wondering if I can just slip out and pretend it never happened.

'Are you awake?' he says softly. He kisses the back of my neck, and I'm relieved. Whatever else happens . . . I'm glad he still seems to like me.

'Um, yes,' I whisper.

'So am I,' he whispers back. He unwinds his arms slowly and checks the time. 'Good. It's early.'

'I should go,' I mutter, but he pulls me in close again and kisses me. As soon as he does that, I'm completely undone: I can't do anything but kiss him back. As he wraps himself tighter around me I can feel that yes, he really is awake . . .

There's a noise. Someone is knocking at the door.

'Hey, man, you there?' Shit! It's Luther!

Sam is gesturing for me to get under the covers, but I'm going one better; I roll off the bed, grabbing a sheet with me, and roll right under it. And just in time, because Luther, who doesn't stand on ceremony, has opened the door and come inside. From where I'm lying, I can just see his feet in the sandals he was wearing the other day. Oh my good God. What is he doing? Did he hear us? What if he sees me?

'Hey, man,' Sam says, sleepily. 'You're up early.' He sounds totally relaxed. How is he doing that?

'Yeah,' Luther says. His feet pace over to the other side of the room and I frantically inch my feet back. Suddenly I see my nightdress, in a pile with Sam's clothes, right by Luther's feet. My bikini is hidden, but you can definitely see my nightdress. Oh, no! No!

'Have you seen Alice?' I hear Luther asking. 'She's not in her room.'

'Sure, she's stashed in my closet,' Sam says. 'No, of course I haven't seen her. Maybe she's asleep. It's early.'

'No, she's not in her room. I looked.'

You cheeky bastard! I think.

'I don't know, man. Maybe she's in the pool? Or went for a walk?'

'I'll go take a look. I want to do an interview.' He sounds preoccupied, and he doesn't make any immediate move to go.

I'm feeling incredibly cramped, and the floor is stone cold where my sheet has left gaps. I focus on a small dust ball a few inches from my nose, trying to keep my breathing quiet. I hope I don't sneeze. Oh, God, please let him leave. Just get him out of here and I'll never do anything stupid again. Ever.

'OK, well, I hope you find her,' says Sam. I can feel the bed shifting above me. 'Mind if I get some more sleep?' He yawns.

Luther doesn't say anything, but slowly the sandals turn

and walk out. I let out a long, silent breath and count to ten, watching the door, just in case he decides to come back. I imagine Sam is doing the same thing, because he doesn't say anything. When the coast seems clear, I slowly emerge from under the bed, clutching my sheet. To my disgust, Sam starts laughing.

'*What* is so funny?' I hiss. 'That was horrific.'

'I'm sorry, Alice. You just looked so spooked – and the way you scooted under the bed – it was like something out of a French farce.' He holds out his arms, trying to take me in them. 'I didn't mean to laugh at you. I know you must've been freaked out. You look very cute in that sheet, by the way.' He puts his hand to my face and pulls me towards him to kiss me. But I can't kiss him back; I'm still too shaken.

'Sam, do you know what would have happened if he'd caught me here? He would have been furious! He would've fired us both!'

Sam sighs and lets me go. 'Maybe. But he didn't, so . . .'

'I'm serious! We're just lucky he decided to knock. Imagine if he'd –' I can't even say the words 'walked in on us'. How the hell would I explain that one to Luther – or, God forbid, Olivia? I wouldn't just be given the boot; I would be hung, drawn and quartered. 'Sam, I think this was a mistake. We should never have done this. If Luther found out . . .'

'It's none of his business.'

'Well, it is, isn't it? I mean, I'm his editor, you're his agent – isn't it a little – unprofessional?'

I can see him flinch slightly at that. But then he leans back and looks at me.

'Is that what you really think? Or do you just not want to be here?' he asks.

I'm about to reply when there's the sound of footsteps

218

going past us in the corridor. It sounds like Luther again. We both freeze, and I crouch down, preparing to duck back under the bed if necessary. But then they go past, leaving me limp with relief and delayed terror.

I get up, still clutching my sheet. 'I've got to go.'

'Alice,' Sam says in a low voice. 'Come on. I understand your concern, but can we just talk about this for a second?'

I shake my head. He's about to say something, but then he stops, and just reaches out to grab my nightdress from the floor and hand it to me. I don't want to drop my sheet to get dressed. He seems to get the message and looks away, while I pull the nightdress on awkwardly. I get up and walk over to the door.

'Wait,' says Sam.

I turn around expectantly, but all he says is, 'I'll check the corridor.' He gets out of bed – now he's got a sheet around him – opens the door and glances out, then closes it.

'All clear.'

'Thanks.' I slip out, avoiding his eye.

TWENTY-SIX

I run myself a cool shower, and shiver under it while I give myself a firm talking-to. *What was I thinking?* Do I actually want to be fired? I'm in enough trouble as it is. If Luther had found out, it would have been a *catastrophe*. He could easily have heard us, or walked in on us – if he'd been any later, God knows what he would have seen . . .

But that thought just leads me right back to Sam. What he was like. Being so near him, so intimate with him. It was so intense. I wouldn't have dreamed he'd be so passionate, but, actually, it isn't surprising at all. My entire body feels like it's humming or vibrating or something. I can still feel his kiss on my lips, and everywhere else.

I turn the shower water to cold, and start scrubbing myself energetically. Yes, it was – great, but it was still a bad idea. We were both drunk, and I was traumatised from my conversation with Olivia, and I did something incredibly stupid. I should never ever *ever* have slept with Sam. It was a total error of judgement and it's never going to happen again.

And if you weren't working together? a voice says inside me. *Would you still feel the same?*

I think I would. It's too much too soon, and also, I feel ashamed now, because I don't know whether he's still going to respect me. I know it's old-fashioned, but I do. But I also meant what I said about it being unprofessional. I don't know why he reacted the way he did. What did he mean when he said, 'Do you just not want to be here?'

I go out to meet Luther feeling extremely nervous and convinced that he'll be able to see what I've been up to. I'm relieved to find he seems oblivious, just very depressed. He's on the back terrace, except that instead of lying in his usual position on the sunlounger, he's looking at a script with his agency's logo on it.

'There you are. I was looking for you,' he says sadly.

I decide not to make any excuse in case he sees through it. 'Sorry. Is that the script for the pilot? Is it any good?' I ask him, sitting down.

'I don't know. I've been flicking through, but I can't bring myself to actually read it.' I've never heard him sound so downtrodden.

'Oh,' I say. 'Pity. The writers sound good.'

'Yeah. Anyway, I'd better face it. This is what the future has in store for me.'

'How do you mean?'

I've had more than enough of my own dramas; I'm quite happy to listen to one of Luther's instead. He sighs and doesn't reply at once.

'Come on, Alice,' he says. 'I'm not where I could be. I mean, yeah, I've made some good movies, but I'm not Matt Damon. I'm not Clooney. I'm not Brad Pitt. I'm a go-to guy for shitty action movies. And in a few years, I'm going to be too old for those.'

I'm genuinely confused. It is true that Luther has done a lot of action films. But he's still a big star. Isn't he? He's just done *Roman Holiday* with Natasha Pullman – that's bound to be huge. And *Total Kombat* wasn't shitty, it was a big success. *The Last Legionnaire* was a monster. What is he talking about?

'Did you see *Star Trek*?' he says. 'The kids in that were half my age. And they didn't even have to move around that much. With all that stuff I did in *Total Kombat*, I massacred my back. I can't kick-box. They don't want me, they want Shia LaBeouf.'

'That's ridiculous! The people in *Star Trek* aren't half your age. They're seven years younger than you. You're thirty-three, aren't you?'

'Yeah. But the kids are just coming up faster and faster, and getting younger and younger. I'm not like that. I'm not on Twitter. I'm not best friends with Lindsay and Paris. But I'm not one of the indie people, or one of the huge leading men either.'

'But what about your new comedy, *The Deep End*? That's bound to be a big hit.'

'I hope so, but who the hell knows? Nobody. Maybe it'll tank. Maybe they'll cut my screen time to zero or leave me off the posters. Maybe everybody will say how great my co-star was and how much I sucked.'

Poor Luther. Suddenly I get it: I get what it must be like to live the way he does – to be so exposed and never to know how much longer your career will be viable.

'Anyway,' he says. '*Roman Holiday* was great, and I hope it does do well. I want to develop. I feel like there's more to me than just action. I feel like my image has just become a straitjacket. I want to do parts that reflect more who I am, you know?'

'Have you spoken to Sam about all this?'

'Not really. I think he's worried I'm not bankable, and that's why he wants me to do TV. You know what? In ten years' time they probably won't even need actors. It'll all be done with CGI. You'll get holograms picking up Oscars.'

'Oh, come on. You're not—'

'It'll be all about the blue people. James Cameron will generate an army of blue actors, and he'll franchise them out

222

everywhere. They'll have their own union. It'll be the Blue Screen Actor's Guild.'

He seems to be spiralling into more and more of a depression, and we've wandered completely off the topic of the book. If only Erica were here to give him one of her pep talks about how he should be glad he's not an orphan, etc.

'Luther, you're just awfulising. I do that a lot,' I tell him. 'You're thinking of one bad thing and it's turning into hundreds. You have a lot of fans. You know we're all incredibly excited about the book. It's going to be huge for us – our biggest non-fiction title of the year, easily.'

This seems to cheer him up, temporarily. I decide to begin our session, and I make sure he sees me switching on the Dictaphone.

'Luther, could we talk about what happened when you – disappeared?'

'When I went to Hawaii, you mean?' he says unexpectedly. 'I know there are all these rumours, but that's basically all I did. I went to Hawaii for ten months and I learned to surf, and I worked in a bar. I grew my hair and a big ridiculous beard. I also got this tattoo.' He points to the dragon tattooed on his right bicep. 'People would recognise me, but I just said I was researching for a part, or on vacation – whatever I thought would get me off the hook.'

I can't believe it. The big revelation, and that was all it was. He was a beach bum for ten months.

'It was pretty peaceful,' he continues. 'I got very into surfing. I sat on the beach, smoked a lot of dope, went to parties. It's beautiful, Hawaii. It's volcanic, like here.' He points to Mount Etna behind us. 'It probably saved my life, to tell you the truth, except the dope started to make me feel even more depressed and paranoid, so I cut back.'

'But what made you go?'

'Everything,' he says. 'It was everything. The break-up with

223

Dom, and the intensity of rehab, *Summer Rain* being such a flop . . . and my performance being pasted. I thought it was a good movie, and that it wouldn't have flopped, if they had cast somebody else. I felt like I ruined it. All these years I'd been thinking I was an impostor, and suddenly I had been unmasked. But what was I going to do? Move back to Queens and work in a store? I couldn't do it. So Hawaii was an escape hatch, a kind of a nowhere place.

'I had this thing I used to say,' he continues. 'That I came from nothing, and that I could go back to nothing, and I wouldn't miss any of it: the applause or the girls or the fame. I don't know, maybe I heard it in a movie or something and I thought it sounded good. But it turns out it wasn't true.'

He's silent for a long time.

'So how did you get back into acting?'

'That's it,' says Luther.

'What is?'

'That's what I don't know if I should tell you about.'

I'm not sure what to say. Luther lies back and lights a cigarette. I decide to wait until he's smoked the whole thing before saying anything else. It's so hard, because I am dying to ask him, but I force myself to stay quiet. Sooner than I expected, he starts to talk again.

'You know, something like this happens, and you can try to forget about it, so it's like it never happened. But it kind of almost gets worse inside your head and starts getting bigger and bigger. You know?'

I nod slowly.

'So, it started when I was working in the bar, in Hawaii. This guy used to come in. He was a producer, there on vacation. We got talking, and he mentioned this movie about a Roman soldier. It sounded great. I didn't see him again after that, but the whole conversation sort of galvanised me into action. So I flew to LA and I started calling people.

'But it was difficult. I went back to my old agent, but I wasn't his hot property any more. He was finding me roles, but they weren't the ones I wanted. But then I met this guy who suggested acting as my manager.' He exhales smoke slowly. 'He seemed really well-connected. He knew about. *The Last Legionnaire*, which was the film I'd heard about, that I badly wanted to do. He was able to get me a meeting, he said, unofficially. So I went and met the director and one of the producers, who was the guy I met in the bar.'

He pauses and turns his head to look out over the sea. I can hear the waves below us.

'Soon after that, my manager rang me and said he had good news. I had the part – nearly. The only thing was that there was a condition. I had to go out on a date with the producer's wife, so she'd put in a good word.'

'A date?' I ask, blankly.

'Yeah, a date,' he says. His expression is unreadable. 'That was what he called it. But he didn't mean dinner and a movie, you know?'

As the reality of what he's saying dawns, I realise that my jaw has dropped, and I hastily close it again. The tape recorder is still running, but I'm too shocked to stop it.

'So you had to . . .'

'Yeah,' says Luther. 'I had to sleep with her to get the part.' He takes a drag of his cigarette. 'You know, when I say it out loud like that it doesn't sound that bad. But I've never told anyone before.'

I don't want to sound judgemental, or blasé, but equally I don't want to sound unsympathetic. Instead I probably manage to sound all three. I say, 'Was she . . .?'

'Attractive? Not particularly. I made sure I could, you know, perform and I forgot all about it as soon as I could. It happened in Hawaii, actually, in their summer place, which I thought would make it easier, like I could leave it all behind.' He shrugs.

'Except I guess I haven't. You know, it just makes me feel like, my entire comeback, so to speak – ever since *The Last Legionnaire*, which was probably my biggest movie – is not based on my talent. It's because I slept with the right person.' He looks down. 'It makes me feel pretty ashamed, I guess.'

I decide to throw aside my role of professional listener and just sympathise. 'You don't have to feel ashamed,' I say. 'They're the ones who should feel ashamed. Although I understand why you would feel bad.'

'Yeah,' he says. 'I did. I do.'

'And you've never told anyone? Not even Sam?'

'Not even Sam. Although you can see why I value him so highly. He's not about to pimp me out to some sleazy producer and his wife.'

'So what happened to your manager?'

He shrugs. 'I got rid of him. As soon as the movie was a success, I found someone else a.s.a.p. I don't really hear about him.'

'And – the producer and his wife?'

'He died actually. About two years ago. Cardiac arrest. I didn't send flowers.' He laughs, but there's not much humour in it. 'I haven't seen her either.'

'I'm so sorry,' I say. 'You didn't deserve that. Nobody does.'

'Thanks. You know, it feels good to tell someone about all this. I knew it would be.'

'Good. I'm glad.' I wait to see if he wants to say anything else, but he doesn't. So I continue, 'You've done incredible work on this book, Luther, honestly. It's going to be brilliant. In fact, you'll be able to read the first draft in the next day or so.'

'I don't think I need to read it.'

I glance at the Dictaphone. If this was one of my typing sessions, it would be one of those moments where I'd rewind and check that was what he actually said.

'You don't need to read it?' I repeat.

'Nah. I'd like Sam to read it, and maybe my attorney. But

226

aside from that, I don't think I want to. I'm not a book person. And I didn't set out to write . . .' He waves his arms, obviously trying to think of a comparison '. . . the *Mona Lisa*. I just wanted to talk through it all. It's been good that way.'

Not for the first time, I'm at a loss for words.

'Let's take a break,' he says. 'Federico's taking out his boat, so maybe I'll join him. I'll lose this script overboard somewhere.' He stands up.

'Of course. You know, Luther, all that stuff about, you know, the producer – that was off the record – needless to say.'

'You think? I don't know, Alice. Maybe this stuff happens, you know? And maybe I should be open about it. Honestly, I don't care. I'll leave it up to you.'

He can't possibly mean that, can he? I won't question him about it right now. Once he's gone, I get up and, after turning off the tape, I lean over the wall, looking out to sea and taking deep breaths. Despite the beautiful view, I feel as if I've been trapped somewhere dark and claustrophobic, deep underground. It's funny, it's happened exactly as I imagined. Luther has told me things he's never told anyone else; as Ruth predicted I've wormed all his dark secrets out of him. But it's not even remotely romantic. How did I ever think it would be?

Poor Luther. Is it possible that he did this entire book just so that he could tell someone what happened to him? That seems the saddest and weirdest thing of all. Surely you would go and see a therapist, rather than sign a book deal? I would, but I don't exactly inhabit the same universe as him. But why on earth would he tell me, of all people, something so scandalous? Isn't he worried about what it will do to his career?

I go inside, get out the laptop and start transcribing. I'm going to leave out the whole scandal and career crisis element of the conversation – it's too horrible and I don't think he meant for it to go in the book. I email it to Brian and Olivia, and explain that in fact the Hawaii episode, which was built up as such a big deal, will only be a chapter. When I'm finished, I literally slump over the keyboard. I have a sudden urge to take a swim or go to the beach or even go for a walk in Taormina. I just want to be somewhere normal, with people having ordinary conversations about normal, boring things.

'Hi!'

I look up from my keyboard and find Sam standing there.

'Um, I think this is yours . . .' He hands me my bikini.

'Oh.' I take it and try to fold it up into as small a ball as possible.

'Are you OK?' he asks. 'You look exhausted.'

'Thanks,' I mutter. 'I didn't realise it was that obvious.'

'Don't be so paranoid. I didn't mean it that way,' he says gently. 'I just meant you look like you could use a break. And so could I. Want to go out somewhere?'

Of course I want to. Despite my worries, he's the person I most want to see in the world. Going somewhere with him right now would be like getting out of prison. But I don't think it would be wise. What would Luther think? And . . . I'm still feeling self-conscious about last night. It would be madness to take this thing with Sam any further, when I'm skating on such thin ice with work anyway.

Sam sighs, interrupting my thoughts.

'Look, Alice,' he says. 'I realise I put you in an awkward position last night . . . and this morning. I'm sorry. I shouldn't have laughed about it. But . . .'

What? But what?

'I'd just like to spend time with you,' he says simply. 'If you don't want to, then just tell me now and I'll – well, I'll probably keep asking you anyway.'

It's the nicest thing anyone has said to me in a very long time.

'No, I do,' I tell him. 'I really do. Just let me go and get my bag.'

TWENTY-SEVEN

'Hey, wait a minute,' he says. 'Do you know where you'd like to go?'

Anywhere but here, I think, *and anywhere with you*. 'I don't mind.'

'Why don't you get ready and we'll decide,' says Sam.

I run and get my bag and throw in a towel, suntan lotion, some lip balm and my wallet. I'm definitely leaving my phone here. I debate changing my outfit but decide not to bother. I don't want to waste a second of the time I could be spending with Sam. I just put my bikini on underneath my clothes, and I'm ready to go. I also take my wrap, in case – hope springs eternal – we stay out late.

His little Fiat is so hot from the sun that we have to leave the doors open for a few minutes to cool it down. Sam opens up a map and spreads it out on the bonnet.

'You haven't been up Mount Etna, have you? Did you want to go?'

'Well, I'm not desperate to go . . .' Actually, I'm sick of looking at it all day.

'Good, me either. So, one thing we could do is drive to Corleone. It's the home town of the Godfather in the movie, and it's actually where Al Pacino's grandparents came from too. It's a pretty long drive because it's all the way over to the west, and it's only a small town but it's still fascinating if you're a fan of the movies. You're a fan, right?'

I don't want to pour cold water on his plan, but I am totally dismayed. Does he really want to drive for hours to a random small town because of *The Godfather*? Well, if it's what he wants to do, I'm willing to go with him. Because – there's no point kidding myself – that's how crazy I am about him.

I think he sees my expression, though, because he says, 'Or, we could go to a nature reserve that's a little closer, just down the coast. Beautiful empty beaches.'

A nature reserve! Even the words sound soothing. I can't imagine anything better, after all the trauma of the past twenty-four hours, than beautiful empty beaches.

'Let's do that,' I say, and we get into the car.

'So I take it you're not a fan of *The Godfather*,' says Sam, as we swing out on to the road. 'Please tell me you've at least seen it.'

'No,' I say. 'My favourite film is *Working Girl*.'

'That is a classic. But you also like *Sunset Boulevard*, right? I remember you mentioned it the other day.'

'It's one of my favourites. It's so macabre and Dickensian. And it's an excellent piece of storytelling. There isn't one scene wasted.'

'You know,' says Sam, 'there is a sort of similarity with what you're up to here. The writer trapped in the house with the movie star, trying to finish the script . . .'

I laugh. 'I'm not exactly trapped, and I don't think Luther's much like Norma Desmond. He's a little younger, for one thing.' Suddenly a bizarre image floats into my mind, of an ageing Luther in a smoking jacket surrounded by hundreds of pictures of himself in his glory days. 'So what's your favourite film? Is it *The Godfather*?'

'*The Godfather* is definitely up there. But I have a few

other favourites. *La Dolce Vita. Bicycle Thieves*. There's a great French movie called *Army of Shadows*—'

'I think I've heard of that. Is it about zombies?' I ask, making a random guess.

'No, it's about the French Resistance,' says Sam. I start to laugh. He glances over at me, grinning, and I can feel myself falling for him even more.

After driving for about half an hour, we park in a little car park overlooking a hill. There is nobody around. Below us, an empty beach stretches around in a golden curve towards a huge rocky headland crowned with olive trees and wild vegetation. I look at my watch. It's already four o'clock but it's still hot. I sniff the sea breeze, drinking it in. We walk down the steps and along the beach in companionable silence.

'It's funny how it's still hot, even though it's late afternoon,' I say.

'That's because their midday was about an hour ago,' says Sam.

We drift towards the water. Neither of us feels like swimming yet, so instead we paddle. I spot a huge bird flying over the headland, soaring in big arcs. It's so peaceful. The only other people around are a young couple with a toddler. We exchange hellos when we hear them speaking English. It turns out they're Americans, from California. Sam tells them he's from Utah and they talk about hiking there.

'Why didn't you tell them you lived in LA?' I ask, after they've gone.

'I didn't feel like getting into it.'

I can understand that. I wouldn't want to meet anyone from London right now. I wonder what they would have said if they'd known what we were doing, that Luther was with us or that Sam was a Hollywood agent. Maybe they wouldn't have cared. Maybe they don't watch many films. Some people don't. In fact, most of the people on this planet have never heard of Luther, or Dominique Rice. I watch the water foaming around my feet and dig my toes into the wet brown sand.

'How about a swim?' says Sam. 'I'll race you to the headland.'

As I strip down to my bikini I'm suddenly a little self-conscious. Thinking of all the models and actresses he must be used to seeing in LA, I wonder how I measure up with my pale skin and English hips. On the other hand, it's a bit late to be coy, and when I think of how he explored every inch of me last night, it's probably safe to assume I don't totally repel him.

The water is heavenly. I'm a pretty strong swimmer, but I don't always like swimming too far out in a sea I don't know. With Sam beside me, though, I feel more adventurous than usual, and we make it all the way to the headland and back.

After we get out, we lie on the beach for a while to get dry. Sam forgot to bring a towel, so I hand him my wrap.

'But I'll get it all sandy.'

I shrug. 'It's so hot, it'll dry.'

'It is true what they say about British girls. You are easy-going. I mean, not easy,' he adds hastily. 'Easy-going.'

As he lies down beside me, I close my eyes. I can hear the sound of the waves, and I can feel him beside me, close enough so that I could reach out my hand and touch him. I have the feeling that he's waiting for my cue, and if I gave him a sign, he would kiss me. I would, but should I? We should probably get back soon, but I never want this day to end.

'What are you thinking about?' he asks.

I laugh. 'I thought only women asked that question.'

'Not necessarily. I'm pretty nosy.' He's propped up on one elbow, looking down at me.

'I was thinking how nice this is,' I tell him truthfully. 'I feel so relaxed.'

'Would you like to take the rest of the day off? Go somewhere after this and have dinner with me?'

I squint up at him, shading my eyes from the sun.

'Do you think Luther will mind?' I say reluctantly. Then, to clarify, I add, 'I mean, if we're not back?'

He doesn't say anything, just shakes his head.

'Then yes. I'd love to.' Seeing the pleasure on his face makes me feel like a million dollars.

'Great.' He throws himself back on my wrap with a sigh. 'Now I can relax,' he adds almost to himself. Smiling, I close my eyes again and just lie there, basking in the sun, feeling incredibly happy.

'Hey,' Sam says. 'You're going to burn if you're not careful.'

'Really?' I open my eyes to find he's rummaging in my bag for my suntan lotion.

'Roll over,' he says.

'Is that how you normally talk to girls?' I say, obeying.

'Only if they're very pretty.'

It's not the smoothest line ever, but it makes me smile. This is what I love about Sam. Luther splashes his charm around indiscriminately, and it doesn't mean a whole lot. I think Sam is just as charming, but it's genuine, and you have to know him for him to turn it on. I like that: it feels as if it's just for me. I don't know if Ruth or Poppy would necessarily see what I see in him, or why I prefer him to Luther, but it doesn't matter. I can see it.

As his hands move over my back, shoulders and neck, I close my eyes and surrender to the feeling. Oh, God, those hands . . . I'm suddenly reminded of my first day, when we went swimming off the yacht and I accidentally flashed

Sam, thanks to that crazy swimsuit.

'Now what are you laughing at?' he asks. 'Ah, yes. I remember,' he says, when I tell him.

I roll over and look up at him. 'You looked completely horrified.'

'Well. Not completely . . .'

I pretend to swat him, he grabs my hand, and there on the empty beach, we start kissing again. It's not in the pounding surf, like Burt Lancaster and Deborah Kerr in *From Here to Eternity*, but it's still wonderful.

Later, we drive to a little town curled around a blue bay like a white cat dozing in the sun, with winding streets climbing up a hill and small houses glowing gold, orange and pink in the setting sun. We have a glass of prosecco in the main square, where children are running riot and screaming while their families stroll around and old men sit and nurse one glass of cognac for hours. It's so much fun just sitting and watching everybody. At one point, three very well-dressed young men nearby become embroiled in what sounds like a dreadful argument, complete with wild gesticulations: hands clasped in prayer, fists shaking, gesturing to the sky. One of them is giving the most incredibly impassioned speech I've ever heard in my life, and I wish I could understand: it must be about religion or politics, or some terrible family feud at the very least.

'What on earth are they talking about?' I murmur.

'Football,' Sam says.

After a while, as the sun begins to go down, we walk a little way up the hill and we find a little restaurant with whitewashed walls and stone tiles and one fatherly-looking waiter with a big shock of white hair. The waiter shows us to a little table in a back alcove, which he indicates with a flourish, and then pulls out my chair for me. The whole place is done out so sweetly – there are all these braided mats, just like the one in Marisa's house, on the floor, and there are little wooden carvings of sheaves of wheat on the walls. But it's empty.

'Oh no,' I say involuntarily.

'What?' asks Sam, looking concerned.

'Just – it's so lovely, but we're the only people here. I hope they're not struggling for customers.'

'No, it's just pretty early by local standards. People won't be eating for at least another half-hour.'

'Oh,' I say, relieved. I hate seeing nice places do badly. I can't explain why but it makes me almost feel like crying. It's worse when they do cute things, like drawing pictures on the specials boards, or putting flowers on the table, or folding menus into glasses. In fact, even when a place is thriving, these things can make me feel melancholy.

'That's a very intense reaction,' says Sam, when I tell him. 'I know what you mean, though. I feel the same way about pet stores. There's one near my apartment that had a sign recently saying, "Puppies at fifty per cent off". Can you imagine? I almost bought the lot of them.'

There aren't any menus. Sam talks to the waiter and finds that they can offer us either pasta followed by fish – he's not sure which fish – or pasta followed by lamb. I opt for lamb. The food, when it arrives, is absolutely spectacular – a melting pasta dish with aubergine and ricotta, followed by the thinnest slivers of lamb, with baby courgettes and tiny roast potatoes. We wash it down with thin, sweet red wine – Sam insisted that we should have red because I'm having lamb, even though he's having fish.

'It's fun to eat dinner with people who actually eat,' he remarks. 'No one eats in LA. Except sushi. Sushi is very big.'

'You never told me why you speak such good Italian.'

'Ah,' he says. 'I could tell you, but then I'd have to kill you.'

'Mob connections?' I ask in a low voice.

'No. I was a missionary for the Church of Jesus Christ of Latter-Day Saints.'

'You are joking.'

'Not at all,' he says. 'I'll give you the short version. My family live in Colorado right now, but I actually grew up in Salt Lake City, Utah, which has a big Mormon population. My parents aren't super-observant – they certainly didn't expect me to do a mission. But, after I messed up my knee and left UCLA I was feeling very lost. I went home for a while, and I decided to do my mission. I got assigned Italy, had intensive training in Italian, and got sent to northern Italy.'

'Gosh.' What else can I say? 'How long did you spend there?'

'It was meant to be two years, but I only did eleven months. My dad got very sick, so I came home early.'

'Oh, no. What happened?'

'He had a heart attack and he had to have several operations. He's a doctor, which almost makes it worse, because he knew exactly how serious it was. They didn't tell me at first, but when I finally found out – I can remember exactly where I was. I was at a public payphone near the Piazza dei Signori in Vicenza, in my suit and everything. I just walked straight back to our apartment, got my bag and left for the airport.'

'Did you get in trouble?'

'Sure. But I didn't care. Things were such a mess at home. My little brother was having a hard time for various reasons, my sister was going off the rails, and my mom was struggling with everything. I felt really guilty for being away, and

I sort of threw myself into things, trying to look after everyone. I probably ended up driving them crazy. But it was the right thing to do. There was no way I wanted to be over on the other side of the world if people needed me at home.'

'Is your father OK now?'

'Yes, he's fine. Thanks. And the mission wasn't a bad experience in a lot of ways. Spending a year trying to convert devout Catholics is pretty good preparation for selling stuff in Hollywood. Plus I got to live in Italy. My paternal grandfather was from northern Italy, near Venice, so I had a feeling at the time that it was a sign.' He shrugs. 'Now I just think it's a coincidence.'

'Your paternal grandfather? But what about your surname?'

'It was Terranova, which means "new land". He changed it to Newland when he came to the States. What are you thinking, with that expression?'

'I was just thinking how everybody I meet these days seems to have had a complicated past, unlike me.'

'Really?' says Sam. 'Nothing? Come on, you've got to have some dark secrets. I've just told you my crazy story. It's your turn.'

'Nothing as dramatic as yours,' I say. But I find myself telling him about secondary school, and about the girls who bullied me for four years, before I made friends with Ruth – my first friend since primary school. Actually, Ruth and I bonded over our crush on Luther, but I don't mention that.

'What did they do?' he asks gently.

I just give him edited highlights of the less awful parts; how one game was to hide my shoes, because they thought it was hilarious that I wore size eight, and how they used to call me names.

'What names?'

'Oh . . .' I'm going red. I have literally never, ever told a man this. 'White Rabbit, because I had braces. Also Big Bird.'

'Are you serious? Those are the lamest nicknames ever,' Sam says. 'Couldn't they come up with anything better?'

'I know. Compared to what girls today probably get called, it almost sounds affectionate, doesn't it?' I don't know why it's never occurred to me before how ridiculous that part of it was. He's laughing, which makes me start laughing too. I've never been able to laugh about it before. It's a good feeling.

For the rest of the meal we chat about other random things. I don't want to talk about work in any detail but, for some reason, I tell him about Poppy and Claudine, and their tussle over the manuscript.

'She sounds like one to watch,' he says. 'Pushy and ruthless. It's an effective combination. Don't make her your assistant, whatever you do.'

'Yes,' I say. Shit. I feel dishonest not telling him that I *am* an assistant, but it's too late now. The thought of Olivia and my disastrous mistake crosses over me like a dark cloud, but I put it out of my mind. I'm determined to enjoy every second of this day with Sam. We talk about our birthdays and our ages. Sam is twenty-eight – the perfect age. He's too polite to ask me how old I am, but I tell him I'm twenty-six. Then we talk about films again, and I tell him how much I loved *Fever* when it first came out.

'You certainly know your dance movies,' he says. 'Have you ever taken classes?'

I'm about to tell him I can't dance, when I remember that's not true – I did dance, with Luther.

'No, I've never got round to it,' I admit. 'But I would like to. Maybe some day.'

We finished eating a while ago, but the waiter has tactfully let us linger. After he finally clears our plates, he brings us over two little glasses with a bright yellow liqueur. He says something very charming-sounding, beams at us and waddles away. The liqueur is ice-cold and tastes intense and sweet.

'It's delicious. I normally hate liqueurs but this is great. What is it?'

'Limoncello,' he says. 'You get it everywhere in Italy. This was on the house.'

'Oh, how sweet. What was he saying about it?'

'It's hard to translate, but something like "A golden drink for a golden, beautiful girl".' He smiles at me. I'm about to make a joke about how that would never happen in London, but I decide not to.

We're the last people to leave the restaurant, and we were the first to arrive. Sam insists on paying, and I let him.

'You can pay for our next dinner,' he says, which makes my heart leap.

As we stroll down through the town, I wonder what exactly he meant by that. I'm really glad he thinks we're going to have dinner again. But when, and where? The book is nearly finished; I'll be going home soon. He did say that he was coming to the Venice film festival in September. Perhaps he could stop off in London en route? Or – or I could go to Venice with him? I wish I could ask him, but I don't want to crowd him. It's probably better to play it cool.

We're heading down a flight of little winding steps towards the main square, when we pass a gorgeous girl with long dark brown hair and huge brown eyes, wearing a long white cotton dress that shows off her astonishing figure – the kind of girl who would turn every head in London. Sam glances at her, and she gives him a look of distinct interest back.

He's busy telling me some story about something that

happened to him and Luther at the Oscars this year. I can't concentrate, though. Was he looking at that girl? If he was, I couldn't blame him. She was gorgeous. Is it my imagination, or is he being a little distant? He's not holding my hand or anything. I'm suddenly paranoid that he's pulling back. *Stop it*, I tell myself, *you're being crazy*. But I can't shake the feeling. Why is he talking about the Oscars, anyway? Is he trying to remind me not-so-subtly that we have different lives and that he lives on the other side of the world?

We're walking through the square, which is now full of kids running around and beautiful men and women catwalking up and down. Right now, with me dressed up and with a tan, and Sam wearing a T-shirt, we probably look like a normal couple on holiday. But we're not. In real life, Sam is a Hollywood agent, who can have any woman he wants, and I'm a scruffy assistant who never has any luck with men. Even if he did decide that he wanted to see me again, I would never be able to afford to visit him, or keep up with him when I got there. He knows Sienna Miller, for God's sake. When he says I can pay for our next dinner, he probably doesn't mean Pizza Express. I think of showing him my bedroom with my home-made cardboard squares, and shudder.

'You have a very expressive face, do you know that?' Sam says.

'Do I?' I ask, startled.

'Yes. Even when you're not talking. In fact, especially when you're not talking.' He smiles at me, and my heart skips a beat. I wonder if he might be about to say something to reassure me – maybe talk about when we're going to meet again?

'You're not worrying about the book again, are you?' he says. 'It's going to be fine.'

'Um, no, I wasn't,' I say, filled with disappointment. God,

the book. I wish we didn't have to talk about the bloody book.

We get back in the car and on to the road. It's night now, and the stars are out. The radio is playing the same Shakira song they played in the nightclub – it seems like such a long time ago.

'So it looked like a pretty gruelling session today,' Sam says. 'What were you guys talking about? If you don't mind me asking.'

'Oh. It was pretty intense stuff. We won't put it in the book.'

'Ah.' He sounds startled. 'Was it serious? Why would you not put it in the book?'

Why does he keep going on about work? A car suddenly overtakes us in the face of an oncoming lorry, missing us both by inches. People drive like lunatics here.

'I just –' I can't tell him what Luther was talking about. 'Just sort of – things Luther's done, things that have happened to him, and – his image, I suppose. He talked about wanting to develop.'

'Wanting to develop his range?' Sam sighs, and shakes his head. 'He and I have talked about that a thousand times. And then he ends up wanting to go for the same old thing. I even had to talk him into *Roman Holiday*, which was the safest bet we got sent all year. Was that all?'

'Well, there were some personal things.' Why are we even talking about this?

There's a long pause.

'Is it something illegal?'

'No! I mean, I don't think so. I don't know. Look, it's nothing.'

'OK,' Sam says. 'I won't pump you for information. I'll speak to Luther.' He looks preoccupied.

'Yes,' I say tonelessly. 'Good idea.' I find myself scratching nervously at something on my arm: a mosquito bite. Damn. I suppose I've been lucky to escape those so far.

'Mosquito bite, huh?' Sam asks. 'They're the worst. Marisa got eaten alive when we were in Rome.'

Marisa got eaten alive when we were in Rome.

Grammatically, there's no way of telling, from that sentence, when they were in Rome. He could be talking about years ago, when they first worked together. But I know, somehow, that he means three days ago.

'You mean – when you were there recently?' I ask. 'On your way to London?'

'Oh, no,' he says. 'I mean when we were there years ago. Working.'

Is he lying? I can't tell. He sounds very plausible, but that doesn't make sense: why would he mention it if it was years ago?

'Oh, right,' I say. I know I should just drop it but, like my mosquito bite, I can't leave it alone, and I can't help adding, 'I kind of got the idea, at one point . . . I thought that there might be something between you two. When I first met you, I mean.'

He's silent for a moment.

'We did date. When we first met, before she got married, we had a brief relationship. It didn't work out. But we stayed in touch.'

I don't say anything. I can't.

'Does that bother you?' he asks, looking over at me.

'Of course not,' I say, too quickly.

But it does. It bothers me because I know I can't measure up to Marisa. She is stunning and intelligent and sophisticated as well as being a genuinely lovely person. That they were together makes sense, because he is out of my league. And at the same time I can't help thinking: is this what he does? Does he just have mini-romances every time he sets foot in Italy, or France, or England? And then leaves, to go back to soulless LA and his hundred-hour work week and no dating actresses? Either way it looks as though I was wrong about his charms only being obvious to me.

I have to change the subject. I clear my throat. 'Listen, you know, we've almost finished with the interviews. Luther tells me that he doesn't need to read the book. Do you think that's true? He suggested you could read it for him.'

He's still looking at me. Then he looks back to the road. 'Sure. I'll read it. He really needs a manager for this stuff,' he adds under his breath.

We drive on in silence, and when we arrive back at the house, I get out of the car as quickly as I can.

'Thanks for a lovely day, and evening,' I say, not meeting his eye. 'Gosh, it's getting cool!' I start walking towards the house, pulling my wrap around me before realising it's all sandy. What a lame excuse; it's a lovely warm night.

'Wait,' he says behind me. I turn around. He's standing beside the car, looking astonished. 'Are you serious? That's it?'

'I don't – I'd better check in with Luther.' And I hurry inside before he can stop me.

TWENTY-EIGHT

I walk out to the terrace to find a scene of domestic bliss: Marisa and Luther drinking tea and playing cards. Marisa kisses me, and when Sam comes in behind me she kisses him too. I have to look away while this happens.

Sam sits down. 'Sorry we're back so late. Hey, did you read that script yet?'

'Alice, *bella*,' says Marisa. 'Why don't we leave these two to chat? We can go inside and watch TV.'

'No, stay,' says Luther.

Marisa glances at Sam. 'Actually,' she says, 'I should go home. Poor Federico will wonder where I am.' She picks up her bag and gets up, saying, 'I'll call you tomorrow,' to Sam.

Marisa goes off to the bathroom, while I check my email. There's a message from Brian. It's the manuscript. He's done his first draft in less than a week. This is unbelievable! I hook up the laptop to the printer and start printing it out, half listening to Sam and Luther talking outside.

'Luther,' Sam is saying, 'We've talked about this. You know I can't make you into Depp or Clooney overnight. But of course you can develop. I just think, if you want to do that, you're going to have to take more risks.'

I don't hear what Luther says then, but Sam continues,

'I'm not so sure. *Roman Holiday* was a good start, but you could do more. Why do you think I'm suggesting this part?'

'That's not a risk, that's TV,' Luther says.

'It is a risk, because it's something different. It's an excellent part. It's a complex character, and it's brilliantly written. That's the kind of risk I think you should be taking – not just following an action movie with a rom-com.'

Luther says something I can't hear. Marisa emerges from the bathroom, and I get up to walk her to the door. As I walk beside her I can see there's a huge mosquito bite on her shoulder. I don't know how I didn't notice it before.

'Were you in Rome recently, Marisa?' I ask her.

She looks very startled, almost shocked. 'How do you know?' she says.

'I just . . . wondered. I know Sam was there recently.'

She sighs. 'He wasn't meant to tell anyone. I can't let Federico find out – will you promise?' She grabs my hand and looks at me imploringly. She seems genuinely apprehensive. God, is she scared of him? How horrible, if that's the case.

'I promise,' I say, feeling awful. 'I'm sorry. I won't say anything.'

'Thanks, *bella*,' she says. 'You're a real friend. *Ciao*.' She kisses me again and slips out the door.

I walk back and sit down at the computer, which is still printing away. So that's that. Sam was in Rome with his beautiful ex, who I didn't even know was his ex until an hour ago. And whatever the reason for their trip – even if it was totally innocent, which I'm dubious about – he lied to me about it. He lied to me, after we'd slept together and spent an idyllic day and evening together.

I'm starting to doubt everything he said. Was he even in London at all? Did he make all that up about walking along the river, looking at my office on a map? I suddenly have a vision of the two of them in Rome at some glossy dinner full of film people, talking shop in a mixture of Italian and English, her in a beautiful evening dress, his hand on her arm. Or wandering past the Colosseum hand in hand . . . coming back to their hotel room late at night, her wearing his dinner jacket . . . oh, God, I feel so stupid.

I wait until the manuscript has finished printing, and I take it in to my room to finish reading it. My room is a total mess – almost as bad as Annabel's was, except with fewer expensive clothes and products. My drawers are still open from when I charged in like an over-excited child and got ready for my day out with Sam. I can't think about that: it's too painful. I take a deep breath and decide to focus, as I should have from the start, on doing my job.

I've read about three chapters when the phone rings. It's Olivia.

'Hello, Olivia,' I say in the smallest, least offensive tone I can manage.

She just says, 'I've finished reading Brian's draft.'

I'm closing my eyes and crossing my fingers.

'It's generally in good shape.'

Hallelujah! In Olivia language, that's practically the Nobel prize for literature. Could this be a reprieve? Is she going to say I'm forgiven?

'There's just one thing,' she continues. 'I am disappointed that there's nothing more behind the whole episode of the year he disappeared. Which, as you know, was one of the subjects we wanted him to cover in the contract.'

OK. Point taken.

'It's just an anti-climax that all he did was sit on a beach. Are you sure there was nothing more to it than that?'

Oh God. It's an obvious, yet terrifying question. I can feel my hand turn damp as it clutches the phone.

'You see,' she says, 'I don't think we can trust him to tell us everything. And now I don't know whether I can trust you.'

'I know,' I mutter. 'But . . . that's all he's said . . . so far.'

'I'm not convinced. I think there's more to the whole thing, and if you value your future with us, you'll make sure to find it out,' she says. And hangs up.

I thought I'd been scared before. I thought I'd been worried about my job before. But I have never felt such terror as now. This is it. If I don't tell Olivia what Luther told me, I could get fired.

I should have told her. It was said during an interview; therefore there is no reason not to put it in the book, if Luther agrees. In fact, surely I would be more to blame if I left it *out* of the book. If Olivia ever finds out what Luther told me, and that I didn't tell her – she wouldn't just fire me. She'd kill me.

But what would it do to Luther's career? And would it be good for him to have it in black-and-white for ever? I remember, uneasily, what I was thinking earlier, about him needing a therapist rather than a book contract.

Well, that isn't my responsibility. If Luther doesn't want it in the book, he can say so. But there's no point in me holding back to protect him. I have to save myself. I go to my computer, and I fish out the tape where Luther talked about the whole sordid thing, and start to type it up. It doesn't take long. When I've finished, I print it out so I can show it to Luther, and I attach it to an email ready to send to Brian and Olivia. My cursor hesitates over the send button. Strange: just by pressing this I can affect Luther's entire career. And mine. And Sam's.

Can I do that? Am I really prepared to ruin Luther's career to save my own?

I'm probably being overdramatic. Luther's career won't

247

be ruined. Anyway, I don't have a choice. I'm just about to press send when I hear a knock on my door.

'Alice?'

It's Sam. I'm not answering.

'Alice? I know you're there.'

He knocks again. A few minutes later, I hear him walk away. I bury my face in my hands. Today has just been too much. I won't send the email yet: I'll send it in the morning.

TWENTY-NINE

I'm awoken by yet another knock on my door. I look at my watch: it's 7.15 a.m. Who is it this time, and what do they want? I can't wait until I'm back in my own bed instead of being here on call twenty-four hours a day.

'What is it?' I call, foggy-voiced.

'It's me.' Sam, again. I go to open the door, hopes rising despite myself. Is he going to tell me that the whole Marisa thing is a mistake? He hasn't shaved yet, and he's wearing his swimming things with a towel thrown over his shoulder, which is distracting.

'Dominique's on her way,' he says.

'What do you mean, she's on her way?' I ask blankly, looking past him as if she might be coming down the corridor.

'I mean, she's on her way here, now. Her manager called me late last night.'

So that was it – the reason he knocked on my door last night. It wasn't to talk to me at all.

'Why is she coming in person?' I say, knowing I sound snappy.

'I have no idea.'

'Well, when is she coming?'

'This morning. She has a few requests.'

'Such as?'

'Helicopter parking. The manuscript printed out in trip-licate on cream-coloured paper. And mentholated cigarettes, and five litres of Fiji water.'

'Very funny.'

'I'm not joking,' says Sam. 'You know, that's not a big ask by her standards.'

'No?'

'No. You got lucky.' He's not smiling.

'We'll do our best,' I say. 'Did she request any brand of mentholated – actually, what am I saying? There's enough madness in her menthols.'

I'm about to turn away when he puts a hand on my arm. Looking down at me, he says, 'Hey. Alice. Did I do or say something to piss you off?'

'No, of course not.'

'Then why are you being so weird with me?' He looks around and continues, in a low voice, 'Yesterday . . . I had a really great time with you, and I thought you did too.'

I consider telling him that I know about him and Marisa, to see if he might be able to explain. But what is there to explain? Even if there is some innocent reason why they jetted off to Rome together, the fact is that he lied to me; he didn't tell me she was his ex until I asked him outright, and he and I are never going to be together again anyway. This whole thing with Sam was just as much of a fantasy as my crush on Luther.

'Is this about me and Marisa?' he says, seemingly reading my mind. 'Look, it was a long time ago, and I can't help having dated other people in the past.'

How dare he be so patronising? Now I'm definitely not going to let him know why I'm upset.

'No,' I say. 'That has nothing to do with it. We did have

250

a good time. I'm sorry if I seem distracted, but I'm here to do a job and I can't afford to get sidetracked.'

He steps back. 'Fine,' he says shortly, looking annoyed. 'Understood.' And he marches off down the corridor. Watching him go, I still feel hurt, but I'm angry too, and in a strange way, that makes me feel better. It's so much better than just feeling hurt.

The rest of the morning reminds me partly of a treasure hunt and partly of those fairy tales where the girl has to spin a barnful of hay into gold, or some such. While Luther sleeps the rest of us run around like mad things. Maria Santa serves breakfast at the speed of light and bustles around making everything look even more spotless. Sam reckons the best thing is if they land the helicopter on the beach, and he goes to look up the tides to see how much longer we have. I don't know what to do about the manuscripts. There is a computer and printer in the house but they're very slow. I swallow my pride and ring Marisa and cast myself on her mercy.

As I knew she would, she comes through. She says her cousin runs a stationery shop, and Federico has a printer in his office so she can print three copies there. She can get cream paper by nine, and can have it around at our place, printed, by ten. She'll also buy the mint smokes, which have seriously made Dominique go down in my estimation. That was what we smoked in school – how is she still on them?

The water is the hardest part. I've looked online, in vain, for suppliers in Italy. I ask Marisa, and she's never heard of it.

'I don't think you're going to find this in Sicily,' she says doubtfully. 'Maybe in Milan, but . . .'

I find myself thinking frantically of how to get water from Milan in time for this morning – FedEx? A concierge service like Quintessentially? But then I think better of it.

251

'Forget it,' I say to her. 'We're not going to be able to get it, and that's that. Let's just get some San Pellegrino.'

When Luther hears that Dominique is coming, he goes very quiet, but I can tell he's excited, and also nervous. He doesn't get involved in all the chasing around getting things straight. Instead, he paces around the terrace a lot. I feel sorry for him. And also nervous, albeit for different reasons. Because if she's come here for some sort of showdown – if she's decided not to co-operate – then we're in deep trouble.

I've realised, there's no point in sending anything to Olivia or Brian until we find out what Dominique is going to say. But meanwhile, I print out the page of what I've written up of the Hawaii story – Hawaiigate, as I'm now calling it – and give it to Luther to show Dominique. If he's OK with it and if she doesn't object, I'll send it to the others.

'You're sure you're OK with this going into the book?' I ask him.

'Sure,' he says. 'And it's good that I can show it to her now.'

I nod, feeling uneasy.

At around 10.30, we see the helicopter arriving. It hovers for what seems like ages, then starts to descend towards the beach.

'How on earth are they going to be able to land there?' I say.

'It's flat and clear of rocks and the tide won't reach it for another eight hours,' Sam says, even though I wasn't asking him. 'It's totally illegal, but they should be fine. They're going to fly back to a helipad inland once they've dropped her.'

I wonder how Dominique is going to arrive up at the house. Is she going to be willing to climb the fifty or so steps? I suppose she could see it as part of her daily workout, which must be fairly punishing, judging from her slender figure. Or will she be carried on a litter or something?

Marisa, Sam and I peer over the terrace edge to look down. Luther is waiting down on the beach. We can't hear anything because of the noise, but we see about six people emerge, one of whom has Dominique's distinctive long black hair. She steps forward and we see her kiss Luther, very formally, on both cheeks, without removing her sunglasses. They all stand around for a few minutes, presumably talking, before they slowly turn towards the house.

'It's like a state diplomatic visit,' I say.

'That's exactly what it is,' Sam replies.

A few minutes later, Dominique and her entourage, plus Luther, emerge on to the terrace. She looks exactly as she does in photographs: immaculate. The only surprise is how tiny she is – like a child. She's wearing cotton cargo pants and a plain white tank top, with her wavy black hair tumbling down her back. Her entourage is made up of men and women, all seemingly laden down with bags and clipboards. It's hard to look at anything but her, though. Her expression seems totally blank, but that might just be the dark glasses.

I feel genuinely nervous. Of all the famous people I've ever met, she is definitely the most famous. Or is 'meet' the right word? I'm not even sure if I am going to meet her at all. Marisa and Maria Santa have made themselves scarce, but Luther is introducing her to Sam. Sam seems to know one person in her entourage, and he greets both her and Dominique very nicely. Dominique extends a hand which he shakes.

Then Luther says, 'And this is my editor, Alice.'

Her face moves in my direction, but it's hard to say if she sees me. Perhaps she has a special kind of vision that can only see important people. There's a faint nod, or twitch, and then she says something to a member of her entourage, who says something to Luther.

'Please,' he says. 'Come and sit down.'

And he leads them all over towards the table under the canopy. I decide not to join them, and stay standing here. But strangely enough, I don't feel humiliated – if anything, I feel excited and privileged to have seen her. I suppose that must be star quality.

Marisa appears beside me. 'How was she?' she murmurs.

'Beautiful,' I whisper back.

We stand together to see how Maria Santa's refreshments go down. She's brought out a big glass decanter filled with water, and Luther and Sam are explaining how, although Fiji water was unavailable, we've got chilled mineral water plus some special naturally sparkling Sicilian spring water which we've decanted into traditional glass bottles. Only Marisa and I know that it's actually San Pellegrino. There's an agonising pause, but then it seems to go down OK.

After a few minutes, we realise that we're standing there like idiots, and we decide to go inside. Once we're in the house, we look at each other and start laughing, but manage to stay quiet.

'It's exciting, eh?' says Marisa in a low voice. 'Like a visit from royalty.'

'Or outer space,' I reply. We both giggle at that, but quietly.

I start doing edits on the book and Marisa plays patience. I don't feel exactly the same about her as I did before, but I'm glad she's still here – the more hands on deck, the better, in case some special request suddenly comes through from the terrace. It would be nicer for us both to be outside by the pool, but we both know, without any discussion, that we need to stay out of sight for now. After about twenty minutes, Sam comes in.

'She wants to read it,' he says.

The manuscripts are waiting on a side table. I hand them to him. 'How is it going?' I ask.

'Hard to say, but at least she wants to see the book,' he says.

Sam goes back to the table, and hands the manuscripts to one of the entourage, who – I can't believe my eyes – hands them to someone else, who takes two of the copies and hands one to Dominique. They then all withdraw, leaving just Luther with Dominique. They talk a few minutes more, and then Luther gets up and walks away ceremonially – almost, it seems, without turning his back. It's like something in a martial arts film.

Dominique changes position to sit cross-legged with her back to the terrace, with the manuscript set out in front of her in a very neat pile. After a minute she turns a page very precisely. I've never seen anyone sit with such a straight back, and I remember reading that she trained as a ballet dancer. From time to time she makes a note in a separate notebook. Marisa and I watch for a while until it starts to become ridiculous, and we go off and resume our work. From time to time, though, I can't help getting up and peeking out at Dominique, still sitting completely upright, reading with extraordinary concentration, a cigarette burning in the ashtray beside her. Luther is sitting near her, perched on the edge of his chair, looking at her.

At around 1 p.m., Luther comes in to us.

'How's it going?' we both ask him.

He shrugs. 'I don't know. She's still reading. She hasn't said anything yet.'

'Can you gauge her reaction at all?' I ask him.

'Nope,' he says. 'She's quite the poker player.' He sounds admiring.

'We should eat,' says Marisa. 'Luther, will we offer her some lunch?'

'I already asked,' says Luther. 'She's not hungry.'

'But what about all her – people?' I say.

'They don't eat if she doesn't eat.'

'Jesus,' says Sam, who's just joined us. 'OK, let's eat in the kitchen.'

So we do. Maria Santa lets us raid the fridge for cherry tomatoes, mozzarella, cured ham and olives, which we eat with slices of bread dipped in olive oil and salt. Looking at Luther hoovering up his lunch, I realise I've never appreciated just how easy he's been to deal with. Sure, he's self-centred, but compared to Dominique, he's Joe Normal.

'Has anyone heard from Annabel?' asks Marisa. 'Is she still with her boyfriend?'

'Oh yeah,' says Luther. 'I almost forgot about her. I had a message from her yesterday. I'll call her back after Dom goes.'

After lunch, Marisa goes off to the beach, and I continue with the editing. It's pretty dismaying to realise how big a part of the book Dominique is – if she's not happy we could end up losing an awful lot. If she makes loads of changes, on the other hand, it could become incredibly bland.

'That's quite a sigh,' says Sam, coming inside.

'Sorry,' I say awkwardly. 'I didn't realise I was sighing.'

'Do you want me to go check on her – scope out the lie of the land?'

That's incredibly good of him. 'Are you sure?' I say, tentatively.

'Yeah. And you can print it out for me too, and I'll start reading it.'

I look at him. He doesn't look very friendly, but he clearly means it. And I realise that no matter what his feelings for me are, or what happened between us, he is still going to keep his promise to me.

'Thank you,' I say. I print him out a copy, and he starts reading it as it comes out.

We both continue working for the rest of the afternoon and early evening. Occasionally, I sneak covert looks at Sam, and wonder if I've made a huge mistake. When I think of how he was with me the other night, and the day we spent together, it does seem hard to believe that he could be having some sort of thing with Marisa on the side. But then I keep coming back to the same thing: why did he lie about going to Rome with her? And something else is nagging at me. How come *she* never told me that she was his ex? We've talked about everything else – why not that, unless there was something she didn't want me to know?

Maybe they're not having a full-on affair; maybe it's something more complicated. Maybe he's planning to marry her so she can get a visa and work in the US, or something. Or . . . Americans always date multiple people, don't they? Maybe he thinks it's fine to see both of us at once, and if I ask him about it, he'll think I'm being unreasonable and unsophisticated and possessive . . .

That thought is just too horrible, so I decide to put it all out of my mind and try and concentrate on Luther's book. In general, I'm really pleased with it. I'm making notes as I go, but aside from bringing out a few more dramatic moments and cutting here and there, there isn't all that much that needs changing.

Except, of course, adding the producer story – the truth of what happened after Hawaii. I get out my email again and go back to the drafts folder where it's waiting, ready to be sent to Brian and Olivia. I start typing a covering email. 'I've just found this out . . .' – it's a lie, but anyway – 'Luther is sensitive about it but I know that I can get him to put it in. It's such a major trauma that we'll have to change the second half significantly, and keep referring back to it, and then give more of an impression that L has "recovered". There are legal issues but they should be resolvable, particularly since the producer is dead.'

I stop, and read back over what I've written. Did I really write that? It's all so seedy and depressing. It will overwhelm the book; it will be all that anyone talks about. And, for the rest of his career, it will be the one fact that people remember about Luther, too. 'Oh, yeah, he's the casting-couch guy.' Is that what we want?

Why did Luther tell me about it? Maybe he just wanted to tell someone, but that's not the same thing as telling the world. Personally I think he was crazy to tell me. But he trusts me, and he would put it in, if I persuaded him. Oh, God. This is not why I wanted to work in publishing. I wanted to work with authors and help them tell great stories. I didn't want to exploit people and harm their careers. I was proud of this book before. I won't be any more, if I do this. Suddenly a really horrible thought comes to me. If I do this, am I really any different from the people who did this to him in the first place?

I can't do it. I'm not going to put it in the book, and I won't tell Olivia what happened. It's not my secret to tell. If Olivia ever finds out that Luther told me about it, and that I kept it from her, then I'll definitely be out on my ear, but I just can't do it. I delete the email. Then I search for the file of our last interview, which I typed up and gave to Luther. Finding it, I press delete, and then I empty the trash folder. It's gone. And I feel as if a massive weight has been lifted off my shoulders.

I've hardly noticed that it's getting dark, until Sam gets up and puts on the light.

'My God. Are they still out there? I'd almost forgotten about them.'

'They're leaving,' Sam says. 'Let's go say goodbye.'

Outside, the entourage are standing around, with Dominique and Luther a little way apart from them. He's holding some notes, which I realise must be from her. We all shake hands with the others, and then they all file down the stairs. Dominique and Luther stay behind last of all, saying their goodbyes at the top of the stairs. Looking at them standing in the half-dark, at the edge of the terrace, with the last light from the setting sun behind them, I think about what a sight this would be for a passing paparazzo. But even if they were caught on camera, there's no way for anyone to know what they are saying.

She leaves, and Luther comes slowly back over towards us, looking at the wad of paper in his hand.

'How was it?' I ask.

'Good,' he says. 'Bittersweet, you know?'

'And did she like the book?'

He nods slowly. 'She did, you know? She really did.' He waves the papers. 'She wants us to change, like, six pages.'

'Six pages? Is that all?'

'Yeah, she's worried when I talk about a friend of ours, and there are some other things that she wanted to change. But she's cool with most of what I said about her and me. She says she hopes it helps other people who are going through similar stuff.'

This is unbelievable. I feel a new-found respect for her: what a star. Suddenly the noise of the helicopter begins. It's completely deafening, and it blows all our clothes against us. We look up at the chopper, lifting higher and higher overhead.

I take the pages from Luther, and examine them, holding them tightly – it would be too tragic if the wind blew them away. Her changes are written in a tiny, neat hand, and they seem to be mostly psychobabble – far-out chat about learning and growth and acceptance and change and other stuff which is going to sound extremely strange woven into Luther's bad-boy anecdotes. But I just don't care any more.

'These look great,' I say to him. 'I can't believe she came out and just did it in a day. Luther, do you know what this means? We've finished the book!' I'm so excited that I'm practically jumping up and down, and Luther is laughing at me.

We get some champagne and open it on the terrace, while Maria Santa is setting up for dinner. I remember the last time someone brought champagne on to the terrace – Luther, when he tried to seduce me after the nightclub. I can't believe that after everything that's happened, all the disasters and detours, we've actually ended up with a publishable book.

'This is such a great feeling,' I say to him. 'Luther, you should be proud of yourself. Are you happy about it?'

'Yeah,' he says. 'Yeah, I am. I feel like I learned and grew, you know?' He's clearly taking the piss, or is he? As ever with Luther, I'm not totally sure, but he looks pretty happy.

I decide that before the others join us, I'd better tell Olivia that Dominique has approved the book. I've just opened up my email, when Sam comes inside.

'What the hell is this?' he snaps.

'What the . . . hell is what?' But I can see. He's holding a piece of paper. In slow-motion horror I realise Luther's told him about the producer story. And shown it to him.

'Sam, I can explain,' I say, realising I'm talking in clichés. 'I changed my mind. I don't think it should go in.'

'Oh, sure you've changed your mind. Right after you asked Luther to show – this – to his ex-wife. How could you do this? He trusted you. How could you encourage him to broadcast such a miserable, shitty story? Didn't you even think about what it would do to him, to his career? I'm just glad he decided not to show it to Dominique.'

'But – I've deleted it! Honestly. You can check my computer.' I turn the laptop towards him with shaking hands.

'I don't believe you,' he says. 'But I get it now. There's the version you gave me, and there's the version that you're really publishing. Well, you can do your own dirty work from now on.'

'So – so are you cancelling the book?' I ask helplessly.

He laughs. 'Of course, that's the main thing: the book. Don't worry; Luther still wants the book. But don't even *think* of including this sordid piece of gossip in it.'

'Wait, Sam! You don't understand. I'm about to lose my job—'

'Skip it, Alice. I know you're under pressure to dig for dirt. Just go dig somewhere else, OK?'

'Please, Sam. I can explain.'

'There's really no need. Luther's changed his mind about the TV; he wants to do it. We fly tomorrow. You've got your book; we're done here.'

And he walks out to greet Federico and Marisa, who've just arrived. I can't speak; I can't even cry. I've lost him.

At dinner, everyone is in a celebratory mood. Federico tells us how his printer kept jamming, and Marisa talks about getting hold of the paper and how her cousin wanted Dominique's autograph. Luther is on great form as well, inventing lots of outrageous anecdotes which he claims he's put in the book. The champagne gets finished surprisingly quickly, and Luther immediately asks for another bottle, and another one. I just concentrate on cutting up my food and making it look as though I'm eating so that nobody asks me any questions. I've already booked my flight, and I've emailed Olivia telling her that Dominique has approved the manuscript, and that nothing else came of the Hawaii story. Now I want to go home.

The others are discussing *Roman Holiday*. In the ending of the original, the Princess and the journalist go their separate ways because they belong to different worlds. In Luther's remake, she hands the throne to her younger brother and they ride off into the sunset together. It sounds awful. Of course I haven't said as much to Luther, but Marisa, who can say things we can't, is telling him they should have kept the ending as it was.

'It was more romantic,' she says. 'Ah, the scene with the press conference at the end – it's beautiful.'

'It's a downer,' Luther says irritably. 'Ours is more uplifting.'

'But not as true,' Marisa argues. She turns to Sam. 'What do you think? More beautiful before, no?'

Sam just makes some generic comment about how he can't wait to see Luther's version. If only I hadn't done that awful thing with the producer story, maybe he would have looked at me and said something meaningful about how the Princess should have ended up with the journalist or something, and I would have agreed and we would have ended up riding off into the sunset together. But he won't talk to me, or even look at me. Seeing him sitting beside Marisa, I realise it's hopeless. There probably is something between them. And even if there isn't, he hates me now.

By 1 a.m., Marisa and Federico are still there, having a whale of a time, and Luther's clearly in for the long haul. When he tries to top me up for the tenth time, I make a move to go, talking about being tired and having to pack.

'No!' Luther protests when I get up. 'Disloyalty to the party!'

The mention of disloyalty makes me blush. 'My flight's at eleven,' I mutter.

'I'm sorry I can't take you to the airport,' Marisa says. 'I have some errands to do. Sam, will you take her?'

'I won't have time,' Sam says shortly. Marisa looks surprised.

'It's OK. I can get a taxi. Goodnight, everyone,' I say.

'Hey. Come on, man,' says Luther, unexpectedly. 'She's worked hard. Give the girl a ride to the airport.'

This sudden kindness, coming on top of what I was going to do to him, pushes me over the edge; I can feel tears collecting in my eyes and a lump in my throat. Sam snaps, 'OK, fine.'

I escape to bed before I break down completely. I'm so relieved. Sam hates me now, but I know that if I can just talk to him properly, I'll be able to explain. I hope so, anyway. I fall asleep practising the way I'll phrase it.

THIRTY

I'm packed. I'm ready. I've looked under the bed and in all
the drawers, and I'm leaving in twenty minutes. I'm leaving
the brown hair-shirt here – I'd like to have a ceremonial
burning of it, but I've left it a bit late. I've decided the neon
swimsuit is something Poppy might be able to carry off, so
I'm taking it with me. I've just come back from saying
goodbye and thank you to Maria Santa when I see Marisa,
jumping out of her car and running towards the house.

'What's up?' says Sam, who's just emerged on to the
terrace with Luther.

'I just talked to Annabel on the phone,' Marisa says. 'She
sounded terrified. She's in Nikos's apartment. She says
they've had a fight, and he's really scared her. She wants
someone to come and get her.'

'Tell her to get a taxi,' says Luther.

'Did he hit her?' says Sam.

Marisa shakes her head. 'I don't know. There wasn't time.
She said she couldn't talk for long, so I just said we would
come and get her. Sam, please will you go and collect her?
She told me where his house is.' She looks at me. 'Oh, wait.
I forgot. You're taking Alice to the airport.'

'No. I think I should help Annabel,' Sam says. And hearing
this, I know that I've lost him for good.

'Damn,' says Luther. 'I knew I should've packed my piece. Never mind, I can go hand-to-hand. Take that Nikos guy down.'

'Easy, Starsky. You're not coming. Forget it,' says Sam, going inside the house.

'What are you talking about?' Luther's following him. 'You need back-up. You're a Mormon, for Chrissake. What are you, going to preach him to death? You need someone from the street, like me.'

'No! Your publicist hates me enough as it is.'

'Come on, *bella*,' Marisa says. 'I'll take you to the airport.'

I knew it. I knew this would happen. Even if Annabel is in some kind of danger, which personally I doubt, her timing sucks. We go inside, where Sam is putting on his shoes and Luther is practising gun-pulling poses in the mirror.

'Hey, so we need to say goodbye,' says Luther. 'Alice, it's been real.' He punches me gently on the arm, then he seems to change his mind and lifts me up in a bear hug. 'Have a safe trip home. Give my love to the Queen.'

'Goodbye, Luther.' I have a lump in my throat.

I turn to Sam. 'Thanks for all your help.'

'Bye,' he says curtly, without even looking up. I walk away quickly, putting my sunglasses on before anyone sees my eyes brimming.

We get into the car, and Marisa starts the engine. Luther comes out, and waves for a second before disappearing back through the archway. As we go up the drive, it hits me: it's all over. I'll never see him again. When Marisa asks kindly, 'Is something wrong?' it's fatal. I try to reply, but I'm crying too hard.

'I'm – sorry,' I say through gulps. 'It's – just – all been so intense.'

'I know. But – ' she's smiling but nonplussed – 'you completed the book! What a success.'

265

I just shake my head.

'Why is Sam being so strange with you?' Marisa asks. 'Did you have an argument?'

I breathe in quickly and drink some water out of my bottle. I realise I have to get it together, or they won't let me on the plane.

'We just argued about the book.'

'Ah.' Marisa looks thoughtful. Then she changes the subject, and for the rest of the drive, neither of us mentions Sam at all.

At the airport, I give her a huge hug. I also ask for her address; I'm sending her champagne, or flowers, or an elephant or something.

'Here's my email address,' she says, writing it down for me. 'It's best you get in touch with me this way first, because . . . I might be moving quite soon.'

She looks down as she says this, blushing slightly. That sounds pretty definitive. She must be leaving Federico for Sam. Perhaps she's even moving to LA. Well, they'll make a good couple. I take a deep breath, determined not to show her how upset I am.

'Thanks so much for everything, Marisa,' I tell her. 'I honestly could never have done this without you.'

'*Niente*,' she says. Nothing. She kisses me, and then waves me off to the departure gates.

The people beside me on the plane keep staring at me. I know I look a sight with my red eyes. I have to order a gin and tonic just to get through the flight. It comes in a nasty plastic sachet and costs about five euros. The plane lands in Stansted at 2.30 p.m.: a random place at a random time. As I shuffle out into arrivals and see all the people being met, I try not to think of Sam meeting me at Fontanarossa.

After the heat and light of Sicily, England is so depressing.

It's raining and grey, one of those summer days that might as well be March or October. I'm freezing in my stripy blazer and navy skirt. One of the cash machines is broken, so I queue there for ages before waiting for the bus to Victoria. The queue for the bus is a mile long; there are children crying behind me and the man in front of me is having an argument with the ticket collector. The longer I stand there, the more it seems as though everything that's happened in the past fortnight has just been a dream.

The journey home from the airport seems to take almost as long as my flight. I have to get the tube all the way across town. I arrive home and dump my bag in the hall, and go to get a glass of water from the kitchen. The sink is piled high with dishes. I can hear football in the background. Martin, my flatmate, trails into the room, wearing a Real Madrid T-shirt.

'Oh, hi, Alice,' he says. 'How was Spain?'

'It was fine. I mean, Italy was fine.'

'Good stuff.' Martin takes a head of lettuce out of the fridge. After inspecting it for a minute he pulls off a leaf, spreads peanut butter on it, rolls it up and starts eating it.

'Um – is Ciara home?'

'Nope. Out with some bloke, I think.' He wanders out of the kitchen, leaving the fridge door open.

I close it automatically. I should be happy that Ciara has met someone, but at the moment it just makes me feel more alone. What to do now? I could make a cup of tea, call Ruth or my parents, unpack, do my laundry, check my emails, but I don't have the energy. I fetch my bag and head into my bedroom, passing through the living room where Martin is watching football. Everything is just as I left it. Here I am again, alone in my room with my DVDs, looking at my cardboard squares. The past two weeks – not even two weeks, in fact – are over, and it's back to real life.

THIRTY-ONE

I really have to psych myself up to force myself out of bed and into the shower the next morning. I'm almost too scared to go into work, thinking of the wrath that is probably going to descend on my head. As I get dressed, I try to think of reasons to be cheerful. Number one: we got Luther's book; number two: they might forgive me now that everything's turned out OK; number three . . . I'll see Poppy again. Those will have to do.

Olivia's already at her desk when I arrive. She looks very pale and even thinner than usual; her Orla Kiely dress is hanging a bit loosely on her. With a flicker of guilt, I realise how stressful it must have been for her, being here and unwell in London while I was on the loose in Sicily. I take a deep breath and go and knock on her door.

'Good morning,' I say quietly.

She looks up briefly. 'Oh. You're back.'

I've brought her some almond biscuits I picked up in the airport, along with Poppy's olive oil, as a peace offering, but now I realise this looks stupid. I'm about to walk away when she says, 'Alice, can you come in and see me at twelve? Just catch up on everything else until then.'

'Of course.'

Well, that wasn't so bad. I go back to my desk, hopeful

for the first time that this whole thing might not end in total catastrophe.

'Morning, Henry,' I say to one of the other assistants, as I turn on my computer.

'Oh – hi,' he says evasively. Normally he would stop for a chat, but he scuttles off, straight back to his own desk.

That's odd. In fact, the atmosphere in general seems odd; I feel people are avoiding me. But maybe I'm just imagining it. It's often the way when you come home from holidays: everyone is interested for five minutes, but naturally enough they're wrapped up in their own lives. Poppy is pleased to see me, but she's in the middle of a nightmare editing job, so she just gives me a quick wave and says she'll catch up with me later.

When twelve o'clock comes around, Olivia puts her head out from behind her door.

'Alice? Can you come in please?'

I walk into the office, and I'm surprised to see a woman there I vaguely recognise. She has chestnut-coloured hair in a bob, and glasses. She's wearing a grey pinstripe skirt and a blue cardigan. And she's holding some kind of file or folder.

'This is Kim Lewis, from HR,' says Olivia.

And that's when I realise something very bad is about to happen.

'Alice,' Olivia says, 'this isn't going to be easy for anyone, so I'll keep it brief. We've had a number of problems recently with you, over this Luther Carson book, and I'm afraid they are so serious that we have no choice but to end your employment with us.'

'What?' I say. I don't get it. For a second I wonder if they're transferring me to another department or something.

'You're being dismissed, for unprofessional conduct,' Kim says.

I'm being fired. I knew it was possible, I had imagined it, but now that it's actually happening, I can't believe it. Olivia glances at Kim, who clears her throat.

'Firstly, there was your decision to fire the ghostwriter,' Kim intones formally. In a detached way, I find myself noticing that she has a very soothing Scottish accent which must help cushion the bad news. I wonder if that's why they picked her for this.

'I didn't fire him,' I say as politely as I can. 'I told him to go and work from home—'

'Yes, but you knew you had no authority to do that,' says Olivia. 'And then, there was the incident with the clause.'

'Leaving out the clause was a mistake, we know,' Kim says smoothly, and I wonder if they've practised this together. 'But it was negligent not to tell your manager about it as soon as you knew.'

They both look at me, as if they're expecting me to say something. But I can't think of anything to say. I feel as if I'm at a play, or watching some kind of double-act, where my participation's not needed. I just nod for them to go on.

'Then there was this picture,' says Olivia.

This is new. What picture? Olivia gets up and looks in one of her wire in-trays. She takes out a celebrity magazine, one of those cheap £1 ones. What is this? Has Luther done something awful? Or – did someone spot me and Sam? Now I'm really scared. My heart is hammering. Is there a picture of me and Sam kissing on that beach?

She hands it to me open at a page. I don't believe this. It's me and Luther, stumbling out of that nightclub. His arm is around my neck with his fingers dangling towards my cleavage in a very lewd way, and I look smashed out of my mind, smiling a weird *Valley of the Dolls* smile. The caption says that Natasha Pullman is distraught because

270

Luther has been seen hanging out in Sicily with a 'mystery blonde'. I can feel my face growing hot.

'Then there was also an email that went around after the picture came out,' Olivia says. 'One of those gossip circulars, about how a certain editor was seen canoodling with her famous author, etc.'

Kim glances at Olivia. I wonder if 'canoodling' is in her approved vocab. And more importantly: what the hell is this blanket media coverage? Why has nobody told me about it? Has it been on the nine o'clock news?

'The email was particularly disturbing because it goes to so many media people. We had lots of calls about it and Alasdair had to go to some length to suppress the story. It has made the company look very unprofessional,' Olivia says.

'It's not appropriate. It doesn't live up to company standards. It damages the company's reputation,' Kim explains, as if I don't know what 'unprofessional' means. I know exactly what it means. It's just about the worst word you can use, isn't it?

Kim now starts talking in legalese, about consultations, and security, and instant this and that. 'Do you have any questions?' she asks finally, in her soothing tones.

'Um . . .' I don't actually, but I suppose I'd better ask something. 'How much notice do I get?'

Kim and Olivia exchange looks again.

'You will be paid until the end of the month,' Kim says. 'But it's probably best if you leave after today.'

'There's a lot of handover to do. Who should I . . .?'

'Just leave written instructions,' Olivia says. 'We can access your email for anything vital.'

I nod again, and get up to go.

'Alice,' Kim says. I turn around. She's brandishing a box of Kleenex. 'Tissue?' she says, in sepulchral tones.

'Um – no thanks.'

I turn around and walk back out. I'm not quite sure what to do or where to go or how to look. People are looking at me, and I realise the rumours have obviously been going around. They know something's up. But I still can't believe that I've been fired.

A big commotion is happening at the other end of the floor. Everyone is gathered around Claudine's desk, and there's much whooping and celebration. If I go back to my desk it will look as if I'm sulking, so I walk over as calmly as I can. At first I think it must be her birthday, but then I hear the word 'promotion'. Maybe it's my imagination, but people seem to stop talking and stare at me as I arrive.

'Congratulations, Claudine,' I say.

'Oh! It's our movie star!' Claudine leans over and gives me a very unwelcome hug. Then she immediately launches back into her story, which is all about how surprised and amazed she was finally to be made editor. I smile as serenely as I can as she meanders on. I notice I'm not the only one: Henry, the other non-fiction assistant, is looking daggers too. Poppy's expression gives nothing away, but she glances over and raises one eyebrow.

I slip back to my desk as soon as I can. I sit down and open up a blank document which I call 'Handover notes'. I stare at it. Where to begin? Then suddenly I do a double-take and realise: I'm not going on holiday, or taking a sabbatical or voluntary redundancy. *I've just been fired.* I don't want to write them handover notes.

I stand up and leave the document open, cursor flashing. I start gathering my bits and pieces together. There's so much, it would take hours to sort everything out. But I don't want to stay for hours. I stuff my ballet flats into my cotton bag, and add my spare lip balms and a few other bits and pieces, some cards from authors, a book or two, and that's it. Four years' work in one crappy cotton book-bag. I'll be sorry to leave my spider plant, but I don't want to draw attention to myself by taking it. I'm definitely leaving the poster of Luther behind. I don't speak to, or look at, anyone. I just walk out, ignoring everyone's stares and the murmur of conversation that gathers to a crescendo behind me. I see a flash of Orla Kiely print as I pass Olivia's office, but I don't look at her.

I'm waiting for the lift when I hear heels clacking towards me. It's Poppy. She's wearing a blue denim jump-suit and silver stilettos, and looks like something out of *Top Gun*.

'Alice! Where are you going? What happened?'

'I've been fired,' I whisper.

'You've been what? *Why*? Why have they fired you?' At the sound of the concern in her voice, I start to cry again, for the second time in twenty-four hours.

'Come on,' Poppy says, bustling me into the lift. She's even had the presence of mind to bring her bag with her. 'You and I are going for a big drink.'

'What about work?'

'I'm on strike,' says Poppy, darkly.

THIRTY-TWO

Poppy suggests the Dog and Duck, but that's always full of work people, so instead we go to the Queen's Head. She orders double gin and tonics and burgers and chips, though I won't be able to eat a thing. I insist that we go to the darkest, most obscure little booth; I don't want anyone from the office to see us.

'I can't believe they've fired you,' she keeps saying. 'The bastards! It's so unfair.'

I manage to keep it together, and tell her everything that happened – just about the job, though. I can't mention Sam; it's too painful.

'I mean, I knew it was a possibility, ever since the clause thing, and Brian, but – I didn't know about the picture, or the email. Did you?' I ask.

'Yes, I did,' she says uncomfortably. 'I saw the picture, and I heard someone talking about the email. It was just on one of those blindbeast.com gossip circulars. You know nobody takes them seriously.'

'Have you still got it? Can I see it?'

Poppy gets out her iPhone and after a few minutes she finds it for me.

After paying a reputed two million dollars for a celebrity autobiography, there must be red faces at this publishing house following rumours that their editor has joined the star's list of conquests. It seems she's fired his ghostwriter so that she can have him all to herself, and they're hiding out in a holiday villa, where they've been seen getting very intimate in a nightclub. Let's hope he tells all in the autobiography.

It's like one of those nightmares where you appear in the supermarket with no clothes on.

'You could sue them, probably,' says Poppy. 'It's obviously completely made up.'

I wince at her last words, and put my head in my hands. 'The thing is – it's not. We were sort of – I mean, it was only one time, but we *were* sort of intimate in a nightclub.'

Poppy puts down her gin and tonic. '*What?!* Tell me all immediately.'

I look around first to check that nobody is listening, and then I tell her: about Luther, and the champagne and dancing, and how I almost kissed him but didn't.

'Good grief,' says Poppy when I've finished. 'You know, that makes me take my hat off to you. He's a hot famous man, he tried it on and you said no. That's amazing!'

'No, it's not amazing. I shouldn't have been there in the first place, drunk, in a nightclub; I shouldn't have sent Brian home – I should have handled the whole thing differently. I was an idiot,' I say, adding quietly, 'I deserve to be fired.'

'Alice!' Poppy cries. 'Would you listen to yourself? *You got the book.* There *was* no book before you went, and you got it and it's going to earn the company millions. So what if you danced with Luther and some stupid photo got taken? And Brian – the man's wife has cancer. What were you supposed to do, chain him to his desk? Who cares how you did it? You got Luther to write his book!'

I'm crying properly now, but I'm so grateful. What would I do without Poppy?

'I think they've been complete bastards,' she repeats. 'You should sue them. And I'll come out and strike in solidarity.'

'No, don't do that.' I know Poppy is just as broke as I am.

'How are you for money? I can lend you . . .'

'Oh, no. That's sweet of you, but I'll be fine for a few weeks. I'll ring Erica. She'll probably help me out.'

'And she's an employment lawyer,' Poppy reminds me. 'I bet she'll help you sue, and you'll win a landmark victory.'

I blow my nose on a paper napkin, and shrug. I'm too depressed for a landmark victory. I want to go home and watch *Murder She Wrote*.

'Hey. This might not be the moment, but – I've got something for you. It might cheer you up – or just give you a few laughs . . .' Poppy rummages in her squashy ponyskin bag and unearths what looks like a condom wrapper.

'Good grief,' I say. 'I know I've been a bit indiscreet lately, but there's no need for the sex ed.'

'No, no,' says Poppy. 'It's the invitation to the *Bitch Done Me Wrong* opening. It's on Friday evening.' Of course: her ex-boyfriend's exhibition. I can see now it's not a real wrapper, just a little square foil that for some reason is made to look like a condom.

'It's pretty gross, isn't it? Typical Crippo.'

When I heard that name, I knew there would be trouble. His real name, I'm remembering now, is Crispin, and he's a lot posher than he likes to let on.

'I'm going to do a quick sweep while in disguise,' Poppy says. 'In and out, an hour tops. Then a drink. What do you think? It might be a distraction . . .'

'Let me think about it,' I say. At the moment I can't think of anything I feel less like doing than schlepping out to the East End to look at some idiot's installation, but I owe Poppy.

If it wasn't for this drink with her, I don't know if I would have made it home without falling apart.

Suddenly I realise something.

'Poppy,' I say. 'How do they know I sent the ghost home?'

'What?'

'That email thing. It said I sent the ghost home. Nobody knew that but you and Olivia, surely?' I look at her and we say in unison, 'Claudine.'

'She must have overheard me talking to you,' says Poppy.

'And she knows Simon,' I say. 'Oh God! He knows the people who send this thing out. I bet you anything she told him, and I bet you he wrote this. It even sounds like him.'

'Oh, shit,' says Poppy. 'Alice, I'm so sorry.'

'It's OK,' I say numbly. 'Look . . . you'd better get back to the office.'

I trudge back to the Tube. It's full of tourists on their way to Heathrow, with huge bags, which reminds me of my lost bag which I never did get back. Down on the platform, I suddenly get a fright when I catch sight of Luther – but it's just a poster advertising his new film, *The Deep End*. I move away so that I can't see it. It feels so strange to be on the Tube in the middle of the day, with nothing to do and nowhere to go. What did Sam call me when he met me? The out of office girl. I really am the out of office girl now. I start doing sums in my head, wondering how much I have left to last me until rent day.

THIRTY-THREE

'OK,' says Erica, putting on the kettle. 'First things first: do you have a copy of your contract with you?'

I shake my head.

'People never do,' she sighs. 'Don't worry, Al. We'll sort you out.'

Erica's left work early and come over to our flat for a crisis summit. Ciara is here too, and Poppy is going to come later. Ruth wanted to come, but she's stuck at a work event, so she's said she'll make me dinner tomorrow night. Ciara's ordered Indian food, and Martin is out – for once.

We go into the living room, and I tell them everything I can remember about the reasons they gave for firing me. Erica gets out a notebook and asks me loads of questions – about whose responsibility the contract was, and other details. Finally she says, 'None of that sounds serious enough for instant dismissal. Especially since the book is satisfactory, and there's no lasting damage to the company.'

It's a big relief to hear her say this. Erica is a lawyer, and if she thinks what I've done isn't so bad, then perhaps it isn't.

'What about gross misconduct, though?' I ask doubtfully. 'They can fire you straight away for that.'

'Alice – that's if you stole something, or assaulted a

278

colleague,' Erica says patiently. 'You've just made a series of mistakes.'

Ciara kneels down opposite Erica and pours out our tea. It's so lovely to see them both again. After Italy, they both look so blonde and blue-eyed. Ciara has the same colouring as Erica and I have, except that her hair is curly whereas ours is straight.

'What I don't understand is *why* you didn't put the Hawaii thing – whatever it is – in the book,' Ciara says. 'He told you during an interview, didn't he?'

'It's just – he didn't understand the consequences. Luther's a bit like a child that way. He wanted to tell someone, but he didn't realise what it would really mean in terms of his career and everything. It would be a catastrophe for him.'

'Well, it's your career I'm more worried about,' Erica says. 'I think you certainly have a case for unfair dismissal. I could represent you, freelance. Though my work insurance wouldn't cover it, so—'

'I don't want to, Erica. It's just not worth it. And . . . there's other stuff that I wouldn't want to come out, if it came to a court case or anything.'

'What other stuff?' Erica asks instantly, putting down her mug.

'I had –' Argh. 'Well, a sort of a thing, I mean a fling . . .'

'With *Luther*?'

'No, no, with Sam. Luther's agent. We had a . . .' I look at them both. How to put it? 'Sort of a one-night stand. Well, it was more than that. I really liked him. So, that's why I don't really want to do the court case thing. In case it came out.'

Both of them are looking a bit stunned.

'I think that's very unprofessional of him,' says Erica. 'How old is this man?'

'And of me, Erica! It took two of us to tango. He's twenty-eight. But now he hates me.'

'I'm sure he doesn't hate you,' Ciara says. 'What happened?'

I tell them, reluctantly, about how Sam thought I was going to betray him and Luther and put the Hawaii thing in the book.

'You should have seen the look on his face. He wouldn't even look at me, wouldn't speak to me. And also – he's interested in someone else.'

'Who?' says Ciara, looking nonplussed. 'Oh, wait, doorbell. That'll be our food.' She runs off to answer it. I explain to Erica about Marisa and how she turned out to be Sam's ex.

'Don't tell Mum and Dad about any of this,' I add.

'It sounds like *Celebrity Love Island*,' Erica says, shaking her head. 'How did any of you get any work done at all?'

'Hello!' It's Poppy, laden down with a box of books and papers I left at the office, and – bless her – my spider plant.

'What did I miss?' Ciara says. 'Who was the other woman with Sam?'

'Sam?' Poppy asks. 'I knew it! All that stuff about how controlling and uptight he was . . . it sounded very sexy.'

'Never mind,' I say shortly. I don't want to talk about it in this way.

They all exchange glances. Poppy looks embarrassed. Erica gets down from the sofa and sits beside me on the floor.

'I'm sorry, Al,' she says, putting her arm around me. 'We know you've had a rough time. You don't have to tell us anything else if you don't want to.'

Ciara pushes over a box of tissues, and Poppy pours me a glass of wine. I start to tell them: about how I hated Sam at first, and then I saw another side of him, and how we ended up together one night, but then I realised he had something going on with Marisa.

280

'The thing is,' I explain, 'I can see how they are more suited. She's much more his sort of person. I mean, she's beautiful and sophisticated, and she knows about the film industry . . .'

'Wait a second,' Poppy says. 'Aside from this trip to Rome, what actual proof do you have that they're anything but friends?'

'Well, she said she might be moving soon . . .' I say uncertainly.

'I don't think that means anything. It sounds to me as if he liked *you*,' says Poppy. 'Running after your every wish, sweeping you off your feet, canoodling on the beach with you, wining and dining you and knocking on your door late at night – that sounds like pretty smitten behaviour to me.'

The idea that Sam might have liked me, and that I ruined it, is too horrible to bear. But I don't think he ever did like me in the first place – not that much. 'Honestly, Poppy, it might sound that way, but Sam really is completely out of my league. And he thought that as well.'

'What makes you say that?' Ciara asks.

'Well . . .' I'm trying to think how to explain it, and I realise I actually don't have much concrete evidence to give them. 'Well, when we went for dinner, there was this gorgeous Italian girl, and he was staring at her.'

'Oh. Drooling at her instead of at his spaghetti?' Poppy says. 'I hate it when they do that.' Ciara nods.

'No,' I say miserably, aware that I sound crazy. 'He just – glanced at her. As we walked past.'

'Right,' says Erica. 'Anything else for the prosecution?'

'Nothing specific. It's just – a feeling,' I have to admit.

'I think you're being paranoid,' says Poppy. 'You're gorgeous and smart and talented and a lovely person. It sounds to me as if this guy wanted to be in your league. Why not let him?'

281

'I don't know. I don't know why I didn't!'

Oops. That came out louder than I meant it to.

'Sorry, hon,' Erica says. 'We don't mean to lecture you about it. But it's probably for the best. I mean . . . I'm sure you could resolve the misunderstanding over the Hawaii thing and what have you. But . . . he lives in LA, doesn't he?'

'Yes,' I say, gritting my teeth. I know what's coming next: long-distance relationships are hard, and we have different lifestyles.

'Long-distance relationships are really hard,' Ciara says, gently.

'And . . . it sounds as if you have rather different lifestyles,' Erica adds.

'But I know all that! I'm the one who's telling *you* that it's a non-event. I don't even have his email address. I've tried to explain things and he won't believe me. And anyway, I know he's with Marisa. So it's well and truly dead in the water.' I wipe my eyes. 'Now, can we change the subject?'

There's an awkward silence, which Ciara breaks by saying tentatively, 'Would anyone like to hear about my love life?'

'OK,' I mumble.

With a quick glance at me, Ciara starts telling us about the new man she's met horse riding. I notice they're all looking at me nervously, as if they're afraid I'll snap at them again. Oh, God. I'd better be careful; at the rate I'm going I'll soon alienate all my friends as well as having lost my job. But I know that Poppy is wrong about Sam. I did think, at one point, that we had something, but like my relationship with Simon, it was obviously a total mirage.

THIRTY-FOUR

It's Friday: the end of the longest week of my life. I've been out all day trekking around temping agencies having interviews, which went OK until we reached the part about why I left my last job. I'm not hungry but I know I should eat something – budget permitting. I've taken my Italian cheque to the bank, but even if it clears soon, it won't last me very long. I didn't know how lucky I was when I could just float across the terrace and see what Maria Santa had rustled up. Thinking of dinner in Italy makes me think of Sam, so I try and think of something else.

I'm standing in Ine Ood Stores at the bottom of my street, wondering what is cheapest and has the least amount of scary preservatives. Martin says that when he moved here first, it was Fine Food, but the Fs fell down so now it's Ine Ood. Poppy's art thing is tonight, but I've cried off – I feel very bad about letting her down, but I can't face people this evening. Ruth invited me to join her and Mike for dinner too, but I'm not in any kind of state to play gooseberry.

I decide to be totally disgusting and buy a frozen pizza on offer for a pound and – what the hell – a mini bottle of red wine, one of those tragic glass-and-a-half ones. Then I see a bag of Minstrels. Why not Minstrels too? It's Friday

283

night. I'm entitled. As I assemble my treats, I think, this really is the classic sad, singleton Friday night. All I need is a DVD of *Bridget Jones* or *My Best Friend's Wedding* and I'll be set. I just hope nobody I know sees me.

I wouldn't believe it if someone told me this but, just as I'm thinking this, I see *him*. Simon. He's at the other end of the shop, with a girl – *not* Claudine, but someone else; I think it's the girl I saw him with on Facebook – debating over the wine selection. I look in horror at the back of his curly head: it's definitely him.

'I think we should get champagne,' the girl is saying.

'No way, babe,' he says. 'Can't turn up with corner shop crap.'

You know those fantasies where you run into your ex and you're looking radiant and casual, yet perfectly groomed? This isn't like that. I tried to dress smartly for my interviews, but all my nice Sicily clothes were still in the wash. So I'm wearing an old green skirt I don't like but can't give away because it was expensive, and a black shirt that isn't as black as it once was. Even if I looked like a model right now, though, Simon is the last person I want to see.

I immediately turn around and pray for the two people in front of me to hurry up so I can pay and leave. Or for him to take ages so that he doesn't catch up with me. But it's too late: they're right behind me in the queue; I can hear them talking. Has he seen me? If only I had a hat or a hood. Or a wig. I'm next to pay. I'll pay and leave without looking behind me. Just a few more minutes and I'll be home free.

The man behind the counter says, 'Three fifty-nine please.'

I hand over a fiver, grab my sad little items and mutter, 'Keep the change.' I'm scuttling towards the door when a voice says, 'Alice!'

I turn around automatically. Damn. Why did I turn around? Why didn't I just run?

284

'I thought it was you. This is Emilia. Emilia, this is Alice.'

What is it with this guy? Does he crave awkward situations? Emilia looks a bit like her predecessor Claudine: she's very tiny, dark, and expensively dressed, with thin lips and, just now, a puzzled expression that says: how does Simon know this dowdy girl?

'What are you doing here?' he asks, which is totally ridiculous. He knows I live around here! What's he doing here, more to the point?

'I live here,' I remind him. 'You?'

'Oh, we're off to supper with some friends of Emilia's.' Simon looks smug. His tone seems to imply that Emilia has very desirable friends.

Good for you. Can I go now? Of course, I don't say this. Instead I say, 'That sounds nice.'

'What about you?' Simon asks, pushing his feet apart as if he's trying to screw himself down into the ground. I'd forgotten he did this; it looks really stupid and annoying. He looks at my bag. 'Having a night in?'

'Yes,' I say. I look down involuntarily at my bag as well, and I'm about to make some sort of self-deprecating remark, when he says, 'By the way – how was your trip with Luther Carson?'

I look up, and when I see his expression, I just know it was him. I see red, and my mouth begins to speak without my strict permission – a bit like it did that time with Luther.

'You know,' I hear myself saying, 'you have some nerve, asking me that. I know you wrote that email. Did you know I've been fired because of it? It wasn't enough for you to dump me in the most horrible, gutless, spineless way possible' – Emilia's eyes are like saucers now – 'but now you've made me lose my job. Well, good for you. He's a real catch,' I add to Emilia.

Emilia's expression has gone from puzzled to utterly

horrified, and she looks up at Simon for guidance. He's looking a little embarrassed.

'Have a good one,' I add, stamping out past them.

As I leave the shop, my heart is thumping from the shock of the encounter. Why did I have to meet him, in a city of seven million people? And what did I ever see in him? He's *awful*. Buttonholing me and asking me if I was having a night in. It was probably crystal clear from my pathetic treats. I shouldn't be worried about it in the grand scheme of things, but I wish they hadn't seen those. Why couldn't I have been buying, I don't know, a litre of cream and a whole smoked salmon? Or a bottle of vodka and six limes? They're probably laughing about it right now. I can't decide whether the fact that Simon's thing with Claudine, which was part of the reason I got fired, didn't last makes me feel better or worse.

I've reached home by now. As I let myself in and put my sad snacks on the table, I suddenly think: *What am I doing?* So I've been fired and my heart is broken. So what? Life goes on. It's Friday night. Even Simon is having a night out, taking a break from ruining people's lives. Poppy's out facing her demons – my friend Poppy, who's been such a star to me. These are supposed to be my golden years. Why, exactly, am I at home with a £1 pizza?

I stick the pizza in the freezer, put the wine and Minstrels out for Ciara and Martin, and dial Poppy's number. She's still at home, thankfully.

'Poppy? I'm on my way. Can you text me the address?'

THIRTY-FIVE

Fifty-five minutes later, Poppy and I are standing at the entrance to the warehouse off Commercial Street where *Bitch Done Me Wrong* is having its grand opening. She wasn't joking about coming in disguise. She's wearing a long blond wig and a pencil skirt with a plain white shirt and a string of pearls, plus big Supernanny-style glasses. It's quite effective: even I didn't recognise her at first. I look a bit different too. I'm wearing the blue beaded dress over boots and black tights, and the biker jacket. I've scraped my hair up into a messy top bun, and I'm wearing a slick of red lipstick and lots of black mascara.

'Are you ready for this?' I ask.

'Listen,' she says, 'I know all this stuff. Question is, are you ready for it?' She pushes down her glasses, and looks at me again. 'Oh my word. Check you out. You're a knockout!'

'Just a little something I picked up in Sicily,' I say. 'Come on, in we go.'

Another thing I'd forgotten is how fashion-forward people are in London. It's astonishing. As we go up the metal stairs, I see people wearing the most incredible outfits: vintage dresses with fur coats and hats, playsuits with platform boots, T-shirts and tweed jackets over sequinned harem

287

pants, all customised with feathers and safety-pins and God knows what. Poppy is very conspicuous in her sexy secretary outfit – I hope people don't recognise her.

We sign the visitors' book – Poppy writes 'Cruella de Vil' – and go into the first room, a big white space. One wall is occupied by a massive, blown-up slide projection of a toddler in a pink jumper – Poppy. She looks very cute, with her hair in braids and a toothless grin. Another wall has a big map of Jamaica. There are different toys strewn around the floor; a Meccano and Lego set on one side, and My Little Pony on the other. Beside the My Little Pony is a small, tattered photo in a cheap frame: a little boy, who I think must be Crispin.

'So far, so weird,' murmurs Poppy, and we go into the next room.

The second room is even bigger. One wall seems to be covered with memorabilia, tickets and receipts, and the other is covered with massive sketches and paintings of Poppy, some of which are quite good. Suddenly a noise starts up on some kind of intercom: 'Hi, my darling . . . just leaving you a message to say . . . miss you. Lots of love. Byeee!' It's Poppy's voice. After a second it continues: 'Hi, my darling . . . just leaving you a message . . .' It plays on a loop for a while, then goes quiet.

'Oh my God,' says Poppy.

'Are you OK?'

'Not sure.'

We look at the memorabilia wall. It's covered with stuff: tickets to exhibitions and gigs, cards, wrapping paper, paper napkins with doodles and messages on them, receipts for meals at cheap cafés, train tickets, cinema tickets, programmes and leaflets. There are also tons of snapshot photos, mainly of Crispin, I mean Crippo, and Poppy. She looks really happy in some of them.

'Look, there's Crippo,' hisses Poppy.

I glance over. It is indeed Crippo, wearing a red lumber-jack shirt, braces, black skinny jeans and twelve-hole Doc Martens, and glasses with heavy black frames. His hair is in a massive quiff. He's holding court to a group of admirers, mostly girls. He doesn't seem to have seen Poppy.

'I'm going to escape,' Poppy stage-whispers, 'into the next room. Coming?'

'Go ahead, I'll join you in a minute.'

Despite its horrible title, I'm finding the exhibition pretty interesting. I take a look at the programme, which is filled with waffle about how Crippo is 'recording his own responses towards emotional upheaval through different found objects'. In a strange way, I feel almost jealous: I can't imagine any of my old flames treasuring one of my used paper napkins, let alone filling a whole wall with mementoes.

I examine a painting of Poppy, where she's wearing a red dress and standing on a green surface. The ground below her feet is covered with hundreds of little red flowers. I lean forward to look and, of course, they're poppies. Not that I've seen her name written anywhere yet.

As I straighten up, the thought suddenly strikes me, out of nowhere, that Sam has been really unfair to me. OK, I *was* going to tell Olivia about Luther's scandal – but I didn't. That's a big difference. He didn't even give me a chance to explain. He was very quick to judge me, especially consid-ering he was still involved with Marisa. I wonder if he knows I've been fired. Probably not, since he's dealing with Olivia now anyway. What a mess.

I go over to Poppy, who is talking to a girl in a 1940s-style tea dress, with what looks like an entire pheasant on her head – it's actually a hat, I see now.

'This is Melissa,' says Poppy. 'Melissa, Alice, a friend from work.'

Melissa has huge eyes and false eyelashes, which she's blinking energetically.

'Oh, right,' she says. 'Which books do you work on?'

'Non-fiction.' I'm not going to tell her I've just been fired.

'Alice has just finished working on Luther Carson's book!' says Poppy.

'Wow! What was he like?' asks Melissa.

It's a good question. What was he like?

'He was great,' I say. 'Good fun, and very down to earth.'

This is going to be my line on Luther; I'm never going to tell anyone about what really happened. It's true, anyway. He was great.

I excuse myself, and drift into the final room of the exhibition. It's quite something. The entire four walls are plastered with sheets of paper covered in Crippo's spidery writing, sometimes with sketches. There are dried flowers – poppies – stuck up everywhere too.

A few feet away from me, I can see a tall woman with long dark hair, who is also looking at the wall. She looks familiar. Then I realise who she is: Caroline Brady. I've seen her picture in the trade press. She's Irish and was previously an editor at a literary publisher, and she's recently founded a new agency with two others. I read a book by one of their debut authors recently and it was excellent.

I know what Claudine would do in this situation. I remember watching her at a launch earlier on this summer, circulating like mad. She'd bounce right over there and probably press her card on to the woman or even suggest lunch. I could never do that.

A little voice inside me says: *And maybe that's why Claudine is being promoted and you've been fired.*

Standing there, I think, not for the first time, about how all of my problems – Sam, work, everything – stem from my crazy lack of confidence. It's ridiculous: I can fly off the handle at Luther, or Simon, yet I can't cross the room to talk to this woman. Why am I such a mouse? Why can't I just go up to her and introduce myself? What's the worst that can happen? I make an idiot of myself and she snubs me. I'm not going to die, am I?

But then I think better of it. It seems so intrusive. She's probably come here to relax, not to be hassled by unemployed people. And what would I say? 'Hello, I know who you are'? And . . . what if she has heard I've been fired? How will I explain it? As I debate with myself, Caroline looks at her watch and half turns, as if to leave.

That's a sign. I have to do it. I'm going to pretend I'm Claudine. No, I'm not. I'm going to pretend I'm a more confident me. I've done harder things than this in the past two weeks. Before I can change my mind, I walk over to her.

'Excuse me,' I say. 'Are you Caroline Brady?'

She smiles. 'Yes, I am. And you are?'

'I'm Alice Roberts,' I say, shaking her hand. 'I used to work at Paragon until last week. I loved that Irish novel you sold recently.'

'Thanks,' says Caroline, looking very pleased. We discuss the book for a while. Then she asks curiously, 'So what sort of work did you do at Paragon?'

I could play safe, and not mention Luther – in case she knows what happened. But what's the point of playing safe?

'I've just been working on Luther Carson's book,' I tell her.

She raises her eyebrows; she looks impressed, but I'm relieved to see there's nothing else in her expression. 'Really? He's a big fish. How did you find that?'

Normally, I would say something extremely self-deprecating here, about how awful or difficult the book was. But then I think of Claudine. She would never do that; she would spin herself for all she was worth.

'It was a challenge,' I say. 'But I'm pleased with how it turned out. He really came through, and we've had some great reactions from the papers.'

'Good for you,' Caroline says. 'And what's your connection here?'

'I know, um, the ex,' I say. 'The subject, I mean.'

'Ah, fair enough. I'm on the groom's side, so to speak. Crispin is a cousin of my husband's. A distant one, though.'

Here's even more proof that Crippo is secretly posh. Only very posh people know who their distant cousins are, let alone invite them to their art launches.

'So what do you think of the exhibition?'

'I like it. It's . . . thought-provoking. I'm assuming that the title is meant to be ironic though.'

She smiles. 'Let's hope so,' she says. 'We've a table booked for dinner so I'd better head off. But let me give you my card. If you're interested in what we do at the agency, you should drop us a line.'

'Thanks very much, I will,' I say, delighted. Caroline says goodbye and I watch her go, exhilarated. It might come to nothing, but it's a step in the right direction. She was so nice! I can't believe she didn't even ask me why I left Paragon.

'Hey,' says Poppy, appearing beside me. 'What have you been up to?'

'Looking at the rest of the exhibition, and networking!' I show her Caroline's card.

'You go, girl! Look at you, working the room. I mean the space.' She looks around. 'I think I've seen enough, and I've even managed to say hello to Crippo. Shall we make a move?'

'Of course.' I don't want to ask her what she thinks of the exhibition. No matter how flattering it is, I can imagine it must be very intrusive.

To my relief, though, Poppy starts to laugh as soon as we leave the building and begin walking towards the nearest pub.

'God, that was surreal. I need a drink,' she says. 'I can't believe we went to an opening without even a box of wine. He is such a skinflint.' She gives me a hug. 'But thanks for coming with me. You're a star. I've got something for you!'

Poppy digs in her bag and produces something. I half expect it to be another art invitation, but it's a card. I take it uncomprehendingly. It's Sam's business card.

'Um . . . Poppy, where did you get this?'

'I nicked it from Olivia's desk while she was at lunch. I know, I know. I'll put it back on Monday. But you said you didn't have his email address. And now you do! Honestly, Alice, if you just emailed him and explained to him properly—'

'Poppy, I'm not going to contact him.'

She looks crestfallen. 'But why not? What have you got to lose?'

I shake my head. I can't explain that even the tiny act of holding Sam's card has brought back all my most painful feelings. I don't want to call him and feel them all over again. I don't want to be the girl in London he hates, or – even if he believes me – the one he feels sorry for, who had a crush on him and got fired. And I don't want to be invited to his and Marisa's wedding.

'Look,' I tell her. 'I appreciate this, I really do, but it's pointless.' And I hand her back the card. 'Now, let's get a drink and forget all these awful men.'

I start to walk on, but Poppy doesn't follow.

'You know, Alice,' she says, 'I've seen you do this before.'

'Do what?' I say warily.

'When a nice guy shows an interest in you, you run a

293

mile. It's as if you think you don't deserve it. Whereas a creep like Simon has your full attention.'

'That's not true,' I say uncertainly.

Turning away slightly, she slips her wig off and puts it in her bag, fluffing out her curls. 'Never mind,' she says. 'Let's get a drink. How about the Ten Bells?'

In the pub, we mainly talk about Crippo and the exhibition; Poppy fills me in on some of the work gossip as well. She tells me that she's helping Olivia out with some of the more confidential stuff, while they interview for a new assistant. That was how she was able to borrow the card.

'You don't mind, do you?' she asks.

Of course I don't mind: I don't care. She doesn't mention Sam again. But on my way home on the Tube, I keep thinking about what she said. *When a nice guy comes along, you run a mile, whereas a creep like Simon has your full attention.*

She's right. I was so scared of getting close to Sam, and not just because I thought he was out of my league. It was also because he was real, and Luther wasn't real – it was just a fantasy about rescuing him. I can remember the panic I felt when I woke up beside Sam – it wasn't just panic that we had done something unprofessional: it was panic that once he got to know me, he would stop liking me, the way Simon did. And that's what happened – not just because of the thing with Luther's story, but because I was horrible to him and ran away from him. And now, even if I send him all the emails in the world, it's too late.

THIRTY-SIX

My first full week of unemployment is pretty awful. The worst part is telling my parents: I've been putting it off but it has to be done. They've never really understood my job anyway, and when I tell them I've been fired for leaving out a clause and sending the ghostwriter home (I'm not mentioning the magazine), they're completely baffled, and indignant.

'I'm putting you on speakerphone,' my mum says. 'I want your father to hear this. Graham! Listen to what's happened to Alice.'

After some rustling at the other end, my dad comes on the line. 'Have you asked Erica's advice?' he says after I've told him what I told Mum.

'I have, Dad, but I don't want to take any legal action—'

'All right,' says my dad. 'Then we'll try and resolve it informally. Why don't we arrange a meeting with your boss – I'll happily come up to London and sit in with you, if you'd like – and just talk through things reasonably?'

It's sweet of him, but the idea of Dad storming up to London in his Toyota Corolla has to be nipped in the bud immediately. 'Dad! No! This isn't school. You can't just ask to see the headmistress.'

'But there must be *something* we can do. This is just

disgraceful of them. Completely unjustifiable. You've been a good employee—'

'Graham, let me talk to her,' I hear my mum say in the background. She comes back on the line, trying to sound reassuring though I know she's really worried. 'Don't worry, darling. We'll sort this out somehow. And meanwhile you can always move back home.'

My situation is bad enough, but to hear my parents so upset and helpless makes it a hundred times worse. Then there's the problem of having to explain, every time I apply for something, why I left my previous job. Erica's given me some phrases to use, but they don't sound very convincing. By Wednesday I can't face doing any more proper job applications, and I find myself scanning my local noticeboards for things like babysitting and dog walking. I also apply for a job as a waitress in a café down the road, but the man says he's looking for someone with more experience.

On Thursday morning I wake up in a state of total despair. I know I should get dressed and start applying for things, but instead I turn on the TV and lie down on the sofa. I'm so engrossed in *This Morning* that I almost don't hear my phone ringing.

'Alice? It's Alasdair White here. From Paragon.'

'Muh-nhuh?' I say, almost dropping the phone out of surprise and clearing my throat because this is the first time I've spoken all day. 'Oh. Hello, Alasdair.' I try to sound polite, but I'm freaking out. What on earth is he ringing about? Do they now want to sue me or something?

'Is this a good time to talk?'

'Ah . . . yes,' I say, putting the TV on mute. Hopefully, if he heard voices he'll think I was in some kind of meeting.

'Alice,' he says, 'this will probably sound surprising, but – we've reconsidered our decision to let you go. I think we've acted somewhat hastily. I was wondering if you would like to come back and work with us again. Not as an assistant,' he adds. 'But as a commissioning editor.'

I'm so shocked that I literally can't say anything. I can't even make a sound.

'I can understand if that doesn't appeal to you,' Alasdair says. 'If you'd like, there is an editorial vacancy in another company in the group, which I think you'd be perfect for. It would be the same role: commissioning editor, non-fiction, celebrity books.'

'What?' I manage to say.

Alasdair repeats, 'There's an editorial vacancy in another company in the group, and I would put in a very good word for you. If you don't want to come back to us, that is.'

'But why do you – why have you changed your mind?' I know it sounds blunt, but I can't think of any other way to phrase it.

'There are various factors,' he says. 'I know that, ah, Luther is keen to continue working with you. He feels that your input was crucial in helping him write his book.'

I look at the TV, where Phillip Schofield is laughing away about something on mute. Is this *really* happening? Has Luther really insisted on having me back on board? I'm feeling shocked, amazed and baffled, all at once.

'Um . . . Alasdair, thank you, but I'm going to have to think about this,' I tell him. 'I mean – it's quite a surprise.'

'I understand,' he says. I hear his dog beginning to bark, and he sounds as if he's standing up. 'You can take as long as you like, Alice. And on behalf of the company, I do apologise. I think we had legitimate concerns but we over-reacted. We would like you to come back. I hope you'll think about it.'

He hangs up, and I'm left blinking at the phone, open-mouthed. I can't believe it. In fact, if it hadn't been for the dog barking in the background, I would have thought it was a hoax. It's like those daydreams where you're suddenly thin and gorgeous and your ex begs you to come back. It certainly feels like a dream come true – my long-awaited promotion. I might even get my own office. Alice Roberts: commissioning editor, non-fiction. It's the answer to all my prayers!

Or . . . is it? Would I want to go back again after what's happened? It was nice that Alasdair apologised – eventually – but what about Olivia? What does she think about it all? Maybe I should take that other job working on celebrity books. Although . . . the idea of going near a celebrity book ever again fills me with dread and despair. Which isn't exactly promising. The conversation's made me feel more energetic, though, and I suddenly feel galvanised to fire off my CV to Caroline Brady. I've spent the past two days drafting and proof-reading my email: now I need the balls to press send.

After I've done that, I hop in the shower and get dressed. The whole time, I'm thinking about the idea of going back to work, and about Luther. If he did say that he wanted me back, it's incredibly nice of him. Or . . . maybe they just realised they were being unfair? Is that possible? I can't fathom it.

'That's great news,' says Erica, when I ring her. 'They've obviously realised they were out of order and they're terrified you're going to sue. So now you can have the promotion and keep quiet, or you can definitely bring a case for wrongful dismissal.'

Oh, God. I have to say neither one of those options sounds all that enticing.

'I'm going to have to think about it,' I tell her.

After I've sent one more application, I clean the bathroom, tidy my bedroom, and then go to Ine Ood to buy a Crunchie. After I've had my Crunchie with a cup of tea, I sit again for a while, staring into space. Ironically, I find the days go very quickly when you have nothing to do: somehow it's already five o'clock. I could do it right now: I could just pick up the phone and tell Alasdair 'Yes'. I could go back to work tomorrow. I wouldn't have to worry about what I'm going to live on next month. In fact, I'd have more money than I've ever had before. It's very, very tempting, but . . . Aargh. I just don't know what to do. I'm drawing up a list of pros and cons, when the phone rings. It's Poppy! Brilliant: exactly the person I want to talk to.

'Congratulations,' she says in mysterious tones. 'I hear you've been made an offer you can't refuse. Or maybe you can. What do you think?'

'I have no idea what to think! Tell me everything, do you know why they've done it?'

'Well,' she says, 'they've obviously realised they were fools to fire you. And of course you have a big fan in LA, baby.'

'So it was him! I can't believe it. It's so nice of him. Do you know what he said?'

'I do. It was when he emailed through the acknowledgements. He was praising you to the skies, saying that if it hadn't been for you the book never would have been written, and that if you did come back, he would recommend Paragon to all his A-List friends, etc. etc. It sounded like the carrot to end all carrots.'

'Wow,' is all I can say.

'There *might* also have been an element of stick.'

'*What?* As in, give Alice her job back or there's no book?' I don't like the idea of owing my job to strong-arm tactics.

'Well – not in so many words, but that was the implication,' Poppy says. 'That's a secret, though. Well, the whole thing's top secret. I was accidentally copied in on an email, and I know that you weren't meant to know about it, ever. He made that very clear. So don't tell him I told you, please.'

I just can't believe it. The idea of Luther going to these lengths for me is so ridiculously touching. Especially since he probably had some strong opposition from Sam.

'I think he must have told them to tell you it was Luther's idea,' Poppy is continuing.

'Yes, I know,' I say, without thinking. Then I do a double-take. 'Luther's idea? What? I thought it *was* Luther's idea! Who said that?'

'Sam did! Who did you think I meant? Sam got you your job back.'

'Sam?' I whisper. I've been walking and talking with the phone, but now I have to sit down. 'But . . . Poppy, that's impossible. He hates me. Last time I saw him, he would barely look at me. Unless he believes me now! But how did he find out I'd been fired? And why would he do it, does he just feel guilty or what?'

'Alice,' Poppy interrupts me, 'You know how I love to chat, but – don't you think you should be asking Sam these questions?'

She's right, of course.

'OK. I'll email him.'

'Do, or you could call his hotel. I've got the number right here.'

'*What*? He's *here*, in London?'

'Yes, for the premiere of *The Deep End*. He and Luther are at the Dean Street Townhouse. But they'll be leaving soon – I think it starts at six-thirty.'

'And when are they flying back?'

'I'm not sure – some time tomorrow morning. Listen,' she whispers, 'Olivia's back. I'd better go. Good luck!'

I open up my email, and type, 'Dear Sam.' I don't know what to put next. I can't believe he got me my job back. I would have preferred to get it back by myself – or, ideally, not have been fired at all – but I'm still very grateful. I want to thank him but more importantly, I want to know *why* he did it when he was so mean to me last time I saw him. And – when I was so mean to him. Perhaps I should call him, as Poppy suggested? But what would I say? Maybe I should email and suggest meeting. But there might not be time, before his flight. I stare down at my list of pros and cons about taking the job. Maybe I should write one about different ways to contact Sam too.

Suddenly I realise something. While I'm writing my pros and cons, drafting emails and biting my nails, Sam is *here* – here in London, just a few miles away, for one night. Tonight is probably our only chance to meet face to face, and talk properly. It's twenty past five. If I leave now I can just about reach him before he leaves his hotel. OK, I'm going to do it. If I don't, I'll always regret it. Without giving myself time to talk myself out of it, or even bothering to change out of my jeans and T-shirt, I grab my bag and run out the door.

THIRTY-SEVEN

Of course, this has to be the day that the Piccadilly line decides to have a meltdown. We sit at Knightsbridge for ages in a packed, sweltering hot train while I look at my watch and realise this was a really stupid idea. By the time we inch into Leicester Square station it's a quarter past six. I'm sure he'll have left by now. And even if he hasn't, I imagine myself rocking up and finding him in the middle of a massive entourage, up to his ears in Luther stuff, asking me what I think I'm doing there . . . OK, I'm going to stop thinking about it and just do it.

I try to take a short-cut through Leicester Square itself but it's packed solid with people waiting for the premiere to start. The irony is not lost on me. For a mad minute I wonder if I should just stay there and try and wave at Sam from the crowd, but that would be too humiliating and, also, he might not see me. Instead I do a detour, into Lisle Street, across Shaftesbury Avenue where I'm almost mown down by a rickshaw driver, until finally I arrive, red-faced, sweaty and panting, at the hotel.

'Can I speak to Sam Newland?' I ask breathlessly. 'He's staying here.'

'I'm afraid we don't have a guest by that name, madam,' says the dark-haired receptionist politely.

'What? But he's here! He's with Luther Carson.' I lower

my voice. 'I know him. Could you just tell him I'm here? Or has he left already?'

'Madam – I'm sorry, but I think you have the wrong information.' In the mirror behind her I can see myself, hair dishevelled, cheeks fiery red, eyes staring. She probably thinks I'm a crazy stalker or an aspiring actress.

I'm about to try again when a voice behind me says, 'Alice?'

It's him. He's alone, and he's looking devastatingly hand-some in black tie. At the sight of him, I can actually feel myself going weak at the knees, heart pounding. Oh God, I really hope I don't faint again.

'Are you – looking for Luther?' he asks.

'No, I was looking for you. I wanted to . . .' I trail off. I had a whole speech prepared, but now that I'm face to face with him, I'm so nervous I can't remember any of it. Should I thank him? Ask him why he did it? Then I notice two things: one, he's staring at me as if he can't believe his luck, and two, he seems incredibly nervous too.

Sam takes a step closer. 'Hey. Could we talk for a minute?'

The receptionist is pretending not to listen, but I can tell she's completely rapt. Whatever this conversation is going to be, I don't think I can have it here, or in a bar. 'Let's go up to your room,' I say, whereupon her eyes pop out on stalks.

As we go up in the lift, I'm feeling ridiculously shy. I don't know where to look or what to say, and he's very quiet too.

'Sorry about that, back there,' he says, as we walk down the corridor. 'I sometimes ask them not to tell people I'm here, when I'm with Luther, you know, just in case . . .'

'It's OK.'

His room is beautiful, with yellow-and-white striped wallpaper, and a four-poster bed, which I avoid looking at. Sam gestures for me to sit in a chintzy armchair, but I decide to stay standing. He leans against his desk, a few feet away.

303

'Thank you for getting me my job back,' I say formally.

He looks down. 'Ah . . . OK. You were not supposed to know about that. How did you find out?'

'It doesn't matter. But thanks all the same.'

Sam shakes his head, and starts talking very quickly. 'Alice. I'm the one who should be thanking you – and apologising. I've been a total asshole. I should have believed you when you tried to explain about Luther. You were about to lose your job and you could have saved yourself by giving them that story, but you decided not to. I can't believe you did that. I mean, I *can* believe it because I know you well enough by now. But I don't know anyone else who would have done it. I owe you more than I could ever repay you. So does Luther. So please don't ever thank me.'

I know I'm blushing, but I'm determined to get some facts straight before I start getting all emotional. 'But how did you find out?'

'I couldn't stop thinking about it after you'd left, wondering if I'd been wrong. I was kicking myself for going to get Annabel – who was fine, by the way, she was painting her nails when I arrived – rather than giving you a chance to explain. I tried emailing you, and I got a bounce-back, saying you'd left. I was just figuring out how to reach you, when I had an email from your co-worker . . . Patty?'

'Poppy!'

'Yeah. She told me what really happened. Though I could have saved myself a lot of trouble just by asking you in the first place. Look . . . I'll be completely honest. I was sore that you withdrew from me, after everything that happened between us. I thought maybe you decided to end things with me because you wanted to dish the dirt on Luther. I can be a stubborn, suspicious bastard, as you've probably realised. I'm really sorry.'

He moves his hand, as if to reach out for mine, but then he drops it back by his side.

'But why did you pull back from me, Alice? If it's just that you weren't feeling it, then you don't have to explain. In fact, don't say anything, and I'll never bother you again. But if it's something I did . . . I need to know.'

My heart is hammering again. I decide to sit down after all. I can't believe we are actually having this conversation. I could, of course, tell him, 'It was because of my crazy insecurities,' but instead, I say, 'I thought there was something going on with you and Marisa. Because of the trip to Rome.'

He groans. 'I knew it. She's just got a job in Rome working for a big studio. That's why we went there. I wanted to introduce her to some people. She asked me to keep it secret, so I did. But I should never have lied to you about it.'

'Why did you? I know she didn't want Federico to know, but you could have trusted me.'

'I know. Look, I take things way too literally sometimes. If someone asks me to keep a secret, I keep a secret.' He smiles ruefully. 'I guess I was being stubborn, too. I didn't see why I should feel guilty about my exes and I didn't know you knew she was in Rome with me. I realised afterwards I'd been pretty stupid. Marisa told me so, in fact.'

'Did she? I suppose I was surprised as well because . . . well, she never told me that you were her ex.'

'I think,' he says, 'that might have been because she guessed that I was falling for you and I didn't know what the hell to do about it.'

I have to look up, at that. The words he's spoken are hanging in the air; I can almost see them. The room is so still I'm sure he must be able to hear my heart thumping.

'But – how do *you* feel?' he asks.

The look of uncertainty on his face makes me melt. This is where, I know, I should be sensible and tell him that of course, if circumstances were different, then great, but we live on different continents and it really wouldn't be wise, but instead I stand up and go over to him and before I can say anything else, he's taken me in his arms and he's kissing me. It's every bit as magical as it was the first time. I never want it to end. Even if it's just for tonight, I'm so happy to be here with him.

After a while, though, I remember something.

'Sam, aren't you late for the premiere?' I say reluctantly.

'Hell, no. I don't even need to be there. Luther has a ton of people with him.' He kisses me again. 'You know, the main reason I came to London was to try to see you. In fact, I just emailed you about half an hour ago, to see if I could meet you tomorrow.'

'Really?' I'm even more thrilled to hear this.

'Yes. So, no, I don't care about the premiere. Unless you wanted to come with me?'

I laugh. 'Are you serious?'

'Sure. Why not?'

'I'm not exactly dressed for it. And wouldn't Luther find it strange if I was there as, um, your date?' More to the point – I don't want to spend my one evening with Sam watching a film. My heart sinks as I remember: we've got tonight, but tomorrow he'll be leaving.

'You could go like that,' he says. 'Or the stylist could fix you up with something. And as for Luther . . . well, I don't know if this is the right moment to tell you this, but . . .'

'God, Sam, what?' I can't take any more shocks.

'I'm not going to be representing Luther for much longer. I've been offered a job at an agency in London. And I want to take it.'

He looks at me for a reaction, but there is none because I can't have a reaction. It's too much. I'm all out of reactions.

'OK. Maybe we can talk about that later. I didn't mean to spring it on you like that. But what do you want to do about tonight?

You want to go? Because we don't have to. We could just hang out, go get a drink, or some food, or whatever you want . . .'

I can tell he's thinking the same thing as I am: we could just stay here and make the most of his lovely hotel room. Order room service . . . It's very tempting. But now that I know we have more time together, I think it would be fun to have a night out. After all, we've got a lot to celebrate.

'No, let's go,' I tell Sam. 'If you're sure it's OK. And congratulations about the job. That's great news!' I kiss him again, he kisses me back, and then, before we get totally carried away, Sam calls the stylist, Roger, who says he can fix me up if I come around to the suite right away.

Forty minutes later, when Sam and I step out of the lift, hand in hand, I see the receptionist do a double-take. I don't blame her: I'm unrecognisable. I'm wearing a gorgeous full-length blue chiffon dress by Alberta Ferretti. My hair is swept to one side in a low chignon, my skin is glowing and Roger has somehow managed to make my eyes look three times their normal size. I've left my jeans and T-shirt in Sam's room. Neither of us has said it but I think we both know I'll probably wear them home tomorrow morning.

'You look beautiful,' Sam says, kissing my cheek.

'Thank you. Oh, Sam, I need to send a text. Do you mind?'

'Of course not. We can be late.'

I fish my phone out of my borrowed Chanel clutch, and text Poppy: 'Off to premiere with Sam!!! THANK YOU SO MUCH xxxxx'. Then Sam and I walk out of the hotel into Dean Street, attracting more than a few looks and smiles in our evening dress. I make a mental note to get Sam to tell me what the film is all about, in case Luther asks me about it later. I know that, with Sam sitting beside me, I'm not going to be able to concentrate on the screen.

EPILOGUE

Three weeks later

'So how did it go?' says Sam.

'Good, I think!' I slide into the chair beside him. We're in Polpo on Beak Street, which is a Venetian-style bar. Sam loves it because they serve Negronis, and an obscure drink called Spritz all' Aperol. I really like it too – although, to be honest, we could be in Burger King on Tottenham Court Road and I'd be just as ecstatic. 'They were really friendly. It's hard to say, but I think it went well. And the whole why-did-you-leave thing was fine, now that I can say I left of my own accord.'

'So when will they let you know?' he says, pouring me a glass of wine. 'This was the second interview. It's time for them to make their decision.'

'Well . . . Caroline said, "Officially, we have another person to see. But unofficially, when can you start?"'

'Hey! So you got it! Congratulations.' He looks delighted.

'I'll wait till I get a definite offer. But . . . fingers crossed.'

Sam was the first person I told when I got the interview. He spent hours with me the weekend before, going over interview techniques, firing questions at me and saying things like, 'You gotta bring your A-game! Bring it!' I told him he was being scary, but I was very touched. I can't imagine Simon ever helping me prepare for an interview.

'So – you do understand why I don't want to go back to Paragon?' I ask him. 'It's good to have it as back-up. But . . .'

'No, I totally get it. You want to strike out on your own and find something you're passionate about.' He smiles at me. 'I think it's great.'

Sam has come to London to work for the sister agency of the one he worked for in LA. I get the impression it's less high-powered what he used to do, but it's less manic and he's finding it really interesting. He's wearing jeans, a faded blue bomber jacket and a white T-shirt that shows the end of his tan. Strangely, he seems to have got younger since he's arrived. With his BlackBerry no longer permanently attached to his hand and ear – well, not quite so permanently – he looks much less stressed. He still works very long hours, but he says it's nothing to the way it was before.

'So tell me,' I say teasingly. 'Are you glad my words of wisdom beside the pool helped you rethink your career?'

'Hey, don't get cocky,' he says. 'It wasn't just you, you know.'

Our food arrives. It's a selection of snacks; gnocchi with duck ragu, gorgonzola and walnut crostini, and arancini, or rice balls, just like we had in Sicily. We start wolfing it down.

Sam continues, 'You were right, though. If I'd continued the way I was going, I would have burned out. At some point in Sicily, I started to think, do I really want to spend all my waking hours policing Luther? I think I was having a kind of early midlife crisis. My old co-workers all think I'm insane – half of them think I've been fired, in fact – but I could care less. I heard from Luther today, by the way,' he adds. 'He's coming over again to promote the book soon, so we should all get together.'

'Mm,' I say. Somehow, I don't think that will happen. Luther was happy to see me at the premiere, but now Sam has told him we're an item, and, apparently, Luther finds it weird, which I can completely understand.

'You know what else? He's met someone.'

'*Has* he?' I'm really pleased. I'm so loved-up right now, I want everybody to be happy.

'Yep. She's a make-up artist. He met her on the TV show. Her name's Jenna and she's Canadian. She sounds like quite a tough cookie, in a good way.'

'I think that's what he needs.'

'Definitely. I was always worried he would go back to Dominique.'

Sam's opinion of Dominique is something I've learned over the last three weeks. I've also learned that he is a wonderful cook – he learned in Italy – and that he hates shopping for clothes. And that he's very tidy, but he doesn't mind if I'm messy, and that he and his brother are fanatical about their football team, the Utes – the season is just beginning and Sam's going to teach me the words to the very cheesy Utah Fight Song. He's not remotely bothered by my cardboard squares – to be honest, whenever he's come home with me, we haven't had time to notice the squares. He wants to go surfing in Devon, and to go to Venice and a hundred other places, and I think he's also in danger of being co-opted by Mike's tag rugby team. I've realised he's frantic to fill the gap that used to be filled with work, but that's OK. Anyway, he's not the only one with hobbies. I've finally decided to start taking dance classes.

'Speaking of Luther . . . check this out.' Sam produces something: an advance copy of Luther's book, straight from the printers. We exclaim over it like proud parents for a few minutes, before Sam says, 'His acknowledgements are at the back. You should read them.'

I flip to the back, and read out: '*I want to thank my agent Sam Newland, who has given me the best nineteen-and-a-half months of his life: Sam, I hope it's been worthwhile.*'

'Thanks, man,' Sam says drily. I skim more names – that's

nice, he's mentioned Brian – until I come to my own: '*I also want to thank my editor Alice Roberts, who believed in me even when I was totally bullshitting her. Seriously, Alice, I could not – and I also probably would not – have written this book without you.*'

'Wow. I never knew Luther was so eloquent. Did you?'

'He might have had some help,' is all Sam will say.

After dinner, we go for a walk down towards the river. Although I'm wearing a summer dress – the pistachio-green one that Marisa gave me – there's a definite freshness in the air that wasn't there even this time last week.

'I can't believe it's already September,' I say.

'I know,' says Sam. 'Hey, I hear the fall is a particularly good time to see Paris. What do you think? Depending on when you start your new job,' he adds.

'If.'

'When.'

As he takes my hand, I try and think how many times we've seen each other since he came to London, and I realise I've lost count. Being with Sam doesn't feel like anything else I've ever experienced. When I think back to my thing with Simon, it seems hard to believe I put up with it. What did I ever see in someone who cared so little about me?

Life certainly can surprise you. I remember how, on the plane to Italy, I had those crazy dreams about having a romance with Luther, and I wanted so much to be promoted. None of those things happened; instead, it's been a hundred times better. I don't know what the future holds for me and Sam. I don't know how long he's going to stay in London – a year? Two? Maybe he will move back to America, and I'll move with him, or something else will happen. Who knows? I only know that right now I'm smiling, and I feel as though I'm going to be smiling a lot more in the future.

ACKNOWLEDGEMENTS

Many people helped me while I was writing this book – either with moral support, practical information or by reading it. I hope I haven't forgotten anyone.

Thank you to all the friends who read early drafts, including: Gráinne Brett, Síofra O'Donovan, Amber Burlinson, Clare Thomas, Hannah Knowles, Natasha Laws, Daniela Buckley, Hilary Attenborough, and, heroically, my brother Barry. I particularly want to thank Frieda Klotz, my very first reader, for her astute and encouraging comments from day one, without which I probably would not have finished the book. Thank you to my sisters-in-law: Santina Doherty for introducing me to Sicily and Anne O'Mahony for straight-talking and insightful feed-back. I also benefited from the advice of Julie Cohen via her fantastic blog, which I'd recommend any aspiring author to follow. For insights into the European and US film industries, thank you to Olaf Gonzáles Schneeweiss, Daniela Buckley, Helen Berger and MF. Thanks also to Mark Dyson. For inside info on Utah and the LDS, as well as LA café suggestions, thank you Jaremey McMullin. For (hypothetical) legal advice, thank you Noel Dilworth, Lucy Miles and Ronan McCrea. Any mistakes are all my own work. Thanks to the staff at Alimentari and The

Salusbury Deli in Queen's Park, who fed me and watered me and got me out of the house.

Thank you to Rowan Lawton and Juliet Mushens at PFD, for brilliant editorial guidance, support and macaroons. Thank you to Sherise Hobbs, for superb edits that have made the book so much better, and to Imogen Taylor and Lucy Foley for welcoming me back to the Euston Road – thanks also to Imogen for thinking of the title! Thank you Rachel Mills and Alexandra Cliff for sending Alice abroad. For early and invaluable support, thank you to Anne Louise Fisher, Joy Terekiev at Mondadori and Nicola Bartels at Blanvalet. Thanks to my lovely colleagues past and present at Hodder and The Folio Society. Lastly, I'd like to thank my parents, who supported me through all my decisions and never minded when I came home to visit and locked myself away writing. And to Alex: thank you for holding my hand through submission and rewrites (not literally of course) and for celebrating with me.